The Librarian
and the Spy

BOOK YOUR PLACE ON OUR WEBSITE AND MAKE THE READING CONNECTION!

We've created a customized website just for our very special readers, where you can get the inside scoop on everything that's going on with Zebra, Pinnacle and Kensington books.

When you come online, you'll have the exciting opportunity to:

- View covers of upcoming books
- Read sample chapters
- Learn about our future publishing schedule (listed by publication month and author)
- Find out when your favorite authors will be visiting a city near you
- Search for and order backlist books from our online catalog
- Check out author bios and background information
- Send e-mail to your favorite authors
- Meet the Kensington staff online
- Join us in weekly chats with authors, readers and other guests
- Get writing guidelines
- AND MUCH MORE!

**Visit our website at
http://www.kensingtonbooks.com**

The Librarian and the Spy

SUSAN MANN

ZEBRA BOOKS
KENSINGTON PUBLISHING CORP.
http://www.kensingtonbooks.com

ZEBRA BOOKS are published by

Kensington Publishing Corp.
119 West 40th Street
New York, NY 10018

All Kensington titles, imprints and distributed lines are available at special quantity discounts for bulk purchases for sales promotion, premiums, fund-raising, educational or institutional use.

Special book excerpts or customized printings can also be created to fit specific needs. For details, write or phone the office of the Kensington Sales Manager. Attn.: Sales Department. Kensington Publishing Corp., 119 West 40th Street, New York, NY 10018. Phone: 1-800-221-2647.

Zebra and the Z logo Reg. U.S. Pat. & TM Off.

First Printing: May 2017
ISBN-13: 978-1-4201-4330-0
ISBN-10: 1-4201-4330-1

eISBN-13: 978-1-4201-4333-1
eISBN-10: 1-4201-4333-6

10 9 8 7 6 5 4 3 2

Printed in the United States of America

To my husband,
Ken,
and our daughter,
Sarah,
the loves of my life

ACKNOWLEDGMENTS

I am so very grateful to those who have helped this book come to be. My agent, Rena Rossner of the Deborah Harris Agency, is superhuman. I thank her for her tireless efforts in getting the manuscript into shape and working her agent magic. I am forever grateful for her love of "quirky." Thank you to the entire team at Kensington Publishing and especially my editor, Esi Sogah, whose enthusiasm for card catalogs knows no bounds. Working with her is an absolute joy, and together we made this story shine. My friends, led by fellow author Lexie Dunne, hold a special place in my heart. If not for them telling me I should write novels, this story wouldn't be. I am also indebted to those who read and provided invaluable feedback on various drafts: Erica, Michael, Russ, Neil, and Kate. I also must thank Authoress, who gets the words of newbies like me in front of agents. Finally, thank you to my family: my husband, Ken, for his constant and unwavering support in everything I do; our daughter, Sarah, who truly is my pride and joy; and my parents, for always, always, always being there.

Chapter One

Quinn's grandfather always said being a librarian is a lot like being a secret agent. Like a good spy, a librarian has to be quick thinking, resourceful, and tenacious. Chester Ellington assured her he knew about such things since he'd read just about every spy novel ever published.

Quinn Ellington appreciated his elevated opinion of those in her chosen profession. To her, though, the comparison was more than a little over the top. She liked to believe she was quick thinking, resourceful, and tenacious, especially since she was known to follow bits of bibliographic data like a bloodhound after a rabbit. But she knew being *just* a librarian would never fully quench the thirst for adventure she inherited from her spy-novel-loving grandfather. As it stood right now, the likelihood of her being called upon to disable a death ray pointed at the White House from space by a maniacal villain bent on world domination was pretty low.

She snipped off another strip of red book repair tape from a roll and used it to attach the swag of fake green garland and colored twinkle lights to the front of her metal desk. She smiled when she thought of how her grandfather would approve of her unconventional use of library supplies, as tame as they might be.

The trimming secured, she crawled under the desk most likely manufactured during the Eisenhower administration and plugged the lights into the power strip. She grunted when her head banged against one side of the desk and a hollow bong reverberated around her as she backed out from the tiny space. Good thing for her skull it sounded worse than it felt.

Clear of the desk, she scrambled to her feet and stepped around to the front again. She folded her arms across her chest, tipped her head to one side, and turned a critical eye on the trimmings. Martha Stewart she wasn't.

She glanced up at the clock attached to the wall of the Bullpen, the large office that housed the desks of the reference librarians at Westside Library, and realized it was time for her to cover her duties at the desk. Any additional decorating would have to wait. After draining the last of the barely warm Earl Grey from a mug with the Dewey decimal number for tea emblazoned on the side, she snagged a book review magazine to peruse in case it was slow at the desk and left the office.

She walked behind the main library counter—a monument to wood laminates that stood at the center of the main reading room—and climbed up onto the high bar stool–like seat. She had just set the magazine down when she looked up to see a thirtyish-year-old man, briefcase in hand, striding toward the desk.

He stopped in front of her and Quinn gave him a smile. In her best librarian voice, she said, "Good morning. What can I do for you?"

"Hello. I'm hoping you can help me," he replied in a BBC news anchor accent that made her heart skip a beat.

"That's why I'm here."

"I need to find out the history and value of a brooch."

Her eyebrows shot up. "A brooch?"

"Am I not the brooch type?" he asked with a crooked smile.

"Well, as long as it matches your tie," she said, nodding at the red vintage convertible sports car repeated over the tie's black background. She also noticed his jeans and brown leather jacket, her favorite look on a man. "You do seem a little too young and male to wear a brooch."

Delight flashed in his sky blue eyes. "Well, for what it's worth, you seem a little young and, ah"—he paused and he squinted at her—"denim wearing to be a librarian."

"I get that a lot." Feeling cheeky, she swung her legs to the side and lifted a foot, showing off her high-heeled leather boot. "You'll also note I'm not wearing sensible shoes today, nor is my hair in a bun." While she occasionally wore her blond hair in a ponytail, today, as usual, it was loose around her shoulders.

"Duly noted."

She lowered her foot and faced forward again. "Now, about this brooch. I have to warn you up front that unless you're talking about tracking down the value of one that's already been appraised, I can't tell you how much it's worth. I'm not qualified. I can help you get a list together of local appraisers if you'd like."

"I understand. That's not what I'm looking for. Can you help me learn more about its history?"

"Again, unless it's a well-known piece, I doubt we'll find much. You'd be better off taking it to a jeweler." But her curiosity was getting the better of her and before her brain could stop her mouth, she found herself saying, "But since you're already here, I guess it couldn't hurt to take a quick look."

"Brilliant," he said. He lifted his briefcase and laid it flat on the counter.

"You have it with you?"

"No, not the brooch itself. I have a photograph of it." He rummaged through the papers in his briefcase.

Quinn tried not to be too obvious as she studied his features. He was extremely handsome, with a wide brow and strong jaw that tapered to a pointed chin. His nose was slightly crooked and sported a small bump. She supposed it had been broken at some point in his life. Still, it in no way detracted from his good looks—if anything, it added character to his face.

"Ah, here it is." He handed her an eight-by-ten.

She blew out a low whistle. "This isn't what I was expecting at all. I thought we were talking gold flowers or gem-encrusted bumblebees. You know, like the brooches Queen Elizabeth wears."

"Yes, well, this is very different than the ones worn by Her Majesty."

She brought the picture close to her face and examined the intricate details of the round, flat ring. Absently, she said, "I read recently that forty-two thousand schoolchildren in Southern Rhodesia donated pocket money toward a diamond brooch to give to then Princess Elizabeth as a present for her twenty-first birthday. It was presented to her when she visited with her parents and sister in 1947. It's called the Flame Lily brooch and apparently it's one of her favorites." She looked up and when she saw the mixture of amusement and bemusement on his face, she cleared her throat and squinted at the paper again.

"I'm no expert, but my guess is this is Celtic. And old." It reminded Quinn a little bit of a belt buckle, only rounder. The flat ring was inlaid with panels of intricately patterned silver. A long, thick pin was attached to the top half of the hoop and appeared to be able to move around the ring. There were a number of empty settings dotting the silver where Quinn assumed gemstones had once adorned the brooch.

"Maybe Anglo-Saxon." She looked up and asked, "What makes you call it a brooch?"

"That's what the inventory calls it."

"Inventory?"

"I work for the insurance company that will be covering it."

"So you need to figure out if it's worth what the client says it's worth? And not something you can buy for twenty bucks on eBay?"

"Or has MADE IN CHINA stamped on the back."

She sighed. "I'd love to dig into this, but like I said before, this is really a job for an appraiser." Her eyebrows lowered when she inspected the photo again. "Or a professor of archaeology, if this thing is authentic." She set the picture on the counter and looked at him. "Doesn't your insurance company have people who do stuff like this?"

He shuffled some of his papers, clearly ordering his thoughts. "It's a bit complicated, with client confidentiality and all. For what it's worth, I can assure you a professional appraiser is already in the process of evaluating this piece." He shrugged. "I want to do my own due diligence."

"You want to see if what they come back with is the same as what you found out on your own?"

"If not the same, at least close. I tried to do some Internet research myself, but almost everything I ran across was new, and for sale on Etsy." His gaze remained unwavering as he considered her. "I need the help of a professional."

A thrill buzzed through her. This wasn't exactly as pulse-pounding as stopping a death ray, but it was by far the most interesting thing she'd been asked to research in a long time. How could she say no? She dipped her head almost imperceptibly and said in a soft voice, "Okay."

Even as she agreed, her mind began to swirl with thoughts of how to best tackle the task at hand, the potential problems they might encounter, the amount of time the search might take, the fact that his cologne was more than a little distracting, and how nice his smile was. Since the last two musings were unprofessional—the bit of flirting she'd indulged in wasn't terribly professional, either—she stuffed them in a crevasse in her brain and focused her attention on the brooch. "Technically, I'm only supposed to help you gather the materials. You need to come to your own conclusions."

"Of course, Madam Librarian," he said with a bow from the waist.

She suppressed a snort and held her hand out across the counter. "Please, call me Quinn."

His handshake was firm. "It is a delight to make your acquaintance, Quinn. My name is James."

"James." She suddenly felt a little self-conscious. When he released her hand, she dropped her gaze to the picture on the counter and pushed her hair behind her ears. Her focus now restored, she said, "Is there a deadline we're looking at? Because to be honest, I'm not sure how long this will take. We might find your answer in twenty minutes, but it could take several days if we need to get books from another library."

"No, there's no set deadline, but the sooner, the better."

"Got it." She couldn't contain her excitement and fairly bounced in her chair. "You don't have any information on it at all?"

"No. It's part of a collection the owner bought at an estate sale. Some of the pieces had paperwork. A lot of them didn't, including this one."

"Okay, then," she said, and rubbed her hands together. "Off we go into the wonderful world of brooches. First, we need some basic information." She turned to the computer in front of her and found an appropriate entry in one of the library's online encyclopedias. She angled the screen so they could both see it. They spent the next ten minutes learning about various brooch styles. After examining the photo again, they agreed it was clearly a Celtic pseudo-penannular brooch used to fasten cloaks.

Quinn went to the library's online catalog and performed a subject browse search. She set her elbow on the counter and rested her chin in her palm while she scanned the results on the screen. After a few more refining searches, the printer to her left whirred to life and spit out a piece of paper.

"Here's the deal," Quinn said. "We don't have any books in this library specifically on Celtic brooches." When she saw the disappointment on his face, she said, "No, no, no. We're not giving up yet."

Quinn jumped down from her stool, snatched the paper from the printer, and took off toward the nonfiction stacks. She stopped, spun around and, reassured he was following her, turned and started toward the stacks again.

Quinn zeroed in on the appropriate section of books like a laser-guided missile. She dodged around a cart filled with books to be shelved, and when she reached the correct aisle, she pivoted and hurried down it, at one point hopping over a metal kick stool.

Despite her quick maneuvers, James managed to keep up. He was in full stride behind her, so when she came to a sudden stop, he crashed into her.

She lurched forward. The paper in her hand went flying. Had James not shot out a hand and gripped her arm to steady her, she would have executed an epic face plant. "Quinn, I'm so sorry."

"No, it's my fault," she said, thankful she hadn't taken a swan dive in front of him. She swept the rogue strands of her hair back in place. "I stopped with no warning. I should have brake lights installed." She was keenly aware of his hand resting on her arm.

He retrieved her paper from the floor. "What are you looking for? I thought you said the library didn't have any books on brooches."

"We don't, but we do have some books on Celtic and Anglo-Saxon designs and their histories. What's been found on stone crosses, illuminated manuscripts, stuff like that." She consulted the paper he'd handed back to her to verify the call numbers. Tipping her head back, she scanned the spine labels. "I thought maybe if we found the design on the brooch in one of these books, you'd be able to figure out when they first appeared."

"And we would know the brooch was made sometime after the first use of those designs," he said as if clarifying the idea in his mind.

"That's the theory anyway. You also might be able to figure out which region it's from, you know, if it's Scottish or Irish or Welsh." When she found the books she was looking for, she said, "Here we go." She slid one from the shelf, the protective dust jacket cover crinkling in her hands. She flipped it open to a photo of a stone Celtic cross on one page and a detailed drawing of its designs on the other.

James peered at the book from over her shoulder. She turned the page and he pointed at a picture. "That looks familiar."

Quinn read the small print under the photo. "It's a Celtic knot." She snapped the book closed. "We have a winner." She scanned the titles of the books on either side of the first's location and took the ones that looked most promising from the shelf.

They exited the stacks and walked toward a nearby vacant table. "Why don't you look through these books and I'll go back to the desk and see what else I can find for you." She placed the books on the table while James set his belongings down next to them. He slipped off his jacket and hung it on the back of a chair.

"This is brilliant." He took a seat and looked up at her. "Thank you so much for your help."

"You're welcome. It's why they pay me the big bucks."

Her heart skipped a beat—again—at the dazzling smile on his face. "I'll check back with you in a little while with whatever else I find."

She hustled back toward the reference desk. She sighed when she realized her research for James would have to wait. Ed Robles, a fellow reference librarian, was already occupied with one patron while two more stood waiting at the counter.

For the next forty-five minutes, a steady stream of patrons kept her busy. Between pointing out the parenting books to the harried young mother with a death grip around the wrist of her scowling three-year-old—the kid was clearly approaching critical mass and a thermonuclear tantrum seemed imminent—tracking down the sports page of the local newspaper to the men's room and having to send Ed in to retrieve it, and helping the man in oil-stained pants find the correct pages for his pickup in a service manual, she didn't have a moment to give James's Celtic brooch a second thought.

When the action at the desk finally slowed, she did some research. She compared James's brooch to a similar one owned by the British Museum and guessed it to be from the eighth or ninth century A.D. Quinn also found the title of a book that looked spot-on and tracked down a copy at UCLA's main research library. It would be a fun field trip to go on campus again and take a look at it if need be.

She set off toward James's table, excited to share the information she'd uncovered with him. She turned the corner and saw the empty chair. Her steps slowed as she scanned the area, thinking perhaps he'd moved to another location. He was nowhere to be seen. She reached the table and noted the books she'd left him with remained. His jacket and briefcase, like their owner, were gone.

Chapter Two

Quinn walked into the Bullpen to find a young woman sitting in her desk chair and spinning herself around and around. Her long, jet black hair moved like a silk curtain in a breeze with each new rotation. "You're late," she said without stopping.

"And you're in my chair," Quinn countered to her best friend.

Nicole Park stopped and faced Quinn. After some rapid blinking to clear the dizziness, Nicole's dark eyes found Quinn's face. "I had to sit somewhere while I waited for you."

"You didn't have to spin."

"What good is a swivel chair if you don't spin?" When Quinn didn't answer right away, she pointed and said, "See? You're totally going to do it all the time now."

There was a reason her friend was a children's librarian. Kids—and everyone else, for that matter—were drawn to Nicole's sense of wonder, ebullient personality, and warm smile. She was a natural fit for the job.

"Who says I don't already?"

Nicole giggled. "The truth comes out."

"Yes, you've found me out," Quinn said, the mock shame

heavy in her tone. She flicked a glance over her shoulder and then leaned in. "When no one else is around, I've spun in my chair a time or two."

Nicole dropped her chin and gazed up at her from under an arched eyebrow. "You wild thing, you."

"That's me." Quinn came around to the other side of the desk and pulled open the bottom drawer. She lifted out the paper lunch sack and pushed at the drawer with her foot. It slid closed with an echoing boom. "Ready?"

"Oh, come on, Q," Nicole said, exasperated. "Not another sad little peanut butter and jelly sandwich."

"You know it's all I can afford right now. Christmas is coming up and I don't want to have to buy my niece and nephews their presents from the library's discarded books sale table. I'm not sure the two-year-old would appreciate the nuances of a steamy bodice ripper."

"You don't know until you try. He might like it."

"Says the most inappropriate children's librarian ever. I'll go with you to the deli, though."

"Deal."

Twenty minutes later, they sat on a bench in front of the library—where its close proximity to the beach meant that most fiction books were returned with sand between the pages and smelling faintly of suntan lotion. They munched on their lunches and soaked up the early December Southern California sunshine.

"So, tell me about the cute guy you were chatting up at the reference desk earlier," Nicole said before she took another bite of her chicken salad sandwich. "That's a nice way to start the week."

"Who? Mr. Ackerman? I guess he's cute for a guy my grandpa's age." She had discovered the whereabouts of the missing sports page on behalf of Mr. Ackerman, the sweet widower who came into the library every day to read the newspaper.

Nicole bumped Quinn with a shoulder. "Don't give me that crap, Q. You know who I mean: brown leather jacket, jeans. Don't tell me you didn't notice the thick, wavy, dark blond hair."

Quinn had indeed noticed the thick, wavy, dark blond hair.

"When we get back from lunch, you should ask him out."

"I'm not going to ask him out."

"Why not?"

"Well, for one thing, he might be married."

"Was he wearing a ring?"

"No, but that doesn't necessarily mean anything."

"You should have asked."

"Not exactly part of the reference interview, Nic. 'Does the owner have any information on the brooch? Oh, and by the way, are you married?'" She took a sip of water from her bottle. "Subtle."

"You're clever enough to have found out without him even realizing it. You're good at getting information from people."

"It's part of the job," she answered with a shrug. "When someone comes in and says, 'I want to find a book I read last year. It's about this guy who's a lawyer and his wife leaves him. Can you tell me where it is?' you have to know how to get more details out of them." Nicole was right, though. Off the top of her head, she could think of at least three different questions she could have asked to find out James's marital status. "Even if I was crazy enough to ask, I can't. He left."

"He left?" Nicole's voice pitched up an octave. "He looked like he was going to be there a while when I saw you with him at the table."

"I thought so, too. I even did more research for him. But when I went to talk to him, he was gone."

"Maybe he went to lunch and he'll be back."

"Maybe."

"And when he comes back, you need to ask him out."

"You know I'm not going to do that. Besides, I don't know anything about him other than he works for an insurance company. He could be a descendant of Jack the Ripper for all I know."

"Why Jack the Ripper?"

Quinn heaved a sigh, knowing full well there was a tsunami-sized reaction coming. "He's British."

"He's British? Oh my God!" Nicole clutched at her chest. "A handsome British guy! Quinn Ellington's kryptonite."

The heads of both the man passing in front of them and the dog he was walking swung toward them at Nicole's hoots. Quinn just closed her eyes and shook her head. Drawing unwanted attention was simply part of the territory whenever she was in public with Nicole. Eyeing the medium-sized dog with a flashy marbled white, black, and copper coat, Quinn said, "Did you know Australian shepherds aren't from Australia at all? They were developed as herding dogs on ranches in the western United States."

"I didn't know that, and don't change the subject. If you don't ask him out, I'll do it for you."

"Don't you dare."

"Come on, Q. He's British, he's cute . . ." Nicole raised a finger as she ticked off each point.

"He's gone, I'll never see him again, and I don't ask guys out . . ." Quinn raised her fingers as she spoke, mimicking Nicole.

"You're so old-fashioned." Nicole popped the last bite of sandwich into her mouth. After she swallowed, she said, "Fine. Forget the British dude. We still need to get you out there."

"No, we really don't. I'm good." The words came out as more of a growl than she intended. Quinn stared at the traffic flowing past.

"Fair enough," Nicole said. "The last guy we set you up with wasn't exactly Mr. Perfect."

"You think?" Quinn said wryly. "I'm sure the feeling was mutual—I thought he was kidding when he said I should become a fruitarian. Turns out he wasn't. Oops."

"I blame Brian. It was his idea to set you up with that dopey friend of his in the first place."

"It's okay. His heart was in the right place. No harm, no foul."

"We'll find the right guy for you someday." Nicole brightened and sat up straight. "Hey! I know. You should go out with Brian and me tonight. We're going to check out the new Korean barbecue place after work. Come with us and enjoy the food of my people."

Quinn cut her eyes toward her friend. "Your mom wants you to check it out and then reassure her that her food is way better, doesn't she?"

"You know it." They stood and walked toward the front steps of the library. "You should come. It'll be fun."

"You know how I feel about being a third wheel."

"I know, but this is no big deal. Just dinner. You've gone out with us before. You like Brian, right?"

"You know I do." Brian practically worshipped Nicole, and the two of them together were adorable.

"Look, you're always talking about how you'd like something exciting to happen in your life once in a while." Nicole paused. "Although now that I think about it, I'm not sure going out for Korean barbecue is exactly what you had in mind."

"Are you kidding? The food of your people is always an adventure. I never know when some superspicy kimchi will turn me into a fire-breathing dragon."

They climbed the steps toward the entrance. "See? You totally want to go now."

"I do, but I can't. No money, remember?"

"Yeah, I know. I could—"

"No. I appreciate the offer, but no." She grabbed the handle and pulled open one of the glass double doors.

"Okay. Promise me you'll go out with us after the holidays when you can afford it."

"I promise."

"Good. I'll hold you to it."

Their conversation came to an end now that they were inside the library. "See you," Quinn said quietly as they split off.

Nicole waved and strode toward the children's section.

As Quinn walked through the main reading room, she couldn't stop herself from glancing at the table where James sat earlier in the day. The books were still there. He was not. The fact she was disappointed and annoyed only served to aggravate her more. Determined not to let it bother her, she tamped down her irritation, lowered her head, and marched toward her office.

The mail clamped between her upper arm and rib cage nearly dropped to the floor as Quinn unlocked the door to her Sherman Oaks apartment and pushed it open. She was plunged into darkness when she kicked the door closed with a foot. She immediately relocked the dead bolt and flipped the wall switch. The table lamp illuminated the living room with a warm, yellow glow.

Rasputin blinked against the light and trotted toward her.

"Hey, how's the kitty?" She walked to the kitchen counter and dumped her purse, keys, and mail on it. After she slipped off her jacket and tossed it over the back of the couch, the cat rubbed his side against her shin and curled his tail around her calf. He looked up at her and meowed in greeting.

She scooped him up and slung his front paws over her left shoulder. He purred in her ear. "You're probably hungry," she said and scratched his head.

Rasputin's nails gripped her shoulder as she carried him into the kitchen and retrieved from the refrigerator the can that contained the other half of the food she'd fed him that morning. After carefully removing his claws from the fabric of her top, she set Rasputin on the kitchen floor and picked up his bowl. A fishy odor wafted around her when she removed the lid from the can. Both sound and smell elicited impatient noises from the cat. She whacked the can against the side of the bowl until the food plopped out.

"Yum. Salmon. Your favorite." Quinn set the bowl on the place mat dotted with black paw prints and smoothed her hand over the cat's back as he plowed into his dinner. Bits of food went flying, some of it sticking to the wall. "You eat like my brothers."

She opened the refrigerator and grabbed a bottle of water, then guzzled half of it in one breath and expelled a loud burp. "Monroe would be proud," she said of the brother who had taught her proper belching technique when they were kids—which reminded her she hadn't listened to her voice mail. She set the bottle on the counter, took her smartphone from her pocket, and touched the voice mail icon on the screen.

"Quincy," she heard her dad's voice say in his usual brusque manner. Nearly everyone who ever interacted with her father was completely awed and intimidated by him. She knew underneath that gruff exterior, he was a big teddy bear. "Call us when you get home."

"Yes, Dad," she said and deleted the message. She'd call him back after she ate dinner, as long as it was before eight o'clock. Anyone calling after that was a hooligan in her dad's book.

She turned on the TV, surfed around until she found a college basketball game, and listened to it while she changed into her flannel pajamas. Now comfortable and barefoot, she padded to the kitchen, stood in front of the open refrigerator, and considered her dinner options. When inspiration failed to strike, she moved and stood vigil in front of the mostly empty pantry. The idea of eating ramen noodles again made her scowl and she'd had a peanut butter sandwich for lunch. She finally settled on macaroni and cheese and took the box from the shelf.

It wasn't long before she flopped down on the beat-up couch and watched the game while she ate her dinner straight from the pot. Her oldest brother, George, first purchased the sofa when he'd furnished his apartment in law school. It had subsequently been passed from one sibling to the next until it now found its home with her. Its best days were clearly behind it, and Quinn didn't even want to know about the origins of some of the larger stains that graced the upholstery. But the couch had been the right price: free.

She refrained from eating the entire contents of the pot—she'd done that once before and the resulting stomachache was one she'd never forget. She put the leftovers in a plastic container. As a bonus to not giving herself a bellyache, she now had lunch for the next day.

Once the dishes were washed, she snagged her phone and returned to her spot on the couch. She'd barely sat down when Rasputin jumped up and began to knead her thigh with his front paws. When he'd apparently come to the conclusion her leg had been sufficiently massaged, he curled up on her lap and purred. She dialed and idly rubbed the thin fur in front of the cat's ears with her pinky and thumb.

"Hello," her father barked, his tone clearly questioning if the caller knew exactly what time it was.

"Hey, Dad." Quinn shot a look at the clock on the bookshelf against a wall. It was five minutes to eight. "Sorry I didn't call earlier. I was really hungry when I got home and ate dinner first."

"That's okay. Was it dark when you left work?"

"Mmm-hmm."

"When you walked to your car, did you have your car key ready to use as a weapon like I showed you?"

"I did." The answer to his next question—they'd had the same conversation many times before—was already formed in her mind. Since her father was also a Marine, this kind of thing was part of her life.

"What are your primary targets?"

"Eyes and throat."

His tone softened. "That's my girl. How was work?"

"It was fun. Among other things, I had a high schooler ask where she could find *Tequila Mockingjay*. After some questions, I figured out she meant *To Kill a Mockingbird*." Her interaction with James was definitely not something she wanted to talk about with her dad.

"Glad you had a nice day." He paused and Quinn heard her mother's voice in the background. "Your mother wants to make sure you're still coming for Grandpa's birthday party this weekend."

"Of course I'll be there. I wouldn't miss it. He'll only turn eighty once."

"Good. Just wanted to make sure since the whole crew will be here."

Her eyebrows shot up. "Really? Even Madison? I thought he couldn't come."

"His *gig* fell through." She stifled a giggle but still grinned at the exasperation in her father's voice and pictured him rolling his eyes. "Maybe this'll knock some sense into him and he'll finally get a real job."

"Dad," Quinn said in a warning tone while she heard her mother say, "Robert," at the same time and in the same way. Quinn heard him blow out a breath. "No matter what he does, I'm supportive of his choices."

Quinn's silent snicker at the rather rehearsed way her father made his declaration shook the cat on her lap. Rasputin's eyelids were opened to little more than slits when he looked up at her and meowed in protest. Her gaze fell on the framed photo of her parents next to the lamp on the end table. "You and Mom have always been there for all of us," Quinn said softly.

"You're good kids," he said and cleared his throat. "It's getting late and you should get to bed soon."

She knew she would never be too old for him to tell her it was time for her to go to bed. Despite the fact it was only a few minutes after eight, she said, "Okay. Say good night to Mom for me."

"Will do. Talk to you soon."

"Good night."

She set the phone down and turned up the volume on the TV. Between watching basketball and scrolling through her various social media accounts on her laptop, she managed to kill the rest of the evening. When a jaw-cracking yawn overtook her, she decided it was time for bed.

She switched off the TV and closed her laptop. Rasputin stood, arched his back in a stretch, and then jumped to the floor, paws thumping lightly on the carpet. She double-checked the locks on the door and turned off the lamp. Pale light from a nearby streetlight filtered into the room through the thin curtains.

After brushing her teeth, she found Rasputin lounging like a king in the middle of her bed. He never moved, even when she slid under the covers and settled back against her pillow. She picked up a book from the nightstand, the latest in a series of spy novels her grandfather had loaned her. She settled in, excited to find out how MI6 spy extraordinaire Edward Walker would escape the clutches of nefarious Brazilian drug lord Teodoro Aguiar Boaventura with only a Bic lighter, a gum wrapper, and an overripe guava.

Chapter Three

Quinn trained her rifle at the middle section of the tree and squeezed the trigger several times in quick succession. She watched where the rounds disappeared into the thick boughs. The way the branches bounced and shook—different than when moved by the breeze—confirmed her suspicion. The bogie was hiding up in the tree.

Whipping her head and rifle back, she pressed her back against the palm tree she hid behind. Pointy bits of bark poked her in the back of the head. She ignored the irritation, and focused on controlling her breathing. That's what Edward Walker would do. She took a deep breath in and blew it out slowly, like he did in *Target São Paulo*. And sure enough, after a few more breaths, the pronounced pounding in her chest began to lessen.

She glanced at her brother John hunkered down behind a shrub a couple of yards to her left. "Hey!" she whispered. He looked at her and she pointed at the tree on the other side of their parents' backyard. "Monroe," she said. He sent her a thumbs-up in reply. She peeked around the palm tree again. A pellet exploded against the trunk inches from her face, the spray splattering the visor of her face mask with blue paint. She snapped her head back and tried to make herself even smaller behind the only thing protecting her from the paint-filled projectiles.

As long as Monroe was hidden behind the leaves of that tree, she and John, the last surviving members of Red Team, were pinned down. Madison had been the first member of their team to go out. But at least he'd taken Tom, of Blue Team, with him. Monroe must have climbed the tree during the skirmish. Quinn hadn't seen since at the exact same moment, she and John had scampered for shelter at the other end of the yard. Now it was two against two. George, Quinn's oldest brother, was hiding behind the far corner of the house.

"George!" John shouted. "Come out from there. You know we're not supposed to get too close to the house. Mom will kill us if we get paint on it."

"Then don't shoot," George yelled back. "If you hit the house you have to clean it up."

"What are we gonna do?" Quinn asked John. "We move from here and Monroe will pick us off."

John shook his head. "Dunno."

A shout of "Hi, Daddy!" drew Quinn's attention to the patio where her four-year-old niece, Bailey—resplendent in the Cinderella princess ball gown Quinn's grandmother had made—stood. She waved at the corner where George hid. "Can you see me waving, Daddy?"

George peered around the edge of the house and waved at his daughter. His mask muffled his voice, but Quinn could still easily make out his words. "Hi, Bailey honey! I can see—Ow!"

A red blotch of paint bloomed on George's shoulder. Quinn looked over at John just as he pulled his rifle back and crouched behind the bush again. Shots of retribution came from Monroe up the tree. Quinn was certain behind his mask, John grinned like the Cheshire cat.

Quinn peered toward the patio again and watched George step out into the open. He ripped off his mask and with a fierce scowl, shouted in John and Quinn's direction "You su—" At the sight of his daughter's big, brown eyes, the word died on his lips. He amended his almost "You suck!" to "Taking me out when I'm saying hi to my daughter? You're the worst."

"Boo frickin' hoo!" John pushed his face mask up onto the top of his head. He remained stooped behind the bush when he shouted back, "You come out of your hidey-hole and I'm gonna pick you off."

George crossed the patio and shed his gear. Once he was paint-free he picked up his daughter and kissed her cheek. "Hiya, pumpkin."

"I'm sorry you got hit, Daddy." Quinn heard a quiver in Bailey's voice.

"It's not your fault. Uncle John's a cheater." He smiled at his daughter. "This way, I get to spend more time with you."

Bailey grinned and hugged his neck. Over her shoulder, George frowned and said, "You're still the worst, John." He flopped down in an empty chair and set Bailey on his lap. Father and daughter joined former combatants Madison and Tom, as well as Quinn's father and grandfather who also watched the battle.

"Yeah, yeah. Whatever," John said. "You're the cheater, not me. And stop impugning my reputation in front of my niece."

Quinn chuckled. Her two oldest brothers had always had a competitive and at times combative relationship. As a little girl, she remembered more than one occasion when they had to spend time in separate rooms to cool off. Their rivalry had mellowed now that they were adults—except, apparently, when paintball was involved.

"Improve your reputation and I will," George shot back.

That triggered a round of "ooooos" from the peanut gallery.

When John looked over at Quinn, she noted his set jaw and the flare of his nostrils. "I can't lose to his team now. I'll never hear the end of it." She hadn't heard that snarl in his voice in ages. "How do we get Monroe out of that tree? You got any ideas?" The way he squinted at her, he looked just like their dad.

Quinn pushed up her mask. She sucked in a deep breath and took in the familiar scent of ocean. It was good to be back at her parents' house in San Diego County, not far from Marine Corps Base Camp Pendleton where her dad was stationed. To Quinn, it would always be home.

"I might," she replied. "You read *The Basque Assassin* yet?"

"Just finished it the other day." He cocked his head and stared at her, trying to work out what scenario she might be alluding to. After half a minute, his face cleared. "You're talking about when Edward Walker shoots the Basque Assassin when he comes out of his hiding place to help that pregnant woman who stumbled and fell, aren't you?" John shook his head emphatically. "No. You can't. What if Monroe doesn't fall for it? He'll take you out in one shot. Your sacrifice will be for nothing."

"I know, but what choice do we have? We're at an impasse. Monroe can sit up there all day, just like we can hide here all day. Something's gotta give and I don't want it to be my bladder. The only way is to flush him out—no pun intended."

He snorted at her quip. Squinting at her again, he said, "Playing a pregnant woman? You trying to tell me something?"

"Ew. No." She grimaced like she'd just slammed a glass of shark chum. "One more crack like that and I'll shoot you myself."

Chuckling, John replaced his mask and said, "Okay. Let's go for it. I'll lay down cover fire. Good luck."

"Thanks. I'll go after one." She tugged her mask over her face and took a couple of deep breaths to center herself. When she did, she realized she sounded a bit like Darth Vader. "'Luke, I am your father,'" she rumbled in as deep a voice as she could muster. After regaining her focus, she looked over to John and held up three fingers. She started her countdown after his thumbs-up.

"Three. Two. One." She gripped her rifle in both hands, spun out from behind the tree, and sprinted toward the wooden swing set. At the same time, John shot one pellet after another at Monroe's position.

Quinn zigzagged across the grass, dodging Monroe's volley. Thankfully, John's cover fire seemed to be interfering with his aim. Monroe missed her every time.

Quinn was almost to the play set's plastic slide when her left foot caught on a clump of grass, sending her sprawling. She lost her grip on her rifle when her hands shot out to break her fall. The air in her lungs gusted out in a whoosh when she crashed to the grass. Rolling onto her back, she ripped off her headgear and tossed it to the side. She stared up at the patchy clouds in the sky and cradled her left wrist against her abdomen.

She heard a chorus of "Quinn! Are you okay?" En masse, the spectators jumped up and ran to her.

Robert, her father, reached her first and dropped to his knees beside her. "What hurts, Quincy?"

"My wrist," she groaned, her face contorted.

He gently probed the bones of her wrist with the tips of his fingers. "It doesn't feel like anything's broken. Can you sit up?"

"Yeah, I think so."

Robert slipped a hand under her shoulders and helped

her sit. From the corner of her eye, she caught a glimpse of Monroe as he sprang down from the lower branches of the tree and landed lightly on his feet.

Four quick shots came from John's position behind her. Four tightly grouped blotches of red materialized on Monroe's vest. Monroe tore off his face mask—his blond hair sticking out in all directions—and looked down at the stains on his chest. Incredulous, he glared at John. "You shot me? Our sister is hurt and you shot me? George is right. You do suck." The second the word slipped out, he winced. His gaze traveled from Bailey to her father. "Sorry."

George shrugged it off and pinned an accusatory stare on Quinn. "Are you even hurt?"

Now she felt bad for making everyone worry about her. She looked up at him sheepishly. "No. I fell on purpose to get Monroe out of the tree."

Tom cast a glance up at the sky and shook his head. Wordlessly, he turned away and headed for the house.

An exuberant grin exploded on Madison's bearded face. He stooped, grabbed Quinn's hand, and hauled her to her feet. "We won!" He gave John, who had just joined the group, a high-five. "Nice shooting, bro." To Quinn, he said, "Awesome fall, sis. I totally bought it."

She smiled at her ever-ebullient brother. "Thanks."

Quinn picked up her equipment and the group started for the house. As she removed her vest and peeled off her camouflage jacket, Grandpa gazed at her. His blue eyes gleamed with approval when he said, "Excellent use of deception, angel. How'd you come up with that idea?"

She lifted a shoulder in a slight shrug. "*The Basque Assassin.*"

"Ah," he said and nodded. "It's on my reading list. I'll get to it as soon as I finish *Code Name: Tungsten.*"

"I can't believe I fell for that trick," Monroe said, looking rather grumpy. He took off his crimson-spotted vest and dumped it on the pile. "Chance Stryker and Petra Vučinića did almost the exact same thing in *The Hercules Transgression.*"

"I haven't read that one yet. I guess I know what I'll be reading after *Down the Spider Hole,*" Quinn said with a smile she hoped would ease the sting of defeat. She plunged her hand into the ice-filled chest of drinks sitting on the patio, retrieved a bottle of beer, and held it out to Monroe as a peace offering. "Thanks for coming down from the tree to check on me."

After a momentary scowl, he relented and smiled at her. "You're welcome." He took the proffered bottle and flicked off the cap with an opener. Before he took a drink, he pointed the top of the bottle at her and said, "It's a big brother's job to look out for his baby sister."

"And I'm really lucky to have five big brothers."

"Well, four who look out for you," George said. "John was willing to sacrifice you if that plan didn't work." Good-natured teasing replaced the pique that had colored his tone earlier.

"Hey! It was her idea. She volunteered," John said and shot a smirk at Monroe. "It was the only way it would work. We all know Monroe would've never come down to check on me if I was hurt."

Monroe lifted his bottle in salute. "True that."

Now that all the battle participants were paint-free and divested of their gear, Robert slid the patio door open and everyone filed past him into the family room.

Once George lowered Bailey to her feet after carrying her into the house, the little girl made a beeline for Quinn. "Aunt Quinn?" Bailey gently patted her aunt's thigh. "Can I ask you something?"

Quinn squatted down and looked into Bailey's angelic face. "Of course, sweetie. What do you want to know?"

Bailey's dark brown eyes rounded and a somber look overtook her face. The four-year-old gulped and said in a timid voice, "Did you lie to us and Uncle Monroe when you said you were hurt but really weren't?"

Oh boy, Quinn thought. Her first instinct was to leap up and shout to George or his wife, Isabelle, that there was a parenting emergency. She held off, though, once she realized she could call in the big guns if she crashed and burned. "That's a really good question, Bailey," Quinn answered, giving herself a minute to think. She reached out and moved one of the long, brown pigtails behind Bailey's shoulder. "You know a lie is when you say something to someone you know isn't true, right? Like, if you broke one of Wyatt's toys and when your mommy asks you who broke it, you say Wyatt did?"

Bailey's eyes grew even wider as she slowly nodded her head. "Mmm-hmm." Her nod morphed into a headshake. "I would never do that."

Quinn smiled and rubbed a hand up and down Bailey's arm. "I know you wouldn't. What I did is a little different. It was a trick. I wanted Uncle Monroe to come down from the tree, so I pretended to be hurt. As soon as he fell for the trick and climbed down, I let him know I wasn't really hurt after all. Does that make sense?" Quinn wasn't sure if it made sense herself.

Bailey's eyebrows drew together. "Kinda."

It was clear the little girl was not convinced. Quinn racked her brain to come up with an example. Fortunately, one came to her when she looked past Bailey and into the living room. It was pretty lame, but it was the best she could come up with. "Say you really, really, really want to see Santa when he comes to your house on Christmas Eve, so during the night you lie on the couch near your Christmas tree and wait. You hear Santa come down the chimney, but you know he'll leave right away if he knows you're awake. So you pretend to be asleep, but peek at him through your eyelashes. By pretending to be asleep, you trick Santa and see him. Do you understand?"

She held her breath as Bailey tipped her head to one side and thought it through. Quinn hoped there wouldn't be any follow-up questions regarding the intricacies of Santa Claus's omniscience.

After what seemed like an eternity, Bailey said, "Yup, I understand." The little girl brightened and chirped, "Will you read me a story now?"

Quinn released a relieved breath and smiled. "I would love to read you a story." She looked over to her mother who moved around the kitchen with the efficiency of a general before launching an attack. With an iron fist in a velvet glove, Marie had raised six kids on her own when Quinn's father had been deployed at different times as she grew up. The woman was Quinn's hero.

"Hey, Mom. Do you need me to help you right now or do I have time to read Bailey a story before we have cake?"

"Go ahead and read. It'll be a little while yet."

"Okay." To Bailey, she said, "Go get a book and meet me on the couch."

Bailey scampered off, Cinderella dress swaying as she ran. Quinn barely sat down on the leather couch when her niece skidded to a stop in front of her. Bailey dropped the book onto her aunt's lap, clamored up onto the couch, and settled in next to her.

Quinn immediately knew which book she'd chosen, despite only having caught a glimpse of the cover. "You picked a great one. I love *Tacky the Penguin*. Grandma used to read it to me all the time when I was your age."

Quinn opened the book to the title page and huffed a half laugh. Her five-year-old self had scrawled her name in large, hesitant letters in the upper right-hand corner of the page. She had obviously misjudged the length of her last name and had only gotten to the second *L* in Ellington before she'd run out of room. Her solution had been to turn the book sideways and finish the rest of her name down the side of the page.

"My friend Nicole is a children's librarian and she says the kids always want her to read them Tacky stories."

Bailey didn't seem particularly impressed by Quinn's observation and wiggled with impatience. Taking the hint, Quinn turned to the first page and read the story of how Tacky the Penguin's nonconformity to penguin stereotypes saved him and his penguin friends from a group of hunters.

After Quinn finished the book, she noticed her grandmother had joined her mother in the kitchen. "I'm gonna go help Grandma and Great-Grandma get Great-Grandpa's birthday cake ready. Maybe I can read you another story a little later."

"Okay. I'm gonna see if Wyatt is up from his nap." Bailey slid off the couch and bolted from the room in search of her two-year-old brother.

"Don't wake up Hunter. Aunt Stephanie and Uncle John had a hard time getting him down for his nap and he still needs to sleep." Bailey and Wyatt's three-year-old cousin hadn't wanted to miss out on the excitement and had battled naptime with every fiber of his being.

"I won't," Bailey called, already in another part of the house.

Quinn joined her mother and grandmother in the kitchen and was immediately put in charge of placing the candles on the cake. An in-depth discussion ensued between the three generations of women as they deliberated the merits and dangers of having eighty burning candles on one cake. It was decided the hazards far outweighed the benefits, and the best course of action was to use two number candles: an *8* and a *0*.

Soon the cake was deployed to the dining room table and the entire family assembled, including Wyatt, still groggy from his nap. Grandpa took his place of honor behind the cake and the group belted out a raucous and enthusiastic rendition of "Happy Birthday." Pictures were taken and the candles were blown out. Within five minutes, everyone had a piece of cake and a scoop of ice cream. Quinn could only shake her head in absolute amazement at her mother's and grandmother's mad cake cutting and serving skills. Sadly, the hostess gene didn't seem to have been passed on to her.

Quinn took her plate and wandered back into the family room. Madison and Monroe sat on the couch and shoved each other as both tried to stab the other's cake with his fork. She had no intention of ending up with frosting in her hair, so she found an empty spot on the floor on the other side of the room and sat.

Carrying a yellow plastic dump truck, Wyatt toddled over to Quinn and dropped the toy in front of her with a clunk. He sat on the floor next to it and stared up at her with the same dark brown eyes as his mother and sister. "Truck."

"Okay. Let's play with your truck." Quinn set her plate on the coffee table and began to load whatever she could find into the hopper: the TV remote, a wadded-up napkin, a rubber ball she'd spotted under a chair, and a pen. She made appropriate engine noises as she crawled across the floor, pushing the truck along. Wyatt's gaze followed her. When she stopped the vehicle, intoned a high-pitched "Beep, beep, beep," and lifted the front of the hopper, its contents slid onto the floor in a pile.

Wyatt bounced and clapped his pudgy hands, squealing with delight. Then he stood and waddled over to Quinn and the truck. He squatted down and began to drop the stuff she'd just dumped out into the hopper again.

"So, Quinn," her sister-in-law started from where she sat. "Are you dating anyone?"

Quinn suppressed a groan. She'd hoped to get through the day without anyone asking her that most despised question, especially since she had nothing to report.

Isabelle had plucked a nerve, but Quinn loved her and refused to be short with her. She knew the question was in no way malicious. She shrugged and said, "Nope. Not dating anyone."

"It's too bad we live so far away. There are some really great guys at George's law firm we could set you up with."

She wasn't sure how to respond. For the first time ever, Quinn was grateful they lived in Seattle. Thankfully, a way out presented itself when she caught a distinctive odor wafting up from Wyatt's backside. Quinn pointed at the toddler and said, "I think someone needs a change."

"Thanks for the heads-up." Isabelle stood and scooped her son up into her arms. "*Ven aquí, chico hermoso.*" As the two headed out of the room, Wyatt waved at Quinn.

She waved back and said, "See you in a few minutes, buddy." She watched them go and reflected on what an odd thing it was to be thankful for a loaded diaper.

Quinn and her grandfather sat alone in the dimly lit living room, illumination coming only from a small lamp and the hundreds of colored lights aglow on the Christmas tree. The house was mostly quiet, except for the sounds of a football game emanating from the TV in the family room and Pot Roast, her grandparents' English bulldog, snoring a few feet away. The lump of a dog rumbled like an idling Harley-Davidson.

"Thank you again for the new book, angel," Grandpa said. "I appreciate it, but you shouldn't have spent money on me. I know how much you struggle to make ends meet."

She pulled her legs up and settled deeper into the cushioned chair. "I couldn't resist getting you the latest Edward Walker novel. And don't worry about the cost." She leaned closer to him and said in a conspiratorial whisper, "I got the library discount."

The wrinkles at the corners of his eyes deepened when he smiled. "Well, no matter how you got it, thank you. And you can borrow it when I'm done."

"Thanks. Those novels help me get my adventure fix, even if it is vicariously."

"No plans to take a trip to some exotic locale?"

"No," she said and heaved a defeated sigh. "I don't have the money. I'm just glad you and Grandma spend the winters here in San Diego so I can see you. I wouldn't be able to afford to fly out to Maryland to visit."

"I have an idea. It might be difficult, but it will be worth it in the end."

"What?"

"I want you to get a jar and put a five-dollar bill in it every single day. I know trying to save a thousand dollars sounds like an impossible task, but if you do it five dollars at a time, you won't notice. By the end of a year, you'll have over eighteen hundred dollars. You could go on a pretty great trip with that much money."

Given her tight finances, she wasn't sure she could pull it off. But it was a great idea and she told her grandfather so. "I'll do my best, Grandpa."

"I know, angel. You always do."

Chapter Four

Quinn typed the search terms into the little box on her computer screen, her fingers flying from key to key like the legs of a water spider skittering across the surface of a pond. The clattering ceased once she hit the enter key with a little more force than was probably necessary. A split second later, the screen filled with the results of her query. Her nose scrunched with disapproval when she skimmed over the list of titles. Fantasy books were definitely not what she was looking for. Partway through the list, she spotted a book that looked promising.

She picked up her mug and sipped the lukewarm tea. When Quinn's gaze landed on her search terms "flat earth" highlighted in red in the online table of contents, she felt the familiar tingle of excitement she got whenever she found the librarian's equivalent of a gold nugget. "Bingo," she whispered and returned the mug to her desk with a clunk.

She switched tabs in her browser and reread the e-mail from a high school student named Cody.

"I have to write a paper about how most people a long time ago didn't really think the earth was flat after all and my teacher won't let me use Wikipedia. I don't know what to do." His confession made her sad. It pleased her he reached out to the library for help, though.

She scribbled down the title and call number on a scrap of paper, jumped up, and headed for the nonfiction stacks. She skirted past the row of patrons sitting at the library's computers and walked toward Mr. Ackerman, firmly ensconced in one of the cushy reading chairs. He lowered the newspaper and peered up at her from under bushy eyebrows.

Smiling down at him, she said in a low tone, "Anything exciting happening in the world?"

"Nah. Same old, same old." He snapped the paper in disgust. "Stupid politicians have their heads so far up their colons they—" He gave her an apologetic look. "Beg your pardon."

She patted him on the shoulder. "No worries. My dad said almost the exact same thing just yesterday."

"Your dad sounds like a smart man." He cocked his head to one side. "How'd the Bruins do last night?"

She hoped his question was conversational and not because the sports page was languishing in the men's room again. "They won, but just barely. Their best three-point shooter had an off game. Hopefully, he'll get hot in the next one."

He nodded and stroked his closely trimmed white beard. "For your sake, I hope he does."

"You know me well."

Without warning, a chill raced up her spine. She scanned the area, moving her head just a fraction. There, next to a table that displayed various books on decorating Christmas cookies stood the head honcho and her boss: Virginia Harris, library director. Magnificent in her black pantsuit, crisp canary yellow top, and black shoes that made no sound when she walked, Virginia Harris was as no-nonsense as the severe bob of her white hair.

Quinn's eyes went round as she glanced at Mr. Ackerman. "I gotta get back to work." The humor she saw reflected back in his eyes told her he understood everything.

"See you later," she said as she moved away.

"Yup." The newspaper rustled and he said in a singsong voice, "Good luck."

She strode off toward the stacks again, hoping not only to locate the book she sought, but also to find protection from Virginia's eagle-eyed scrutiny. Along the way, she glanced toward the table where James had sat the week before. She wasn't angry he'd left without a word. How could she be? He was under no obligation to tell her anything. What she felt was disappointment—due to the unresolved question of the Celtic brooch, of course. When she'd mentioned this to Nicole, her best friend had rolled her eyes and said, "Yeah, keep telling yourself that."

Quinn ducked into the appropriate aisle, skimmed the call numbers, located the book, and took it from the shelf. On her way back to her desk, she turned the corner at the end of the stacks and pulled up short. Her boss blocked her path.

"Good morning, Virginia."

"Good morning, Quinn." The bespectacled woman peered down at her from behind lenses so thick they made her light blue eyes appear much larger and rounder than they actually were. *Gollum* was the first thing Quinn thought whenever she looked into her boss's eyes. Fortunately, she had sufficient brain-to-mouth impulse control to keep that little bon mot to herself. "I haven't received your statistics from yesterday yet." Virginia's gaze traveled over Quinn's jeans. She sniffed with mild disapproval.

Quinn clamped her jaw shut. She was a librarian, but that didn't mean she had to dress in some horribly shapeless atrocity and wear her hair in a bun. Her male colleagues wore jeans all the time and Virginia never gave them a second glance. Quinn swallowed her frustration and replied, "I'm sorry. I'll turn them in as soon as I finish what I'm working on right now."

"See that you do. And be sure to mark you took that book off the shelf," Virginia ordered. "Statistics are the lifeblood of a public library. It's how we show the city council we're important to the community and keep our funding."

Although Virginia was as prickly as a pineapple, Quinn knew she spoke the truth. With so many people believing every question in the universe could be answered with a simple Google search, the relevance of and need for libraries was being questioned all too frequently. She met Virginia's eyes with a steady gaze. "You're absolutely right, Virginia. I always log everything I do, every material I use, and I will make sure to get my report to you before I leave today."

"Very good," Virginia said. Quinn detected a nearly indiscernible change in Virginia's stiff carriage. Apparently satisfied Quinn sufficiently grasped the importance of data collection and was taking it seriously, her boss was now a slightly less tightly coiled spring.

After a beat of awkward silence, Quinn held up the book and wiggled it. "I, um, I need to go answer this e-mail reference question."

"Yes, of course," she said with a nod. "Carry on." Virginia's sights were now set on some new, fresh horror. She stalked past Quinn, leaving the faint scent of powder and book glue in her wake.

Quinn drew in a deep breath and expelled it slowly. She'd landed her job at the library two years before—a job any twenty-four-year-old fresh out of library school would envy—and still Virginia Harris intimidated the living crap out of her.

She shook off the residual negative emotion that almost always clung to her after any interaction with her boss, crossed the main reading room, and returned to the Bullpen. When she reached her desk, she flopped into her chair and opened the book to the appropriate chapter.

The words on the page immediately engrossed her. She had just gotten to the part that explained how Washington Irving's nineteenth-century fictional account of Christopher Columbus setting out to prove the world was round became entrenched as fact in history books, when a voice from the doorway made her jump. She peered around her monitor and saw Rosemary from Reference poking her head through the doorway. "A patron at the desk is asking for you."

"Okay, thanks. I'll be there in a minute."

Quinn typed a quick response to Cody, informing him she had a book for him and that she'd put it on hold at the reference desk. Virginia's statistics would have to wait. She rolled her chair back, grabbed Cody's book, and strode out the door. Her footsteps slowed and the book nearly slipped from her hand when she saw James standing alone at the far end of the reference desk.

Her mouth went dry. When his gaze landed on her, the smile that formed on his face made her stomach flip. She took a deep breath and returned his smile with a tentative one of her own. "Hi" was all she could think to say.

James's smile never faded as he took her hand and shook it in greeting. "I'm so glad you're here. I wasn't sure if you were working today, but took the chance and stopped by just in case."

"Well, here I am," she answered with an awkward shrug.

"I want to apologize for leaving here without a word. I received an urgent call from my boss and had to return to London immediately. I wanted to tell you, but you were busy," he tipped his head indicating the desk, "and I didn't want to interrupt."

A less than eloquent "Oh" was the only response her suddenly blank mind could form. The way he held her hand in both of his caused the synapses in her brain to completely misfire.

"I just arrived in L.A. late last night and came here first thing." He dipped his head and looked into her face. "I was hoping you could help me with some more research."

As though a magician had snapped his fingers, her muddled brain sharpened in an instant. She was a professional. "Of course I can help you."

But before either of them could say anything else, Virginia charged at them. Quinn was instantly reminded of the children's book *The Story of Ferdinand,* the way the woman's breath whooshed from her nose. Virginia shot a disapproving look at James and grasped Quinn by the elbow. She steered her off to the side and glared at her with Gollum eyes. "Ms. Ellington, I would appreciate it if you and your boyfriend would refrain from conducting your private affairs during business hours. You're making a spectacle of yourself in front of the patrons."

Quinn jerked her arm from Virginia's clutches. "He's not my boyfriend," she whispered sharply. "He *is* a patron. I helped him last week." Quinn's fingernails dug into her palms when her hands balled into tight fists. "I'm doing my job."

Virginia blanched and took a half step back. "I'm sorry. I assumed. The way you two—"

"Yeah, well, don't."

From the corner of her eye, Quinn saw James cautiously step toward them. He wore a chagrined look as he shook Virginia's hand. "I'm so sorry. I seem to have gotten Quinn into a spot of bother, haven't I? I was here last week and she was so very helpful. I was asking her for additional assistance in finding materials in this fine repository of knowledge."

Quinn nearly smiled when she detected the subtle way James's voice had turned smoother and how his British accent became more refined and aristocratic. He studied Virginia and then said with a slight smile, "You have a keen eye for talent if you were the person who hired Quinn." Apparently, James had decided to launch a full-charm offensive on Virginia.

"It *was* me and yes, Quinn *is* one of our best reference librarians," Virginia gushed. "Her talents were obvious to me the moment I met her."

Quinn held back a snort. Her boss had never once complimented her in the two years she'd worked there.

"Of course," Virginia purred, "if you'd like to work with someone who has much more experience, I'm available as well."

When Quinn heard Virginia utter those words in that suggestive tone, her eyebrows shot up. In her life, she never believed she would observe Virginia Harris, library director, go from overbearing boss to prowling cougar. *Ick.*

"As tempting as that is . . ." James paused and waited for her to fill in her name.

"Virginia Harris, library director," she said, her voice coming from deep in her chest.

"As tempting as that is, Virginia," James continued, "Ms. Ellington is already familiar with my inquiry."

Quinn died a little inside when she heard him call her "Ms. Ellington." She hadn't told him her last name. That meant he'd heard every word Virginia had said, including the word "boyfriend." Spontaneous human combustion appeared to be the only viable way to escape the humiliation.

"And I'm sure," James continued, "that you, as library director, are irreplaceable in your other duties."

Quinn managed to keep from rolling her eyes when Virginia pursed her lips, nodded, and said, "That is so true."

"I'm glad I had this chance to speak with you because I was hoping, if it's acceptable to Quinn of course"—he glanced at Quinn and then looked back at Virginia—"that I could use her research expertise on a more permanent basis." He turned to Quinn and said, "I have a number of items to examine, not just the brooch. Would you be willing to work with me exclusively when I'm here?"

Quinn stared at him. The offer was completely unexpected and the entire situation was rather surreal. But there was no way she was going to pass up a chance to do something fun and different. "I'd love to work with you."

The library director in Virginia resurfaced. "This is highly irregular. I'm not sure I can approve of such an extraordinary request. I need Quinn to assist other patrons." Virginia narrowed her eyes at James. "Perhaps if you could reimburse the library for Quinn's time. I could use the money to staff the reference desk with another librarian while she's with you." Quinn could practically see the dollar signs flashing in Virginia's eyes. "We have a 'Friends of the Library' fund."

From the front pocket of his jeans, James removed a wad of cash secured with a silver money clip. He deftly slid the clip from the bills and flipped them up as he counted. Quinn gaped at the hundred-dollar bills.

When he slipped the clip back on the remaining money, Quinn observed his stash included wider, more colorful notes. Pounds and Euro notes, she noticed.

"I do hope two thousand dollars is sufficient for now," he said, holding out the cash.

Quinn shot out a hand and pushed the money back against his chest. She turned to Virginia and said, "I want confirmation. When Mr.—" She stopped and looked at him. "I'm sorry, I only know you as James."

"Lockwood."

She dipped her head in acknowledgment and turned back to Virginia. "When Mr. Lockwood is here at the library, I have permission to assist only him. We can use any and all resources at my disposal for our research."

"Yes," Virginia said, eyeing the money.

"And we have total autonomy in conducting the research in any way we see fit."

"Yes."

Quinn's voice was flinty when she added, "And I will suffer no professional repercussions because of this arrangement, and my position here as a reference librarian will not be endangered in any way."

"No, your job is secure." Virginia's eyes flicked to Quinn's face before they returned to the money in James's hand.

Quinn looked at James. "Agreed?"

He wore a serious expression, but his eyes twinkled back at her. "Agreed," he said and held the bills out toward Virginia.

"Agreed," Virginia said. She snatched the bills from his hand, folded them in half and then half again, and clutched them in her fist. Quinn had to bite the inside of her cheek to keep from hissing *"My Preciousssssss."*

"Brilliant," James said. "Now, if you'll excuse us, Virginia, Ms. Ellington and I have some business to attend to. Is the coffeehouse across the street acceptable for a meeting? My treat."

She could barely contain her excitement. "Why, yes, Mr. Lockwood, I believe it would be a lovely place for a meeting. Let me get my coat." She hurried to the Bullpen, grabbed her jacket, and slipped it on as she made her way to the door. As she walked she saw Mr. Ackerman grinning. She smiled and winked at him. He saluted her with a surreptitious thumbs-up.

Quinn rejoined James and the two strode side by side toward the front of the library. As they walked past the children's section, Quinn caught a glimpse of Nicole sitting on a tiny chair and holding up a picture book she was reading to a group of little ones sitting cross-legged on the floor in front of her. Nicole glanced up and did a double take worthy of any TV sitcom as she watched them pass by. Quinn gave it five minutes before her phone would start to buzz. It took two.

Hipster indie music filled the inside of the coffeehouse, where people tapping away at their laptops occupied the majority of the tables. Quinn lifted a large green ceramic cup to her lips and blew across the surface of her hot chocolate before sipping it. "My boss just pimped me out for two thousand dollars."

James's face twisted like he'd just been socked in the stomach. "It sounds dreadful when you say it that way. Please know I never intended to offend you. If you've changed your mind, I'll go away and never bother you again."

"No!" she said a little too loudly. Moderating her voice, she started again. "No, you're not bothering me and I haven't changed my mind. I just had no idea Virginia was so mercenary."

He relaxed against the back of his chair and crossed one long leg over the other under the table they shared. He sipped his coffee and said with a slight smile, "She's a bit like Gollum with the One Ring, isn't she?"

Quinn's eyes widened. "Oh my God! I thought the exact same thing. It's the gigantic eyes behind the thick lenses, right?"

"It is." The sunlight streaming into the café made his eyes a lighter shade of blue.

"I guess that's why I feel like she's always watching me." Quinn shivered. "She's really intimidating."

James shook his head. "I find that hard to believe. From what I saw, you are the force to be reckoned with, not her."

"I've never thought of myself as intimidating at all. I'm not big enough to be scary."

"Size has nothing to do with it."

She was about to make what was probably a too lewd quip, given their brand-new acquaintance, when her phone buzzed for the tenth time in the last two minutes.

"I think you'd better answer. That person seems pretty insistent."

She felt a blush creep up her cheeks. "Sorry." She took her phone from her pocket and furiously jabbed at the screen under the table. In no uncertain terms, she warned Nicole that if she didn't stop, there'd be a details embargo.

"Boyfriend? Roommate?"

Quinn shifted forward in her seat and returned the phone to its pocket. "No, best friend with boundary issues." When he cocked his head in an unspoken question, she crooked up an eyebrow. "She doesn't have any." She smiled when he laughed at her joke. "And the guy I live with doesn't have a cell phone."

"No cell phone? That's surprising."

"It's just as well. If he had one, he'd be texting me all day complaining about the emptiness of his food bowl and the abysmal condition of his litter box."

"I'm relieved I don't have to worry about someone misconstruing our business arrangement and ending up with a black eye." Just before he sipped his coffee, he said, "There's no need for you to worry since I don't have one either."

She knew what he meant, given the way they'd unabashedly flirted with each other. But she also couldn't ignore the hanging curveball. She didn't even try to stop the wicked smirk that overtook her face. "A boyfriend?"

He snorted, and by the way he started to cough, he seemed to have sucked half of his coffee into his lungs. He grabbed a napkin, slapped it across his mouth, and hacked into it.

"I'm sorry. Should I get you some water?"

He waved the napkin and croaked, "I'm okay." After a moment of throat clearing and wiping his watering eyes, he managed to suck in a lungful of air and release it without triggering another coughing fit. "I see I'm going to have to be careful around you."

"That's probably a good idea," she answered with a grin. Nicole would never forgive her if she didn't seize the opportunity to ascertain his relationship status, so she said, "And you still haven't answered my question."

"I do not have a boyfriend, nor will I ever be interested in having one." He held up both hands and added, "Not that there's anything wrong with that." He smiled when she snickered. "I don't have a girlfriend, either. Or a wife. Or a fiancée," he said, adding to the list. "See? I'm already learning to be more precise around you."

"Nicely done," she said with a dip of her head.

After a beat, James said, "Why don't we move on to the business at hand?"

"Sure." She absently spun her mug. "The truth is I'm a little puzzled why you've coughed up so much money for my help. I hardly did anything when you were at the library last week."

"I saw what you did in such a short time. If your enthusiasm for research is any indication, my money has been well spent." He leaned back in his chair again and gave her a smug look. "I bet you found the brooch."

She shrugged. "No, not the exact one."

"But found something," he prompted.

"About when it was made, yeah. I compared its style to similar ones held by the British Museum. My best guess is that it's eighth or ninth century A.D."

He leaned forward and rested his elbows on the table. "The designs on the brooch. Did you find any strange markings, ones that seemed out of place?"

"I'm sorry, but you're confusing me with someone who has an eidetic memory," she answered. "Which, by the way, is different than my almost superhuman ability to recall worthless bits of trivia."

He closed his eyes, sat back, and shook his head. "I had the photograph of the brooch with me this entire time."

"Yup."

"Well, now that I'm back, photo in hand, we can examine the designs together. But I want to hear more about this gift of yours."

She huffed a laugh. "My friends would say it's more of a curse than a gift."

"I'll decide that for myself."

How was she supposed to demonstrate when the way he smiled at her almost made her forget her own name? "It's not like I can just conjure them up at will." She stared into her now nearly empty cup and chuckled when a bit of information tucked away in one of the wrinkles in her gray matter escaped. "Because of his belief in the health and nutritional value of chocolate, Thomas Jefferson wrote to John Adams in 1785 saying he believed chocolate would become a more popular drink in America than coffee and tea."

"Obviously, Mr. Jefferson was wrong."

"Obviously." She watched him tip his cup back and finish his drink. "But the queen's going to strip you of your British citizenship. You're drinking coffee."

His lips pursed as if he'd just sucked on a lemon. "She'd never. No self-respecting Brit can choke down that colored water you Yanks call tea." He paused. "Do you like tea?"

"I do. I drink it every day."

"And you use those nasty tea bags?"

"Horror of horrors, I do."

"Tragic," James said solemnly and shook his head. "After

I've brewed you a proper cuppa, you'll never be able to drink that other dreadful stuff again."

His comment was innocent, but the thought of him brewing tea for her made a squadron of butterflies perform aerial stunts in her stomach. "You sound pretty sure of yourself."

"It will leave you stunned and amazed," he replied confidently as he picked up his briefcase and stood.

The butterflies swooped and dive-bombed. That was exactly what she was afraid of.

Chapter Five

It only took a couple of days for Quinn and James to establish a work routine. The time difference between Los Angeles and London meant James was busy in the mornings, leaving Quinn free to answer e-mailed questions and staff the reference desk until he arrived after lunch. Then they would find a table, cover it with photographs, books, and laptops, and renew their research.

Their arrangement was, of course, a great curiosity to everyone who frequented the library. Quinn's colleagues were both amused by the situation and gracious in covering her usual shifts. Mr. Ackerman winked at Quinn whenever she passed him, and it came as no surprise to Quinn that Virginia was never far away. At first it was irritating, the way Virginia watched her like a sentry on patrol. But when James started calling her Professor Umbridge under his breath, it was much easier to smile whenever they spotted her lurking about. Both Quinn and James were red-faced with giggles the day Virginia prowled the library dressed in pink from head to toe.

Quinn also caught Nicole prairie dogging over the children's stacks to peer at them. For the first couple of days, her phone was under siege. A constant barrage of texts came through from Nicole wanting to know all the details. Finally, Quinn sent a terse response that there would never be anything to tell since she and James had a working relationship only. And Nicole, apparently sensing she'd touched a nerve, immediately ceased and desisted.

Quinn wasn't trying to be snippy, but the situation was hard enough without Nicole's pestering. On the one hand, she was attracted to James and had been from the moment he'd first approached the reference desk. But she was also a professional and needed to act as such. Besides, once he was done working in L.A., he would return to London. So it really was best for her to keep him at a friendly yet professional distance.

She did an admirable job of it too, even though the more time she spent around him, the more her secret crush deepened. They had an easy rapport as they worked together, growing excited when the other unearthed a helpful piece of information and "arguing" over whether a vase was late Ming or early Qing dynasty. She'd never had so much fun at work before.

It could have been a real problem, had James given her any indication he saw her as anything other than a professional collaborator. But all their interactions were focused on research and at the end of every evening, he'd bid her good night and leave the library before she did. It was just as well. It made it easier for her to keep her feelings under wraps.

Pushing her musings aside, Quinn glanced over at the reference desk. It was pretty dead around the library. Apparently, everyone was out Christmas shopping. Ed looked more than a little bored as he sat at the desk and flipped through a magazine.

Returning her attention to the papers spread out all over the table, Quinn watched James slide a photograph of a marble bust of Plato in front of him and scrutinize the inscription on its base. It jogged loose something that had been lurking in the back of her mind.

"I have a question," Quinn said. "If we're doing research to insure all these items now, does that mean they're not currently insured?"

He answered without looking up. "No, the entire collection is covered by a blanket policy while we're gathering appraisals for each individual item."

"And these pictures are part of the documentation for each item?"

"Mmm-hmm."

"Do you take the pictures?"

"I do."

"So why don't you use an iPad or your computer to display the pictures when we're doing our research? It'd be easier to zoom in on the detail."

"It's what the client wants. I have permission to take pictures and print them out on a printer at his house. The camera and the card in it stay there."

"Doesn't he know you could just scan the pictures and have digital copies anyway?"

"I'm sure he does. But if even one of the items that's part of his collection here in L.A. is somehow leaked, I'll be unceremoniously sacked."

"We don't want that."

"No, we don't."

"Wait!" she said, her eyebrows pulling together. "You just said 'part of his collection here in L.A.' There's more somewhere else?"

James looked over at her. "Yes. This is about a third of it."

"A third?" Her voice rose in pitch. "Are the other items in England?"

"Mmm-hmm. It's best not to have an entire collection in one place in case some kind of disaster happens, like a fire or flood. The rest of the collection is split between his place in London and his estate in Northamptonshire."

"You already inventoried his collection in England?"

"No, not me. One of my colleagues, Ben, is doing that while I'm here." His head jerked up. "Which reminds me. Ben wants to talk to you."

"He wants to talk to *me*? Why?"

"He knows I've been working with you and I've told him how good you are at digging up information on the most obscure objects. He's got an item he could use your help with."

"Oh, sure. Okay." Her eyebrows pulled together in question. "Why doesn't he just shoot me an e-mail like the masses that send me questions over the Internet while they're still in their pajamas?"

He gave her a roguish smile. "Better than them not wearing any pajamas at all."

"Ew!" Quinn said quietly and shoved his shoulder. "There's an image I could do without. You got any brain bleach?"

"Sorry, no."

She looked at him side-eyed. From the curl of a smile lifting one corner of his mouth, she knew James wasn't sorry in the least.

"He could just e-mail I guess, but Ben said he wants to meet you."

"Okay. I guess it could be fun to meet one of your colleagues."

"Brilliant. Let's see." James glanced down at his watch. "It's a little after seven in the evening in England. I'll text him to see if he's available to video chat with us."

While James sent Ben a message on his phone, Quinn surreptitiously scanned the area for Virginia. Sure enough, she was shooting them furtive glances from the audiovisual department. She was also wearing the ugliest Christmas sweater Quinn had ever seen. Actual jingle bells were sewn onto Rudolph's harness and Santa's suit was adorned with red sequins and white faux fur trim. Why the sweater's designer didn't include a working red lightbulb to make the reindeer's nose glow, Quinn couldn't understand.

"We can't talk to him here. Virginia will flip if we're too loud."

"Afraid you'll be blackballed from the secret librarian cabal if shushed by another member?" That crooked smile of his just about did her in.

"Oh yeah. We're a ruthless bunch."

"Clearly." James's phone buzzed. "Ben's not available right now, but will be in around an hour. Why don't we go have lunch at the deli across the street and then talk to him from there?"

Quinn was already gathering her things. "Sounds like a plan."

An hour later, James and Quinn sat at a corner table at In A Pickle where they had just finished lunch. Quinn gave a tentative smile to the man looking back at her from the screen of James's open laptop. Ben Baker was fortyish with brown hair and gray eyes that twinkled with mischief. She had a feeling she was going to like him.

"Thank you for taking the time to speak with me," Ben said in an accent that was slightly different from James's. Based on her years of watching *Downton Abbey,* her guess was Yorkshire, but she didn't know for sure. "James tells me you're a wizard at research."

Her smile was shy. "That's nice of him to say."

"He wouldn't say it if it weren't true. Would you, James?" Ben didn't wait for an answer and forged ahead. "Quinn, I've been working with a handwritten copy of Arnold Schoenberg's opera *Moses und Aron.* I'm specifically interested in

learning more about a recitative in the second act. I searched
WorldCat and found a monograph that should answer my
questions. It's a dissertation and there's a copy at the UCLA
Music Library. If I e-mail James the call number and the
information I'm looking for, can you help me?"

"Monograph? WorldCat? You sound like a librarian,"
Quinn said.

Ben chuckled and said, "That's because I am a librarian, though I now use my research skills to make more
money in the private sector."

"Interesting." Quinn wondered just how much more
money he made.

"Thanks for helping James out, by the way. His research
abilities are stretched to the limit when he uses Google to
find the closest pub."

James shot Ben a sardonic look. "Thanks for that, mate."
Ben just grinned back at him.

"Give him some credit. I've seen him use Google to find
gas stations, too."

"*Et tu, Brute?*" James said, squinting at her.

First Harry Potter and now Shakespeare. It was as if he
had a secret file on her that listed all her favorite things and
was sprinkling them into their conversations to make her
like him even more. Not that he needed to work at it.

"Just kidding," she said and bumped James's shoulder
with hers.

Addressing Ben, she said, "I'm glad James isn't an expert
researcher. If he was, he wouldn't need my help."

"Fair point," Ben said with a nod. They chatted for a few
more minutes and ended the call with Quinn promising to
get the information Ben requested as soon as possible. She
couldn't work out why he wanted to know more about a
passage of dialogue in a German opera when he was supposed to be authenticating artifacts. But if he was anything

like her, he probably wanted to sate something that had piqued his curiosity.

But why would he be taking time out for a video chat for a purely personal matter? Something didn't add up.

James closed the laptop and looked at Quinn expectantly. "Ready for our outing?"

"Our? You want to come with me?"

"Of course. Why wouldn't I?"

"It won't be very exciting. I'll grab the dissertation off the shelf, skim it until I find what Ben needs, and copy those pages."

"I've never been to UCLA. I'd like to see it. I hear it's beautiful."

"I'm biased, but yeah, it is." She was secretly thrilled at the idea of showing him around her alma mater.

"Also, I can take pictures of the pages on my phone and text them to Ben. That way he can see them right away. If it's not exactly what he needs, we can keep looking."

"Okay. That's a great idea." She picked her purse up from the floor. "Westwood, here we come."

Chapter Six

It was late Friday afternoon and Quinn and James were wrapping up their research for the day. Quinn made a note that she'd requested a book on antique clocks through inter-library loan and considered checking with Nicole to see if she wanted to go out after work.

Her deliberations were interrupted when James grumbled, "I'm starving." He closed the book he'd been reading with a thump. "Have dinner with me tonight. Please?"

She stopped typing, not expecting that at all. They'd had a great time at the music library the day before, and after retrieving the information Ben had requested, walked around campus together. But upon their return to the West-side Library, James immediately bid her good night and left. And yet now he was asking her to dinner.

He sat up straighter and his eyes widened. "It's not a date or anything. I just can't stand the idea of another night of eating alone."

And there it was. He'd asked her because he didn't know many people in L.A. She almost laughed out loud when she realized how foolish she'd been. It didn't mean she'd say no, though. "Sure."

"Great! I want to try this hamburger place I keep hearing about. I hear their double cheeseburgers are unparalleled."

She immediately knew the place he was talking about. She folded her hands together and eyed him. "Everything you've heard is true." The gravity in her voice made it sound as if they were discussing a matter of national security. "But you must be warned. The Double-Double is the gateway drug. Soon, you'll be ordering your fries Animal Style and asking for Neapolitan milk shakes. I won't be held responsible when you climb onto an airplane at Heathrow, all wild-eyed and jittery, muttering you have to get back to L.A. for In-N-Out."

"You paint quite a picture," he said, his smile lopsided. "Will it live up to the hype?"

She slapped a hand to her chest. "You wound me deeply."

He chuckled quietly as she saved the work on her laptop and closed it.

"You want to drive, or should I?" she asked.

"I'll follow you in my car. That way I can go straight back to my hotel."

Right, she thought. Why ride in the same car when it wasn't a date? "Good point." She stood and gathered her things from the table. "Come with me to my desk so I can get the rest of my stuff. We can sneak out the back door to the parking lot."

He followed Quinn's lead, picked up his papers, and placed them in his briefcase. "Invited into the library's inner sanctum? I'm honored."

"You should be," she said. "Upon crossing the threshold, the secrets of the universe will be revealed to you. It's where we keep them. Job security."

"That explains a lot," James shot back, his tone equally wry. He tossed his jacket over his arm, picked up his briefcase, and looked at Quinn expectantly. "Lay on, Macduff."

More Shakespeare, and quoted correctly, although they

weren't in the middle of a swordfight. *How was he even real?* she wondered as she led him toward the Bullpen.

Once at her desk, she went about the business of preparing to leave while James stood in the space between her and Ed's desks.

"What *is* that?" he asked.

Quinn glanced at him from over her shoulder and followed his gaze to the snowman figure atop Ed's desk. "We've decided it's the evil spawn created from the unholy union between an orc and Frosty the Snowman."

He bent forward to get a closer look. "I think they were going for whimsy when they gave it a toothy grin. But it's just creepy."

"Exactly."

"The snow arms and legs don't help either. Snowmen really shouldn't be mobile." He straightened. "If I may ask one question."

"Why?" she asked with a smile as she tugged the purse strap up over her shoulder.

"Yes."

"You've met Ed, right? The guy who says his first job was at the library in ancient Alexandria?"

James laughed. "Yes, I've met Ed."

"Last year he brought in a terrifying Santa as a Christmas decoration. It had these red, glowing eyes that followed you like the all-seeing eye of Sauron. I begged him not to bring Sauron Santa in this year and he promised he wouldn't."

"So he brought this instead? I'm not sure Frosty the Snoworc is an improvement."

Quinn smiled. "When he promised no Sauron Santa, he warned me he would buy the most horrifying decoration he could find to replace it."

"I see he was successful," James said. "That has to be one of the most disturbing things I've ever seen."

He swept his arm out to the side, indicating she should go

first. They exited out the back door and into the parking lot. James followed her ancient 4Runner in his rental through two miles of rush hour traffic to the nearest In-N-Out. Quinn called it a win since she was only cut off three times.

Once parked, they dodged between cars lined up in the drive-thru and walked toward a white building with lighted red letters and a yellow arrow above the door.

"Wow," James said under his breath when they joined the line to order food.

Quinn glanced around the crowded dining room. "This is busy, but you should see it at lunchtime. I sometimes eat in my car because I can't find a place to sit." One of the red apron-wearing employees shouted a number from behind the counter. She watched a man in a brown UPS uniform shoulder his way through a cluster of people to retrieve his food.

"I take it you eat here often?"

"I think I'd better plead the Fifth on that," she answered with a half smile.

They shuffled along until they reached the counter and when she dug into her purse for her wallet, James took out his fold of cash, peeled off a twenty-dollar bill, and handed it to the cashier. "Please, allow me."

"At least let me pay for my half," Quinn said.

He waved the request away with a hand. "No need. I'll expense it."

She wanted to say something snarky like *You sure know how to impress a girl,* but instead she merely thanked him. She reminded herself, again, they were work associates and nothing more.

After securing a table, James went to the counter when their number was called and returned with a red tray laden with food.

Quinn watched James take a Double-Double and peer down at it. It must have passed inspection since he lifted it in salute, said, "Cheers," and took a bite.

As he started to chew, his face remained neutral. At first. But then his jaw slowed and his head tipped back, ever so slightly. His eyelids fluttered and a euphoric hum bubbled from his chest.

She giggled at his reaction, pleased but not at all surprised. Now that he was forever firmly under the enchanting spell of the Double-Double, she took a bite of her own. Her reaction was similar to his. When he took another bite and grinned at her as he happily chewed, Quinn fought the urge to reach across the table and wipe off the blob of sauce on his cheek.

A companionable silence settled over them as they ate with gusto. When Quinn had plowed through most of her burger and downed at least half of her fries, James said, "Please don't take this the wrong way, Quinn, but I've never seen someone as petite as you eat like a lumberjack."

"I've got five older brothers," she answered with a shrug. "If you don't eat fast, you don't eat at all."

"Five brothers? That's a big family. Are you the only girl?"

"Mmm-hmm. And the baby." She breathed a laugh. "My parents thought they'd never have a girl. They could hardly believe it when I was born."

"They must have been thrilled."

"They were, but it caused some drama, too, when it came time to name me. My parents had a naming scheme, so when I finally came along, I threw a monkey wrench into it."

"Really? How so?" With a cheeky smile, he asked, "They ran out of names that start with the letter Q?"

"Ha! That'd be a trick, wouldn't it?" she said, grinning at the thought of it. "Quixote, Quimby, Quirinius . . ."

"Quentin."

"That's only four. We need one more." Her eyes darted around the dining room. When her gaze landed on a dark-haired boy who looked to be eleven or twelve years old, she stated, "Quirrell."

He nodded in approval. "Harry Potter."

She smiled and nodded. "But as cool as it would be for all of us to have names that start with Q, that's not it. My brothers' names are George, John, Thomas, Madison, and Monroe." With an arched eyebrow, she asked, "See a pattern?"

He sipped his drink, deep in thought. "The first two could be Beatles, but the rest don't fit."

"Madison would love to be Ringo, but nope. What if I gave you a hint and told you George's middle name is Washington?"

It wasn't long before his face lit up and he snapped his fingers. "Let me guess. John's middle name is Adams."

"Ding, ding, ding, ding," she said and toasted him with her cup. "My dad's a huge American history buff and my mom thought the naming scheme was fun."

He cocked his head. "Not that I'm biased or anything, but why is Madison not James?"

"He was going to be, but he and Monroe are twins."

"Ah. That's brilliant, actually. How does Quinn fit in?"

"It's short for Quincy."

Understanding gleamed in his eyes. "John Quincy Adams."

"Yup, next on the list. My parents were going to chuck the whole 'name-the-kid-after-a-dead-president' thing and use the girl's name they'd picked out years before. But the story goes when my brothers came to see me in the hospital right after I was born, George took one look at me and said, 'You have to name her Quincy. She's bald just like John Quincy Adams was.' So Quincy it was. It got shortened to Quinn almost right away. My dad has always called me Quincy, though."

"That's a fantastic story."

"Thanks. I'm impressed by your knowledge of American presidents."

"Don't be. I only know the first few." He scratched his cheek and added, "I took an American history class at university."

"Well, you still know more than most Americans." She needed something to do with her hands, so she stuck a French fry into her ketchup and swirled it around. "What about you? Is there a story behind your name?"

"Do you mean was I named after an American president? Sorry, no."

She wadded up a napkin and threw it at him. "Smart aleck."

"Perhaps you need to be more precise with your words," he shot back with a wry smile.

"I'll keep that in mind."

"To answer your question, as far as I know, my parents simply liked the name."

"That works, too. Do you have any brothers and sisters?" Quinn already knew the answer to her question, and several other bits of information she'd gleaned from her research on him Monday evening after he'd "hired" her. Nicole had deemed it "some world-class Internet stalking." Quinn preferred to call it effective use of her professional skills. Besides, it was smart for her to know a little more about the person she'd be working with.

"I have a younger sister, Sophie. She's finishing up her last year at university." James glanced around and said, "I think we'd better go. There are a couple of chaps who are eyeing our table." He hiked a thumb over his shoulder toward the restrooms. "I'll be right back."

"Okay."

James slid out of the booth, leaving his jacket on the seat and his phone on the table.

Was it her imagination or had he dropped the subject of

family like a hot potato? Maybe it was a painful subject for some reason? She'd try to curb her curiosity.

Quinn decided to clear out and open up the table for the lurkers waiting to sit. She reached out to pick up his phone. It buzzed and she jerked her hand back in surprise as a text message flashed on the screen.

It wasn't her fault she could read upside down. When she saw the text was from someone named Shawna asking James to meet up, Quinn's cheeseburger-filled stomach leapt to her throat and her mind jumped into overdrive. Who the hell was Shawna? Had James lied when he told Quinn he didn't have a girlfriend? Had Shawna come all the way from England to surprise him? Maybe he hadn't lied about not having a girlfriend but had met Shawna in the past couple of weeks, just like he'd met her. Who knew what he did once he left the library every evening? Maybe he hooked up with this Shawna person after working with Quinn all day.

Hurt and anger burned in her chest, although she knew she had no right to feel either. They only worked together. He had every right to do whatever he wanted. Still, it felt like someone had kicked her in the gut.

Quinn continued to struggle with her emotions when James returned. Sitting across from her again, his brow furrowed with concern. "Are you okay?"

She gave him a wan smile. "Just a little tired, I guess."

"Then it's time we get you on your way home." He picked up his phone and pressed the front button, checking it. Other than a slight flare of his nostrils, his features were inscrutable as his thumbs moved over the screen. He slid his phone in his back pocket and smiled. "Shall we?"

They slid out of their booth and James dumped their trash into the bin as Quinn slipped on her jacket. Once outside, she tugged the front of it closed to ward off the chilly evening air.

Quinn pushed aside the questions swirling in her mind and said, "Thanks for dinner. It was fun." At least until the end, she added silently.

"You're quite welcome."

She waved the keys in her hand and mumbled, "I, um, I guess I'll see you Monday." The library was closed all day Sunday and she wasn't scheduled to work Saturday. Since James hadn't mentioned anything, she assumed he would be taking the weekend off. At least now she knew why. He'd be spending it with Shawna.

"Yes. Right. Monday." She expected him to say good-bye and walk off toward his car. Instead, he stayed glued to the asphalt and rubbed the back of his neck with a hand. "I was wondering if you might have some free time tomorrow."

Her eyebrows shot up in surprise. Maybe he didn't have plans with Shawna after all.

Before she could answer, he said, "There are a few more pieces I need to document, and I thought you might like to come along to the client's house and see some of the things we've been researching in person."

Of course it was about work. But when the thought hit her that if he were with her, he wouldn't be with Shawna, she said, "Sure, I'd like that."

"Brilliant," he said with a grin she assumed was his happiness at not having to work alone.

Something he'd mentioned the first time he came into the library pushed itself to the front of her mind. "What about your client's confidentiality?"

"I assured the majordomo you were both very discreet and highly unlikely to steal anything, so he approved."

"Thanks for the sterling character reference. Wait. There's a majordomo?"

He nodded. "The client has a man who takes care of his house and affairs here in L.A. I'll text you the address,"

James said. "Meet me in front of the house at ten o'clock tomorrow morning?"

"I'll be there."

"Great. See you then." With that, he spun on his heel and strode off toward his car.

Quinn climbed into her truck and craned her neck, to watch the interior light go on and off as James got in his car. Her truck's engine roared to life as he drove past her on his way to the exit. She backed out of her spot and turned just in time to see James make a right and join the flow of traffic. She threw her car in gear, stopped, and took a deep breath.

The way home was left. She turned right.

Chapter Seven

Just as Edward Walker had done when he followed Mai Nguyen in *Death's Dossier*, Quinn kept at least two cars between her and James. It wasn't stalking, she told herself. She needed—no, she *deserved*—to know what the hell was going on. Sure, she had no claim on James. But he had, in no uncertain terms, told her he didn't have a girlfriend. If he'd lied to her, she'd go to the client's house tomorrow only long enough to confront him, tell him to shove those arti- facts up his colon, and kick his ass to the curb. And if she was wrong and he returned straight to his hotel, or Shawna turned out to be only a friend or coworker, Quinn would keep this little escapade to herself.

She squinted against the oncoming headlights and kept her eyes on the gray sedan. Her middle churned with uncer- tainty, but at the same time she vibrated with excitement. Sure, she loved being a librarian. But this momentary adventure, this little taste of what it must be like to be a secret agent—tailing a subject, trying to not be detected, assessing situations, making snap decisions, the risk of being exposed—thrilled her like nothing else.

A few blocks later, James made a right and then a quick left into a small parking lot behind a building that housed three businesses fronted on the street. Quinn made the same right but not the left. Instead, she drove past and watched James exit his car. He adjusted his jacket and started for the front of the building.

Quinn scanned the signs above the back service entrances of the three businesses and immediately eliminated the yarn shop and thrift store. James was headed for a place called Red's.

She circled around and parked on the next street over. When she reached for the door handle, she hesitated.

What the hell was she doing? Her hand dropped to her lap and she leaned forward until her forehead clunked against the steering wheel. Staring down at the floorboard, it hit her that it wasn't so much about a lie, but about the truth. If James was there to hook up with Shawna, Quinn needed to know. Seeing him with another woman would allow her to finally rid herself of the stupid crush she'd been nursing.

With renewed purpose, she lifted her head and opened the door. It was just as well, she told herself. He lived in London and would be gone soon. Either way, she needed to shed her feelings for him. As much as it would hurt, seeing him with Shawna would be a good thing.

Still, she didn't want to die of humiliation if he caught her. When she reached the corner of the building, she stopped and stood with her back against the wall. She peeked around to see if James was waiting for Shawna on the sidewalk. He wasn't. Blowing out a relieved breath, she spun around the corner and walked to the front entrance. The red neon martini glass above the red door confirmed Quinn's suspicion. Red's was a bar.

Her next problem was getting inside while not being seen. She loitered outside until a sufficiently large group of people approached. As they entered the bar en masse, she joined the pack at the back. That was one good thing about being short. It was difficult to spot her in a crowd.

She stayed with the group until they passed where James sat at the bar. When they stopped at the pool table at the back of the room, Quinn claimed an empty bar stool. While those around her sat with their backs to the shelf and watched the pool game, Quinn faced the wall. It probably looked strange for her to sit like that, but it was the best she could do.

Quinn flipped up the collar of her coat to obscure her face and peered over the top edge of the material. James sat with his back to her and facing the most beautiful woman Quinn had ever seen in real life.

Even sitting down, Quinn could tell the woman she assumed to be Shawna was tall and slender. Like a beauty pageant contestant about to explain how she would end world hunger, she sat perched on her seat with ankles crossed. The heels she wore were glamorous and spiky. Quinn snorted at the thought of how ridiculous she herself would look teetering around in shoes like those. Shawna's impeccable business suit fit her perfectly and her long, brunette hair was thick and luxurious. The woman belonged in a shampoo commercial. When Shawna smiled, the set of straight white teeth nearly blinded Quinn. She added toothpaste commercial to the list.

Between the loud music, boisterous conversations, clinking ice, and clacking billiard balls, Quinn couldn't hear a word of their conversation. But based on Shawna's body language, she was in full flirt mode. She laughed and tossed her head, dark hair cascading over her shoulders.

Quinn sighed. No wonder James had never shown any interest in her. Quinn had no chance against a woman like that.

Shawna rested her hand on James's arm.

"Blech," Quinn grumbled. She was about to turn away from the scene when James unexpectedly jerked up his arm and flung off Shawna's hand. A slash of red from glossy fingernails arced through the air.

Shawna's green eyes widened with shock.

Quinn's weren't much different. She'd been so focused on Shawna she hadn't studied James's body language at all. Watching him now, she noted that rather than leaning in, he sat with his shoulders squared. In fact, it appeared he was actually tilting back, as if trying to put distance between them. Quinn could practically see the tension radiating from him.

Interesting.

Quinn shifted her attention back to Shawna, whose face was now pinched and tight. Shawna's mouth dropped open when James furiously jabbed his finger in the air at her. And when he slowly leaned toward Shawna, his body still rigid, Quinn guessed he wasn't whispering sweet nothings in her ear. He was pissed.

Shawna pressed a hand to her chest and shook her head, clearly pleading her case. She broke eye contact with James and glanced around the room in distress. For a split second, Quinn's and Shawna's eyes locked.

Crap. Quinn ducked behind her upturned collar and spun away. *Crap. Crap. Crap.*

She set her elbow on the ledge and shielded the side of her face with her hand. Mind racing now, she weighed her options. She could bolt out the back door, but it would be pretty obvious. She would sit there for a few more minutes and hope Shawna saw Quinn as a nosy nobody watching a couple argue. The more pressing question was, Had James turned to see who Shawna was looking at? If so, in a matter of seconds James would tap her on the shoulder and demand to know what the hell she was doing there.

She closed her eyes and listened to her pulse whooshing in her ears. A few seconds passed. The laughter, the music, the cadences of the conversations in the bar hadn't changed. The room hadn't fallen silent, like saloons did in old Westerns when there was about to be a shootout.

"Hi there," a voice right next to her said.

"Shit!" An explosion of adrenaline nearly sent Quinn rocketing through the ceiling like a missile. She slapped one hand over her thumping heart and gripped the shelf with the other to keep from falling off the bar stool. After catching her breath, she looked into a face sporting a thick, dark beard. "Sorry. You scared me," she said.

The poor guy looked like he was about to be slammed by an oncoming bus. "Oh, jeez. I'm so sorry. I didn't mean to." He shoved his hands in his pockets and stared down at his shoes. "I'll go away now."

"No," Quinn said quickly. "No, you don't have to do that." Talking with someone would make her less conspicuous. Plus, if James did see her, she could claim them being at the same bar was purely a coincidence. She smiled. "You surprised me, that's all."

"Yeah. Again, sorry," he said, still looking a bit rattled.

Quinn glanced over her shoulder in time to see James leap up from his seat, dig out his money clip, and throw a wad of bills on the bar. Then he stormed out the front door, leaving Shawna alone and visibly shell-shocked.

Quinn had to let some time pass to ensure James had cleared out of the parking lot before she could leave, so she decided to keep the conversation going with the bearded guy for a while longer. She turned back toward him and offered her hand. "I'm Quinn."

He relaxed and his faltering smile turned confident. He shook her hand. "Josh."

They exchanged pleasantries and as they talked, Quinn learned Josh was an aspiring actor. So far, being a zombie extra in a low-budget flick Quinn had never heard of was his biggest claim to fame.

Quinn peeked over her shoulder again to check on Shawna's status. The wetness that had glistened on her cheeks only a few moments before had dried. Shawna's megawatt smile was back on full tilt and she batted her eyelashes at the broad-shouldered man with black, wavy hair now occupying the bar stool James had vacated. When he closed in and whispered in her ear, Shawna grinned and slid her hand up his thigh.

Shawna seems to be handling her heartbreak pretty well, Quinn thought sardonically.

Quinn spun back around when Josh asked, "Can I get you a drink?"

She seriously considered staying for a while longer even though she figured she was good to go. But after the stalking, the spying, and having the crap scared out of her, she'd had enough for one night. "I'm sorry. I'm kind of tired, so I'm just gonna head home."

Josh's face fell. "Oh. Okay." Not giving up completely, he asked, "Can I at least have your number? Maybe we can get together for coffee or something sometime."

Josh really did seem like a nice enough guy. James wouldn't be around much longer and he'd made it clear they were only business associates. Quinn had no reason not to go out with him. "Sure." She dug in her purse and handed Josh her business card. "I'd like that."

She smiled when he beamed at her. *At least there's one guy in L.A. who wants to go out with me,* she thought. They said their good-byes and as Quinn gathered her things, she noted how Josh received several congratulatory pats on the back when he returned to his friends and showed off her card.

Quinn slid off the stool and strolled toward the front door. When she passed by Shawna, though, she dipped her head and rubbed her fingertips over her forehead to hide her face.

Outside, she drew in a deep breath of cool night air and took off toward her truck. Once settled in the safe confines of the driver's seat, she let her head fall back against the headrest and stared out the windshield. Her mind was a muddled mess.

She didn't know what Shawna and James's relationship was exactly, but at that point it didn't really matter. His actions had made it pretty clear he wanted nothing to do with her. And that made Quinn giddy with relief.

She sat forward and stuck the key in the ignition. "Crap."

Chapter Eight

The air was crisp and the sun shone bright in a cloudless blue sky. There wasn't a hint of the storm that brewed off the coast and was expected to hit later that night. It was the kind of December day Quinn knew was envied by other parts of the country blanketed under inches, if not feet, of snow.

On the downside, her patch of the world would never look like the winter wonderland portrayed on Currier and Ives holiday cards. There was a secret part of her that would love to experience, just once, a Christmas where she could ride in a horse-drawn sleigh past barren trees, branches laced with snow, and farmhouses with warm light glowing from the windows. Since the likelihood of that ever happening was infinitesimally small, the sleigh bells chiming in the Christmas song filling the interior of her truck would have to do.

Traffic was light that Saturday morning, so Quinn made good time as she drove west toward the Pacific Ocean on a curving, tree-lined section of Sunset Boulevard.

The night before, when James forwarded the address to her, she knew she'd be venturing into one of the most expensive and exclusive enclaves in all of Los Angeles. Pacific Palisades was an area less-than-wealthy librarians feared to tread. This was her chance to see that world from the inside.

She turned left off of Sunset and slowed the truck so she could read the house numbers painted on the curbs. The residences were either large, well-maintained homes with perfectly manicured yards or hidden behind walls and copses of trees.

Parked in a driveway was one of the most amazing cars she'd ever seen. The sapphire blue convertible supercar was sporty and sleek and looked as fast as it was expensive.

She spotted James's rental and pulled up behind it. She'd barely come to a stop and he was already yanking open her door. Had he seen her at Red's the night before after all and was about to call her out? She was ready to plead temporary insanity and hope for the best.

"Did you see that incredible machine?" He pointed at the supercar gleaming in the sunlight.

"I did." She shut off the engine and silently celebrated the fact her exploits from the evening before were not the featured topic.

"It's a Lamborghini LP550-2 Gallardo Spyder. It has 550 horsepower and can go from zero to sixty in three point nine seconds." His boyish excitement was adorable.

"That's impressive. Now I know what to get you for Christmas."

"Yes, please. One with a big red bow on the bonnet, like in the adverts."

"Big red bow. Got it."

"It will only set you back about a quarter of a million dollars."

Her eyebrows shot up. "Yikes. Pricey." She grabbed her computer bag and purse and slid down from the seat. As they walked together toward his car, she said, "Since I'm unwilling to rob a bank to buy you a car like that, how do you feel about me knocking off four zeroes from the car's price tag and buying you a Lamborghini necktie instead?"

"It would be one of my most cherished possessions," he said without a hint of sarcasm. His sincerity took her aback and she made a mental note to look for a Lamborghini tie online.

He stooped and rummaged around the front seat of his car. Quinn couldn't help but admire the view. James certainly wore his jeans well.

She smiled innocently when he straightened up and held out a plastic-lidded cardboard cup. "I brought you some Earl Grey."

"That's thoughtful. Thank you." She took the cup in her free hand and sipped. It was warm and pungent and wonderful.

He dove into the car again, extracted his briefcase, and slammed the door.

They walked through the wide gap in the stucco wall at the front of the property and up the driveway. She jumped at a noise behind her and glanced over her shoulder. A gate hidden in the wall slowly slid across the opening.

Another stucco wall stood between them and the house. James pressed a button on the intercom panel next to the security door. While they waited for a response, Quinn blew out a breath.

He lightly rested a hand on the small of her back. "Are you okay?"

"Yeah," she answered. Her eyes darted from the intercom to the camera pointing at them from above and finally to his face. "I feel a little out of place."

"You may feel out of place, but you don't look it." His smile was warm and his touch comforting.

The intercom crackled and a male voice drawled, "Yawp."

James's hand remained on her back when he looked straight up at the camera. "James Lockwood here, with my associate, Quinn Ellington." She lifted her tea toward the camera in an awkward salute.

"Hey, James!" the voice boomed. "Come on in."

The door buzzed and they stepped into a courtyard. To their right, water burbled up from the top of two hexagonal stone pillars that stood in the middle of a square pond. Water flowed from it through a foot-wide channel to the front of the house.

They strode up the walkway that ran alongside the trough. The front door opened before they arrived, revealing a short, middle-aged man with wild, curly hair, and a friendly smile. "Great to see you again, James."

"You too," he answered as they stepped into the house and shook hands. "Paul, this is my research associate, Quinn Ellington. Quinn, this is Paul Shelton. He's my client's business manager and takes care of the house when he's away."

"Nice to meet you, Mr. Shelton," she said and extended her hand. When James had called Paul a majordomo, she'd pictured a tall, thin, dour man in formal wear. In reality, the man shaking her hand was the very opposite in faded jeans, green rubber flip-flops, and a black Pink Floyd hooded sweatshirt. She mentally kicked herself for allowing a stereotype to color her expectations. It was something she was always fighting as a librarian, so she couldn't believe she'd just done the very thing that drove her crazy.

"Please, call me Paul." His eyes were riveted on Quinn when he said, "James, I can see why you've been spending so much time at the library. You told me you were working with a lovely librarian. You didn't tell me how exquisite she is."

Quinn felt her cheeks grow hot. She almost spun around to see if he was talking about some other librarian behind her.

She glanced over at James. His ears were beet red.

Paul's gaze darted between their faces and a knowing smile formed. He released her hand and asked, "Quinn, can I give you a quick tour of the place before you get to work?"

Happy to move out of the Entryway of Awkward Greetings, she said, "I'd like that. Thank you."

"James, do you want to come with us? Or should we meet you in the office in a little while?"

"I could go on another tour."

Amusement twinkled in Paul's eyes. "I thought so."

They ventured farther into the house. The channel of water continued all the way to the backyard. If not for the thick, clear plastic covering it as it flowed under the floor, a midnight run to the refrigerator could be a dangerous proposition.

She gazed up at the soaring ceiling and then at the formal sitting room to their right. Colorful modern art paintings hung on stark white walls. A black grand piano sat near the floor-to-ceiling wall of windows that ran the length of the house. The glass allowed for a spectacular view of the backyard and the ocean beyond.

White, black, gray, and chrome were the featured shades throughout the house. As they walked, Quinn noticed some of the items she and James had researched. While it was fun for her to see them, they only reinforced her overall impression she wouldn't want to live there. It was too much like a museum. Wealthy, sophisticated people threw swanky cocktail parties in houses like that. She couldn't picture Wyatt rolling his toy dump truck across the cold, marble floors.

"Thank you for the tour," Quinn said at its conclusion. "This is the most incredible house I've ever seen."

"It is something special, isn't it? I'm glad you enjoyed," Paul said. "Well, I'll leave you two kids to your work. If you need anything, I'll be in the backyard soaking up some sun." He gave them a quick wave and walked outside through the sliding glass doors.

Quinn followed James down a long hallway to the office. It, like all the other rooms in the house, was enormous. Black leather sofas lined two walls. Several framed paintings leaned against one. A large, black lacquered desk sat at the center of the room. The items they would be examining were laid out atop it: the antique shelf clock she'd begun researching the day before, coins, a pair of flintlock dueling pistols in a green felt-lined wooden box, and military medals attached to faded ribbons.

There was one object that stopped her dead in her tracks. She gaped at the jewel-encrusted item and asked in a voice barely above a whisper, "Is that . . . Is that a Fabergé egg?"

James removed his laptop from his briefcase, set it on the desk next to the camera already there and opened it. "That's what we're here to find out." He smiled, clearly enjoying how awestruck she was.

As mesmerized as she was by the probably authentic Fabergé egg, a different object brought a smile to her face. The item that had started this unexpected adventure: the Celtic brooch.

She set her computer bag down, unzipped a front pocket, and removed a pair of white cotton gloves.

James chuckled and shook his head. "Why am I not surprised you have a pair of those with you?"

"Why wouldn't I?" She slid the glove on her left hand and flexed her fingers. "I rarely go anywhere without these, book tape, scissors, a ruler, and book glue."

"For any book repair emergencies you may encounter at the grocery store?"

She tugged on the other glove. "Sure, you laugh now. But someday you'll thank me when my roll of book tape and I are all that stand in the way of global chaos and certain doom."

"Of this I have no doubt."

She picked up the brooch and held it in her open palm. A thrill buzzed through her. She held an object over a thousand years old. She hefted the brooch and found it to be heavier than she expected. At six inches in diameter, it easily covered her entire hand. She studied the detail on the front. The photograph hadn't done justice to the craftsmanship she now beheld in person.

She turned the brooch over and traced a gloved fingertip over the runic lines scratched into the silver. "Ragnar owns this brooch," she whispered, echoing the inscription. James had been especially keen to translate the runes and it was the first thing they'd worked on earlier that week. They'd spent several hours poring over books and websites before finally translating the etched Old Norse. It was a bit of a letdown when the inscription turned out to be nothing more than a statement of ownership. Still, the fun of the journey more than made up for their less-than-earth-shattering findings.

She felt James's gaze fall on her and he said softly, "I'm sure Ragnar wore that brooch on his cloak with great pride."

Quinn studied the runic letters and pictured Ragnar sailing a dragon-headed longship toward the northeastern coast of England. "I'm sure he did," she answered quietly. "I feel bad for the guy he pillaged this from. It must have been terrifying to have big, brawny Vikings rampaging through his village."

"Indeed." His voice turned contemplative. "Think of the journey that brooch has taken over the centuries so that you, Quinn Ellington, at this very moment can hold it in your hand."

Her breath caught and she looked at him. "That's really quite profound."

"I have my moments," he replied with a modest smile.

They held each other's gaze until her hammering heart warned her she was venturing into dangerous territory. Flustered, her mouth engaged. "Did you know 'Ragnar' is the name of the mascot for the Minnesota Vikings?"

At the odd look he gave her, she added quickly, "It's a football team."

His eyebrows rose halfway up his forehead.

"American football, not what you call football and what we call soccer." She cringed and set the brooch back on the desk. "What, um, what do you want to tackle first?"

"You've already done some research on the clock. Why don't you start there?" He moved the clock in front of the black office chair. "Have a seat."

She rolled it back and sat. "Wow. This won't make my derrière go numb like the torture device at work does." She ran a hand over the supple leather. "Do you think Paul would notice if I accidently took it with me?"

James chuckled as he unfolded a piece of gray felt cloth and laid it on the desk. "I'm sure you rolling it down the driveway wouldn't draw his attention at all."

She laughed at the thought of it and turned her attention to the clock. The white lacquer case was rectangular and about two feet tall. Tiny red flowers were painted along the front edges and arch above the dial.

Quinn looked up and watched James place a coin on the felt. "Your client must be a seriously wealthy dude. The guy's got a Fabergé egg, for Pete's sake. I can see why he's installed so much security."

James picked up the camera, pointed it at the coin, and snapped a picture. He lowered it and said, "Most of his items are irreplaceable."

"You're doing an excellent job of keeping his identity a secret, by the way. I'm inside the guy's *house* and I have no idea who he is." Quinn hadn't spotted one personal photograph in the house—candid, formal, or otherwise. "Just so you know, from now on I'm going to call him 'Mysterious Art Collector Guy.'"

James removed the coin from the felt and replaced it with another. "I'm sure if he knew, he'd be quite amused."

Quinn set her elbow on the desk and dropped her chin into the palm of her gloved hand. With a sly look, she said,

"You know I could find out who owns this house if I tried. A few searches, a couple of phone calls . . ."

"I know you could," James answered. He raised the camera again and took another photo. "I've witnessed the impressive amounts of information you can uncover when you set your mind to it."

"So why shouldn't I use my skills to find out who Mysterious Art Collector Guy is?"

His eyes snapped up to meet hers. The amusement she'd grown accustomed to seeing in them had vanished. "Because I'm asking you not to." The seriousness in his tone startled her.

She didn't know what was behind his strong reaction, but she trusted him all the same. "Okay," she said with a tight nod.

His face relaxed into a soft smile. "Thank you."

She returned his smile and pointed at the clock. "I guess I should get back to it." She stared at the masted sailing ship painted on the front for a moment to allow her unsettled feelings to pass.

Focus restored, Quinn turned the clock around and carefully pulled open the thin wooden door to inspect the inner workings. There were ratchets and gears and a couple of levers on the front of a brass box with more gizmos inside it. She knew nothing about clocks and was about to close the back when she spied a small brass peg sticking out of the wooden base. It looked like a tiny metal mushroom.

She leaned in to inspect it more closely. Curious how tightly it fit into the wood, she put her finger on top of the peg and wiggled it. Without meaning to, she pushed it down. She jumped when a thin drawer popped out at the bottom of the clock. "I was *not* expecting that."

James looked up from the camera. "Where did that come from?"

"I pressed on a little peg and a drawer slid out."

He set the camera down and raced around to her side of the desk. "Is there anything in it?" Their heads nearly touched when he bent forward and leaned his elbows on the desk.

Her eyes crossed when his divine scent enveloped her. Despite the distraction, she tugged the drawer out farther. Inside it was a yellowing piece of paper.

"Do we take it out?" she asked.

"Why wouldn't we?"

"We don't know how brittle the paper is. It could crumble the second I touch it."

He looked at her side-eyed. "You mean you could shut it back up and leave it there without reading it?"

"Hey, I'm just looking out for you. It's your butt on the line if this goes south."

"Thank you for showing concern while throwing me under the bus at the same time."

"You're welcome." She turned her face toward him and was treated to the strong jawline of his profile. "What'll it be?"

"Executive decision. We open it."

"Because no one else knows about it and if it turns to dust we keep this to ourselves? No harm, no foul?"

"Exactly."

"Works for me." Her gloves caused her to lose a significant amount of dexterity. She didn't want to take the chance of crumpling or tearing the paper, so she tugged them off and set them aside. "Here goes nothing." She pinched the paper between her finger and thumb and slowly lifted it from the drawer. Once it was safely on the desk, she exhaled the breath she'd been holding.

"There's a ring. It was hidden under the paper."

"Well that's a fun twist." She held it up. From its small size and delicate design, it was clearly a woman's ring. "The silver's really tarnished," she said, noting the darkened metal of the band.

"That's not surprising. Think how long it's been hidden away in that drawer."

She rotated the ring slightly to allow the light to catch the facets of the red gemstone. "What do you think? Ruby or garnet?"

"I'm sorry. I left my jeweler's loupe in my other trousers."

She snickered and nudged his shoulder with hers. "Maybe the note will tell us." She set the ring down and with great care unfolded the paper. Sharply angled cursive handwriting covered the page. The black ink had faded, but was still easily legible.

"'My dearest love,'" James read. "'My ardor and affection for you has only grown during our torturous and most wretched separation.' Well this just got really interesting."

"It sounds like a line from a steamy romance novel."

"Know a lot about those, do you?"

"Hush, you, and keep reading."

"If I do both, I'll be reading to myself."

She heaved a mock put-upon sigh. "Fine. Read aloud, please."

He cleared his throat with dramatic flair and continued. "'How my arms ache to hold you to my bosom so that I may enchant you with whispered endearments and declarations of my passionate and undying love for you.'" James grinned. "I'm not sure 'endearments' and 'declarations' are what she's hoping for."

Quinn laughed.

"'Oh, the hours pass so slowly as I yearn for such rapturous time when we can be together again, even now with your husband remaining in London.'" His eyebrows shot up. "Scandalous! She's a married woman."

"Five bucks says he's married, too," she said evenly.

"I'll take that bet and defend the honor of my gender against such slander."

Her only response was an assured smile.

"'Until then, my heart fills with joy each time I hear the peals of your sweet laughter ringing through the halls of Summerfield. You are like the shining sun piercing through the joyless and lugubrious gloom that is my wife.'"

"Told you," Quinn said, her tone smug.

"Yes, yes. I owe you five dollars." It was clear he was attempting to appear peeved, but the glee in his eyes completely negated it. He looked down at the paper again. "'I am tormented daily by the knowledge that I married the wrong sister.'"

"No!" they shouted at the same time.

"He hooked up with his wife's sister," James said in disbelief.

"You don't have to pay me five dollars. Neither gender is looking too good in this."

"Not even a little. Do you want me to finish reading it?"

"Yeah, we still don't know what the deal with the ring is."

"Sure, Quinn," he said with delighted skepticism. "It's all about the ring."

An eyebrow arched.

He laughed. "Hint taken. 'Until we may partake in our much-anticipated reunion, please accept this ring as a token of my humble esteem and most ardent love. Yours in sincere adoration, H.'" James picked up the ring and mused, "She never took the ring from their clandestine drop box. What do you suppose happened? The husband showed up from London unexpectedly?"

"Could be. Maybe H's wife found out and shut it down." She shook her head. "Man, that's rough. She not only finds out her husband is cheating on her, but he's doing it with her own sister? That's an episode of *Dr. Phil* just waiting to happen."

"For all of their sakes, I hope it turned out better than we fear it might have."

"I hope so, too." There was a dangerous edge to her voice when she said, "I'll tell you what. If I found out my husband was cheating on me, he'd be walking funny for a year after I got through with him."

"He'd deserve it," James replied without hesitation. "Any man who would cheat on you is an idiot and a fool."

"That's sweet of you to say," she said quietly. She brushed at a strand of hair that fell across her forehead and added with a wry smile, "You can come bail me out after I get arrested for assault."

"I would be honored to be your phone call," he said and returned her smile with a warm one of his own. "Why don't we just make sure you marry a man who would never do such a thing instead?"

"That's a much better idea." The conversation needed to move to safer ground, so she said, "We need to tell Paul about the note and ring. I bet Mysterious Art Collector Guy will be excited by it."

"I'm sure he will. I'll photograph the note, the ring, and the drawer and add everything to the inventory."

"I guess I'll get back to work, too, although I'm not sure anything will be quite as exciting as finding a torrid love note and a ring in a secret compartment of an antique clock."

They worked for the next hour, the relaxed silence between them broken only by a question or comment about the item one of them was working with. Around noon, Paul strolled into the office to take their orders for lunch and was thrilled by their unexpected find. Quinn watched with interest as Paul read "H's" note. She and James shared knowing smiles when Paul's eyes grew the size of saucers and said, "His sister-in-law?"

Later, the three ate take-out Chinese food on the backyard patio. They chatted about the weather, football, and the upcoming Christmas releases of various blockbuster movies. After lunch they worked a couple more hours before James announced they were done for the day.

Quinn packed her things and went off to use the bathroom before the twenty-five-minute drive to her apartment. "That's a huge bathroom," she said upon returning to the office. "Seriously, I think it's bigger than my entire apartment."

She looked over at him when she didn't receive a response, witty or otherwise. He stood motionless in the middle of the office. His features were taut and a thin sheen of perspiration glistened on his forehead.

"Are you okay?" she asked.

From the mildly green tint to his face, she wondered if the Chinese food had disagreed with him.

"I was just, um, I was wondering if you're free for dinner tonight."

A wave of relief washed over her. It didn't exactly thrill her that having dinner with her made him look nauseated, though.

Before she could answer, he said, "I know it's last minute and you probably already have plans, but I just thought I'd ask."

"I—"

"If you're busy, or don't want to, you know, for whatever reason, it's okay."

"James—"

"It's just that there's this Italian bistro on Santa Monica I drive past every day and I really want to try it."

"I—"

"I haven't eaten there yet because from the minute I saw it, I knew . . ." He stopped, gulped, and swiped his sleeve across his forehead. "I knew I wanted to go there with you. On a date."

"What?"

He took a step toward her. "I want to take you on a proper date, Quinn. I want to drive to your flat, collect you, and take you to Lucrezia's because it has white twinkle lights on the awning and candles on the tables."

"James—"

"I know this is completely out of the blue since I made a point to say it wasn't a date when we went to In-N-Out last night. I was trying to convince myself I could spend time with you and keep it strictly professional."

"James—"

"But I can't. I've never had more fun or felt more comfortable with anyone than I do with you. I just want to spend as much time with you as I can before I have to go back to London. Please say you'll go out with me tonight."

With a soft smile, she asked, "Are you through?"

He vigorously nodded. His lips were clamped closed, as if he was afraid to utter another syllable.

"I feel the same way about you."

His apprehension melted into a heart-stopping grin. "Really?"

"Yeah, really." It was too late to guard her heart. His return to London would leave a crater in her life no matter what. "I'd love to go on a proper date with you."

"I'll make a reservation and ring you to let you know when I'll come by to pick you up."

"Are you sure you want to drive that much? You'll already be in Santa Monica. Why don't I just meet you at Lucrezia's?" When his smile wavered, she realized she and her pragmatism had stepped in it. He was clearly committed to giving her the full and proper date experience. Backtracking, she said, "Although now that I think about it, you should get Rasputin's approval before we go out."

"Rasputin?"

"My feline roommate."

"Right. I hope I pass muster."

"I'm sure you will." She picked up her bag and slung the strap over her shoulder. "Walk me to my car?"

He smiled and hefted his briefcase from the desk. "With pleasure."

Chapter Nine

Quinn raised the mascara brush to her right eye and swiped it under the upper row of lashes several times, being careful not to cake it on so thick it would turn into a clumpy mess.

"I don't know why you wouldn't let me come do your makeup for you," Nicole's voice said from Quinn's phone lying on the bathroom counter.

"'Cause the one time I let you, I ended up looking like a hooker."

"Hey!" Nicole's huffiness came through loud and clear.

The brush stopped and hovered in front of her eye. Quinn scowled at the phone in mild exasperation.

"Yeah, okay. You're right. It was awful."

"And what did we learn?"

Nicole sighed and said in a flat tone, "Blue eyes and blue eye shadow don't mix."

"Thank you." Quinn switched and applied the black goo to the lashes of her left eye. "And James and I are just going to dinner. It's not a big deal." Simply saying the words made her stomach lurch with excitement. "I mean, we're not exactly walking the red carpet at a movie premiere." It was a good thing, too. She hated dresses and the mere thought of wearing a long, formal one by a designer she'd never heard of nearly made her break out in a sweat. She was grateful to instead be wearing comfortable black jeans and a gray cable-knit pullover sweater. "Thanks for helping me decide what to wear, by the way."

"You're welcome. Is it sad I know exactly what's in your closet without even being there?"

"You see me at least five days a week," Quinn answered, her defenses up. "You've seen me wear everything in my closet at least a hundred times."

She regarded herself in the mirror. Her naturally light lashes, now augmented with the mascara, were darker and fuller. She had to admit the more expensive brand of mascara Nicole told her to buy really did make her blue eyes pop. But she decided to keep that revelation to herself. Otherwise it would embolden Nicole and before she knew it, it would be The Hooker Incident all over again. So she stayed silent, screwed the cap back on the tube, and dropped it in the open drawer.

"You'll need to get some new clothes if you start going out with James all the time." Quinn could practically see her friend preen when Nicole added, "Which is funny since about two weeks ago, you weren't interested in the dating scene."

"I changed my mind." Quinn rummaged around in the drawer and found a tube of lipstick. She pulled off the top and recoiled when garish red lipstick—a leftover from The Hooker Incident—twisted up. She tossed the tube back into the drawer as fast as humanly possible.

Quinn smiled as she thought about the man who had changed her mind. "Can you blame me?"

"Not even a little. James would change my mind, too," Nicole answered. "I'd dump Brian in a heartbeat if James asked me out."

"You would not," Quinn said, calling her friend's bluff.

She found another tube of lipstick and checked the color. It was sheer, just the way she liked it.

"You're right," she heard Nicole sigh. "I wouldn't."

Quinn swiped the lipstick over parted lips.

"Besides, it would never happen. The man hangs on to your every word."

Quinn made a face. "He does not." She slipped the tube in the front pocket of her jeans in case she found an occasion to reapply after dinner. Then she raked her fingers through her blond hair a couple of times in a vain attempt to fluff it. She rolled her eyes. There was really no use. Until she had a personal stylist—and why would she ever—it would always be flat.

"Yeah, keep telling yourself that," came Nicole's reply, complete with an incredulous snort. The teasing dropped from Nicole's voice and Quinn heard the sincerity in it when she said, "I'm really happy for you, Q. I hope you have a good time tonight."

She picked up her phone and flicked off the bathroom light. "Me too." As she walked through her bedroom, she said, "I gotta go. If you promise not to text me twenty times before dessert to ask me how it's going, I'll give you a call tomorrow and give you details. Deal?"

"Deal. Talk to you soon."

"Bye." Quinn touched the screen to end the call, slipped the phone into her back pocket, and checked her watch. It was a couple of minutes before seven and James would be there any minute. From the doorway of her bedroom, she surveyed the living room. It would never be featured on the glossy pages of *Architectural Digest,* but at least it was clean.

Too nervous to sit, she puttered around the apartment until the intercom buzzed. When James announced himself, she pressed the button to allow him in. She considered opening the door and waiting for him in the doorway, but that seemed too eager. Instead, she stood behind the closed door and waited the twenty seconds until there was a knock. Her hand rested on the doorknob as she drew in a deep breath, held it for a few seconds, and then gusted it out. She unlocked the door and opened it.

James stood before her with his hands deep in his front pockets and a shy smile gracing his face. He looked more handsome than she'd ever seen him, in a dark blue V-neck cashmere sweater and blue jeans. It was only by divine intervention she didn't actually whimper. She unstuck her tongue from the roof of her mouth and said, "Hi."

"Hi."

She took a step back. "Please, come in."

"Thank you." He stepped through the doorway and as he passed her, his scent made her toes curl. "You look lovely."

"Thanks. You look really nice, too." She might have sounded completely lame, but *nice* was the only word her thoroughly addled brain could come up with besides *dreamy*. She was trying hard to avoid coming off like an eleven-year-old girl gushing about her favorite member of a boy band, so *nice* would have to do.

James glanced around the apartment. "Nice place. Why am I not surprised by the packed bookshelf?"

"Occupational hazard," she replied with a shrug.

His gaze settled on the two-foot-tall artificial Christmas tree sitting at the center of the square card table that served as her dining table. "Very clever. I like the scaled-down size of the ornaments," he said of the decorations that looked like very small, very shiny gold, red, and green wrapped packages.

"It's a good thing I like trimming it, too." When his brow lowered in confusion, she clarified, saying, "Every time I come home from work, Rasputin has somehow managed to scatter them all over the apartment."

"You realize he's got you trained." He laughed.

She grinned and said unabashed, "Completely."

"Speaking of Rasputin, I believe I need to gain his approval before we can leave. What happens if I don't pass inspection? Am I going to have to return to Santa Monica alone?"

"Why? Are you not feeling confident about your cat-whispering abilities?"

"Oh, I'm ready," he answered. The look he gave her melted her insides. "There's just a lot riding on it, that's all."

"I wouldn't be too concerned," she managed when she found her voice. "I pay the rent, so I have veto power. Besides, I'd hate for you to go back to Santa Monica alone."

"I appreciate the consideration."

"I have to admit I'm also curious about how he'll react to you. I don't have a lot of company, so he's not around new people very often."

"Happy to be your test case," he said.

"Okay, here we go. Kitty, kitty, kitty," she called. A half a minute later, Rasputin prowled out of her bedroom and slowly approached, his tail trailing behind him, tip curving up. About five feet from where Quinn and James stood, he stopped and stared at them with amber eyes.

James didn't advance to greet the cat. Instead, he squatted down, reached out his arm, and pointed his index finger at Rasputin. He turned his head slightly to the side, stayed completely still, and waited. After thirty seconds or so, the cat started forward again, his supple shoulders rolling as he strode straight for James's extended finger. When the cat reached the outstretched fingertip, he sniffed it, and then touched it with his nose.

Impressed, Quinn watched the greeting continue as Rasputin rubbed his cheek against James's finger and then his hand. After the cat pushed his face against James's hand a few more times, he scratched Rasputin under his chin. Still in a crouch, he twisted around and looked up at Quinn. "I believe I've just survived the crucible of the Feline Gate-keeper."

"With flying colors."

James stood and the cat immediately wove between James's feet and rubbed his sides against James's shins. "Obviously, Rasputin is an impeccable judge of character."

"Obviously."

There was a short pause while they both watched Rasputin continue to mark James, leaving a few stray strands of cat hair on his jeans in the process. James didn't seem the least bit concerned. When the cat moved away to rub against the corner of the couch, James asked, "Ready to go?"

"Almost," she answered and reached for her jacket draped over the back of the couch.

James's phone blinged as Quinn slipped her arm into one of the sleeves. She noted the uncertainty clouding his face, obviously not knowing if she would be bothered if he responded. "Go ahead and check it if you want," she said. She shrugged on the jacket and flipped her hair out from under the collar. "I don't mind."

His features cleared. "It's probably nothing, but since it's the middle of the night in Britain, it's best I check."

"Of course." She watched his face as he tapped the screen with his thumb and grew concerned when his eyebrows puckered as he read the message. "Is there a problem?" she asked. "Do we need to take a rain check for tonight?"

He stared at the phone a few seconds longer before shaking his head. "No, no, it's fine. It's my sister. I'll text her back now and ring her later." His thumbs moved across the screen as he filled Quinn in. "She's at a Christmas party at a friend's house and couldn't wait to tell me the chap she fancies has been chatting her up. She's quite thrilled."

"And you don't like him."

"No, I don't. I find him to be obnoxious and tiresome." He slipped the phone into his back pocket and returned her gaze. "It's that obvious?"

"Let's just say I recognized the big brother face you were just wearing. I've seen it myself a time or two. As a little sister, I can tell you Sophie might act like it annoys her when you go all big brother on her, but deep down she appreciates you care and are looking out for her."

"Thanks. It's nice to know a baby sister's perspective."

"Happy to help." She picked up her purse and keys from the kitchen counter. James went out the door first. She made sure the lamp on the table was on, closed the door, and locked the dead bolt with her key.

They walked past the row of town houses on their right. When they'd traveled about halfway between Quinn's apartment and the front gate, a man in long shorts and a sweatshirt came up the stairs from the complex's parking garage below. He carried two canvas bags full of groceries. "Hey, Quinn. Going out tonight, huh?" The man smiled while giving James a quick inspection.

"We are. Rick, this is my friend James. James, Rick is the complex manager. He lives here with his wife and two munchkins."

Rick set one of the bags on the sidewalk and the two men shook hands. "Where are you off to tonight?"

James smiled over at Quinn and said, "I'm taking this lovely lady to dinner at a little Italian place in Santa Monica."

"Well, that sounds like fun," Rick replied. Even in the dimness, Quinn saw his eyes twinkling at her.

Never comfortable being the center of attention, Quinn moved the conversation along. "What are you and the family up to tonight?"

"We'll be popping and stringing popcorn while we watch Christmas movies." He chuckled and added, "With a six- and an eight-year-old, there might be more eating than stringing." He picked up the bags by the handles. "I'd better get inside before they send out a search party. It was nice meeting you, James. You two have a nice evening." He started up the steps to his front door. She knew the man could barely wait to get inside and tell his wife, Emily, Quinn was actually going out on a date.

"Thanks. Tell the kids I said not to eat too much popcorn."

"Will do," he called back just before the door closed.

"He seems like a friendly neighbor," James said as they started walking again.

"They're a nice family. I babysit the kids once in a while in exchange for them taking Rasputin when I go out of town." Quinn reached the front gate and pushed it open.

"That seems like a fair trade," James said and opened the car door for her. Once she'd slid into the passenger seat, he shut it, ran around to the driver's side, and climbed in the car next to her.

The conversation stalled and the silence that descended wasn't the laid-back quiet that settled over them on other occasions.

Quinn snuck a side-eyed glance at James. His relaxed posture and the slight smile on his face as he accelerated and merged the car onto the 405 Freeway seemed to indicate he didn't feel the same level of discomfort she did, or any at all, for that matter. That alleviated her mind a little since he didn't appear inclined to pull the car over, make her get out, and end their date right there on the spot due to her lack of sparkling conversation skills. It still didn't stop her from overcoming the silence by putting voice to a trivia dust bunny that kicked up in her brain when they zoomed past a green freeway sign announcing the distances to the upcoming off-ramps.

"Did you know Mulholland Drive is named after William

Mulholland? He supervised the building of the Los Angeles Aqueduct in the early part of the twentieth century. L.A. wouldn't be the city it is today without the water that first aqueduct brought." After her short and somewhat blurted history lesson, she swallowed and hoped he didn't find what she'd said completely lame.

"That's interesting," he said. "He must be revered around here."

"I think most people don't even know who he was," she said, pleased he seemed interested in her bit of brain lint. "Plus, some of the things he did to secure the water rights up in the Owens Valley where the water came from were pretty sketchy. And one of the dams he personally inspected collapsed and the water killed hundreds of people. So there's that."

He looked over at her for a split second before he turned forward again to face the sea of red taillights from the cars in front of them as they sped over the Sepulveda Pass. "I enjoy your bits of random trivia. Your ability to remember information like that is indeed a gift."

She smiled and the nervous knot in her stomach fully untangled when she realized he was referencing their conversation at the coffee shop.

"Okay, so you've seen me use my superpower a couple of times. What's yours?"

He tilted his head in thought. "Hmm. I'm not sure I have one."

"I'm sure you do." She studied him and then snapped her fingers. "I know. You can get any cat you meet to instantly like you."

He took one hand from the steering wheel and rubbed the back of his neck with it. "Yeah, well, about that. I got lucky. I didn't have the first clue about how to make friends with a cat, so I read what to do on the Internet. I'm surprised it worked."

"You could have fooled me. You looked like a natural. Maybe it really is your superpower."

"Perhaps." After a short pause, he nodded. "I know what my superpower is. You saw it earlier today, and I'm not talking about cats."

She assumed he wasn't talking about his ability to charm the socks off her, so she filtered that out. "Give me a minute." She stared out the window and thought back to earlier that day. She'd first seen him outside of Mysterious Art Collector Guy's house. Her gaze fell on the tall, cylindrical building at the Sunset off-ramp. Every time she drove past it, it reminded her of the air filter that went in Tom's 1990 Camaro. He was always tinkering with its engine and she'd sometimes helped him by passing him whatever tool he needed. A spark ignited in her brain and the two memories fused. "Supercars," she said. "Your superpower is knowing all about supercars."

Warmth spread through her at his smile. "Very good. I've loved cars since I was a little boy. I can't help but be fascinated by their look, their sound, their speed, the engineering that goes into them." James peered over at her and popped a shoulder up and down as if embarrassed by this revelation. "I'll never be able to afford one, but I guess it doesn't hurt to admire them from afar."

"Maybe you won't be able to afford the Spyder we saw this morning, but a Lotus Evora might be doable someday," she said blithely.

She felt an immense sense of pleasure at the shock he showed when he sat up straight. "How do you know about Lotus?" He sat back and sighed. "Why am I surprised? I should know better by now."

"There's a British car show I channel-surfed past one night when the three hosts and their racing driver—"

"The Stig," he said, supplying the name of the show's enigmatic and mute driver whose identity was hidden behind a white helmet with a black visor. James practically bounced in his seat with excitement.

Quinn grinned. "Yes, the Stig. Anyway, the four of them were racing through central London, each using different modes of transportation to see who got to the city airport first. From then on, I was hooked."

They spent the rest of the drive chatting and laughing about the show, its hosts, and the different races and challenges the three had been on. As James parked the car on the street not far from the restaurant, Quinn sighed and said, "Someday, I'd love to go on an adventure like those guys have, like to South America or Africa. Shoot, I'd be up for driving from London to Edinburgh, for that matter. I'm not picky."

"What's stopping you?"

"Money, or lack thereof. My grandfather and I were talking about my love for adventure at his birthday party last weekend. He was in the import/export business and traveled a lot. When I was little, he and I would pore over this ratty old map of the world and he'd regale me with stories of what it was like in those exotic places he'd visited."

"So he understands your desire for adventure."

"Since he was the one who fanned the flames in the first place, yeah." An affectionate smile flitted across her face when she recalled those times when she sat at her grandparents' kitchen table, absently munching on the warm cookies her grandmother made while her grandfather spun stories that kept her completely spellbound. "Anyway, he said I should put five dollars in a jar every single day and at the end of a year, I'd have enough money to buy a plane ticket to just about anywhere I'd want to go."

"Have you taken his advice?"

"I can't afford the jar."

James snickered, shut off the engine, and looked at her. "I hope someday you will go on your great adventure." He held her gaze and smiled. "I don't know about you, but I'm hungry. Shall we?"

"Mmm-hmm."

They walked a block to the dimly lit restaurant, and once inside, they picked their way through a crowd of people to the seating hostess. Their reservation confirmed, James's hand rested at the middle of Quinn's back as they followed the menu-carrying young woman to a table for two next to a window.

James held Quinn's chair for her and once they were both seated with menus in hand, she took a moment to absorb the atmosphere. As promised, white twinkle lights were strung around the windows and twisted through the leaves of the potted ficus trees placed throughout the restaurant. Rather than kitschy, they worked in concert with the white table-cloths to give the place a casual yet elegant ambiance.

"I don't care if the food here turns out to be marginal, I love this restaurant," she said.

James raised his gaze from his menu and beamed at her. "The fact every table is full and people are waiting makes me think the food will be excellent."

Quinn nodded and began to study the menu when a young woman about her age arrived at their table. "Good evening. My name is Molly. I'll be your server tonight. Can I get you something to drink while you look over the menu?"

The innocuous question flooded Quinn with anxiety. She rarely drank alcohol, and when she did, it was usually some microbrew her brother John had run across and insisted she try. It was clear the place had an impressive and extensive wine collection, as evidenced by the giant floor-to-ceiling racks filled with hundreds of bottles housed behind a glass wall. She really did want to take advantage of the collection and try something, but had no idea what to order.

Quinn eyed the thick folder containing the restaurant's

wine list lying on the table as if it was a coiled rattlesnake about to strike. Deciding the best course of action was to kick the can down the road, she said, "I'll just have water for now."

"For me as well," James said.

The waitress moved off and neither spoke as they perused their menus. She wondered if this was the kind of restaurant that served minuscule amounts of food on giant plates. When she snerked, James looked at her and asked, "What?"

She bit her lower lip in embarrassment. "I'm sorry. That was involuntary. I was just wondering what the portion sizes are here and it reminded me of the time I talked my dad into taking my mom and me to a swanky seafood restaurant in San Diego for her birthday a couple of years ago."

"I can't wait to hear," he said. His gaze settled on her in anticipation.

Quinn couldn't stop the grin at the memory. "My dad ordered salmon, asparagus, and potatoes, right? He's all ready for a big old slab of fish, especially since he didn't eat his salad." Quinn pinched her face in a scowl and lowered her voice to imitate her father. "'I'm not gonna eat a salad that looks like the pile of weeds I pulled out from the planters yesterday.'"

James laughed. "I know exactly what he's talking about."

She nodded excitedly. "Right? So anyway, the waiter arrives and with a grand flourish, sets the plate the size of a serving platter in front of my dad. At the center of this huge plate was a piece of salmon about the size of a quarter. Three skinny little spears of asparagus were off to one side and two golf ball–sized boiled potatoes were on the other. That was it." She laughed. "I felt so bad for him. The look on his face was priceless. He stared down at his food with this mixture of confusion, disgust, and betrayal."

James's eyes rounded. "Oh no."

"You know what, though? He didn't say a word about it.

He would never do or say anything to ruin my mom's birthday, and since he'd already made a snarky remark about the salad, he cleaned his plate in about a minute and that was it. Although later I did overhear him tell my brother George prisoners of war get more food than that place served."

James barked out a laugh and then ducked his head when a couple at a nearby table looked over at them. He lowered his voice and leaned forward. "I assume your mum knew what was going on."

"Oh sure. She knew he wasn't thrilled, but she also wanted to honor the sweet thing he was doing for her, so she didn't say anything about it. On the way home from the restaurant, she said, 'Robert, thank you for taking me to such a lovely restaurant for my birthday. It was a wonderful treat. And as much as I enjoyed the birthday flan at the restaurant, what I'd really like right now is a chocolate milk shake from In-N-Out. Would you mind stopping? You and Quinn can get something, too, if you like.'"

"That was her way of giving him permission to eat something else."

"Mmm-hmm. 'Well, Marie,' he said. 'It is your birthday and I'm not going to stand in the way of getting anything you want. I don't want you to eat alone, so I'll get a little something for myself.'"

A smile split James's face. "He ate a Double-Double, didn't he?"

"Yup. Animal Style. Mom said it was one of the best birthdays she'd ever had."

James leaned back in his chair. "You're quite close to your parents, aren't you? They sound like a remarkable couple."

"I am and they are. To me, they're the model of what makes a marriage work: love, commitment, respect, faithfulness, self-sacrifice, gratitude, trust, grace, forgiveness." She wondered if she'd completely freaked him by uttering the "M" word, even in the context of making an observation about her parents' marriage.

To her relief, he didn't run screaming from the restaurant like his hair was on fire. "You're lucky to have such a great example."

Intrigued by his comment, she was about to ask him a question about it when Molly, their server, returned with their waters and asked if they were ready to order.

"I'd like the *pollo pomodori secco,*" Quinn said, sure she was slaughtering the Italian pronunciation.

"Very good. And you, sir?" Molly asked.

"As tempting as it is to order the salmon," he said, and sent a wink Quinn's direction that nearly knocked her out of her chair, "I believe I'll have the ciopinno."

"Excellent." Molly collected the menus and turned to leave. She took a step, stopped, spun back around, and pointed the tip of her pen at James. "You look familiar. Have we met?"

Taken aback, James looked up at Molly and said, "I don't think so."

"I feel like I seen you somewhere before. Do you live around here?"

"No, I'm sorry I don't, although I have been here in Santa Monica the last week or so. Perhaps that's it."

"Maybe. I must be wrong since the person I thought you were didn't rock a cool British accent and lived in Colorado," Molly said and playfully wrinkled her nose at James.

Quinn didn't know whether to laugh at the woman openly flirting with her date or punch her in the mouth. While the second option would have been much more satisfying, it was the less reasonable course of action, so she rested her clasped hands on her lap and pasted a placid smile on her face.

For his part, James wore a polite smile that didn't reach his eyes. "I'll be on the lookout for my American doppel-gänger."

"If you find him, let me know," she replied in a husky voice. She glanced over at Quinn who continued to watch the exchange with a bland expression. Molly seemed to realize she wasn't actually in a singles bar and said in a vaguely chastened tone, "I'd better go put this order in for you." She hurried away.

James winced. "Quinn, I'm so sorry about that."

"It's not your fault. You can't help it if women flirt with you all the time." She was guilty of it herself. "Molly probably shouldn't expect a big tip from me, though," she said in a dry tone.

He crossed his arms over his chest, leaned back, and narrowed his eyes at her. "And I suppose you didn't notice every eye of the male population in this room on you as we walked to our table."

Her response was to guffaw and roll her eyes. "No, all eyes were on the seating hostess in the low-cut number."

"Trust me. They were on you." He paused before rocking forward and resting both elbows on the table. "But let's forget all that and start again." With a devilish twinkle, he said, "Tell me about yourself, Gwen."

She laughed, delighted at the way he dispelled the strain brought on by Molly the Flirtatious Waitress. "It's Quinn, actually. Quinn Ellington." She set her elbow on the table and rested her chin in the palm of her hand. With a playful smile, she said, "I'm twenty-six years old and a librarian." She paused to enjoy the brilliant grin that erupted on James's face. "I love pizza, a good book by a roaring fire, and long walks on the beach." After a beat, she finished with "Oh! And all I want for Christmas is world peace."

Still grinning, James said, "James Lockwood. I'm twenty-eight and I work in insurance. I like fast cars, a pint of porter, and a good book by a roaring fire." Quinn's insides turned to goo when his smile went lopsided. "And all I want for Christmas is a Lamborghini necktie."

"I'll be sure to talk to Santa about that tie," she said. "So, James, how did you get into the insurance business?"

"Nepotism, pure and simple. My uncle is my boss. My mum hounded him until he hired me. I didn't think I'd like it since it sounds incredibly boring, but it's turned out to be a pretty good job."

"How'd you get lucky enough to be the one picked to come here and work with Mysterious Art Collector Guy's collection?"

"I'm the only person in the office without a significant other, so my being gone for any length of time wasn't going to be a hardship. Some of the people actually thought this would be a difficult assignment." He waggled his eyebrows. "I'm not finding it difficult at all."

She blushed and hoped her face didn't glow like a hot ember in the dim light. To combat the sudden onset of cottonmouth, she sipped some water.

"What about you?" he asked. "What made you decide to become a librarian?"

"I was a sophomore at UCLA and had no idea what I was going to do with my life," she said and set her glass down. "I was at the library studying one afternoon and the table I was sitting at wasn't far from the reference desk. It wasn't long before I wasn't studying at all. I just sat there and watched the librarian help people who came in with all kinds of questions. I remember thinking, 'What a cool job. I want to do that.' So I went over to the librarian and asked him what I'd have to do to work at a reference desk. He told me I needed to go to grad school and get a master's degree in library and information science." When James's eyebrows rose in surprise, she chuckled and said, "Who knew, right? Anyway, from that moment on, I knew it was what I wanted to do."

"You're very good at it."

She smiled her thanks. "I guess my work this past week was worth the money?"

There wasn't a hint of doubt in his voice when he answered, "Every penny."

Chapter Ten

After dinner they strolled the few blocks to the place where Santa Monica Boulevard met the Pacific. There, at the edge of the small park, they found a bench that overlooked the beach and the water beyond. Quinn felt like they sat at the cusp of two worlds: a continent ablaze with the lights of civilization behind them and the vast darkness of the ocean before them. She couldn't help but feel insignificant.

Quinn pulled the front of her jacket tight and gave voice to her musing.

James reached over, gently pulled her hand out from where it was tucked, and laced their fingers together. Resting their entwined hands on his thigh, he closed his other hand around hers, too. He said, "You might be a tiny speck on this big planet, but you are by no means insignificant." His voice was as warm as his hands.

Her stomach somersaulted so ferociously she could barely breathe. They were holding hands. She tried not to read too much into it. Maybe it was just a gesture of friendship. But judging by the way their evening had gone, the undeniable chemistry between them, the way he sometimes looked at her, she was fairly certain this was something more than friendship. She'd never felt anything like it. She was thrilled and overwhelmed and happy and terrified all at the same time. And overarching her jumble of emotions was the whispered feeling she and James simply fit.

Her words came haltingly and her voice was thick with emotion. "You're important to me, too."

The soft squeeze of her hand was his wordless and perfect response.

They sat hand in hand and watched the white foam appear with each breaking wave and then disappear as the surf rolled up the sand. It was as if they both understood words would break the tenuous, magical spell.

It was only when the hour grew late and they felt a spit of rain that they finally rose from the bench. They walked back to James's car, holding hands the entire way.

They were in a contented, mellow mood during the drive back to Quinn's apartment and chatted quietly over the soft music coming from the car's speakers. When James parked in front of her building, she was disappointed. It meant the evening was coming to an end.

She slipped her hand into the crook of James's arm as they sauntered along the walkway toward her door. James dug his hand into his pocket, pulled out his money clip, and peeled off a five-dollar bill. He held the note between two fingers and offered it to her. When she gave him a puzzled look, he said, "Seed money for your great adventure jar."

She stared down at the money and murmured, "James, that's very sweet, but I can't."

"Please. Take it. It would be my honor to help you get started. Perhaps you'd consider putting London at the top of your list of places to visit."

She couldn't hurt his feelings by refusing. "I think I can do that." She took the bill and tucked it into the front pocket of her jeans. "Thank you."

"You're welcome."

Her heart rate increased as they climbed the steps and

stood on the landing outside her door. She wasn't sure what to do next and surprised herself by asking, "Would you like to come in for a little while?"

"I would, but it's getting late and I don't want to overstay my welcome."

"Oh, okay." She swallowed and said, "Thank you for a wonderful evening."

"You're welcome. I had a great time." His eyebrows rose. "Can I ring you tomorrow?"

"Of course. I'd like that."

"Great. Talk to you tomorrow." He bent and pressed his lips to her cheek. "Good night."

Her legs went a bit wobbly, but she managed to stay upright and murmur, "Good night." She turned, unlocked the door, and opened it. "That's weird," she muttered when she saw her apartment was completely dark. She was sure she'd left the lamp on. She flipped the switch up and down. Nothing.

"Quinn? Is something wrong?"

"I think the bulb in the lamp went out while we were gone." She left the door open to let in some light, walked to the kitchen, and dropped her purse and keys on the counter. When she flicked on the lights and looked into the living room, adrenaline exploded in her chest as she let out a strangled yelp.

"Quinn!" James bolted to her side. "What—"

She was barely aware he was there. All she could see was her overturned couch, her lamp lying broken on the floor, and every book from the bookcase strewn about.

James sprang into action. He lifted the hem of his jeans and slipped a pistol from an ankle holster. "Stay here," he said in a low voice. Gun raised, he hurried toward her bedroom. The second he disappeared into the room, she heard a shout, followed by a crash, then thumping and grunting.

"James!" She was about to run to her bedroom when a man in a black hoodie barreled toward the front door with her laptop tucked under his arm.

Without thinking, she grabbed her keys, stepped in front of him, and stabbed her car key at his face, ripping through the flesh of his cheek.

He crashed into her and sent her stumbling backward. She slammed into the wall.

He dropped her computer and slapped a hand over the gash. "Bitch!" he spat and lunged at her.

When she could smell onions on his breath, she pushed away from the wall and rammed her knee up into his danglers so hard, he grunted out a strangled "oof."

Wild-eyed and red-faced, he doubled over in pain. Blood seeped through the fingers clamped over his cheek while his other hand clutched his injured privates.

Quinn raced past him. Edward Walker could turn any object into a weapon. She scanned the living room hoping to do the same. Inspiration struck when she spotted one of the two large hardcovers from her set of the *Compact Edition of the Oxford English Dictionary*. She hefted the eight-pound "P-Z with Supplement and Bibliography" volume with both hands. The intruder turned around and charged at her again. She reared the book back and swung it like a baseball bat. It caught him solidly on the side of the head. There was a resounding crack. He dropped to the floor like a bag of rocks and didn't move.

She heard grunting and scrabbling coming from the bedroom. She spun, and still armed with her reference book, burst into her bedroom just as James threw a haymaker at the face of the second, bigger man. His head snapped around at the force of James's punch.

Quinn saw her chance. She took dead aim at the man's jutted chin, stepped into her swing, and brought the book up from below. The spine of the book connected squarely with its target, sending the second man crashing to the floor. Blood dribbled from his mouth and collected in a dark pool on the carpet. Paralyzed, the only thing she could think was that she'd never get her cleaning deposit back when she moved out.

She glanced around the bedroom and noted the open window and smashed-in screen. Her vision went wonky and the book dropped to the floor. The shaking that started with her hands swiftly overcame her entire body. She would have joined the tome on the floor were it not for James's arms around her. She was vaguely aware of his voice imploring her to stay with him.

Quinn wasn't sure how long they'd stood like that when the shivering stopped. The fog in her brain lifted and she found that her head was resting firmly on James's chest. The side of her face was wet and his sweater was damp from the tears she'd been shedding. She lifted her head, swiped her hands across her cheeks, and ran a palm over the wet spot on his chest. "I'm sorry. I got you all soggy."

He squeezed her tightly and kissed the top of her head. "I'll be your handkerchief anytime." He loosened his embrace and leaned his head back. With a finger under her chin, he tilted her face toward his and searched it with worried eyes. "Are you hurt?"

"No, I'm okay." She sucked in a gasp when she saw the rapidly swelling cut on his lower lip. "We need to get you some ice," she said and lightly brushed her fingertips over the angry red mark on his jaw.

"Maybe later." A smile flickered on his lips. "You're pretty lethal with that book of yours."

"My trusty OED."

"Did you take out the other guy with it, too?"

Her lips pressed together in a hint of a smile and she lifted a shoulder.

"Whoever said, 'Sticks and stones may break my bones,

but words will never hurt me' never met Quinn Ellington."
His smile faded and he asked again, "Are you sure you're
okay?"

She nodded and, although he seemed reluctant to do so,
he released her. He walked over to the far corner of her
room, picked up his pistol, and slid it back into his ankle
holster.

Her stomach tightened. "You need to tell me why you're
carrying a gun."

He squatted down next to the unconscious burglar and
rifled through his pockets. Coming up empty, he grabbed
the man by the wrist and rolled him onto his stomach. He
continued his search as he said, "I'll explain later." He
removed a piece of jewelry from the criminal's back pocket.
He held it in his open palm for her to see.

"Hey! That's my great-grandmother's cameo. The other
jackass tried to run out the door with my laptop."

James's face turned grim.

"We need to get the police here," she said and took the
phone from her pocket.

James leapt up and put his hand over the phone. "No."

"What? Why not?"

When he hesitated, she threw his hand off hers and said,
"I'm calling the cops."

"I can't let you do that."

Icy tendrils of fear slithered around her heart. She backed
away from him. "James, you're scaring me."

"Trust me, Quinn. It'll be okay," he said in a calm, soothing tone. "I just need you to not call the police and let me
handle this."

Her head spun. Two men had broken into her apartment
and were now both unconscious on her floor. Her date had
a gun. All she knew was that she had to get away from them.
All of them.

She wheeled around and raced for the door. She was halfway across the living room when she heard what sounded like a muffled gunshot. A sudden and intense pain exploded in her right shoulder blade. She dropped to her knees and fell forward, flat on her face. Her final thought as her vision went black was that this was definitely the worst ending to a date. Ever.

Chapter Eleven

Quinn floated in the gauzy twilight between slumber and wakefulness. She felt wonderfully warm and relaxed. The thought that she shouldn't be, though, nibbled at her contentment. When she drew in a deep breath, she smelled dust and pine. Had she died and gone to heaven? She burrowed deeper into the coziness with both mind and body.

Why had she wondered if she'd died? All at once, reality yanked her into full consciousness. She bolted upright and struggled to catch her breath.

Dizziness engulfed her. Flashes of the evening exploded in her vision. James. Dinner. The ocean. Intruders. A gunshot. She reached a hand around and touched her shoulder blade. Her fingers probed where she expected to feel a bullet hole and warm, sticky blood. There was no hole, no blood. Her shoulder was only tender to the touch.

A wave of nausea swept over her and it felt as if an ice pick had been jammed through her left eye. The spinning and the nausea and the pain were too much. She flopped back onto a pillow and concentrated on her breathing.

When she first heard the voice calling her name, it was hollow and distant. But as the roiling in her stomach abated and her breathing steadied, the voice drew closer and became more insistent. When she tried to tell the voice she heard it, her slurred words came out as nothing more than low moans.

Quinn wasn't about to make the mistake of sitting up again. Instead, she decided the best course of action was to merely open her eyes. She drew in a deep breath to steel herself. She cracked her eyes open and blinked at the low light until the two amorphous shapes swimming in her vision melded into one. When the edges of the figure sharpened and she realized it was James, a mortar of fear exploded in her chest. He'd shot her. She had to get away from him and struggled to sit up.

"Shhh, Quinn. Take it easy. It's okay," James said.

She managed to right herself. The stabbing pain in her eye was still there, but at least it wasn't as sharp as before. Quinn squinted at James. His face was pallid and etched with worry. The dark circles under his eyes made her think he didn't feel much better than she did. His lip had fattened and the bruise on his jaw was purple. His bearing toward her was neither threatening nor hostile. If anything, it was the opposite.

Her fear morphed into anger. She tossed off the blanket and leapt up from a couch she knew was not hers. The pain and dizziness returned. Bubbles of white light formed and popped in her vision. Quinn's fingernails dug into her palms. The withering glower she fixed on James could have melted the polar ice caps. "You . . . you *kidnapped* me!" Her words came out strangled.

"Technically, maybe. Actually, though, I saved you." Despite her furious stare, he smiled and blew out a massive sigh of relief. He reached behind him and picked up a bottle of water. After removing the cap, he held it out to her.

"I don't want your water!" she shouted, her voice so loud it made her head throb harder. "I don't want anything from you!"

He winced and set the water on the table.

"You shot me!" The hurt and betrayal mushroomed like a nuclear bomb. "I trusted you, you son of a bitch!" Now trembling, her rage consumed her. She gripped the throw pillow her head had been resting on and walloped James on the side of the head with it. The pillow was surprisingly dense and when it caught him cleanly, the force of it sent him falling to one side.

Wielding the pillow like a club, she rained down blow after blow, trying to beat the living hell out of him. James ducked and raised his arms above his head to protect himself.

"I can't believe you shot me!"

"Okay! Okay!" he said as she unrelentingly continued to pummel him. "I shot you, but not with a bullet. It was a tranquilizer dart."

"So you took me down like a rampaging moose!" With a backhand swing, pillow and shoulder connected with a satisfying thump.

"I'm sorry I shot you," he said from behind a protective arm. "I had no other choice. You were freaking out."

"Of course I was freaking out, you idiot. You had a gun strapped to your ankle." She paused for a moment, and when he lowered his arms, she smacked him with the pillow again. "Take me home. Now!"

"I can't."

"Why not?"

"I can't tell you."

She snarled in frustration and gave him one last wallop before zinging the pillow past his head with the velocity of a high, inside fastball. "That's not good enough. I'm outta here." Despite her dizziness, she stomped across the room and threw open the door. It was pitch-black outside and snowflakes swirled around her, carried in on a gust of cold air.

"Snow?" she said, incredulous. The door slammed and

she whirled around. "We're someplace where it snows?"
She stabbed a finger in his direction. "Tell me where the
hell I am. Right now!"

"A cabin near Lake Arrowhead."

"*What?*" Quinn stormed across the room and stood over
him.

He sat motionless, as if afraid to make any sudden movements.

She glowered at him and punched her fists to her hips.
"You just toss me in the backseat of your car like a sack of
dirty laundry and haul me up to the San Bernardino Mountains?"

"I did not treat you like a sack of dirty laundry. I would
never do that," he said. His voice remained even, but she
still picked up on the hurt that seeped through.

His hurt did little to dull the anger that still churned in
her gut. She did, however, finally take a moment to study
the room. Given her circumstances when she lost consciousness, she assumed she'd wake up dead, in a hospital
bed, or strapped to a chair in a dark, dank, windowless
warehouse.

It was, in fact, the very opposite of a dank warehouse.
Just as James said, they were in a pine log cabin. The couch
she woke up on, the coffee table he was currently perched
upon, and an armchair were all log framed. A faded, tattered
area rug covered the hardwood floor.

Weak flames licked at barely scorched logs set on the
grate in the brick fireplace. It was clear it had only recently
been lit and had not yet had time to overcome the lingering
chill Quinn felt in the air.

Despite the charm of the rustic setting, her aggravation
roared back. Her apartment had been broken into, she'd
been tranquilized by her date, and dragged off to heaven
knew where. Her nostrils flared and she growled, "You
turned my life upside down, James. I deserve answers. Now."

When he stayed silent, she let out a long, frustrated snarl and started to prowl the room like a caged tiger. She slid to a stop in front of the small kitchen when the electronic ring of a phone rent the silence.

James picked up a phone from the cushion of the armchair. It wasn't the one she'd always seen him with.

"Yes?" He looked directly at Quinn as he listened. "Ms. Ellington is awake and has had no ill effects from the tranquilizer." He nodded. "So am I." After more listening—during which time Quinn's ire rapidly turned into deep curiosity—James said, "You're correct. She's quite insistent she be told exactly what's going on and why." He stretched and threw his shoulders back. "If I may say, sir, I agree with her. She deserves to know."

During the ensuing pause, the pressure built in Quinn's chest until she felt like she was about to explode.

"Can I tell her everything?" he asked. When his shoulders lowered and he smiled and winked at her, she started to breathe again. "Thank you, sir." The smile faded and James's eyes grew cloudy with concern. "No, it's been seven hours since I last heard from him. I tried contacting him during the drive to our current location, but he didn't answer. I was about to try again when Ms. Ellington woke up." His smile returned and he nodded. "Yes, sir. It'll be gone in a minute. Good-bye."

During James's phone conversation, she'd been inching closer to him. "What?" she asked cautiously.

He pressed a button and dropped the phone back on the chair's cushion. "Please, sit," he said and swept a hand toward the couch.

She narrowed her gaze at him and considered her options. When she realized she didn't have any, other than listening to whatever it was he had to say, she took her place at one end and folded her legs under her. He sat at the other end and faced her. He swallowed hard and gave her a rueful smile. Finally, he said, "I don't really work for an insurance company. I work for the United States government." His British accent was gone and he sounded as American as she.

The room lurched and Quinn gripped the cushions to keep from listing off the couch. She blinked, fighting the sudden sting of tears. "You've been lying to me." Her voice was flat.

Crestfallen, he lowered his head and stared at his hands. "James Lockwood is my cover for this op."

"You're a spy?"

His head bobbled from side to side. "Covert operative."

"So everything is a lie." The threatening tears spilled over and coursed down her cheeks

He looked completely gutted by her pain. "No, not lies. My cover. And my name really is James."

She brushed a finger over her wet cheeks and worked to regain her composure. "If you tell me your last name is Bond, I'm gonna punch you in the throat."

It gave her perverse pleasure to watch him slowly lean back, as if moving out of her reach. "No, not Bond. Anderson. My name is James Anderson."

Her anger flared again. "Well, James Anderson, I suppose you're happily married to some former Miss Peach Blossom and have a kid on the way and I'm just some pain in the ass you have to deal with until the op is over?" She felt like a complete fool for believing he cared for her. "You've been playing me this whole time."

He flinched. "I'm not married, I don't have to 'deal' with you, and I'm not playing you. I really do like spending time with you."

"How am I supposed to believe that?" She scowled at him. "You could be feeding me a load of crap right now."

"I could be, but I'm not."

She dismissively waved a hand. "You're trained to say

anything to get me to go along with whatever the hell all this is."

"No, that's not what this is," he said with a deep frown. "Look, your dad's a Marine, right? I'm sure there are lots of things he knows, things he does, places he goes he can't talk about to anyone, even to your mom."

"He would never lie to her," she shot back.

"He'd maintain his cover if he was in the middle of a covert op and she was someone he'd never met before. It's nothing personal. It's part of my job." When she didn't have a response, he said, "Let me explain everything and when I'm done, hopefully you'll understand."

Against her better judgment, and because her curiosity was actually going to kill her, she said, "Okay, tell me. Which agency do you work for? NSA? FBI? CIA? Homeland Security? DEA? Why me? Why am I mixed up in all of this? Was it just a fluke I was at the reference desk the day you came in? Is this connected with Mysterious Art Collector Guy?"

"Whoa, slow down," he said. "On our way up here, I called my boss and my boss called his boss to get approval to tell you everything. That phone call was my boss saying I've got permission to do just that."

When she opened her mouth to speak, he raised a hand to stop her. "The thing is, this is the U.S. government and it wants to ensure secrecy and protect itself from any liability. So, before I tell you anything else, they're sending a document for you to sign that says you're willing to be monitored twenty-four/seven to make sure you don't leak anything I tell you, and I mean *anything,* including what you learn about me, to anyone."

"Watch me twenty-four/seven? How are they gonna do that?" The minute the words passed through her lips, she said, "Stupid question. Forget I asked."

James's face remained inscrutable, although Quinn thought

she saw a flash of humor in his eyes. "Secondly," he said, pressing on, "if you get hurt in any way because of what you hear, it's not the government's fault."

"CYA," she said, referring to the abbreviation for covering one's backside.

"The greatest acronym of them all."

"What if I refuse to sign it? Let me guess. You've got a neuralyzer in your pocket and I'll inexplicably feel a desperate need to go to Cambodia and get a lobster dinner for a dollar?"

"Sorry, I don't track down rogue extraterrestrial aliens. That's a different agency," he deadpanned. "Seriously, Quinn, even if you don't sign and walk away, the danger doesn't disappear. We can keep you safe."

"All of the phone calls, all of this"—she waved a hand around, indicating the cabin—"has been happening in the middle of the night?" She glanced at her watch. It was 2:30 in the morning.

"Yes."

"Am I really this important?"

"Yeah, you are. And you're especially important to me."

She wanted to believe him and the look in his eyes seemed so sincere. But she *knew* James had been lying to her and she had no way of knowing if what he said now was the truth or a lie.

He stood and walked to where his briefcase sat open on the floor. He retrieved a tablet much like an iPad, only sturdier. He swiped his finger over a scanner at the bottom of the device and tapped at the screen. Then he held it out for her to take. "Here, read this."

On the screen was a cover letter. The letterhead prominently featured a round seal that included a shield and eagle's head. "CIA, huh?" She took the tablet and set it on her lap.

The letter acknowledged—but didn't apologize for—her

current circumstances and outlined what James had told her: sign or she'd be on her own. The document itself was peppered with words like *indemnification, liability, obligation,* and *confidentiality.* The phrases "bodily injury or death," "national security," "act of treason," and "federal detention and/or imprisonment," also caught her eye. "They sure know how to paint a rosy picture," she said.

"They like to be thorough."

She ran her hands through her hair in frustration. "How do I know all of this isn't some kind of elaborate scam? People make stuff up with Photoshop all the time."

"No offense, Quinn, but why would we scam you? You yourself implied you live paycheck to paycheck."

"You could be trying to scam Mysterious Art Collector Guy." She dragged a hand over her face. "And now I'm an accessory."

"You're not an accessory to anything." He shook his head and huffed a mirthless laugh. "I'm afraid it might be impossible to convince you I'm telling you the truth no matter what I do. But I'm going to try one more thing."

He rose from the couch and lifted out the false bottom of his briefcase to reveal a cache of currencies and passports from different countries. He picked up a black leather wallet and returned the briefcase to its normal state. He held the wallet toward her and said, "I hope this is enough to prove I'm not a scoundrel. If you're still not convinced, I'll get the agency director on video chat."

Her eyebrows shot up. "The director of the entire Central Intelligence Agency? You can do that?"

"It'll take some time, but yes, I can. And will." The confidence on his face gave her the impression he really could make such a thing happen. "Like I said, you're that important."

She had no idea why. She took the proffered wallet and opened it. A gold badge with the words *Central Intelligence Agency* was clipped to one side. The heft of it told her it hadn't been stamped out of an old pineapple tin. A rather run-of-the-mill picture ID with the name James Anderson was secured under clear plastic opposite the badge. It was no more interesting than a driver's license. She had to really scrutinize it to see where it indicated that James worked for the "Directorate of Operations." Neither the badge nor the ID screamed, "This man is a secret agent!" which, she supposed, was kind of the point.

There was still a part of her that was wary, but it was hard to argue with the evidence. She decided to sign. If it turned out to be a scam, she would claim she was as much a victim of it as Mysterious Art Collector Guy. She had nothing to lose.

She set the wallet on the table and picked up the tablet. She scrolled to the bottom of the document to the signature page. With the tip of her finger, she signed her name on the line. "There," she said and handed the tablet back to James.

He took the device and said, "Just a couple more things." He turned it toward her again. "Swipe your thumb over the scanner." After she did, he said, "Hold still," and aimed the small lens on the back of the tablet at her right eye. A blue light filled her vision. Then he touched the screen, presumably sending the document and accompanying biometrics to his superiors. When he finished, he looked at her and said, "All set."

"That's it? You don't need me to pee in a cup, too? Pledge my firstborn to the agency?" An eyebrow rose. "Pinky swear?"

He smiled. "We save the pinky swears for the super top secret stuff." The smile turned wistful when his gaze lingered on her face. He flicked a finger at a piece of lint on his jeans. "You still don't trust me."

"I'm sure you understand why."

His head jerked in a halting nod. "I do." With renewed vigor, he straightened and looked her dead in the eyes.

"That's why I'm going to make sure you speak directly with the director as soon as possible. Then you'll know for sure I'm not playing you, Quinn."

Her breath caught at the intensity in his eyes and the vehemence of his tone. In that moment, she almost believed him. Almost. She didn't know what to say, so she picked up the bottle of water and took several long pulls.

He cleared his throat and asked, "Are you tired? It is the middle of the night. You should sleep. You can take the bedroom. Your stuff is already in there." He pointed toward a short hallway.

"My stuff?"

"I grabbed some clothes and threw them in a bag I found in your closet. I'm not sure how long we'll be up here, so . . ." He shrugged as his voice trailed off.

She blushed at the thought of him going through her underwear drawer. While most of her things were tame and utilitarian, she did own a few items Nicole had talked her into buying that were on the racier—and lacier—end of the spectrum. "Thanks." All at once, a terrible thought hit her. She slapped her hand over her mouth and gasped, "Rasputin! Did they hurt—? Is he—?"

"No! No, they didn't hurt him," James said in a rush. "He's fine. He was hiding under your bed the entire time. I coaxed him out and took him to your neighbor's place."

She heaved a huge sigh in relief. "Thank you. That poor cat. He must have been terrified."

"I wish I could tell you he wasn't, but he was pretty freaked out. His eyes were huge. I hope he'll be okay."

"I'm sure he will. He's a pretty tough guy. What did you tell Rick?"

"I told him you were busy packing and asked me to bring Rasputin over. I said we got a lead on one of the items we've been researching and needed to go out of town for a few days to track it down." A corner of his mouth pulled up in a

smile. "I don't think Rick believed me. When I handed over
Rasputin, he said, 'I'm happy for you two. I hope you and
Quinn have a great time *researching*,' and went like this."
James proceeded to demonstrate by bouncing his eyebrows
up and down.

She chuckled. "I can imagine. He was already about to
come out of his skin when we left for dinner." It seemed like
days had passed since they'd eaten at that little Italian place.
"How did you explain the, um . . ." She pointed first to her
lip and then her jaw, mirroring where James had been hurt.

"I told him we were walking around the Third Street
Promenade and a rogue Santa tried to steal your purse. I
protected you." James sat up straight and puffed out his
chest. "Rick was quite impressed with my bravery."

"My hero," she said drily.

He smiled and leaned against the back cushion again.

"Rick didn't hear anything? Not even the gunshot when
you hit me with the dart? No one called the police?"

"No. He and the family had a movie playing pretty loud
and wouldn't have heard it. My guess is your other neighbors were out or if they did hear something, didn't want to
get involved."

"What happened after you tranquilized me? What did
you do with the two guys who broke in?"

"I put some of your book tape across their mouths to
keep them quiet and used it to tape their wrists and ankles
together. I called a couple associates who took them into
custody. They'll make sure your apartment gets cleaned
up, too."

"Ask if they can clean under the refrigerator while they're
at it." She returned James's smile before asking, "You think
my two burglars have something to do with your mission?"

"Yes. After what happened at your apartment, the agency
sent people to my hotel room. It'd been tossed, too."

"Your cover's been blown," she stated.

"It looks that way, yeah. I don't know how it happened since everything was okay until tonight. But now you've been compromised, too. Whoever it is knows where you live. I had to get you out of there to someplace safe. That's why we're here."

"Thank you for that, even if you did shoot me with a tranquilizer," she said, and rolled her sore shoulder.

He frowned. "I'm sorry you got dragged into this."

"Yeah, about that. Why would you even go to a public library for help? You must have lots of researchers at the CIA who can help you."

"I'm undercover. I can't have any contact with the agency while I'm in L.A. I only did today because I needed backup. James Lockwood, British insurance guy, would absolutely go to a public library for help."

"So my library was close and it was random when you came up to me?"

Her heart flopped like a fish out of water when he hesitated.

"It wasn't random?"

"No."

"What?" she yelped. "Why me?"

"I don't know."

"What do you mean you don't know?"

"I was told by my boss to go to you, specifically you, for help."

She slumped back against the couch, flabbergasted. "I don't know anybody at the CIA. How am I even on their radar?"

James shrugged. "I have no idea. I did what I was directed to do and went to you for help."

"That's so weird."

"We have a library at headquarters in Langley. Maybe there's a librarian there who knows you."

"You have a library? With librarians and everything?"

He nodded and smiled. "Cool job, right?"

"Okay, yeah, that's a really cool job." She scowled at him, but in a teasing way. "Don't change the subject. You still haven't told me anything about this op of yours. What's the deal with Mysterious Art Collector Guy? It has something to do with the collection we've been researching, doesn't it?" When he unsuccessfully stifled a yawn, she noticed the thin red veins in the whites of his eyes. "You look exhausted."

"I'm okay," he replied. "If you need to know about the op before you sleep, I'm ready to tell you. If you want to go get some sleep and talk in the morning, that's okay, too. It's up to you."

"I hate to make you stay up, but I'll never be able to sleep until I know."

"That's fine."

"But I need a pit stop before we continue."

"Yeah, sure. The bathroom is across the hall from the bedroom."

It pleased her to know the cabin wasn't so rustic that she'd be hiking to an outhouse. She padded across the floor and peeked into the tiny bedroom. It was sparsely furnished, with only a quilt-covered bed with a log headboard and a lamp on a small nightstand. Her overnight bag was at the foot of the bed.

She turned around, went into the cramped bathroom, and practically had to stand on the toilet seat to make enough room to swing the door closed.

As she washed her hands in ice-cold water, she caught a glimpse of herself in the mirror above the sink. She nearly shrieked in horror. The mascara Nicole had talked her into using may have made her lashes look longer and thicker, but the black smudges rimming her eyes proved it was not waterproof. She bent over the sink and caught the frigid water in her hands. The cold stung her cheeks as she splashed it onto her face and scrubbed her fingers over her eyes. She lifted her head and rechecked herself in the mirror. Much better. She turned off the water and patted her face dry with a small hand towel. The water had refreshed her and at 2:45 in the morning, she felt more alert than she did most days at 2:45 in the afternoon.

Quinn inhaled and expelled the air in a gust, bracing for what was to come. She opened the door and strode into the sitting room, ready to hear why she was currently squirreled away in a government safe house.

Chapter Twelve

Only a few hours earlier, Quinn and James sat hand in hand on a bluff above the beach. In that moment, she had felt like her life was on the verge of being perfect. Between then and the present, her life had taken a surreal turn. Now, she sat on a couch in a cabin in the San Bernardino Mountains at three o'clock in the morning with a handsome undercover CIA officer.

"I'm sorry about the rather deplorable snackage," James said as Quinn took a Ritz cracker from the package he'd set out on the coffee table and picked up a can of Easy Cheese. "There's not much to choose from. The cupboards are pretty bare."

She shook the can, poised it upside down over the cracker, and depressed the nozzle with a finger. As the unnaturally bright orange viscous cheeselike substance was extruded, Quinn swirled a glob onto the cracker. "That's okay. It's not like you could call ahead to make sure there would be trays of appetizers ready for when we arrived." She tossed the cheese-laden cracker in her mouth and crunched. The familiar cheesy tang transported her back to her under-grad days when she and her roommates would binge on it—and a variety of other less-than-healthy foods—during midterms, or when they had boyfriend problems, or when UCLA lost in football, or it was Thursday. "Besides, you had an unconscious librarian to deal with."

"That's true," James said. "I considered stopping off at a convenience store on the way to pick up a few things, but I didn't want to leave you alone in the car."

"Alone and unconscious," she finished for him with a slight dig.

He moved a shoulder and said, "Yeah. That."

"Don't worry," she said as she squirted another blob of cheese on a cracker. "I don't have a particularly finicky palate. I'm sure whatever we find to eat around here will be fine." She popped it in her mouth and washed it down with the last of the water from the bottle James had opened for her earlier. "I have loads of questions, James, but maybe you should just start at the beginning. Hopefully a lot of them will get answered."

"Okay. Feel free to interrupt and ask me anything."

"Good, because I was going to anyway."

James went quiet for a moment, gathering his thoughts. "This all started when I was in Moscow a few months ago," he began in a soft voice. "I was reading a newspaper and saw a short article about the widow of a Soviet general who had just sold her deceased husband's art collection to a wealthy British businessman."

"Mysterious Art Collector Guy," Quinn said.

James nodded. "His name is Roderick Fitzhugh."

"Ah," Quinn said, finding it satisfying to finally know. "A wealthy guy buying art doesn't seem particularly note-worthy."

"It wasn't. That's why it was such a short article. The general, Yevgeni Dobrynin, has been dead for about fifteen years. He was killed in a car accident." When James said the last two words, he flexed two fingers on each hand to make air quotes.

"So, not a car accident."

"We don't think so." He waved a dismissive hand. "How he died isn't the issue. The fact that he amassed a fortune by selling Soviet weapons he took control of during the dissolution of the Soviet Union in the early nineties and the political crises that followed is."

"'Took control' sounds like a euphemism for 'stole.'"

"Basically, yeah. He was an arms dealer."

Quinn wondered if the CIA had anything to do with Dobrynin's "accident." She wasn't about to ask.

"Fast forward fifteen years after his death," James said, plowing forward with the story. "His widow and children are strapped for cash—"

"—and a lot of Dobrynin's wealth is tied up in his art collection, so the family decides to sell."

"Exactly. They sold the entire lot to Roderick Fitzhugh for fifteen million pounds."

Quinn blew out a low whistle. "That's some serious dough." She cocked her head and squinted at him. "I still don't get why the CIA would be interested. The general is dead and not a threat. If his wife and kids are strapped for cash, they haven't continued in the 'family business.' Otherwise, they'd have plenty of money."

"You're right. We don't think the Dobrynin family has anything to do with this. The thing is, Fitzhugh is a weapons dealer, too."

"Did they know each other? Friend or enemy?" She sat up straighter and exclaimed, "Oh, I know! Dobrynin screwed Fitzhugh over in some arms deal, so Fitzhugh had him offed. All these years later Fitzhugh's able to exact his final revenge by buying Dobrynin's cherished art collection."

James grinned. "Excellent theory, Ms. Ellington. It's wrong, but excellent."

"What do you mean it's wrong?" She huffed. "It makes complete sense."

"It does if the two men knew each other. There's no evidence they ever did business together or even met, for that matter." His smile remained in place as he looked at her expectantly. "Care to come up with another hypothesis?"

She kept her face neutral. "I get the feeling I'll never guess, so I think I'll pass."

"Fair enough." He downed several gulps of water from his bottle before starting again. "I immediately recognized Fitzhugh's name. He's been on our radar for a while. It seemed really odd to me that one arms dealer would buy the art collection of another, so I did a little more digging on the dearly departed Yevgeni. I found out there's a long-standing rumor he'd hidden away major weapons somewhere. The intel on what it is exactly is pretty murky. It might be a huge stash of conventional guns, suitcase nukes, or a biological or chemical weapon of some sort." He blew out a breath and shook his head in frustration. "We have no idea what, and as far as we know no one else does either."

She found herself leaning forward as if straining to hear the last bit of information that would make all of these seemingly random pieces fit together.

"The rumor also says Dobrynin put the whereabouts of these weapons, whatever they are, into some kind of code and hid them in his art collection."

The "Hallelujah Chorus" played in her head when the final piece fell into place. "Fitzhugh heard the same rumor and bought the collection on the chance it was true," she said.

"That was my feeling, too. I forwarded all the intel and the connections I'd made about it to my boss. He and a roomful of analysts concluded it was credible and to move on it. Since I was the one who brought it to them, they let me plan the op."

Her head felt like it was about to explode as she began to comprehend it all. "You came up with a way to examine the collection and figure out the code before Fitzhugh could by going undercover as an employee of an insurance company."

"The entire company is a CIA front," he said, nodding. "Ben is my partner on the op. He's undercover in England doing the same thing."

"That's why we spent so much time on pieces with writing and designs. You thought those might be the codes." Her eyes widened to the size of saucers. "The first thing you brought in was the brooch with the runic writing. And that explains why Ben wanted more research on the words of that Schoenberg opera. That's brilliant. The entire setup is brilliant."

He smiled at the compliment, but it was short-lived. "Not brilliant enough, since obviously something went sideways. Otherwise, we wouldn't be holed up in a safe house right now."

"Do you think Ben's cover's been blown, too?"

"I don't know. I've been trying to contact him, but he's not answering his phone. The last I heard from him was last night at your apartment."

"So it wasn't your sister who texted you. It was Ben," she said, remembering the moment. "If you were concerned, you should have blown me off."

He pulled a face. "I wasn't going to blow you off. If I seemed a little put off by the text it was because of the time he sent it, not what it said."

"What did it say?"

"It said, 'Good luck.'" He peered sheepishly at her. "He knew I was taking you out to dinner."

She tried not to read too much into it, but if Ben wished him luck on their date, James must have confided it had some level of importance. "Oh," she said softly.

In the quiet that hung between them, Quinn heard snow tapping against the window. And while it was cold and blustery outside, the fire James had built earlier now fully engulfed the logs and chased the chill in the room away. She gazed into the fire and watched it lick up from the wood. It was all quite cozy and comfortable.

"And then while we were at dinner, my apartment gets broken into." She tore her eyes away from the flickering flames and looked at James. "You assumed the two guys who broke into my apartment were connected to your op somehow and not your run-of-the-mill burglars. That's why you didn't want me to call the police."

"When you told me one of them tried to take off with your laptop, I figured they wanted to find out what we knew. It was all too much of a coincidence."

"But why trash the place? It was like they were looking for something besides my computer."

James rubbed the back of his neck. "They might have been looking for the letter we found in the clock. It might contain the codes, so I took it to examine more closely."

"And if Paul works for Fitzhugh and is looking for them just like you are, he might have had the same thought. When he saw it was gone, he assumed it was you." She pursed her lips. "But why not just call and ask if you took it?"

"My guess is my cover had been blown by then. Maybe he already suspected me." He closed his eyes, sagged against the couch, and dragged a hand over his face. When he opened them again, Quinn could see him struggling to focus. He looked absolutely exhausted. "I don't know. There're still gaps in all of this we need filled. I need to talk to Ben."

When he reached for his phone, she admonished him with a gentle "No, you need to let your buddies in Langley talk to Ben. You need to get some sleep."

Her words seemed to rouse him. "Langley? You believe me?"

"Yeah, I do. It's so unbelievably crazy, it has to be true."

"I still want you to video chat with the director."

"James, that's not necessary."

"I don't want you to have any doubts."

"I really don't have any, but if you insist, we'll talk to him after we both get some sleep."

He nodded in agreement.

She flung the blanket off her legs and tossed it toward James. "I'm not going to be a martyr, though," she said with a hint of teasing. "I'm taking the bed. You get the couch."

"I wouldn't want it any other way."

With a smile, she said, "Good night, James. Today was an adventure."

"That it was," he replied. His return smile was as soft as hers. "Good night."

She walked to the bedroom and closed the door behind her. She turned around, leaned against the door, and tipped her head back. It was good to get some distance between herself and James and the fire and the blanket and, well, everything.

Now in the bedroom, she noticed the drastic change in temperature. The heat of the fire hadn't traveled beyond the sitting room. She wasn't at all opposed to the idea of simply crawling under the covers in what she wore to stay warm. She wondered what James had packed for her to sleep in, though, so she unzipped the top of her bag and pulled it open.

Her heart skipped a beat when she saw the copy of *Down the Spider Hole* from her nightstand resting on top of the clothes. In what had to have been an insanely tense situation, James had done something incredibly thoughtful. She swallowed at the unexpected thickness in her throat and with a watery chuckle, chalked up her spurt of emotion to exhaustion.

There were no pajamas, but she certainly didn't take the omission as a salacious hint on James's part. She felt she knew him well enough to know he either didn't want to rummage through her pajama drawer or didn't have time. What she did find was a pair of sweatpants and her navy blue UCLA hoodie. It was like discovering a chocolate doughnut buried in a basket of gluten-free bran muffins.

In less than a minute, she stripped off her jeans and sweater, pulled on her sweats and dove under the covers. She let out a quiet yelp when the cold from the frigid sheets seeped through her socks. She jerked the hood up over her head and pulled the drawstring tight so that only her nose had to brave the cold. Knees drawn up, she curled into a ball to conserve body heat. Once the burst of shivers subsided, she reached out and switched off the lamp.

Now alone and in the dark, she prepared for the onslaught of fear and anger and betrayal and doubt and the myriad other negative thoughts and emotions that would keep her awake the rest of the night. To her great surprise, however, the attack never came. Instead, she found she was filled with a strange mixture of exhilaration and peace. And despite the rather dangerous circumstances she was in, she felt a sense of security. Lulled by the unexpected sensation of well-being, she drifted off to sleep.

Chapter Thirteen

The light that filtered through the white curtains covering the bedroom window slowly brought Quinn to wakefulness. She reached out a hand and searched the quilt for the warm ball of fur always curled up next to her.

When she didn't feel Rasputin, she opened her eyes and took in the wooden walls of the cabin bedroom. She was in a safe house with James Anderson, CIA covert operative. It was all completely ludicrous.

The calm she'd felt when she fell asleep had abandoned her. Her emotions rose to the surface. Would she burst out in maniacal laughter or uncontrolled sobbing? Both at the same time seemed like a real option.

Through sheer force of will, she did neither. She wasn't naïve enough to think people like Roderick Fitzhugh and Yevgeni Dobrynin didn't actually exist. She'd grown up with her father being deployed to fight those kinds of people. She'd just never been directly confronted by them before. In that moment, she resolved not to allow the reality of a seemingly insane situation turn her into a blubbering mess. She gritted her teeth, threw off the covers, and rolled out of bed.

Despite the determination that burned in her chest and propelled her forward, she was keenly aware that she was, first and foremost, in desperate need of a shower. She went to the door and cracked it enough to poke her head through and peek down the hallway into the sitting room. The couch was empty and the blanket was folded and placed on one of the cushions. The rattling noises coming from the kitchen gave her James's location, so she quietly shut the door again and lifted her bag onto the bed. She gathered some clean clothes and bolted across the hall to the bathroom. She twisted the shower's hot water knob to the left as far as it would go and hoped for even a little warm water. Otherwise, she was about to take the fastest shower in the history of mankind.

To her great relief, steam began to billow up and fill the bathroom. She found a small bottle of shampoo and bar of soap that appeared to have been liberated from a hotel. Once in the shower, the hot water cascading over her felt glorious and she stood under the soothing spray longer than she should have. Not wanting to completely drain the hot water heater, she reluctantly shut off the water and snagged a towel. She dried off and tugged on a pair of clean jeans and a long-sleeved cotton top.

With no comb, brush, or hair dryer to be found, she wiped the steam off the mirror, combed out her wet mane with her fingers, and put it into a French braid. She had no choice but to forgo makeup. Plus, she'd already looked like a raccoon in front of James, so in the grand scheme of things, going au naturel could only be an improvement.

She hung her towel over the shower door to dry—there was already a damp one on the rack, evidence that James had showered—and left the bathroom. She pulled on a pair of socks and ambled down the hallway. Her stomach growled like a grizzly bear's and she hoped there was something they could scrounge up to eat other than cheese in a can and Ritz crackers.

A black laptop, different than the one she'd always seen James with, sat closed atop the dining table. Out the window, Quinn saw snow still falling at a steady rate. It didn't appear they'd be going anywhere anytime soon.

James's back was to her when she arrived at the kitchen, his head down as he read the back of a box he held. She cleared her throat.

He spun around, looking completely gobsmacked the second he saw her. "Hey, Quinn. You look great. I like your hair," he said with delight in his eyes. "Did you sleep okay?"

"I did, thanks. And your accent is still American. It's going to take me a while to get used to it."

"Uh-oh. Sounds like James Anderson has some competition from James Lockwood."

She squinted at him and then shook her head. "It's too early in the morning for multiple personalities."

"Then if it's okay with you, I'll be Anderson today."

"Fine by me." She noted his hair was still damp and he hadn't shaved. The morning stubble along his strong jawline made her mouth go dry. He wore the same jeans from the night before, but a T-shirt and a black zippered hoodie had replaced his cashmere sweater. On the front of his hoodie was a yellow shield with a rearing black stallion on it. She dipped her head toward the insignia and said, "Ferrari?"

"Yeah," he said with a smile. "I always carry a bag with some extra clothes in the trunk of my car in case something like this comes up." He pointed at a teakettle on the stove. "Can I get you some tea? I found a box of tea bags and there's hot water in the kettle."

"I'll get it. Thanks." She took down a mug from the cupboard, dropped in a bag, and poured the hot water. She turned back toward him and leaned against the counter. "What have you got there?" she asked, referring to the box in his hand.

"Pancake mix. Just add water. It expired a couple of months ago. Do we try it? We don't have many options."

She shrugged. "I'm game if you are."

They spent the next twenty minutes working side by side. James measured out the mix and water and stirred the contents in a bowl while Quinn heated up a frying pan on the stove.

Pancakes made, and with a bottle of syrup they found in the pantry, they sat down at the table to eat.

"Were you able to get in touch with Ben?" Quinn asked before putting a bite of pancake in her mouth. They were surprisingly good for an expired mix. Or maybe she was just really, really hungry.

"Not yet. I'll try calling him again in a little while."

They continued to chat while they ate, the easy manner they'd enjoyed before her tranquilizing restored. When James finished his breakfast first, he set his empty plate off to the side, slid the laptop in front of him, and opened it. After he swiped his thumb over the biometric scanner, the screen flashed to life. From where she sat, she was able to see a log-in box on the otherwise black screen.

He rose, went to his briefcase, and returned with his phone and a short cable. He plugged the phone into the computer, dialed a number, set it on the table, and tapped at the keyboard.

Quinn was about to take the plates into the kitchen when James frowned at the computer screen and muttered, "What the hell?"

"One of your CIA buddies sent you a picture of a dog about to sneeze?" Her stomach dropped when he didn't even crack a smile.

She leaned over to get a better look at the screen. An e-mail was displayed, the sole content of which was a long number of at least fifty digits. Her eyebrows pulled together. "Why would someone send you a bunch of ISBNs all strung together?"

His head snapped toward her. "Send me what?"

"ISBNs. It stands for International Standard Book Number. Nearly every book that's published in the world has one. Each ISBN is a unique thirteen-digit number." She pointed at the screen and said, "That's just one long string of ISBNs all smashed together."

"How can you know that by glancing at it for two seconds?"

"I'm a librarian, remember? Books? I kinda do them for a living." She jumped up, ran to the bedroom, and snatched her book from her bag. Upon her return, she dragged her chair around next to James's, and sat. She held the book so they both could see the back cover. "Look, the first three digits of this book are 978. That's the beginning prefix for almost every ISBN," she said, pointing to the string of numerals above to the black vertical lines of the barcode. "The same first three numbers of the number in the e-mail."

He moved his finger across the screen as he counted thirteen digits. "Doesn't work. The next three numbers aren't 978."

"That's because they started using 978 in 2007. Before that, ISBNs were ten digits and didn't have the 978 prefix. See?" From where James had left off, she counted off ten more digits. "There's a 978 again." More counting, another ten-digit number and then another one with thirteen. "As soon as I saw 978 repeated several times, I knew they were ISBNs. Plus, look," she said, growing more excited. "All of the 978s are followed by a zero or one. That tells me the books are in English. If the numbers were just random, what are the odds 978 would always be followed by a zero or one?"

James stared at her in astonishment. "You're remarkable."

"Not really," she said with a shrug. "I'm just a librarian."

"No. Not just a librarian," he replied quietly.

"Who, um . . ." She stopped and swallowed at the sudden dryness in her throat. "Who sent this e-mail to you?"

He blinked and moved his gaze back to the screen. "Ben. He sent it from his cover e-mail account to mine. From the time stamp, it was sent about the same time as the text he sent last night. With everything that's been happening since dinner, this is the first chance I've had to check my e-mail." He ran his hands through his hair. "Okay, so we've got these numbers. Now what?"

"We find out what books these ISBNs belong to."

"How?"

"We could probably use Google, but that's so pedestrian," she said and smiled when he breathed a quiet laugh. She went to put her fingers on the keyboard, but jerked them back as if she were about to touch a red-hot stovetop. "I don't know if I'm allowed to touch your superfancy, top secret, government-issue laptop."

"Usually not, but since you're read in on this mission, go ahead."

"Okay." She opened a blank text document, copied and pasted the long string of numbers from the e-mail and put spaces between the ISBNs, whether they were of the ten or thirteen-digit variety. "Looks like five books are listed here," she mused aloud. After opening a browser, she typed in a web address. "I'm going to use WorldCat."

"I remember Ben mentioning it when he asked us to find that dissertation on *Moses und Aron*."

"It's the world's largest union catalog. Ten thousand libraries across the globe have their online catalogs linked to it. Anyone can search for books, DVDs, serials, you name it, and find out which libraries have them in their collection." She went to the advanced search page, selected "ISBN" as the field to search, and pasted the first book number into the box. A split second after clicking "search," the result displayed on the screen.

"It's a book called *On the Run*," she said. She clicked on the title link, which took her to a new page with more bibliographic information. "Well, that's interesting," she said, noting the subject headings. "It's a biography of a CIA intelligence officer." She scrolled down the page to the short summary. James's head moved closer to hers to get a better look at the screen as they read about a disillusioned operative who had written an exposé of the agency forty years before. *On the Run* was his life's story subsequent to those revelations. Quinn looked at James. "What do you think Ben's trying to tell you? Is he about to blow the whistle on something?"

He peeked back at her and shrugged. "It makes no sense for him to tip me off if he was about to do something like that. He knows I'd report it." The tension radiating from James was palpable. His voice was tight when he asked, "What's the next ISBN?"

She repeated the steps for the next number. "It's a detective mystery called *Man on the Run*." Without being asked, she plugged in the next number. "This one is called *On the Run,* too, but it's by a different author and it's fiction." The final two numbers were both novels called *Gone to Ground*.

"I don't think the stories are what's important," James said with urgency in his voice. "*On the Run, Man on the Run, Gone to Ground*." He pivoted in his chair. A jolt of electricity thrummed through her when his knees brushed her thigh. "His cover was blown and he knew it."

"This was his way of telling you he was taking off?"

"Yeah."

"Why all the subterfuge? Why not just send you an e-mail that says, 'Gotta go'?"

He pondered her question. "Maybe he wasn't sure his cover was blown, but knew they were suspicious and figured it was better to take off," he replied. "If they intercepted this e-mail, or someone saw it since these e-mail accounts aren't secure, they wouldn't know he'd taken off since they wouldn't know what the numbers meant. It might have given him the head start he needed to get away."

"But why send an e-mail to an unsecure account? You must have a supersecret one that only works with a mouth swab of your DNA or something."

"He might not have had time to access his agency computer. Even if he did, it takes time to get past all the security measures."

"That makes sense, but why ISBNs? How could he be sure you'd figure it out?" As soon as the question passed through her lips, she rolled her eyes at how stupid it sounded. "You would have forwarded it to CIA cryptographers and they'd have figured it out in no time."

"Not faster than you did," he said. He rubbed a hand over the stubble on his cheek. "My guess is Ben assumed you would see it."

She turned her face away and looked out the window, hoping he wouldn't notice that her entire head had gone the color of a ripe tomato.

At James's sharp intake of breath, her head snapped around. Eyes round, he looked like he was about to be impaled by a charging rhinoceros. "Oh no! No, Quinn, that's not what I"—he gulped—"what I meant. Ben knew how much time we've been spending together is all. Not that we'd be, um, spending the night together, ah, or anything."

When she stared at him mutely, his eyes somehow grew

even rounder. "Not that I wouldn't want to sleep—I mean, you're certainly—we would be so—" Unable to finish a sentence, he screwed his eyes shut. "I'll stop talking now," he said in a low, mortified voice.

She bit her lower lip, trying to keep the smile at bay. The idea that she made him flustered and tongue-tied both delighted her and made her a little light-headed. "You're not exactly James Bond with the ladies, are you?" She made sure to keep her voice teasing, not wanting to add insult to injury. "Don't they teach you how to be all suave and smooth and charming at the Farm?"

"Hey!" His eyes flew open. "I was totally Mr. Smooth the first time I came into the library and met you."

"Yeah, you were." She deflated a little when she realized she didn't really know James, the real James, at all.

As if reading her thoughts, he sobered and said, "James Lockwood might be confident and charming, but it was the sweaty, blithering idiot James Anderson sitting before you that asked you to dinner." He sighed and returned to the subject at hand. "Anyway, now that we know Ben has gone to ground, I need to contact my boss and tell him in case they don't already know." He angled the laptop back toward him and began to type.

Leaving him to his work, Quinn killed time by cleaning up from their meal. Sitting down at the table again, she asked, "You told your boss what we figured out about Ben?"

"Yeah."

"What do we do now?"

"Wait."

"For what?"

"Whatever he wants me to do next."

"What about me? I can't hide out in this cabin forever. I've got a job to get back to."

"I know. I'm sure the agency will figure something out."

"Okay. In the meantime, I guess I'll read." She grabbed her book and sunk into the armchair next to the fire. Despite the fact she was hiding from a nefarious international arms dealer, reading a spy novel by a roaring fire wasn't a terrible way to spend a Sunday morning.

Chapter Fourteen

Quinn read for an hour before a chirp from James's computer interrupted the quiet.

She kept her head down, but peeked over at James. He looked at his laptop and said, "Good afternoon, sir."

"James," a man's voice said from the computer. "Your report indicates Ms. Ellington was instrumental in deciphering Ben Hadley's e-mail." Upon hearing a different last name for James's partner, Quinn realized Baker was Ben's cover name just as James's was Lockwood.

"Yes, sir," James said. "She recognized that the string of digits broke down into ISBNs and figured out Ben sent it to inform me he was going into hiding."

"Excellent work," the voice said. "Is Ms. Ellington available? I'd like to thank her personally."

He twisted around in his chair. "Quinn? My boss wants to talk to you."

She put her bookmark between the pages and closed the book. As she cautiously approached, James stood and offered her his seat. She sat and saw a gentleman in his fifties with brown, curly hair graying at the temples looking back at her. Behind him was a row of books on a shelf. She wished she could read the titles, knowing she'd learn a lot about the man from the books he kept. The head of a golden retriever briefly appeared at the lower corner of the screen.

"Ms. Ellington, I'm Aldous Meyers. It's nice to meet you."

"It's nice to meet you too, sir." She hoped the forced smile plastered on her face didn't reveal her serious case of nerves.

The smile on the man's face was friendly in return, but his eyes were as sharp as his features. He was evaluating her even through the monitor. "We're sorry unforeseen circumstances have forced you into your current predicament."

"Things don't always go the way they're supposed to." She shrugged.

"Regardless, we appreciate your ability to roll with the punches, as it were." After a beat, he added with a trace of amusement in his voice, "And land a few as well."

The only response she could come up with was another tiny shrug and a less than eloquent "Um, okay."

"James has informed me that you were instrumental in decrypting Ben Hadley's e-mail. Well done."

"Thank you."

"From what I understand from James's reports, you have been quite an asset to him."

"Doing research is kind of in my wheelhouse. I enjoyed it."

"And from what I can tell, you're quite good at it."

"Thank you. I try."

"Which is why I'm asking you to continue to work with James by accompanying him to London."

The gasp from behind her was almost as loud as her own. Had she heard him right? "I, uh," Quinn said, reeling, "I was under the impression from here I would go back to work in L.A., but have protection with me until James's mission is complete." Was it her or had the world gone slanted?

"We need you in London."

"Why would we go to London?" James asked from behind.

"We need you to ascertain why Hadley went off grid."

"He hasn't told you?"

"He hasn't made it to any of our safe houses."

Quinn peeked over her shoulder. James wore a grim expression. It was obviously a bad thing that Ben wasn't in a safe house. Where would she be if not for the cabin in which she was securely tucked away?

"There's no good reason why he's not in a safe house, is there?" she asked James.

James shook his head. "No." After a pause, he said, "I still don't see what this has to do with Quinn going to London. She's not a trained operative."

"I want her to look around Ben's apartment to see if she notices anything that will tell us why he went off grid and where he was going."

"Haven't you already sent people to search his apartment?"

It was time for Quinn to speak up. "You think there might be bits of information or clues a librarian might see but others would pass over. Is that it, sir?"

"Yes, that's exactly it."

"That sounds like a long shot," James said.

"Not at all," Meyers said. "He's already sent you a message coded in such a way only another librarian would easily uncover its meaning."

"I understand why he did it that one time," James said. "But to assume he did other things like that is a huge leap."

"It is a huge leap," Meyers responded. Quinn watched the man's features grow stern. "We will be pursuing every avenue to ascertain why he went into hiding and where he might be. For this one, we need Ms. Ellington's expertise."

James wasn't backing down. "So send an agency librarian."

"Ms. Ellington is already up to speed with this op, she

has clearly demonstrated her ability to take care of herself in a scrape and"—his steely expression gave way when a smile twitched on his lips—"none of the librarians are willing to leave the library."

Quinn couldn't help but smile.

"But—" James tried again.

"This isn't your decision, Anderson," Meyers snapped. "It's Ms. Ellington's and hers alone." He folded his hands and leaned closer to the screen. To Quinn, he said, "I know this is a lot to process and you'll need some time to think it over. If you could get back to me by the end of today, I'd appreciate it. Weather data indicates the snow in your area will end soon. That means you should be clear to leave by tomorrow at the latest. If you choose to stay in L.A., protection must be in place for your arrival. If you choose to go to London with James, preparations for that need to be made as well."

"I don't need to think about it," she said without hesitation. "I'm ready to help James and your agency in any way I can."

Behind her, James groaned.

Quinn balled her fists and fought the anger flaming in her chest. Why was James being such a jerk about this?

"Very good, Ms. Ellington. Your country and the agency appreciate your assistance. I'm sure you comprehend you may be putting yourself in danger."

"Yes, sir. I do."

"And since you are a civilian, your taking part in an active operation puts us in a bit of a predicament when it comes to, ah, liability."

"I'll sign whatever forms you need me to."

"Excellent," he said. "We'll get those sent to you on James's tablet as soon as possible."

"I don't have a passport," Quinn said.

"Not an issue. We'll have one prepared for you."

While she and Meyers spoke, James paced behind her.

Meyers raised his voice to get James's attention. "Anderson."

James stopped and stood directly behind her again.

"It's clear you have some problems with Ms. Ellington continuing on this op with you. I don't know what they are, nor do I care." Meyers's nostrils flared. "Get them squared away. You two will be spending a lot of time in each other's company. Make it work." He gave James a long, pointed stare. "We'll speak again later today to discuss the specifics regarding your travel to London." With that, the video feed ended and Meyers disappeared from the screen.

The room fell silent.

Quinn leapt up and whirled on James. "What the hell was that all about?"

"I don't want you going to London," he stated flatly.

"Yeah, I got that. Loud and clear," she snapped. Her head throbbed. "What I want to know is why? I think I've been pretty cool dealing with the steady stream of crap you've flung my way. And now all of a sudden, when everything finally makes sense and I'm on board, you say no?"

He turned his head and stared out the window. The way the muscles in his jaw worked, Quinn could tell he was fighting some kind of internal battle. After a long pause, he said, "It's complicated."

She huffed a mirthless laugh and crossed her arms. "Try again." When he remained silent, she asked, "Is it because I'm not a spy? The agency obviously doesn't care. Neither should you."

"I'm the one who has to protect you."

"So I'm an albatross."

"You're not an albatross. If anything, you're a natural at all this. You're brilliant and perceptive and intuitive and frustratingly fearless."

She blew out a breath, not knowing what to make of that.

"So why do you want to leave me behind?" A rock lodged in the pit of her stomach. "You don't want to be around me that much."

His shoulders sagged. "It's the opposite. I do want to be around you. So much. That's the problem." He looked into her face. "The way I feel about you scares the hell out of me. If something happens to you . . . I can't go through it again."

"Go through what again?"

"I can't . . ." It felt like a dagger jammed through her heart when she saw the storm of agony raging in his eyes. "I can't," he said again. He walked to the door and stepped out into the swirling snow.

Chapter Fifteen

Quinn stood at the window and watched the falling flakes. She blew out a deep breath—fogging the glass—and tucked her hands between her arms and rib cage to keep them warm. And despite the cold penetrating the window, she remained rooted to the floor with her eyes pinned on James, or at least the back of him. When he'd first marched outside, he'd prowled back and forth in front of the cabin like an agitated panther. After a few minutes of tromping a path in the snow, he'd stopped and stood completely still facing the woods with his back to the cabin. And that's exactly how he remained, like a statue with his hands stuffed deep in his front pockets. Maybe he was actually frozen solid, she thought, noting how the snowflakes had accumulated into tiny piles on his shoulders and uncovered head.

How could he not be freezing? He was only wearing his black Ferrari hoodie, jeans, and street shoes. And yet he stood there, motionless, staring at the tall pines.

She wasn't sure what she should do. She wasn't his mother, wife, or girlfriend. She wasn't even sure she was his friend. Besides, he was a grown man, and a CIA officer. And she didn't need a degree in psychology to know he needed some time to clear his head and think through whatever was bugging him.

Still, it was obvious he was upset and not paying attention to the fact that if he didn't come inside soon, he was going to end up with hypothermia and lose a digit or four to frostbite. Quinn came to the conclusion that James's physical well-being was top priority. He'd just have to think or sulk or do whatever he was doing inside. She turned on her heel, hurried to the bedroom, and pulled on her boots.

Her head popped through the neck of her sweatshirt and she was in the process of shoving her arms through its sleeves when she heard the front door open and close. She ran her hands over her hair, resisting the urge to bolt down the hall. It was best to approach him slowly, so as not to spook him and send him scampering outside again.

That was the plan, anyway, until she got close enough to see him standing in front of the fire in the throes of a full body shiver. His shoes were soaked, snow clung to his jeans, and he had that I-can't-move-my-face rigidity to him. She grabbed his hand in both of hers and felt how stiff and cold it was. "Oh my God, James. You're a human Popsicle."

She dropped his hand, tugged down the zipper of his hoodie, and yanked it off. "I should have gone out sooner and dragged you back inside," she said under her breath. She ran her palms across his shoulders. The wetness had soaked through to his T-shirt. "Standing out in the snow. What are you, nuts?" She grabbed the hem of his shirt and barked, "Arms up."

He did as ordered and raised his arms over his head. Quinn peeled his shirt off and dropped it to the floor. When James lowered his arms again, she found herself staring directly at his broad, bare chest. His arms and shoulders were muscled and only a wide, fading scar on his left side marred his hard, flat abdomen. She gulped, which was only slightly less embarrassing than the alternative: drooling.

Her gaze landed on another scar, a three-inch long, thin red line that stretched across his right bicep. Without thinking, she reached out and delicately traced a fingertip along it. At the coolness of his skin, she jolted from her trance and jerked her hand away.

She stumbled back a half step and her awkwardness ratcheted up a notch when she said, "You need to get out of those wet jeans." She cleared her throat and peered into his face. "Do you, um, have another pair?" For the sake of her blood pressure, she really hoped he had another pair.

For the first time since coming inside, the glazed look in James's eyes disappeared and he focused on her. "In my bag."

She spun around and spied the bag on the floor near the couch. She knelt next to it, pulled out a pair of jeans, and tossed them over her shoulder. The only thing she saw for him to put on his upper body was the sweater he'd worn the night before. The black mascara splotch from when she'd used him like a Kleenex during her meltdown in her bedroom was still there. It might not be clean, but at least it was dry.

She heard the distinctive sound of ripping Velcro. She twisted around and saw James removing a pistol in a black ankle holster from his leg. He set it on the coffee table and repeated the process for the weapon strapped to his other ankle.

"One's got bullets and one's got darts?" she asked as she stood.

"Yeah." He set the second holster on the table, and took off his wet shoes. Standing close to the fire had done him good. The color was returning to his face and he'd stopped shivering.

She thrust the dry clothes against his chest. "Go put these on."

Her anxiety about his condition lifted when he gave her a teasing look and said in a husky voice, "I can't change here by the fire?"

"Sure you can, if you want," she said. "I've got five brothers."

"For both our sakes, I'll go change in the bathroom."

It was a good thing he didn't call her bluff.

"It's just as well," he called out as he walked down the hall. "Because you never know. I might be going commando."

James's wet T-shirt and hoodie hung off the backs of two dining room chairs Quinn had positioned close to the fire. His jeans were laid out flat on the brick hearth and bookended by his soaked shoes.

Quinn opened the fireplace screen and set another log on the fire. With an iron poker, she jabbed at the already-burning logs and stirred the glowing embers under the grate. She watched for a time, and once the newly introduced log began to snap and pop, she returned the poker to the stand and closed the screen.

She picked up her steaming mug of tea from the coffee table and curled up in the armchair. She sipped her tea and studied James over the rim of the mug. He sat hunkered on the floor in front of the hearth. A blanket was tucked tightly around his shoulders and he stared into the fire.

She lowered the mug and wrapped both hands around it to warm them. She breathed deeply, hoping to calm her emotions. He was grappling with something, and from what he'd said before he stalked outside, she had only the barest inkling of what it might be.

"Unless you were hoping to catch a glimpse of a real live

Frosty the Snoworc, I get the feeling there's another reason you stood outside in the snow until you almost froze."

He'd been gazing mutely at the flames for so long, it surprised her when he finally spoke. "I'm sorry I overreacted."

"Look," she said, "I know spies are supposed to be mysterious and brooding and stoic and all that kind of crap, but I've never gotten that constipated Jason Bourne vibe from you." She dipped her head to look at him. "Do you want to tell me about it?"

James's eyes squeezed shut and he took several deep and deliberate breaths through his nose. His entire body tensed and she thought he might bolt again. He didn't. Instead, his shoulders sagged further and he exhaled in surrender. When he opened his eyes and looked into hers, the profound sadness she saw there gutted her. "It was about a year and a half ago. We were on a mission in . . ." He stopped and blew a half laugh through his nose. "I can't tell you where."

"That's okay. Can you tell me who 'we' are or is that off-limits?"

"The 'we' was my partner. I can't tell you her name, so I'll call her Claire. We were undercover." He stared down at his hand and rubbed the thumb of one hand into the palm of the other. "We were, ah—" He stopped and carefully considered his words before beginning again. "We were betrayed by someone we were told we could trust. We both ended up getting shot. I survived. She didn't."

"I'm so sorry, James. That must have been devastating for you."

He nodded. "We'd spent so much time together. We went through training together at the Farm and once we finished, they paired us up. We were a good team. We had a couple of successful ops together before . . ."

Silence hung between them, only interrupted by the

staccato pops of the fire. "Were you two, um . . ." Quinn worked her tongue in an attempt to get some saliva going. "Involved?"

His head lowered and he shook it. "She had a serious boyfriend."

Ah. "Did she know how you felt about her?"

His head jerked up and he stared at her. His surprise morphed into a knowing, fleeting smile. "Of course you'd figure it out." He sighed and his smile faded. "No. She never did. No one did. We were professional partners only."

James had wanted more with Claire. Now Quinn wondered if he wanted more with her in the same way. If their date was any indication, she would have to say yes, he did. It was all beginning to make a lot more sense.

"You're afraid if I go on this op with you, the same thing might happen to me that happened to Claire?" No wonder he looked like he was going to throw up when he asked her to dinner. He was scared of letting himself get close to her, to anyone. And now he was facing the very thing that petrified him the most, going on an op with a partner he cared about in more than a professional way.

"Yeah." He dragged a hand over his face.

"I get it," she said with a gentle smile. "But just because something terrible happened to Claire doesn't mean it will happen to me, too."

James shook his head. "You're not even a trained operative. If this thing goes sideways at some point, I can't promise I'll be able to keep you safe. I can't do that to myself again."

"I don't need you to protect me."

"Really."

Without a word, she set her mug down, slid out of the chair, and knelt by the coffee table. She picked up one of James's firearms and slipped it from the holster. When he tried to protest, a dangerously arched eyebrow shut him down.

"Nice," she said. She studied the weapon, being sure to

keep her right index finger away from the trigger by resting it on the slide. "The Glock 33's a cute little pistol." With her thumb, she pressed the magazine catch, slid it from the grip, and set it off to the side. "Three-fifty-seven SIG cartridges pack a pretty good wallop. No wonder they call it the Pocket Rocket." Next, she pulled the slide back and locked it open. After visually checking to ensure the chamber was empty, she stuck her pinky into it. "You can never be too careful," she said, winking at James who stared at her slack-jawed.

"Gaston Glock is Austrian, you know," she said in a light tone. "His first pistol, the Glock 17, was called that since it was the seventeenth set of technical drawings for the company."

She somehow managed to suppress a smile at how utterly and completely confounded he looked. Assured the gun wasn't loaded, she released the slide. It popped forward with a click. She made sure to point the barrel in a safe direction and pulled the trigger. The resulting click was innocuous and uneventful.

"I know some people don't like to dry-fire their weapon since it can damage the firing pin, but since the Glock has a safe action trigger, it has to be done to field strip it." As she spoke, she gripped the top of the slide with the fingers of her right hand and moved it back a little. "Once in a while doesn't hurt it, right?" With her left thumb and forefinger, she pressed down on the lock and let go of the slide with her right. There was another harmless click, after which she removed the entire slide from the frame. She set the lower part of the gun down, flipped the slide over, deftly removed the recoil spring assembly, and popped out the barrel.

Quinn squinted, checked out the barrel, and made a clucking noise with her tongue. "The feed ramp's got some schmutz on it," she said and scratched at the buildup with her fingernail. "You might want to clean that."

James looked as if his cranium had just been smacked with a two-by-four.

She'd made her point. She replaced the barrel and recoil spring assembly, guided the slide back onto the frame, and ratcheted back on it a couple of times to make sure it was working properly. Finally, she slapped the magazine into the grip. Once the pistol was back in its holster, she carefully set it down on the table where she'd found it. She folded back up in her chair and gave James an innocent smile.

"How do you—? I don't understand how—" His stammering was adorable. "God, you're hot," he breathed. The second the words slipped through his lips, he blushed. "Sorry."

The heat crawling up her neck told her she was probably as red-faced as he. Not knowing how to appropriately respond to his slip, she ignored it and said, "My dad's a Marine. I've been around guns my entire life. As soon as I was old enough, he started teaching me gun safety and then how to shoot, first with a BB rifle and then a .22. By the time I was in high school, I was shooting pistols and revolvers with him at the firing range. And I know it's not exactly combat, but on most family occasions, my brothers and I engage in some pretty epic paintball battles."

"Is there anything you can't do?"

"I hate shopping for clothes, I'm terrible at applying makeup, and my cooking skills would be classified as 'good-enough-to-make-it-edible-so-you-won't-starve-to-death.'" She shook her head slowly when she intoned, "And you do *not* want to hear me sing."

"There goes going undercover as the lead in a West End musical."

"Am I to take from that comment you've finally accepted the fact I'm going to London with you?"

"You've shot down, no pun intended, most of my concerns."

With a mock sigh of defeat, he said, "Yes, we're going to London."

She grinned as a surge of excitement sent a raft of chills through her.

"I'm still going to do everything I can to protect you and keep you safe." One corner of his mouth lifted when he said, "Think of the avalanche of paperwork I'd have to deal with if something happened to you."

She hurled the pillow at his head.

He snatched it easily from the air before it could hit him in the face. "Seriously, though," he said, dropping the pillow to his lap. "You might be handy with a pistol, but you're still not a trained operative. You have to follow my orders."

"Yes, sir," she replied crisply and she threw him a smart salute.

"I know you're kidding around, Quinn, but this isn't like the spy novel you're reading. This is real life with real bad guys who can hurt you. You have to do what I say. I can't let anything happen to you."

Her frivolity dropped away at the gravity in his voice. She nervously rubbed one thumb with the other.

"What's the matter?" James asked.

"Well, the good news is we worked out our problems like Meyers wanted us to."

"I guess the bad news is now that we've, ah, cleared the air between us, things have gotten a bit more"—he paused and gave her a significant look—"complicated."

"Yeah."

"Let's look at it this way. This isn't a vacation. It's a CIA op. We're going to London to figure out what's going on with Ben." The seriousness in his tone told her CIA operative Anderson was speaking. "We need to stay focused on that. Any distractions, personal or otherwise, can't be a part of this."

That was exactly the reset she needed. "I agree. From here on out, it's all about the mission. You and I will be nothing more to each other than professional partners, right?"

"Right."

"Like the way you and Ben are partners."

"Exactly. Although Ben and I've never made pancakes together."

"We'll have to make pancakes with Ben after we track him down so he won't feel left out."

For the first time since he sat down in front of the fire, his smile reached his eyes. "Now that's a plan." His phone rang and he answered it with a curt "Anderson."

Quinn watched James's gaze roam the room as he listened. "Depending on the snow, it would be about"—he drew out the last word as he glanced down at his watch—"two and a half hours or so at the most. Traffic shouldn't be an issue since it's Sunday."

When his eyes settled on her, she mouthed, "Where?"

"Airport," he replied silently. "It'll be cutting it close, but we'll be there," he said into his phone. After another moment, he said, "I understand," and then ended the call. He tossed the pillow onto the couch, shrugged the blanket off his shoulders, and stood. "Grab your stuff. Our flight to Heathrow leaves in five hours."

Chapter Sixteen

The first few miles of their trip to the airport had Quinn white-knuckling it as James navigated the snow-covered twists and turns of the road. He, on the other hand, seemed completely unfazed and drove as though they were cruising through the mountains to take in the scenery on a lazy Sunday afternoon. He reminded her he'd received extensive training at the Farm for driving in all sorts of conditions and circumstances, including snow and ice. Still, she didn't lessen her death grip on the door handle until the road was completely devoid of frozen precipitation.

Once they descended the mountains and returned to civilization, they both admitted they were starving. A few crackers and some pancakes were all they'd eaten since dinner in Santa Monica the night before. It was a cause for celebration when Quinn located the nearest In-N-Out on her phone and directed James to it. They stopped only long enough to get their food and for him to wolf his Double-Double down in two minutes flat.

Soon, they were rocketing west on the freeway again. Quinn washed down the last bite of her Double-Double with a sip of root beer and tossed the wadded-up wrapper in the bag at her feet. "Are you sure we can't stop by my apartment so I can pick up some clothes and check on Rasputin?"

"I'm sorry, but we can't. Rick thinks we're already gone and if he sees you, it blows up our time line for last night." James snagged a couple of fries and popped them in his mouth. "Trust me. The agency will make sure you have everything you need."

"That's what I'm worried about. Some wonk gets the order to 'go buy a librarian some clothes for London' and I end up with a suitcase full of wool skirts, tweed jackets, and cardigan sweaters." Just the thought of it made her shudder. "Although on the plus side, if the queen calls, I'll be all set to go up to Sandringham Castle for Christmas."

"That's the spirit." He shot her a quick glance. "And give those wonks a chance. They might surprise you."

"Now I'm really worried." She decided if the clothes were completely intolerable, she could pick up a few things in London.

"Speaking of librarians, we need to let Virginia know you won't be in the library at all this week."

Quinn expelled a loud groan and dropped her head back against the seat's headrest. "She's gonna flip."

"Do you want to call her or should I?"

"She'll take it better if it comes from you." She peered at him side-eyed and added in a husky tone, "She's putty in your hands, you know."

Quinn laughed when his face twisted like he'd just licked the inside of a Dumpster. "I just threw up in my mouth a little."

This, of course, only made her laugh harder. When she got herself under control, she asked, "Is there a chance you can pony up another donation for the Friends of the Library? Money seems to soothe her savage breast."

"Already on it."

"Then I guess I should make that call." She dusted the salt

from her fingers, took out her phone, and called Virginia's direct work line. Once her boss's outgoing message was playing, she put her phone on speaker.

After the beep James said, "Good Sunday afternoon, Virginia. James Lockwood here." It was a little jarring to hear him switch back to his British accent, though it never ceased to charm the socks off her. "I wanted to inform you that Ms. Ellington and I will not be in the library at all this week. Some information regarding one of the items we're researching requires us to travel out of town. I understand this is a huge inconvenience for you since Quinn is such an integral part of your team." He winked at her, eliciting a monster eye roll. "To compensate you for her time away, I've arranged for five thousand dollars to be delivered to you tomorrow as a donation to the Friends of the Library fund."

Quinn's entire body jerked and she stared at him in complete shock. "Five thousand dollars?" she mouthed.

James nodded and made a face that conveyed, "Totally worth it."

Her face in reply said, "You're crazy."

It was obvious he disagreed with her, given the way he frowned and shook his head. "Thank you, Virginia, for being so willing to allow Ms. Ellington to assist me. You are a credit to your profession." At that, Quinn pretended to stick her finger down her throat. He finished with a jovial "Cheerio."

She touched the screen and ended the call. "There's a part of me that wishes I could be there when she listens to that message. My guess is steam will come out of her ears when you say I won't be in, and then she'll fall out of her chair when she hears about the five grand."

"Do you think she'll believe we're working or will she think I'm paying her off so I can sweep you off to some exotic locale."

"As long as the money keeps rolling in, she wouldn't care if I never came back."

"I doubt that." A cheeky smile pulled at the corner of his mouth. "Although now that I think about it, I might have to find someone cheaper to work with. You're getting pretty expensive to keep around. Ow!" he yelped when she playfully slugged him on the arm.

"Stop making me sound like I'm some kind of kept woman."

He rubbed the spot where she'd punched him and huffed a wry laugh. "Believe me. There's not a man on this planet who can keep you."

"Good," she said, mollified. She tossed a couple of fries in her mouth, trying to finish off the rest before they went completely cold. "Is it okay if I call Nicole and tell her I'll be gone?" she asked. "I promised I'd call her today and I definitely don't want her hearing about our impromptu trip from Virginia tomorrow. I'm pretty sure she'd hunt me down, hurl Korean curse words, and then pummel me."

"If I hadn't met her myself, I'd say you were being a little overdramatic. You need to call her, but just keep the party line about why we'll be gone."

"Got it." Not wanting James to overhear whatever inappropriate comments Nicole was sure to make, Quinn plugged her earbuds into her phone and stuck them in her ears. Then she slipped off her boots and got comfortable in her seat. She breathed deeply to mentally prepare herself and placed the call.

The phone had barely connected the call when Nicole shouted, "Do you know what time it is? I've been waiting for you to call me all day, Quinn. All day!"

"I know. I'm sorry. I called as soon as I could."

"As soon as you could? What the heck do you mean by that?" Nicole was certainly worked up and Quinn expected the swearing to start any second. "Wait, were you out with James all night or something?"

"Actually, I kind of was."

Quinn winced when Nicole cut loose with a thundering, "You were out with James all night? Oh my gosh. Did you sleep with him?"

"What? No!" she replied, matching Nicole's volume level.

"Well, what am I supposed to think? I've never known you to be out all night with a guy before." At least Nicole's reply was at a volume that no longer threatened to rupture Quinn's eardrums. "So what *did* you do all night?"

Quinn warned her off with a drawn-out "Nic."

"Okay, okay. Backing off. How was dinner?"

"It was really nice. After dinner we walked down to the little park at Ocean and Santa Monica and sat on one of the benches for a while."

"Oooo, romantic. Did he kiss you?"

Had that question come from anyone else, Quinn would have informed that person in no uncertain terms it was none of their business. However, having gone through Nicole's postdate interrogations a couple of times before, she indulged her. "No."

She harrumphed. "Did he at least hold your hand?"

"Yes."

"He did? Was it like when you're holding a little kid's hand when you cross the street or were your fingers laced together?"

The memory of it made Quinn's pulse race. "The second."

She grimaced again when Nicole screeched like a pterodactyl. Even with the earbuds, James's chuckle told her he'd heard Nicole's enthusiastic response. At the mildly smug look on his face, she gave him a light shove on the shoulder.

"You two are so cute," Nicole gushed. After a brief pause, she said, "Wait a second. Your answers are even shorter than usual. Why are you being so—" It was like a destructive pressure wave after a bomb detonation when she yelled, "You're still with him now, aren't you? Is he right there?"

"Yes." Quinn giggled and pictured the flailing that surely accompanied the unintelligible gurgling coming from her friend. She waited patiently until they subsided and said, "Maybe I should finish my story."

"Yes, please."

Quinn imagined her friend literally bouncing in her seat.

"After the park, James drove me home and on the way he got a call about one of the items we've been researching."

"Late on a Saturday night? That's weird."

Quinn scrunched her nose. It was kind of weird. Thinking fast, she said, "Apparently, this person is even worse than me when it comes to not stopping until he finds the answer to something. He probably didn't realize what time it was when he called." She pulled a face and held her breath as she waited for Nicole's response.

"Yeah, that does sound worse than you. You're a close second, though."

Quinn silently released her breath and forged ahead. "Anyway, it's really important we track this lead down as soon as possible. Since we need to do it in person, we stopped off at my apartment, picked up some clothes, dropped Rasputin off with Rick, and hit the road. I called not only to check in with you, but to tell you I won't be at work at all this week."

"The entire week? Does Virginia know?"

"Yeah. James called and left her a voice mail."

"Tomorrow should be fun at work," Nicole said. "Where are you going, by the way?"

"I can't say. Client confidentiality and all that."

Quinn knew it was a lot for Nicole to process. Even so, the silence that followed was unnerving. When it dragged on, Quinn ventured with a tentative, "Nic? You still there?"

"Quincy Ellington, I can't believe you'd lie to me."

Her stomach clenched. Nicole couldn't possibly know the truth. "Wha—Um, what do you mean?"

"You two are obviously road-tripping to Vegas to get married."

At the droll tone she heard in Nicole's voice, she let out a hearty, relieved laugh. "Yeah, you're on to us. We're totally eloping." James jerked and Quinn had to brace herself against the seat when the car swerved. "Easy there, big fella." She chuckled and patted his arm.

He shot her a wounded albeit amused look. In his James Lockwood voice, he said loudly, "That's not funny, Nicole."

Nicole laughed and shouted back, "It is, too." After Quinn passed along to him her friend's retort, Nicole's voice turned serious. "Look, Q, I have every reason to believe you're on your way to track down information on some dusty old artifact. But even if you're not and it's just some lame-ass excuse you told Virginia so the two of you can run off and spend the week together doing God knows what, your secret's safe with me. I've seen the way you two are together and I gotta say, kiddo, it's magical. And you're happy. I can tell."

"I am," Quinn answered quietly, her voice raspy from the sudden swell of emotion.

"Good. You deserve it. Have fun this week and give me a call when you get home."

"I will. Thanks, Nic," she said and smiled. "You're the best."

Turning sassy, Nicole said, "You two can thank me by naming your firstborn daughter after me."

Quinn snorted and said, "We'll take it under advisement. Bye, Nic."

"Bye." She touched the screen and tugged out her earbuds.

"We'll take what under advisement?" James asked.

She laughed and shook her head. "You *really* don't want to know."

He alternated between studying her and keeping his eyes on the freeway. When she judiciously kept her gaze forward and stared out the windshield, he nodded and said, "Okay. I don't want to know." After a short pause, he asked, "Anyone else you need to talk to?"

"My parents."

"Go for it. You did a great job with Nicole, you'll do fine with them, too."

"I don't like keeping the truth from anyone, especially my parents."

"From what you've told me about them, I'm sure they would understand, especially if they knew why."

She nodded, stuffed the earphones in her ears, and placed the call. Quinn only spoke with her mom who explained her dad had unexpectedly been called to the base for a meeting. This was followed by a news report about the latest sick relative and how things were going with her work, helping spouses and families learn to cope when their loved ones were deployed. When her mom asked how she was, Quinn started at the beginning and spent the next five minutes telling her what she'd been up to with James the past week. Even when Quinn told her she'd be traveling with him, there was no commentary from her mother other than "Well, that sounds really interesting, honey." After a few more minutes of chatting, the call ended and she removed her earbuds.

"That's it?" James asked. "No third degree? Nicole grilled you more than your mom did."

"My parents are always there for me, but they don't inject themselves into my life. My dad always says, 'You're an adult. Falling on your keister once in a while is a good way to learn about life.'"

"Spoken like a true Marine." He glanced at her and asked, "Are you concerned your decision to go on this mission will be a 'fall on your keister' kind of thing?"

"No," she answered without hesitation. "This isn't about me paying too much for car insurance or getting blowback for something stupid I did or said at work. This is probably the most important thing I'll ever do. I know I made the right decision. And if something does go sideways, I'll learn from it and move on."

"That's a good attitude to have, because missions like these never go the way you think they will. Take a look at last night."

"Yeah. Last night I learned never to turn my back on my date. Especially when he's a handsome spy wielding a tranquilizer gun."

"I'm still really sorry about that," James said ruefully. "Speaking of the op, since we have some time, I'd like you to examine the letter we found in the clock more closely. It's in my briefcase in the backseat. Can you reach around and grab it?"

She twisted around and maneuvered the briefcase onto her lap. She found the envelope and from the weight of it, knew the ring was in it, too. "Handling this letter with fingers that have been eating French fries inside a moving car is probably not the greatest idea in the world," she said as she returned the case to the backseat. She rubbed her fingers on her thighs hoping to remove any residual salt and oil.

"We don't have much choice. I'm handing it off before we get on the plane. The agency needs to analyze it. This is our only chance to take another look at it."

"Ooo, like a secret handoff where you bump into someone and you pass it to them without anyone noticing?"

"Something like that."

"Cool." She carefully slid the note from the envelope and unfolded it, doing her best to only grip the outside edges with her fingertips. She read the contents of the letter out loud again and when she finished, added, "The guy was such a slimeball." When James looked at her side-eyed and conspicuously cleared his throat, she sighed, "And so was she."

"Thank you," he said and dipped his head with faux magnanimity. "What we need to do now is look at it not as a love letter, but as a coded message."

"Like skipping words or reading every other line?"

"Mmm-hmm. If it's a more complex code—if there's one at all—agency cryptologists will work it out. I know it's a long shot, but it's worth a try."

"Agreed." Over the course of the next fifteen minutes, she read the letter out loud over and over again. She skipped every other word, then every second word, every other line and different combinations of skipping lines and words. Nothing made sense. Quinn blew out a frustrated breath. "The only locations mentioned are London, which doesn't narrow it down at all if we're looking for a suitcase nuke or something like that, and this Summerfield place." She searched Summerfield on her phone, which turned up nothing helpful.

"Summerfield might be a house name. Unless it's a fairly large estate, it probably won't show up on any searches. And trying to track it down without access to property records at the county level would be almost impossible."

"That sounds like something the analysts at the agency could do," she said.

"Or librarians with the right kind of access."

Being an agency librarian was rapidly becoming her new dream job. She absently stared out her window and watched the scrub brush and the billboards pass by as she mulled over the letter. After a couple of minutes, she looked at James and said, "Dobrynin was Russian. What if Summerfield is a town in Russia, or maybe one of the former Soviet republics? Since you were in Moscow, I assume you speak Russian."

"*Da.*"

Her insides bounced. Now she knew how he'd felt when he watched her field strip his Glock. Based on her reaction to him uttering a single Russian word, she was going to have to turn her brain-to-mouth filter up to eleven for the next few minutes. Who was she kidding? she thought with an internal eye roll. Their decision to keep their relationship purely professional over the course of the op meant her filter would have to be set to eleven for the foreseeable future.

She sipped her root beer and dragged her brain back to the problem at hand. "What's Summerfield in Russian? Maybe that's what we should be searching for."

He was quiet for a moment. "I don't think there's an exact word for 'Summerfield'. But if you break the two words apart, 'summer' is '*lyeh-tah*' and 'field' is '*po-leh.*'"

"That's how they're pronounced. I might need to search them in Cyrillic." She scowled at her phone perched on her thigh. Doing the kind of research she needed to do was going to be laborious on such a limited device. And it would take hours. Still, there had to be a way.

"I know what that librarian brain of yours is thinking, Quinn. Don't even try."

"But—"

He held up a hand. "It's a brilliant idea and I know you want to keep going with it, but there's no way we'll get to the bottom of it in the next thirty minutes. Why don't you write down your idea on a piece of paper and put it in the envelope with the note? Let the agency analysts do the heavy lifting."

Humming her reluctant agreement, she found a pen and a scrap of paper and scribbled out a note. She held the love letter up to the light coming through the window and scrutinized the paper. "I'm sure you considered invisible ink might have been used."

"Yeah. That's the main reason I snagged it instead of just taking a picture of it and leaving it at Fitzhugh's house. It was really the first thing we found that fit what we were looking for. But it was a gamble that apparently blew up in my face."

"Don't say that because we don't know what happened." She lowered the letter and returned it and her note to the analysts to the envelope. "My guess is the gamble was worth it and this is an important clue."

"I hope so."

"Wait, did you say thirty minutes?" She'd been so engrossed in the note she hadn't been paying attention to where they were. "We'll be at the airport in thirty minutes?"

"A little less now, but yeah."

Going to London on a CIA mission hadn't sounded that crazy to her a few hours ago. But now, as they neared the airport, the reality of it all dropped on her like a pile of bricks. Anxiety crept up on her and the blood drained from her face. "This is all a weird dream, right? Or, some kind of elaborate practical joke and I'm gonna end up on one of those prank shows that make unsuspecting people look like idiots so other people can laugh at them. Right? That's gotta be it. Come on. Tell me the truth." When she heard the way her voice was rising in pitch and the panic edging into it, she grew even more agitated. "This can't be real."

James slowed the car a little and looked at her, his face filled with worry. "Quinn, it is very real, but it's gonna be okay." He reached over, dropped his hand over hers, and gave it a reassuring squeeze. His touch was comforting and pulled her back from the brink. "You don't have to do this, you know. You say the word and I'll hand you off to our officers at the airport. They'll keep you safe here in L.A. until it's all over."

In a flash, his words made her realize how much she loathed the notion of staying behind. "No." With gritted teeth, her resolve returned. "I can do this. I *want* to do this."

"Are you sure? I completely understand if you change your mind. I'm sure Meyers would, too." He gripped her hand tighter. "You know how happy I'd be if you stayed here."

"Yeah, I know." She blew out a slow, cleansing breath. "I'll be okay. I *am* okay." With a wry smile, she said, "A little temporary insanity keeps you sane, right?"

"Right," he said, sounding less than convinced. He lessened the grip on her hand, but didn't remove it from where it rested atop hers. "If it makes you feel any better, from here on out, I won't let you out of my sight."

"I'm not sure how that will go over with the women in the ladies' rooms I'll visit, but it does help."

"To be honest, you continue to amaze me." He glanced at her with admiration in his eyes. "That little blip of nerves just now is nothing compared to how jumpy I was before my first op. I swear it was like I'd downed a six-pack of Red Bull. And I'd been trained and prepped up the wazoo for it."

She missed his hand on hers when he returned it to the steering wheel. "I'll have to tell you all about it, or at least the parts I *can* tell you about later though, because it's almost go time."

Her trepidation was replaced by excitement. She slipped her boots on, sucked down the last few swallows of her root beer, and shoved the detritus from lunch into the paper bag.

"I need to put a couple of things in my clothes bag. Can you haul it up here?"

As she had done with the briefcase, she did as asked.

James reached down with a free hand and removed the pistol and holster from his ankle. He handed it to her and said,

"Clear it and stow everything in the bag." She removed the magazine, checked the chamber, and placed the weapon on top of his still slightly damp clothes.

"You're not bringing your weapons, even in your checked bag?"

"No. There are rules and permits needed and I don't want to call attention to us. I'll be rearmed soon after we land." Next, he handed her the tranquilizer pistol.

She secured it as she'd done with the Glock. "What'll you do with this bag?"

"It'll get passed off before we go through security. I need you to put the letter and ring in there, too."

She made a face at the thought of putting such a fragile and important piece of paper unprotected in a bag full of damp, dirty clothes and a couple of guns. She glanced around the interior of the car, looking for something she could use to protect the letter. Not finding anything, she checked the glove box. It was painfully devoid of anything useful. In a last-ditch effort, she rooted through her purse and chirped a quiet, "Yay!" when she found a thin plastic bag from the grocery store stuffed in a pocket.

"Why do you have a vegetable bag in your purse?"

"To make a toy for Rasputin. I tie knots in it until it's kind of like a ball. It's just the right size for him to carry around in his mouth and the soft plastic has some give on his teeth. Sometimes I tie a string to one and jerk it around so he can pounce on it." She snapped the bag to unfurl it and slipped the envelope inside. "He shreds them up pretty fast, so I'm always having to make new ones."

"Hours of fun, huh?"

"Yup, although not quite as fun as catnip." Her voice turned conspiratorial. "We don't talk about that. Almost had to put him in rehab. It was awful." She put the now protected letter in James's bag and zipped it closed.

James snickered, looked over his shoulder, and changed

lanes. "You need to put your wallet and anything with your name on it in your bag that'll get passed off, too. Can't take the chance of going through airport security and having them find you with two sets of IDs."

This wasn't a surprise since he had previously informed her that for her own safety the agency would give her an alias. "You don't know what my cover will be?" she asked as she traded his bag for hers.

"Not exactly. They're working all of that out while we're in transit. I'm sure they won't do anything that will be too drastic of a change from who you already are. Most likely just a slightly different name. You're new to all this. Making too many changes just increases the chances of slipping up."

It seemed like overkill and completely unnecessary, but since the agency was in charge of making up all of her travel documents, she had no say in the matter. Reluctantly, she stuffed her wallet and checkbook in her bag. "If I get a charge on my credit card for one of those late-night infomercial juicers, I'm coming after you."

"Nah, not a juicer. My money's on a giant chocolate fondue fountain. Just in time for the agency holiday party."

She smiled and shook her head.

His rascally smile disappeared. "You have to put your phone in there, too. You can't have any Quinn Ellington personal contacts and photos."

She growled at him.

"You'll get a new one in London and the agency will forward any calls and texts to it so your friends and family won't worry."

She shut off her phone and stowed it in her bag. "They won't notice any difference at their end?" She unceremoniously tossed the bag over her shoulder and onto the backseat.

"No. Everything will be relayed through the agency." He glanced at her and then back at the road. "Why? Are you worried you might miss a call from the guy you met at Red's the other night?"

She flinched. *Oh no.* "What?"

"You know, the bar you followed me to when I met with Shawna. You saw her text asking to meet me," he stated.

There was no use pretending. "Yeah." Humiliated and unable to look into his face, she stared at the dashboard. "I thought you might have lied to me when you said you weren't married or didn't have a girlfriend, so I followed you."

"Ah."

"You're not mad?"

"Nah. I would have done the same thing."

"Fair enough." Cocking her head, she said, "Okay. I spilled my guts. Your turn. Who's Shawna?"

His head wobbled from side to side, deciding what to say. "I know her through the agency," he said without elaboration. "We went out to dinner once while I was at Langley planning this op. It was no big deal. Right after, I came here. You know when I disappeared for a week after I came into the library the first time? I got called back to Langley for some meetings. While I was there, Shawna was after me to go out again. I told her I wasn't interested." He snuck a peek at Quinn. "There was a librarian I'd just met who I wanted to spend more time with."

She smiled. "Ed, right?"

"Yeah, Ed," he said with a laugh. Eyes on the road again, he continued. "Anyway, she went kinda stalkery and flew out here to see me." He scowled and his voice was snapped with pique. "She texted my cover phone. With the crap she was pulling, she could have blown the whole op."

"That's why you were so angry with her."

"Yeah. She was way out of line. I knew she wouldn't back off until I met with her. When I did, I told her to get the hell away. I was undercover, for God's sake, and she put everything at risk the minute she contacted me. I informed Meyers before I even met with her. I think he's more furious with her than I am. She'll be disciplined for breaking protocol."

"What about me? You gotta admit, I went a little stalk-ery, too."

"Not really. You only followed me when you were faced with conflicting information about my cover."

More or less, she thought. "And for the record, I don't have any interest in getting a phone call from the guy from Red's."

"Good to know."

The conversation lulled while his full attention was given over to navigating through traffic as they neared the airport. At the same time, Quinn tried to keep the knot of nerves and excitement from completely overwhelming her.

James drove to the appropriate rental car return area and stopped behind a row of cars waiting to be processed. After shutting off the engine, he took her hand and shifted to face her. "You're gonna be great," he said. "You remember what we talked about, right? You're clear on what's gonna happen as soon as we get out of the car?"

"I am," she answered with a surprising amount of confidence. "I stick right next to you and follow your lead."

He grinned and squeezed her hand once more. "Here we go."

Ten minutes later, they stood waiting to board the shuttle bus that would transport them to the terminal. In front of them, the father of a set of twin toddler boys—both adorable and sporting mops of hay-colored hair—worked feverishly to load the family's luggage and kid paraphernalia onto the vehicle. One boy straddled his mother's hip while she held the hand of the other in a tight grip.

James dropped his bag on the ground next to Quinn's feet and handed his briefcase to her. "Here, let me help," he said to the dad and sprang into action. He picked up a car seat in each hand and stepped around the dad and into the shuttle. After stowing them on the luggage rack, he helped the driver stash the bags before making one more trip to the curb. He snagged the double stroller, leapt into the bus, and set it on top of the car seats.

"Your boyfriend is very sweet to help us," the woman said. Before Quinn could correct her, the other woman lowered her voice and said, "We just finished the first half of our grand Christmas tour at his parents' and now we're off to mine." With a weary laugh, she asked, "Is it January yet?"

Quinn gave her a sympathetic look. "Sorry. Only about halfway through December." She reached out and gently bopped the nose of the little one on the woman's hip with the tip of her finger. He giggled, turned bashful, and buried his face in his mother's shoulder. "I'm sure your parents love seeing them. Mine appreciate it when my brothers and their families visit, especially knowing how much work it is. Entire countries have been invaded by armies with less stuff than what they bring along."

"It's nice to know we're not the only ones," the woman replied.

"You're not. Not by a long shot," Quinn said as James stepped down from the shuttle and rejoined her. Both parents thanked him and stepped up into the bus. From over his mother's shoulder, Quinn received a shy wave from her new little friend. She smiled and waved back.

"Charming the entire male population again?" James asked as he took his briefcase from her and picked up his bag.

She watched a businessman in front of them lift the first of his two suitcases through the shuttle door. "Hardly, although I will cop to being quite the rock star with the three-and-under crowd."

"And those of us who are a little older," he said. He swung his briefcase toward the shuttle, indicating she should board before him now that the man's second bag was loaded and out of the way. As soon as they boarded, the doors closed behind them. There were no empty seats, so they stood as the bus roared off toward the terminals.

Travelers unloaded at each stop—the family with the twins offloaded at Terminal One—until they reached the Tom Bradley International Terminal. It was there that Quinn and James, the businessman with the two suitcases, and a retired couple disembarked. Working together, the shuttle driver handed the bags to James who set them on the sidewalk. Once everyone was sure all of their bags were present and accounted for, the shuttle zoomed off. The retired couple found their suitcases, thanked James for his help, and hurried through the sliding doors into the building.

It surprised Quinn when James left his bag untouched on the sidewalk and instead pulled up the handle on one of the businessman's rolling suitcases. Then he went to the other suitcase, a black one, extended the handle, and tipped it onto its wheels. His eyes darted to the first suitcase, a red one, and then fell on Quinn. "Shall we?" He still made no move to pick up his duffel bag, so Quinn left hers on the sidewalk next to his.

"Mmm-hmm." Her concern over leaving her bag with her wallet, checkbook, and phone in the wide-open evaporated when the businessman picked up their bags and strode off down the sidewalk. A few seconds later a black SUV pulled up alongside him. The vehicle's door swung open and he disappeared into the front passenger seat. The door closed and the SUV sped off.

Quinn wanted to make a quip about how very superspy it all was, but instinctively knew to remain silent. Instead, she took the handle of what was now her suitcase and looked at James expectantly.

They entered the building and were immediately confronted by travelers standing in long queues at airline ticketing counters. She followed James to an open area off to the left. Without a word, he unzipped a side pocket of his suitcase and removed a navy blue passport with the United States seal stamped in gold on the front. He flipped it open, glanced at it, and then shoved it in his back pocket.

Quinn followed his lead and unzipped the same pocket of her suitcase. There, she found a passport. Anticipation shot through her like a kid right before tearing into a Christmas present. She opened it and the first thing she noticed was her photo. It wasn't her driver's license picture as she'd expected. In fact, she didn't know when or where that photo had been taken.

Next, she glanced at her name. She was now Quinn Riordan of Santa Monica. Like James, she slid the passport into her back pocket.

Then she removed a tan leather wallet from the suitcase pocket and opened it. In it, she found a driver's license, a couple of credit cards, and a half-dozen business cards with Quinn Riordan's name on them. They informed her she was a UCLA reference librarian. She approved immensely. Finally, she checked the money slot and pulled out a wad of cash that included both dollar bills and pound notes. She thumbed through them and counted two hundred dollars in twenty-dollar bills and five hundred pounds in twenty- and fifty-pound notes. There'd never been so much money in a wallet of hers in her life. Too bad it wasn't actually hers.

She replaced the cash and when she did so, her finger touched a stiff piece of paper. She slid it out and gaped at a photo of her and James, arms around each other and blissfully grinning at the camera.

"Quinn," James said just loud enough to catch her attention. Still stunned by the picture gripped between her fingers, she looked up at him and immediately followed his gaze to the glinting gold on his open palm. Unblinking, she stared at three rings and instantly knew what they were: a diamond engagement ring, a thin gold wedding band, and a larger, wider one.

She looked into his face again and whispered, "James Riordan?"

His eyes widened a fraction and the nod was nearly imperceptible. As easy as it would have been to stand there utterly dazed and unmoving, her brain shouted at her that James holding her wedding rings in the middle of the airport was an oddity. The notion compelled her to close her wallet and shove it in her purse. She swallowed hard, took the smaller two rings, and slipped them onto the third finger of her left hand. James did the same with the larger gold band. Only two words came to mind as she stared at the rings flashing on her finger: *holy crap*.

Chapter Seventeen

It seemed like forever since Quinn had taken a shower. She knew she'd done so at the Lake Arrowhead safe house, but the actual number of hours that had passed since then completely eluded her. Despite the fact that she was in London—a city she'd wanted to visit for as long as she could remember—getting clean was the first thing she wanted to do now that she and James were settled in their hotel room in the well-heeled district of South Kensington. She'd marinated in the grime of two airports, the nasty, recycled air of a crowded airplane, and the oppressive humanity of the Underground long enough.

"There's a part of me that wants to take a flamethrower to the clothes I'm wearing," Quinn said as she lifted her suitcase and plunked it on the bed. "But I'm afraid I might need them since this is probably full of librarian clothes." It was with no small amount of trepidation she unzipped the bag.

"Could be worse," James said as he punched a series of numbers into the keypad of the hotel room's safe. "You could be going undercover as a nun."

"I would rock a habit and you know it." She decided not to prolong the agony and flipped open the suitcase. "Um, wow," she said softly when she saw that there was no wool tweed to be found. Instead, the suitcase was neatly packed with several pairs of jeans and slacks, some fun, colorful knit sweaters perfect for the cold English December weather, a number of other tops, and a blazer. Everything appeared to be exactly the right size and in fact, nicer and better quality than her own clothes.

"I'm impressed. Whoever pulled all of this together not only did it fast, but has better taste than I do, which, you know, isn't saying a whole lot."

James swung the safe door open, reached in and removed a Sig Sauer P226 secured in a leather holster. He set it on the foot of the bed and raised an eyebrow. "Told you to give them a chance."

"I stand corrected," she replied with mock solemnity. "I am curious, though. How did they know exactly what to get for me, even down to the right sizes? I wouldn't think they would have paid attention to that when they cleaned up my apartment. They didn't know then that they'd be buying clothes for me."

"My guess is they went through your credit card records and figured out where you shop. From there they hacked"—he cleared his throat—"I mean, searched those stores' data-bases to get the details of exactly what you've bought in the past, the sizes you wear, and everything."

"Well, that's ingenious and disturbing at the same time. I think I'll pay with cash from now on." Her eyes followed him back to the safe where he reached in again and took out a subcompact Glock and ankle holster similar to the ones he'd left in L.A. "And maybe find a nice cabin to hole up in in Idaho."

"Don't you think you'd get bored after about three days?"

"Probably." She rested her hands on her hips. "What's the plan for the rest of today?"

"We need to go to Ben's flat as soon as we can."

When her shoulders slumped, he added with an understanding smile, "After your shower, of course."

She bounced on the balls of her feet, giddy with the thought of not only getting out of the clothes she was wearing, but putting on the new, cool clothes she'd neither had to shop nor pay for. It was only a few minutes later that she stood under a stream of blissfully warm water.

Hair dried and government-supplied makeup on in near record time, she strode from the bathroom refreshed and ready to go dressed in black skinny jeans and a crimson top.

A pleased smile tugged at her lips when James caught a glimpse of her and his expression morphed from stunned to admiring. That look would never get old, she decided.

"You look great," he said and made a show of looking down at his clothes. "I guess I'd better shower and change, too, if I don't want to look like a bum next to you." Just before he disappeared into the bathroom, he said, "The phone on the bed is yours, by the way."

While James showered, she took the opportunity to check out Quinn Riordan's phone. Leaning back against a pile of pillows on the bed, she perused the downloaded apps. The agency had obviously examined the phone she'd left in her bag, since the one in her hand had most of the same apps, including several games. She was disappointed her e-books were missing, but doubted she'd have much time for reading anyway.

Curiosity gnawed at her as she squinted at the icons she didn't recognize. She wanted to open them to see what they did but held back. What if one was some kind of panic button and once pressed, their door would be busted in and she'd find herself swarmed by a squad of assault weapon-wielding Navy SEALs? With that image firmly planted in her brain, she decided she could definitely wait until James explained what each one did.

She noted her music library was exactly the same, but the pictures in the photo albums were completely different. Gone were the snapshots of Bailey, Wyatt, and Hunter, all goofy-faced and hamming it up for the camera. Instead, there were doctored candid shots of the happy couple—James and Quinn Riordan at the beach, at dinner, and hanging out at home. The pictures looked so genuine, she could almost conjure the reality of the scenes in her mind. She had to hand it to the graphic artists who'd mocked up the pictures. They had done a remarkable job. If the opportunity arose over the next few days, she'd try to take a few of her and James together to lend more authenticity to her photo album. That's what she told herself anyway.

When she heard the bathroom door open, she clicked off her phone. James came out, looking incredibly attractive in a pair of blue jeans and a long-sleeved dark gray Henley.

"You look great," she said, echoing his words to her from earlier. If she had tried to say anything more specific than that, she was sure she'd embarrass herself. She called it a win since she'd managed not to drool onto her shirt.

"Your phone okay?"

"Yeah, it's fine." Quinn watched him tug up his pant leg and strap the ankle holster on his left calf. "There are a couple of apps I wanted to ask you about."

James picked up the Sig, reached around, and tucked the holstered firearm inside his waistband just behind his right hip. After clipping the holster to his belt, he pulled the hem of his shirt over it and looked at her. "Which apps?"

"I thought you spy types didn't use waistband holsters. Superspy Edward Walker just shoves his gun in his pants."

"A fictional spy might do that. I prefer not to accidentally put a very real slug in my ass."

Quinn swung her legs off the side of the bed and stood. "You clearly lack a sense of adventure."

"Clearly," he replied. James went to the small closet and

hauled out two black overcoats. "As for the apps, I know there's one that gives you the exact location of my phone. It uses a transmitter that works even if the phone is off." He tossed one of the coats onto the bed and held out the other to Quinn. "You have one in your phone, too."

"Why?" She slipped her arms into the sleeves and shrugged into the coat. The hem hit her legs just below her knees. Another fantastic fit and style. She hoped the agency would allow her to keep the clothes when the mission was over and call it compensation for her time. Quinn could just imagine the stupefied look on Nicole's face if she explained her new wardrobe by saying James had "bought her something pretty." That was additional incentive to keep them. "I thought we weren't supposed to be out of each other's sight."

"We're not, but you never know. Were you expecting to be in London on an op for the CIA a few days ago?"

"Good point." Quinn picked up James's coat and held it open for him. He turned his back to her and shoved his hands through the sleeves. She ran her hands across his shoulders and down his back to smooth the fabric. At least that's what she'd claim if he called her on it.

He didn't. Instead, he secured their laptops in the room's safe while Quinn put her phone in her pocket and slung the strap of her bag over her shoulder. Out the door and down the stairs, they strode through the elegantly appointed, marble-floored lobby. The perky desk attendant who'd checked them in earlier chirped, "Enjoy your evening out, Mr. and Mrs. Riordan."

"Thank you," Quinn said and smiled, fighting off the surprise at being called "Mrs."

Without missing a beat, James grinned, waved at the clerk with one hand, and took Quinn's hand in the other. "We will."

Once outside, they skipped down the front steps to the

sidewalk. James lifted their still-entwined hands out a little as they walked. "I hope you don't mind, but I'll need to do this a lot. It's good for our cover and I don't want to take the chance of us getting separated."

He held her hand tight as they threaded their way through a crowd walking in the opposite direction.

"I think I can handle it," Quinn said once they emerged from the pack. The evening air was cold against her cheeks and she was more than happy to have one hand warmed by his while the other was stuffed deep inside the pocket of her coat.

"And you're sure you're okay with our"—he cleared his throat and said barely above a whisper—"marital status and living arrangements?"

"I am and quit asking." She squeezed his hand. "I appreciate your sensitivity, but you've asked me that, like, five times now. I know it's for my protection and the best way for us to be together at all times without anyone questioning it." While the idea of pretending to be married had rattled her at first, she'd seen plenty of evidence throughout the day that proved it had been the right call.

Plus Quinn couldn't deny the unadulterated satisfaction that burned through her when she dealt with a flight attendant who chatted with James a little too long. Without saying a word, Quinn smiled sweetly at the interloper, reached across James with her left hand, and making sure her rings were plainly visible, handed the woman an empty soda can. The sparkling rings worked like a charm. James gave no indication he'd noticed her not-so-subtle rebuff. Even if he had, she didn't care. James might only be her pretend-husband, but no one else knew their true status. It was only right she respond to any potential poachers accordingly.

"I trust you. There's no reason to walk on eggshells around me, okay?"

His uncertainty vanished and was replaced by a quiet confidence. "Okay."

"Okay," she repeated with finality. Now more relaxed, they walked at a brisk pace, past restaurants and pubs, American fast-food joints, tiny retail shops, and a bank. "I take it it's not a coincidence that we're able to walk to Ben's flat from our hotel?"

"You're right. It's not." James practically hurtled over a bicycle locked to a rack on the crowded sidewalk. "Ben needed to look like he could afford to live in a nice area, but not be über-wealthy, so his place is small. And Fitzhugh's house is only a couple of Tube stops from here."

When they reached a wine-and-cigar shop, James pulled her inside and bought a bottle of German Riesling.

"What's up with that?" Quinn asked.

"In case anyone is watching, we're just a couple joining a friend in the building for dinner."

"You think Ben's flat is being watched?"

"I have no idea, but it can't hurt to look like we belong there."

They rounded a corner and started down a narrow residential street. On both sides were unbroken stretches of tan brick, three-story Georgian buildings. At regular intervals, white columns adorned sets of steps that led from the sidewalk to the two side-by-side front doors.

"How well do you think those neighbors get along?" Quinn asked, pointing at one particular duplex on their right. On one side, the exterior was pristine, sporting power-washed bricks and a coat of white paint that brightened the window frames. The other side was grungy, with chipped paint and dirty, dilapidated steps.

"I'm thinking the British version of the Hatfields and the McCoys."

"Accurate," she said with a laugh. "Ben didn't rent an entire town house, did he?"

"No. A lot of these places have been converted into individual apartments." He slowed and looked up at the door with the number *25* on it. "And here we are."

Quinn noticed the four-buttoned intercom panel to the right of the door. "Do you have a key to the front door?"

"No."

"How do we get in?"

He gave her a knowing smile, led her up the steps, and pressed the button next to the name tag for flat C, "Baker, B.," Ben's cover name. Unsurprisingly, there was no response. He pressed it again with the same result. Next, he punched the button for flat A. While they waited for an answer, Quinn peered down at a basement window she hadn't noticed from the street.

"Yeah?" came a man's voice from the speaker. He sounded bored.

"Good evening," James said. "My wife and I are here to have dinner with a friend. We've rung a couple of times, but he hasn't answered. Could you let us in so we don't have to wait for him in the cold?"

Out of the corner of her eye, Quinn saw the sheer curtain below move. "Yeah," the voice said again a few seconds later. James opened the door when it buzzed.

They stepped through the door into a small entryway. To their immediate left was a door with a brass *B* affixed to it. "I think we're up one flight," James said. He took the lead and they climbed the narrow flight of carpeted stairs. They reached a small landing and the door to Ben's flat.

"Now what?" Quinn asked barely above a whisper.

"You hold this," he said and handed her the bottle of wine. He took a small black case from his coat pocket and unzipped it, revealing a lock pick set. "Keep your eyes and ears open." He dropped to his knees in front of the door, took out a couple of tools, and set to work. "If anyone comes up or down the stairs, nudge me."

"Why? What are you going to do, pretend you're proposing?" She instantly cringed. Her brain-to-mouth filter had utterly failed.

"Actually, I'm going to pretend I'm tying my shoe. Any man who proposes on a staircase landing in an apartment building would be deserving of public humiliation."

Quinn leaned back against the wall and recovered from her mortification. "I gotta agree with you on that. This staircase isn't exactly the height of romance."

"Not even close."

"Pretending to propose got Chance Stryker out of a jam in *The Tango Protocol,* though." In actuality, what had saved Chance had been the pulse-pounding kiss that hid his face from his pursuers *after* the fake proposal. Not wanting to put her size sixes in her mouth again, she kept that last bit of information to herself.

"Chance Stryker? What happened to Edward Walker?"

"He's still there. You don't think I only read one book series, do you?"

"Now that you mention it, I don't think that for even a second. And, if it worked for Chance Stryker, I'm sure it would work for us, too." James grimaced as he turned the picks in the lock. There was a click and Quinn could see the tension in his body dissipate. He turned the doorknob and pushed the door open a crack. "There." After returning the implements to their case, he rose to his feet and slipped the case into his pocket. He stepped back and swept his arm toward the door. "After you."

She pushed herself away from the wall and walked into the dark apartment. Once they were both inside, James quietly closed the door behind them.

"We'll need to keep our voices down and walk lightly to keep anyone from knowing we're here."

Quinn nodded, set her purse and the bottle of wine on top of the short bookshelf next to the front door, and waited for her eyes to adjust to the dark. She glanced at the front window and noted the weak light from the street lamp filtering through the closed mini blinds. "I guess we can't turn the lights on if someone might be watching the flat."

"Hang on," he answered. James disappeared and returned a moment later with a quilt slung over his shoulder. "I need your help." He picked up a dining room chair, carried it across the room, and set it down on one side of the window.

She tiptoed across the floor and climbed up onto the chair. At the same time, James bounded onto the couch and stood on the arm. It took a couple of minutes and some binder clips he'd found in a desk drawer, but they eventually secured the quilt over the window.

Quinn didn't move until James maneuvered blindly to the switch next to the door and flicked it on.

Once her eyes adjusted, she quickly surveyed the room. It was a bit smaller than her apartment with only enough room for a sofa against one wall, a small TV on a stand, and a round glass dining room table. Two sets of built-in bookshelves ran the height and length of the wall opposite the couch. A small gray fireplace separated the two sections of shelves.

"No wonder Ben picked this flat. It's like librarian heaven."

From her vantage point atop the chair, she could easily skim the titles on the top two shelves. The very top shelf held several computer manuals and the rest was filled with books on library science. She nearly squealed out loud when she saw Ben owned the same book on acquisitions and collection development she'd studied in library school. She lightly stepped off the chair, moved it closer to the bookshelves, and remounted it.

There were books on research methods, reference work, cataloging, metadata, and information storage and retrieval systems. She couldn't wait to talk to Ben about library stuff in person.

Which reminded her of why she and James were in Ben's flat in the first place. She climbed off the chair and wandered down the short hallway to the bedroom. There she found James rummaging through a dresser drawer.

"I'm sorry, James. The agency flies me all the way to London and all I'm doing is nerding out over Ben's books." She glanced around the room. Besides a double bed and the dresser, a very small desk sat against the wall. "Where do you want me to start?"

He straightened, looked over at her, and shook his head. "I'm not going to tell you where to look. I don't want to filter you or direct you on what or where to look for anything. You're here to search this place as a librarian. I trust that mojo of yours. Use your instincts."

"So, you want me to be part Sherlock Holmes and part Melvil Dewey?"

"Sure, as long as you're 99.98% Quinn Ellington."

"That, I can do." Deciding the desk seemed to be as good a place to start as any, she sat, opened a drawer, and pulled out a packet of receipts paper-clipped together. She studied each one by one and learned that Ben's trips to the grocery store resulted in him buying breakfast cereal, milk, and a variety of fresh fruits. He was partial to eating dinner at the local pub and had recently suffered from a head cold.

Nothing about the receipts jumped out at her, so she left them on the top of the desk and pawed through the rest of the contents of the drawer. It contained pencils, pens, rubber bands, paper clips, and a few postage stamps. She rapped her knuckles on the bottom of the drawer to check for a false bottom. It sounded solid. She closed it and moved to the next one.

She smiled when it revealed a bottle of book glue, several rolls of book tape, and a box of cotton pull fasteners that looked a little like shoelaces. She knew they were used to strap books with their pages falling out together. "Once a librarian . . ." She lifted out a pH pen and examined it, never having seen one in person before.

James came to stand next to her. "That's a weird-looking pen."

"It's used to check the pH level of paper. Paper high in acidity turns yellow, gets brittle, and crumbles when it gets old." She snickered. "And in my head, I just heard my grandpa say, 'So do I.'" Quinn returned the pen after tapping the bottom of the drawer and slid it closed. She craned her neck to look up at him. "Any luck?"

"No." He raked his fingers through his hair. "You?"

"Nope, although we might want to check out the pub Ben eats at all the time."

"That's a good idea. Find out what he's been telling the regulars."

"The food must be pretty good, too, if he eats there a lot."

"Or maybe he enjoys the service more than the food." He wiggled his eyebrows for emphasis.

"Oh, are you admitting to the James Bond stereotype—hooking up with at least one woman during every op?" she asked, narrowing her eyes at him.

He threw his shoulders back and raised his chin. "I'm no more like James Bond in that regard than you are an old lady librarian who wears her hair in a bun and goes around shushing people all day."

"Touché," she said, chastened. "You've been nothing but a complete gentleman and I apologize."

"It's okay. We both have stereotypes to battle against. Are you finished with the desk?"

She raised her arms over her head and stretched, twisting first one way and then the other. "Not quite. I'm going to check the undersides of the drawers to see if anything is hidden." Her hands dropped to her lap and she rolled her shoulders. She sagged back in the chair and stared at the receipts piled on the desk.

"You look whipped. Let me do that. Why don't you go take a break for a few?"

"We need to keep up the search."

"We will, but five minutes won't make a difference."

He was right. Five minutes wouldn't make a difference. "Okay." She left the bedroom, went to the kitchen, and found a bottle of water in the refrigerator. The cold liquid revived her somewhat, but the effects of the day that wouldn't end were beginning to catch up with her. Her legs ached. She knew if she sat down, there was a good chance she wouldn't get back up again until sometime next week, so she ambled back out to the front room and headed toward the book-shelves.

She picked up where she'd left off, starting with the writings of the great philosophers throughout history, from the ancient Greeks to the modern era. Next came a couple of Bibles, a stretch of books on Christianity, the spiritual life, Church history, comparative religion, and monographs of the sacred texts of various Eastern religions.

When the subject of the books jumped from philosophy and religion to politics, she laughed out loud and shook her head. "Ben, you're a bigger library geek than I am." He'd arranged his books in perfect Dewey decimal order.

The way the rest of the shelves were ordered came as no surprise to her. After politics came different foreign language dictionaries, books on astronomy, symptoms and diseases, opera, and a large section of fiction. Finally, there were some old atlases, a few biographies, and a number of history books.

Curious about what kind of fiction Ben read, she went back to the beginning of the section and examined the titles more closely. Overall, he seemed to have pretty highbrow taste. Most of the novels were American and British classics. He also appeared to be a huge Stephen King fan.

"That's weird," she murmured when she spotted a book that was clearly out of place. A copy of *Anglo-American Cataloguing Rules, Second Edition,* known in the library world simply as AACR2 had been shelved between the tomes *Different Seasons* and *Dolores Claiborne.* "That doesn't belong there. Not by a long shot." She took the book from the shelf and studied the cover. She'd never seen such an old copy before. Curious, she flipped the book open.

Excitement thrummed through her. "Hey, James?" she called out in as loud a voice as she dared.

His voice floated from the bedroom. "Yeah?"

"Have you ever seen the movie *The Shawshank Redemption*?"

"Yeah. Why?"

"You know the part where after Andy Dufresne escapes from prison, the warden opens the Bible and finds the pages perfectly carved out in the shape of a rock hammer?"

He stood next to her and responded with a puzzled, drawn-out "Yeah."

Quinn moved the open book so he could see the small, perfectly edged rectangle hewn into the pages. But it wasn't empty. Securely secreted inside the obsolete book was a USB flash drive.

Chapter Eighteen

"I'm not complaining, but I have to admit I never thought my first meal in London would be from Burger King," Quinn said before she took another bite of her chicken sandwich. She stood directly behind James who sat at the desk in their hotel room. When a few rogue crumbs sprinkled down onto his back and shoulders, she brushed off the offending bits with her fingers. "I'm sorry. I'm giving you sesame seed dandruff."

"That's okay," he replied as he stuck the flash drive they'd found in Ben's apartment into the USB port of his laptop. "The pigeons will love me." He took a pull of his drink through the straw and then another bite of his Whopper. "And I promise at some point, we'll eat food that doesn't come wrapped in paper."

"We're not here on vacation and finding out what's on this flash drive takes priority over the time it'd take to eat at a restaurant." Given the angry growls that had come from her stomach as they'd walked back to the hotel, Quinn was happy to eat anything.

A window on the laptop opened to show there was only one file on the thumb drive.

"I'm surprised it's not encrypted," Quinn said.

"It is. This computer has the same encryption/decryption algorithms as Ben's."

"What would happen if we put that drive in my computer?"

"It would explode."

"Really?"

After a pause, he snickered and said, "No, not really."

She pushed at the back of his head with a hand, which made him laugh harder. "You're a doofus."

"Sorry." Still chuckling, he tapped at the keyboard. "I couldn't pass up the chance at a little spy humor."

"Very little."

"Oh, burn," he said, drawing out the second word. "To answer your question, your computer would recognize a drive had been inserted, but it wouldn't be able to open it. You wouldn't see anything." As he finished speaking, a spreadsheet opened on the screen. James looked at the document for a few seconds before he sighed and said, "Nothing is ever straightforward with Ben. This is just another incomprehensible mess of letters and numbers."

Quinn bent forward and with her head next to James's, examined the page. The spreadsheet contained two columns. The one on the far left was a list of three-digit numbers. After a quick scan, Quinn noted the same numbers—082, 100, 850 and sometimes 852—repeated as groups. There were about a dozen of these sets in total.

The next column contained a list of numbers, letters, a word, or a combination of letters and numbers.

"Ben likes multiple layers of security, doesn't he?" Quinn said. "And since I know he's a librarian, I'm positive these are MARC tags."

"They're what?"

"MARC tags. MARC stands for Machine Readable Cataloging. Every book, DVD, audiobook, or whatever a library holds in its collection has its own bibliographic record. A record contains fields where the cataloger fills in information about an item, like author, title, publication date, call number, subject headings, stuff like that. All of those records make up the library's online catalog."

"Okay," he said. "It's not that I don't believe you, because I trust that magical librarian juju you've got going on, but nowhere in this spreadsheet do I see anything that says author, title, or call number."

"And you won't because MARC was developed in the computer dark ages. In the 1960s, Henriette Avram, a systems analyst and programmer—who incidentally worked at the NSA at one point before she ended up at the Library of Congress—designed a way for libraries to use computers to catalog materials instead of having to type up cards."

"Impressive."

"She was." Quinn remembered being in awe of Henriette Avram when she learned about her in her cataloging class. "Anyway, Henriette used really simple three-digit numbers called tags to indicate field names instead of the actual words like title or author. Computers back then were really slow and couldn't store much data. Using numbers instead of letters made for faster computing and didn't take up as much space." She stared at the spreadsheet. "These aren't complete MARC records, though. He's listed only a few tags. That's why it might seem confusing because you aren't seeing the whole picture." She huffed in frustration. "It'd be easier to explain if I just showed you a complete MARC record." She came around and bumped him with her hip. "Move."

"So bossy."

She smiled and slid into the chair when he stood. After opening a browser, she went to her library's online catalog and typed in the search box, "*To Kill a Mockingbird.*"

When the record filled the screen, James said, "I still see words like author, title, and publisher."

"That's because library software companies make the GUIs—the Graphical User Interfaces—for both the end users and the catalogers easy to use." She moved the cursor to the top of the page and clicked on the words, *MARC Display.* "Voilà," Quinn said, feeling a little like a magician revealing the truth behind the illusion.

"It looks like computer code."

"It is. It's what makes the library world go round."

James pointed at the column of thirty or so three-digit numbers on the left. "So these numbers are the MARC tags?"

"Mmm-hmm. The three-digit tag for a field will be the same in every record. For instance, see the 100? That's always used for the author's name. In this case, 'Lee, Harper.' Basically, 100 means author."

"I think I get it." He pointed a little farther down the list and said, "The 245 tag is the title."

"Exactly."

"What's with the vertical line and the *c* after it?"

"That's a subfield. A lot of fields are broken up that way. But subfield codes and indicators are too inside baseball for what we need to know for figuring out Ben's tags."

"So you understand what all of these tags mean?" He sounded impressed.

"The main ones, yeah. I don't remember the specifics of what some of the tags at the top of this record are for. They're control information, record identification numbers, stuff like that. I'd have to look them up to know for sure."

"Hey, look," James said, sounding as if he'd made a great discovery. "The tag for the ISBN is 020. There's the 978."

She grinned at the proud look on his face. "Yup. See? Soon you won't even need me around anymore."

He made a noise at the back of his throat. "So not true. I knew you were amazing, but I had no idea just how mysterious you librarians really are."

"Not mysterious," she answered, chuckling. "Well organized."

"Okay. I'll give you that." His arm grazed her back when he rested it across the top of her chair. "Now we need to figure out what Ben's tags mean."

Quinn returned to the spreadsheet. "Ben's used 082 several times. That's the tag for the Dewey decimal number assigned to an item." She pointed at the places where it recurred. After doing a quick search on the three different Dewey numbers Ben had entered, she said, "The numbers here are for medieval manuscripts, illuminated manuscripts, and Latin."

"Am I reading this right? It looks like he's entered the same author's name for several different books," James said, moving his face closer to the screen.

"Yeah, the ones on Latin. Someone named Dudley."

James hovered his finger in front of the screen and moved it down the list of tags. "The 850 tag is used a bunch of times with either UkLoKC, Uk or UkOxU. What's that about?"

"I think I know, but let me double check first." Back to the browser, she did a quick search. "850 is 'Holding Institution.'" The room fell silent except for the sound of clicking keys. "Bingo," she said in a low voice when she found a pdf file of a list of MARC organization codes for the United Kingdom.

She scrolled through the list. "Let's see. Uk is the British Library here in London, UkOxU is the Bodleian Library at Oxford University and UkLoKC is the Royal Borough of Kensington and Chelsea Library Service."

Quinn looked at James and said, "I bet these are Ben's notes on one of Fitzhugh's items he was researching."

"I agree. Notes he didn't want anyone to understand, even if they were able to get past the encryption on the thumb drive."

"And based on the Dewey numbers, he didn't want anyone to know he found a medieval manuscript."

"That might be why he went off grid," James said. "He found something important in a manuscript and took off with it."

"Wouldn't he contact the agency to tell them he found something, though?"

James stared at the screen and then shook his head. "Maybe we're looking at this backward. What if Ben's cover wasn't blown after all? He couldn't take the chance of communicating with the agency in case he's wrong about whatever he thinks he found and wants to be able to go back to Fitzhugh's if he needs to. Ben could have told Fitzhugh he needs to go on a trip to do more research. We told everyone in California the same thing. That would also explain why Ben's flat wasn't tossed."

"If that's the case, they might not think Ben had anything to do with the disappearance of the letter you and I found in the clock."

"And why he's not in a safe house. He may not actually be in danger." He expelled a loud breath. "It's a lot of speculation, but it's possible."

"Do we stop looking for Ben and go home?"

"No. Until we have some solid answers, we stay on it. We might be wrong."

"Okay, so what do we do next?"

"We follow up on the only lead we have. How do you feel about visiting a library or two tomorrow?"

"I thought you'd never ask." The idea of visiting the British Library made the room spin a little. "I don't think getting into the Kensington Library will be a problem since it's probably a regular public library. The British Library might be a little more restrictive. I need to find out more about what kind of access we can get." She returned her fingers to the keyboard.

James gently gripped her wrists and moved her hands away from the laptop. He closed it. "Not tonight you're not." He stood, took her hands, and pulled her to her feet. "Time for bed." His eyes roamed her face. "I know sharing the bed is weird, so you take it and I'll sleep in the chair or on the floor."

"No, you won't," Quinn said without hesitation. "You can't possibly get any sleep in that tiny, uncomfortable chair. I'm sure you spy types are trained to handle sleep deprivation, but I'm not going to be one who inflicts it on you. Plus, I can't live with the guilt if you contract hepatitis from lying on a germy, bodily fluid–soaked carpet." Jerking her head toward the bed, she said, "Look, we wouldn't even have to sleep near each other—that king-size bed is bigger than a life raft."

"That's true."

"It also seems only right that a pretend husband should sleep in the same bed as his pretend wife."

"Okay. You've convinced me. I'll sleep in the bed," he said. "We can pretend to be one of those couples who've been married for so long, all they do in bed anymore is sleep."

With a wicked glint in her eye, she said, "Oh, sweetie, believe me. When I'm married, that will *never* be me."

The water Quinn downed before bed would not be ignored. Despite her exhaustion, she had no choice but to climb out of the warm bed and stumble to the bathroom. She had no idea what time it was; all she knew was that she wasn't about to turn the bathroom light on for fear of the excruciating pain of burned corneas.

Once finished, she flushed and opened the bathroom

door. She let out a yelp when in the dimness, she saw James filling the doorway wearing nothing but boxers and a smile. Heart pounding, she stood there, frozen, and stared into his face. His smile never wavered and he seemed to be in no hurry to move out of her way. There was only one thing for her to do.

Quinn flung her arms around his neck and smashed her lips on his in a searing kiss. He caught her up in his arms, crushed her body to his, and deepened the kiss. Her entire body exploded with intense, burning desire. Never in her life had she felt anything like it. She caressed the side of his face with one hand while the other roamed over his bare back. When she raked her nails across his skin, he shuddered and moaned with pleasure.

How it was possible she didn't know, but James somehow intensified their kiss. She wasn't aware of anything but his mouth on hers, kissing her hungrily, his fingers tangled in her hair, his skin sizzling under her touch. It didn't matter how tightly she clutched him. She couldn't get close enough.

James broke the kiss, lifted her up, and she wrapped her legs around his waist. Clinging to him, she lowered her mouth to his and kissed him with passion. He carried her to the bed and in one swift movement, he laid them both back on the rumpled sheets and rolled on top of her. His lips moved from hers and he lightly trailed the tip of his tongue along her jaw and down her neck, her entire body racked by a bone-rattling shock wave. She lolled her head to the side and when he nipped the curve at her neck with his teeth, she arched against him and blurted a surprised, "Oh!"

The sound of her own voice woke her up. Her entire body hummed and her heart was racing. With a hand resting on her forehead, she gave in to a mighty shiver and stared wide-eyed at the ceiling. She closed her eyes and struggled to get her ragged breath under control. She hoped her erotic dream–induced outburst hadn't disturbed James.

If he had heard her cry out, she was fully prepared to lie her head off and tell him she'd dreamt she was being chased by a pack of snarling, ravenous wolves. It would at least explain the heavy breathing.

She rolled onto her side, opened her eyes again, and saw James on his side of the bed. He wasn't actually in bed, though. Instead, he was stretched out on top of the covers still fully dressed. He lay on his back and the hand resting on his chest rose and fell with his steady breathing. His face was slack and tranquil with sleep. She only hoped from now on she could look at him without her face glowing red like Rudolph's nose. That dream was going to be with her for a long time. She breathed a sigh in the dark. Who was she kidding? That dream would be burned into her brain forever.

She lay there for a few minutes and hoped against hope that she would fall back asleep. At the realization she really did have to go to the bathroom, she grumbled silently to herself, and slid from the bed. To prove to herself she wasn't reliving the dream, she flicked on the light. When she finished, she slowly turned the doorknob and cautiously swung open the door.

She was mostly relieved and yet slightly disappointed to find that James was not standing on the other side of the door waiting for her. She stealthily crept back toward the bed. As she passed around the foot of it, she glanced at the clock on the nightstand. The luminous green numbers informed her it was exactly 2:23 A.M.

Once she was settled under the covers again, she peeked over at James and was pleased to see he was still asleep. In fact, he was in the exact same position as when she woke up. His breathing was on the brink of actual snoring, deep and heavy, but hadn't quite achieved that buzz saw noise like her grandparents' bulldog, Pot Roast. She was a little surprised by how deeply he slept. From all the novels she'd read, she'd always been under the impression spies slept with one eye open, ready to leap into action. Maybe the dead-bolted hotel door and unholstered Sig Sauer on his nightstand made him feel secure enough to fall into a truly deep and restful slumber.

The Sig on the nightstand reminded her how dangerous the world she'd been sucked into was. And yet despite that danger, she always felt safe with James. She'd noticed how he exuded competence and confidence everywhere he went. His eyes were always moving, assessing threats, scanning faces, formulating potential escape routes from any given area. When she thought about the times they'd been in public before yesterday, she realized he'd always done that. At the time, it hadn't occurred to her to even wonder about it. She'd seen her father do the same thing her entire life and never really thought about it. After a few minutes of ruminating, she fell into a deep, and thankfully dreamless, sleep.

Chapter Nineteen

"I can see you're really broken up about not eating a breakfast that comes wrapped in paper and delivered on a plastic tray," James said, smiling at her from behind the rim of his teacup. He took a sip and set the cup back on the saucer.

Quinn shoveled another forkful of fried egg in her mouth and grinned at him across the white cloth–covered table. She waved her fork toward the long buffet covered with breakfast foods at the center of the hotel's dining room and after swallowing, said, "Hey, I'm just trying to fit in and eat what's offered. I don't want to be one of those ugly Americans that complains about how it's not like the food at home."

"So you're chowing down like a Marine for the good of your country."

"Exactly. It's a sacrifice I'm willing to make." She squinted and pointed her strip of bacon at him. "And don't talk smack about the Marines or this military brat will kick your ass. Oorah." She tore off a hunk of bacon with her teeth and smiled as she chewed.

"I know you would." James looked at her plate piled with eggs, bacon, mushrooms, baked beans, and toast. "I have to say, you're doing an admirable job." A mischievous look came over his face. "I don't see any black pudding, though. If you really want to fit in, you should eat some of that. You know, for your country."

She didn't know what black pudding was, but from the sound of it, it was most likely something her mom would graciously call "an acquired taste." After doing a quick search on her phone and seeing the words *blood sausage* and *congealed*, she stuck her tongue out between her teeth. "I'll, um, save that for another morning."

"Uh-huh."

"Uh-huh." Quinn filled her and James's cups with more tea from a silver teapot and sighed. "I could get used to this."

"What?"

She poured a dash of milk into her tea and stirred, watching the liquid turn the color of caramel. "Traveling. Seeing new places. It's cool." Quinn shook her head in disbelief. "I still have a hard time believing this isn't all a dream, that I'm really drinking tea in London." She silently cursed herself for saying the word. Steamy images of her lusty dream flashed in her mind. Her cheeks warmed and she lifted the cup to her lips. "Why we're here is even more unbelievable," she added in the hope of refocusing her thoughts.

"Speaking of why we're here, what did you learn about the libraries while I was in the shower?"

She was eternally grateful she'd had something to occupy her mind while he'd been in the shower. "The Royal Borough of Kensington and Chelsea library system is a public one like mine. It has a central library with five smaller branches. As for the British Library near St. Pancras, we can get in, but they restrict access to the books. We'd have to get passes to be allowed into the reading rooms."

"Would being a librarian from the States here to do research get you in?"

"I think so. But they'd want to know what books I want to look at before I visit. That could take some time."

"What about Oxford?" James asked and popped a grape in his mouth.

"It's even more restrictive than the British Library. There are two different forms to fill out and we'd have to explain why we can't get access to the materials anywhere else."

"You think we should start with the public library?"

"I do. You used a public library in L.A. to do the same kind of research Ben was doing here. It makes sense he'd use one with easy access first and go to the more specialized ones if he needed to."

He slathered some butter on his toast. "Which Kensington library do we start at? There are six, right? Does each have their own holding institution MARC code so we know which one Ben was at?"

"Look at you talking about MARC codes. I'm so proud."

The roguish smile and wink he shot her before he bit into his toast nearly had her sliding under the table. By some miracle, she was able to stay upright and form words into sentences. "They don't have individual codes, but their catalog indicates which of the libraries has a copy of each title. I did an advanced search on the authors' names and the general subjects from Ben's spreadsheet and found out there's a copy of each of the books at the Kensington Central Library."

"Then I guess that's where we start." After a few seconds, James sat up straighter. "What if Ben checked the books out? We didn't find them in his flat. What if he took them with him when he went off grid? Then we're dead in the water."

"Nope, we're not," she said and sipped her tea. How they made it taste so different and so wonderful, she didn't know.

"How can you be so sure?"

"They're reference books. They can't be taken out of the library. 'Not for loan.' Says so right there in the catalog."

"You librarians are a sneaky bunch, aren't you?"

"I don't know about sneaky. It all makes perfect sense to me."

"I'm glad it does to one of us," James said and glanced at his watch. "I guess we should go." He drained the rest of his tea, set his napkin on the table, pushed back his chair, and stood. Quinn did the same.

After a quick trip back to their room to retrieve their coats, they left the hotel and strode off toward the nearby Underground station. When James took Quinn's hand as he had done the evening before, she involuntarily jerked.

James released her hand like it was a hot potato. "I thought—"

"I'm sorry. It's totally okay," she said and laced her fingers with his. "It surprised me is all. I guess I'm still getting used to being Mrs. Riordan." She hated lying to him, but there was no way she was going to tell him she was still a little jumpy from the R-rated dream she'd had about him.

He regarded her as they walked. "You sure everything's okay?"

This won't do, she thought, angry with herself that a dream had flustered her so much she couldn't be around him without being completely distracted. Jaw set with resolve, she looked James in the eye and answered with a confident, "Yeah, I'm sure."

"Good. Because I have the feeling the real fun is about to start."

"What do you mean the fun is about to start?" she asked as they hurried down the steps of the Tube station. "How is learning about MARC records not fun?"

"Never. It's never not fun," he answered quickly.

"Nice save, Mr. Riordan."

"Thank you, Mrs. Riordan." He dipped his head.

The train arrived and a few people disembarked before they boarded and found two seats together.

Before long, they walked through a tall archway and into

the redbrick building that was the Kensington Central Library. Once inside, Quinn was struck at how similar it was to the library she worked at, with its industrial carpet, laminate-topped tables, and rows of book stacks.

"I know you can take us straight to the books we need to look at," James said, "but I'd like to talk to the librarian at the desk to see if he, or any of the other librarians, remember Ben being here."

Quinn agreed and they waited a respectful distance behind a slightly hunched older gentleman who seemed to be hard of hearing. She felt bad for the man behind the desk. Libraries are supposed to be quiet so people can work and study without distraction. She and her colleagues had perfected their "librarian voices," the volume at which conversation could occur without disturbing others. All that went out the window whenever she'd tried to help a patron who was hard of hearing. When she heard the older man loudly complain he couldn't find the sports section of *The Times,* she stared down at her boots and dug her teeth into her lower lip.

"What? You're trying not to smile," James said in her ear. The low rumble of his voice and his lips hovering near her ear set off a wave of tingles.

She rose up on her tiptoes. James dipped his head and her lips brushed his ear when she said in a throaty whisper, "Experience tells me they should go look for the sports section in the men's room." She felt a sense of deep satisfaction when she noticed he had to rub his neck after she tilted her head away.

Their tête-à-tête was interrupted when a woman in a wool skirt and tweed jacket took her place behind the reference desk. She adjusted her glasses and looked at James and Quinn with a smile. "How can I help you this fine morning?"

"My wife and I are wondering if you had any books on manuscripts we could look at."

"Are you asking about how to write a book manuscript? Or do you mean you're looking for information on medieval and illuminated manuscripts?"

"Um, whatever they have on display in museums," James said. "We were told we'd be seeing some manuscripts during our trip here and we wanted to have some more background on what we'll be looking at."

"Is there a difference between medieval manuscripts and illuminated ones?" Quinn asked, playing along as an uninformed tourist.

"In the strictest sense, an illuminated manuscript is one where the pages are decorated with gold or silver, giving it a luminous quality," the librarian said, her voice taking on a professorial tone. "The term has been broadened to include any manuscript that is illustrated with miniature paintings, borders, portraits, and the like."

"Aren't most medieval manuscripts illuminated?" James asked.

"Not always, no. Those are the most interesting to look at, of course. Owning a splendid illuminated book was often a status symbol, much like owning a large house or driving an expensive car is today. Some manuscripts were beautifully adorned like a . . ." She appeared to be searching for the right words.

"Like a Rolls-Royce?" James offered.

"Yes! Outstanding example," she said, the creases at the corners of her eyes deepening when she smiled. "Other manuscripts were more workaday, like legal documents which wouldn't be ornamented. I suppose you could consider those more like a Dacia."

"I guess we'll probably see some of both, don't you think, honey?" Quinn offered.

James nodded.

"We've got some books in the reference section that should be more than adequate for your needs," the librarian said.

"Great! My cousin, Ben, told us this library would be able to help us," James said.

"Ben?" the woman asked as she came around the end of the desk and walked toward the reference section with James and Quinn in tow.

"Yes, Ben Baker. He told us he's been coming in here occasionally to do research for a work project. Different items of art, I think." James's words were spoken so casually, Quinn would have never known he was actually digging for information.

"Oh, yes! Mr. Baker. He's been coming in fairly regularly the last few weeks. It's great fun to help him. I assisted him with the provenance of a jade Buddha just last week."

"We haven't had a chance to see him yet, we only just arrived from the States yesterday. Maybe we'll run into him here," James said. "Has he been here in the last few days?"

"He was here Thursday. I didn't see him on Friday and I wasn't here Saturday."

The librarian who had gone off to help the elderly gentleman find the sports section was heading back toward the reference desk.

"Gareth," the woman called out quietly. "You were here Saturday, weren't you?"

"I was." The trio stopped. Gareth joined them.

"Was Mr. Baker here, the man doing the research on the art pieces?"

"He was. He was here with another man, a research assistant perhaps? Big bloke. I remember they were both here until five o'clock. I had to roust them out when we closed."

The other librarian chuckled quietly. "That sounds like Mr. Baker. Always here to the last minute."

Gareth nodded and moved on while James and Quinn followed the woman to the reference stacks. After pointing out a dozen or so books on illuminated manuscripts, she bustled away.

Quinn located the specific books listed in Ben's spreadsheet, took them off the shelf, and set them on a nearby table.

"Are we reading for content? Looking for notations?" she asked in a whisper as they each took a seat.

"Both, don't you think?" James slid one of the books from the top of the pile in front of him and opened it. "I'm hoping we'll know it when we see it."

"Me too." She flipped past the first few pages of the book before her and skimmed the table of contents. "Do you know who the big guy Gareth mentioned is?"

"No."

"Not an associate of yours?"

"Not that I know of. If Ben was working with someone here, he would have told me."

"You think he was one of Fitzhugh's men?"

"Probably."

"Do you think he was suspicious of Ben and wanted to keep tabs on him?"

"Possibly."

For the next hour, they scoured through their respective books.

When Quinn came to the index, she closed the book, disappointed she hadn't encountered a single scrap of paper, pencil scribbling, or mark in the margins.

"I now know the difference between breviaries, books of prayer, psalters, and bestiaries, but nothing caught my eye," she said. "Well, other than the slightly off elephant some thirteenth-century clerk painted. It's actually kind of impressive since he probably never saw one in real life." She rolled her shoulders, shoved the book off to one side, and slid the next one in front of her. "How're you doing?"

"The same." James squeezed his eyes closed and rubbed them with his fists. When he looked at her again, the light streaming in from the windows turned his eyes a startling shade of blue. "I was reading about *The Book of Kells*. Do you know it?"

"It's an Irish Bible, right?"

"Yeah. It's basically the four Gospels produced by monks in the early ninth century. It's one of the most important illustrated manuscripts of them all and I can see why. The work is incredible, but staring at the intricate details is making me go cross-eyed." He blinked a couple of times as if to make his point. "On the plus side, I recognized a bunch of the Celtic designs and motifs we learned about when we studied Ragnar's brooch."

"Ah, Ragnar's brooch," Quinn said with a hint of nostalgia. "The thing that started it all."

"Yeah. I'll never be able to look at the queen or the Minnesota Vikings mascot ever again and not think of you."

"I'm pleased to be the one who linked that unlikely pair in your mind."

"I'm sure you are."

They bent their heads over their books again and after another hour passed, James said, "Both books I looked through were about specific famous manuscripts held by either libraries or museums. I wonder if one of them was stolen and Ben found it in Dobrynin's art stash. But how could we figure out which one?"

"I could search newspaper databases to see if anything about those manuscripts pops up. Do the books have indices of the manuscripts and which institutions own them?"

He nodded, turned to the back of one of the books, and angled it toward her.

She scanned the list. "What if Ben went to one of these cities?"

James blew out a breath and slumped back in his chair. "Dublin, Paris, Baltimore, Berkeley, Harvard, Oxford, Aberdeen, Los Angeles. Which one?"

Quinn closed her eyes and rubbed her fingertips over her temples. "We're missing something."

"We are." When James stared at her, she could almost see the gears turning in his brain. "There are still some books over there that weren't on Ben's list, right?" At her nod, he said, "Why don't you go get the relevant ones and we'll go through them? Maybe Ben was being supercareful and didn't put the most important book on the list."

"At this point, I wouldn't put it past him. He does seem to want to be as cryptic as possible."

"I think your idea about checking to see if any of the manuscripts have been stolen is a good one. I'll take some quick pictures of the manuscript lists in these books."

"And I'll go get the rest of the reference books." She went to the short bookshelf, knelt, and skimmed the titles of the books on either side of the gap they'd made when they removed books earlier. When she pulled six more from the shelf, she heard a *thwap*. It was the unmistakable sound of a book falling flat on the shelf, which was odd since none of the books on either side of the gap had gone over.

A book stuck behind others on a shelf was nothing new and she wondered how long the one she'd heard fall had been hidden. More than once she'd seen her coworkers rejoice like fathers at the return of a prodigal son when a previously believed lost or stolen book was found in such a way. *We're so easily pleased,* she thought with a smile.

Of course she couldn't allow the book to languish there. She set the books in her hands on the floor, reached into the dark space, and felt the cover. Unexpectedly, her fingers touched leather. She pulled the book from its hiding place and sucked in a sharp intake of air.

The book was old. Unbelievably old. It was about twelve inches from top to bottom, ten inches from side to side and around two inches thick. Intricate designs were tooled into the leather cover. There was no label on the spine, and when she lifted up the leather straps that held the book closed and checked the inside cover, there were no obvious markings of ownership. She turned to a random page and gazed at exactly what she'd just been studying. On the parchment were the thick black letters of handwritten medieval script, glowing gold designs, and several fanciful-looking animals in the margins.

She closed the book and tried not to appear too suspicious as she glanced over each shoulder to see if anyone was watching her. Assured no one was paying her one iota of attention, she placed the book flat on her lap and then set the other six books on top of it. She casually carried them all back to the table and sat in her chair. The reference books went on the table, but she left the manuscript on her lap. When James finished taking a picture, she leaned back so he could see it. "Look what I found behind the books on the shelf."

James's features remained neutral, but his eyes flashed with interest. "What is it?"

She opened the book long enough for him to see the writing and illustrations. The book closed again, she pressed her rib cage against the edge of the table to hide it from anyone who might pass by.

"Do you think Ben put it there?" she asked.

"It would be a pretty amazing coincidence if he didn't."

"It might belong to this library and was just misshelved. Or it was taken from their rare books area and not returned properly. We should show it to them."

"What if it doesn't belong to the library? They'll take it and keep it until the owner comes looking for it. If Ben left it, we have to take it. Otherwise, we've lost our only clue."

"I know, but I can't stand the idea of stealing a book from a library. What if we get caught?" It made her queasy just thinking about it. "There are security gates at the doors. If this book has an electromagnetic strip on it, we'll trigger the alarm."

"Can you tell if it has one?"

"I might. If it's tucked deep between two pages, I probably won't see it. I don't want to destroy the book finding out."

"Then we have to chance it." James's tone left no room for argument.

"You're right," she sighed, resigning herself to potentially committing a most loathsome library crime. "What do we do if the alarm goes off?"

"Honestly? Drop the book and run."

That elicited a quiet groan from her and she dropped her head in her hand. "I'm officially the worst librarian ever."

He rubbed her shoulder. "No, you're the best. I would have never gotten this far without you. And if we were one hundred percent sure the book belonged to the library, we would leave it here."

"You're right." She looked at him and sighed. "I know I'm making too much of this. It's not like we're trying to smuggle heroin."

"No, I get it. Look, if we find out Ben had nothing to do with it being here, we'll send it back with an anonymous note or something. I promise." He scooted his chair closer to hers. "And to assuage your guilty conscience, I'll carry it out. I'll fold my coat over it so I can ditch it quick in case it sets off the alarm. Does that help?"

"It does." A mischievous smile formed on her face. "And if they catch us, I'll claim I didn't know I'd married a reprobate."

He gazed at her from under hooded eyelids. "Ah, my

loving wife. Ready and willing to throw me under the bus at the first opportunity." Even as he teased, he reached over and moved the book from her lap to his. "Do you want to put the reference books back on the shelf?"

"We should leave them in case they keep usage statistics."

"I guess we're ready to go." His gaze was steady and it imbued her with a sense of confidence. "We strolled in. Now we stroll out."

After the tiniest of nods in response, she steeled her nerves and stood. At the same time, James took his coat from the back of the chair next to him and draped it across the book on his forearm. It was completely hidden from view when he stood.

Quinn folded her coat over her arm as well and after pushing in their chairs, the two ambled toward the exit. As they passed the reference desk, Gareth raised a hand in acknowledgment. She sent him a smile—or at least what she hoped was a smile, even though she was afraid she looked more nauseated than anything else—and a small wave in return. A bead of nervous perspiration trickled between her shoulder blades.

To help her walk at James's steady pace, she slipped her free hand into the crook of his bent elbow. He covered her hand with his, which helped steady her nerves. She held her breath as they approached the tall electronic security gates standing like sentries on either side of the exit doors. She was fully prepared to bolt at the first high-pitched whine of an alarm.

To Quinn's great relief, no beeps or sirens sounded as they passed through the electromagnetic crucible. No snarling pack of angry librarians chased after them as they left the library. Still, it wasn't until they reached High Street that Quinn's hypervigilance subsided and she finally gusted out a breath.

James, who never broke a sweat the entire time, grinned down at her. "You did great. See? Piece of cake."

"I'm not so sure I'm cut out for this cloak-and-dagger stuff," she said, her voice as shaky as her legs.

The hand covering hers tightened. "I know you are."

Chapter Twenty

Quinn threw one last glance over her shoulder as they climbed the front steps of their hotel.

"Still worried the librarian goon squad is following us?" James asked.

"A little."

"If they caught you with a poached manuscript, what manner of punishment would they exact? Forty lashes with an eyeglasses chain?"

She chuckled and squeezed the hand that held hers. "Much worse. I'd be locked in a windowless room and forced to catalog hand puppets, inflatable globes, ukuleles, and animal skeletons."

"Sounds terrible." He pulled open the front door. "Glad you're in the clear. You ready to examine our find instead?"

"I am so ready," she said as they strode across the lobby toward the staircase. "I can hardly wait to get upstairs."

She caught the desk clerk's sly smile as they passed. It was clear her out of context comment had him concluding their afternoon activities would involve something other than scrutinizing a filched illuminated manuscript.

Once in their room, James hung the DO NOT DISTURB sign

on the handle and shut the door. "I don't want someone walking in on us with what appears to be a valuable manuscript. Plus, I don't want to disappoint the desk clerk."

Quinn's gaze followed him as he walked across the room. "You saw his smirk, too, huh? At least we know we're doing a bang-up job selling our cover as a happily married couple."

"*Very* happily married," he replied with a crooked smile as he joined her on the bed.

They both sat cross-legged and stared at the book atop the bedspread. Quinn's mood swung from lighthearted to foreboding. "We were wrong. Ben didn't take the manuscript with him when he disappeared." Quinn noticed James's frown when she glanced at him. "That's not a good sign, is it?"

"No, probably not."

"Let's not lose hope," she said. "Maybe our finding the manuscript was all part of Ben's master plan." She took his hand and laced her fingers with his. "You know what I think? I think he's probably stretched out on a lounge chair on a beach somewhere sipping a drink with an umbrella stuck in it, laughing his ass off that he got us to do all his legwork for him."

"If you're right, once we find him, I'm gonna kick his ass."

"I don't blame you. But first we need to get to the bottom of this mystery and the only way to start is to see what the deal is with that," she said, indicating the book with a tip of her head. "Shall we?"

When he nodded, she released his hand, carefully undid the straps, and opened the cover. "Leather straps with pins or metal clasps were used to keep books closed tight so the parchment wouldn't buckle," she said. She tapped the wood board the leather was stretched over with a fingernail and studied the cords that bound the folio pages together.

At the center of the first page was a wide column of text written in carefully rendered medieval calligraphy. There was so little space between words, it was difficult to tell where one word ended and another began.

"How's your Latin?" she asked.

"*E plurbis unum. Carpe diem. Caveat emptor.* How's yours?"

"*Semper fidelis. Illegitimi non carborundum.*"

He frowned and furrowed his brow.

"'Don't let the bastards grind you down.'"

"Words to live by," he said with a nod. "That's all the Latin you know? I thought you librarian types knew everything."

She lightly smacked his leg with the back of her hand. "We don't know everything. We just know how to find the answers." The second she heard her words, the penny dropped. Quinn sat ramrod straight. "I bet that's what some of Ben's entries on his spreadsheet are about. Maybe he doesn't speak Latin, or at least not well enough to decipher this, so he contacted—or was going to contact—someone who could help him."

"Dudley from Oxford. He was doing what a librarian does. Finding the answers."

Happy to have hopefully solved a small mystery, Quinn squinted at the elaborately decorated initial on the first page of the manuscript. It was a large golden *Q* with tiny gold leaves surrounding it. "I approve of the first letter."

"Of course you do."

James carefully turned the next few pages. Borders of colorful geometric designs were repeated, along with more odd creatures, and some recognizable ones, including a porcupine, an ox, and a snail.

"I'm sure there's a good story behind why a snail battling

a knight would be painted on a manuscript, but I can't figure out what it would be," James said.

When he turned the page again, Quinn said, "Meanwhile, this poor dude is halfway down the gullet of a dragon. That can't feel good." She pointed at the peach-colored structure painted in the margin and said, "There's a tall, skinny castle turret."

James tilted his head to the left and then to the right. "And over here's an ice-cream cone without the ice cream."

"Maybe the illuminator had a geometry test the next day."

He chuckled and turned the page. Surprisingly, it wasn't text, but instead a diagram of seven concentric circles surrounding a yellow orb at the center. Smaller red, blue, and green spheres were painted on the rings. Two of the spheres had C's at their centers, four contained X's, and one had an I.

"Planets, maybe?" she asked. "The solar system? Or at least what they thought it looked like at the time?"

"Looks that way." James turned page after page, each similarly decorated. A man drove several oxen with a train of two covered caravan wagons behind them. Men wielded swords and spears in battle scenes. Portraits of assorted people were painted inside decorated initials. Several miniatures featured what looked to be the same man, an armor-clad knight, in various poses: in supplication before a regally dressed man, astride a horse, alone in a room, and interacting with various men. The manuscript also included a number of crude maps with rivers, mountains, and castles sprinkled throughout. Unfortunately, none of the features on the maps were labeled.

James closed the book. "If Ben saw something important in that, I sure didn't," he said and expelled a loud breath.

"Me either." Quinn scratched her head and stared down at the book.

"Look, Quinn, I have every confidence that you could

decipher this text, and I know how much you'd like to dive into it, but—"

She held up a hand. "But we don't have the time. I completely agree with you. We need help."

"We do. I think right now, your magic librarian skills would be best put to use by tracking down Dudley the Latin scholar."

"On it." She swung her legs off the bed, retrieved her laptop from the room's safe, and jumped back onto the bed in fifteen seconds flat. She flipped open the laptop and rubbed her hands together.

"Here we go," she said, and opened a browser. Starting with the clues from Ben's spreadsheet, she went to World-Cat and searched author Dudley and subject Latin.

"And the winner is . . . Gemma Dudley. She's written a couple of books and some journal articles on Latin, including medieval Latin." After another quick search, she said, "She has a D.Phil from Oxford University and is a member of the Classics Faculty there, specifically Merton College. Here's her phone number. Do you want to call her or should I?" She glanced over at James, who looked like he'd been zapped by a Taser. "What?"

"How did you . . . ?" He pointed toward the bathroom. "I was going to . . . I didn't even get off the bed and you . . ." He smiled and slowly shook his head. "You're amazing."

"I'm nothing special. Lots of people can do what I just did."

"That might be true." His smile softened and when his eyes gazed into hers, she stopped breathing. "But you *are* very special."

The room went still, neither of them moved. Quinn found herself staring trancelike at his lips. She forced her eyes to look back into his. Breathing again, albeit shallowly, she swallowed at the lump knotted in her throat. "So are you," she managed in a whisper.

After what seemed like an eternity to her, he cleared his throat before saying, "You should call her."

Quinn blinked sluggishly a couple of times.

"You should call her," he repeated and licked his lips. "The Latin professor at Oxford."

She ran her fingers through her hair and said, "Right. Um, why me?"

"You have a better grasp on all of this manuscript stuff than I do."

"I'm not sure about that, but okay." She took her phone from her pocket, staring through it as she gathered her thoughts. With considerable effort, she pushed aside the almost kiss and scripted her greeting to Professor Dudley in her mind. She took a deep breath, blew it out in a gust, and dialed the number.

After one ring, she heard a woman's voice say, "This is Gemma Dudley."

"Good afternoon, Professor Dudley. My name is Quinn Riordan. I hope I haven't called at a bad time."

"No, it's fine." Quinn heard caution in the professor's voice. "What can I do for you?"

"I've recently run across what appears to be a medieval manuscript. I was hoping you could help me by looking it over and telling me what it says."

"I assume, then, the text is Latin."

"Yes, and my Latin skills are lacking. To be honest, they're nonexistent."

"I might be able to help you. What makes you think it's medieval?"

"I'm a librarian who enjoys a good mystery and have done some research on it. From the script and illuminations, including a miniature of a knight on horseback, marginalia with some pretty wild grotesques and animals straight from a bestiary, I'm pretty sure it's medieval. At this point, though, the Latin has me stymied."

"Not an uncommon problem." The tightness in the other woman's voice lessened. Apparently, Quinn's liberal use of the manuscript terminology she'd learned earlier in the day had convinced the professor she wasn't a crank.

"With a little more research I discovered you're one of the premier medieval Latin scholars in England. I figured, why not start at the top?"

Professor Dudley chuckled and Quinn heard the woman relax further. "Why not indeed? And, yes, I would be happy to help you. I'm pleased to have an excuse to put off marking this pile of end-of-term exams stacked on my desk. Are you calling from the States?"

"No, I'm here in London. My grandmother died recently." Completely winging it, Quinn widened her eyes and made a face at James. "My husband and I were cleaning out her attic when we found this leather-bound book in a box. Would it be possible for us to come to Oxford and meet with you sometime soon? We'll only be here for a few more days."

"I understand. Let me see." At the professor's pause, Quinn assumed she was reviewing her calendar. "Would dinner this evening be too soon? My husband has a meeting tonight and I find the prospect of eating alone rather dreary."

"Oh," Quinn said, sitting up and looking straight at James. "Dinner tonight"—she paused for a split second, and when James nodded emphatically, said—"would be great. Thank you."

"Wonderful. Shall we meet at a pub called the Eagle and Child?"

Quinn gripped the bedspread to keep from tumbling sideways off the bed. "Did . . . did you say the Eagle and Child?"

"From your reverent tone, I'm given to believe you're familiar with it," Professor Dudley said, clearly amused. "Are you a Tolkien or Lewis fan?"

"Yes. Both. All of the above."

"The Bird and Baby it is. Seven o'clock?"

Quinn mouthed the proposed time to James. He nodded after glancing at his watch. "We'll be there," she said.

"I'll be the woman with the curly, ginger hair."

"I'll be the awestruck blonde and my husband will be the handsome guy trying to stop me from embarrassing myself."

"Brilliant! I look forward to meeting you both," she replied, her smile evident in her voice. "Cheers."

"You too. Good-bye." Quinn tapped the screen and dropped the phone on the bed. "We're having dinner at seven in Oxford with Professor Dudley at a pub called the Eagle and Child."

"This is why it was better for you to make the call," James said. "You were fantastic."

"Thanks," she said and bounced off the bed. She could barely contain her eagerness when she said, "Get a move on, Mr. Riordan. We've got a train to catch."

Chapter Twenty-One

During their hour-long train ride to Oxford, Quinn explained to James the significance of the pub they would be visiting. A group of writers called the Inklings, the most famous of whom were C.S. Lewis and J.R.R. Tolkien, used to meet for lunch at the Eagle and Child. For their fans, it was a place of pilgrimage.

Exiting the train station, they braved the cold and damp weather and walked the half mile to the pub. They were a little early for their dinner appointment, so they ducked into the nearby news shop to pass some time and find warmth. Quinn left James intently studying a car magazine and wandered down another aisle, perusing the array of periodicals. She cupped her frigid hands together and breathed on them, promising herself if she spied a pair of gloves, she'd snap them up.

Quinn ambled over to a rotating display rack filled with cheap Christmas ornaments. She spun it slowly, her gaze drifting absently over the decorations until an especially shiny, metallic one caught her eye. It looked like a copper chicken egg, with the front top half featuring the silver face of an infant. The baby had rounded eyes, an open, gaping mouth, and bright red lips. It appeared to be utterly terrified as it emerged from—or perhaps was trapped in—an alien cocoon.

"Pssst! James!" Quinn hissed and waved him over.

He walked toward her, eyebrows raised in question. When she mutely pointed at the monstrosity, James recoiled. "What the hell is that?" he whispered, face twisting like he'd just swallowed a bug. He hunched forward to get a closer look at the ornament. "I had no idea babies went through a larval stage."

Quinn covered her mouth and shook with silent, uncontrolled giggles. "Maybe alien babies do," she said in a low voice when she finally was able to speak. "I think this is how they travel to Earth, sent by their alien overlords bent on world domination."

His brilliant grin nearly knocked her flat. "And the first thing these evil overlords send is horrifying alien spawn to gain supremacy over Ed's Christmas tree?"

"That's what I'm thinking. Who are we to deny fate? Besides, nothing says Merry Christmas like a nightmarish pupal sprog." She plucked it from the rack and hooked the loop of thick golden thread over her finger. She held it up for them both to admire. "It's perfect."

They approached the cashier, a young woman with her nose deep in a thick paperback copy of *The Brothers Karamazov,* and set the ornament and car magazine on the counter. The cashier glanced down at the items and cried, "Bloody hell! That's a fright." She peeked up at them and shrugged in embarrassment. "No offense."

"No worries," Quinn said. "I'm buying it as a joke for a friend."

"Oh," the young woman said, now smiling as she rang up their purchase. "That's a relief. I mean, to each his own, you know? But that's more than a bit terrifying, isn't it?"

"It is," Quinn answered as she paid for their items. Her treasure now safely wrapped in tissue paper and placed in her purse, she and James wished the young woman a pleasant evening and left the shop.

They were still laughing about their epic find as they approached the entrance to the pub. An oval sign hung from a black wrought-iron arm attached to the wall above the door. It featured an eagle against a blue sky, its wings out-stretched in flight, and carrying a baby slung in a blanket clutched in its talons.

James stopped and faced her. "You okay? You ready for this?"

She fiddled with her wedding rings and nodded.

"Just remember that you're Quinn Riordan and the rest will come naturally. You'll be great."

She nodded again and crossed her arms. "Did you know that pubs put pictures on signs for customers who couldn't read?"

James reached out and rubbed her arm. "I didn't know that, and now I know you're ready." His hand slid down her arm and he intertwined their fingers. As soon as they stepped into the pub his easy demeanor dropped and he shifted into spy mode. He never let go of her hand as they continued weaving farther back into the long, narrow pub.

They came to a small room with a short bar on the right where three men stood waiting to order. Beyond that was a dark timber entryway with a sign attached to the crossbeam. It said RABBIT ROOM.

The room was small—it only sat about ten people—a bench lined one wall with a couple of tables in front of it. Dark wood paneling covered the bottom half of the walls, and small, framed pictures and plaques decorated the plas-ter top half. Quinn would have liked to stop and study the photos, but since there was no red-haired woman in the room, James kept them moving. Quinn knew they weren't on vacation, but that didn't stop her from soaking in the atmosphere.

They walked down another hallway and into a narrow room, stopping for a moment to scan the guests at the tables lining one wall. Still no professor. They pushed on to yet another room beyond.

The room at the back of the pub was obviously a newer addition. The ceiling was glass, the floor was tiled, and the walls were painted brick.

Quinn easily spotted Professor Gemma Dudley at a table against the back wall. Her mane of auburn ringlets was unmistakable. The professor recognized them immediately as well. She smiled, slid out from the bench, and stood. After greetings, introductions, and handshakes were exchanged, James held out a chair for Quinn.

"No, please," Professor Dudley said. "You two sit together. I'm solo tonight. I'll sit there." Before they could argue, she moved her pint of ale to the other side of the wooden table and took the chair.

Quinn knew James preferred to sit where he had full view of a room anyway, so she wasn't about to argue. They removed their coats, scooted across the bench, and settled in. James set his briefcase with the manuscript in it on the floor.

"I hope you don't mind if we sit in this area, Mrs. Riordan. It's not as publike, but it's a little quieter. Unfortunately, it might deprive you of the complete Bird and Baby experience."

"Not at all," Quinn said. "Though I may jump up at some point and gawk at the pictures and plaques on the walls. And please, call me Quinn."

"And James."

"And I insist you call me Gemma."

"It would be an honor, Gemma," Quinn said. "And we

both want to thank you for being so generous with your time. We figured it was a long shot to even speak with you when I called. To be sitting here with you tonight is incredible. So, thank you."

"You're very welcome. I enjoy being able to apply my niche Latin skills in the real world when the opportunity arises. In fact, I was scheduled to meet a man yesterday to look over a manuscript, but he never arrived."

When Quinn flinched at the professor's comment, James rested his hand on her thigh and gently squeezed it.

"That's too bad," he said without missing a beat.

Quinn mentally kicked herself for reacting upon hearing of Ben's probable contact with Professor Dudley. It wasn't exactly smooth spycraft on her part. Time to stay quiet and let the professional handle things.

The conversation was put on hold when their server arrived. All three ordered fish and chips and James ordered a pint of porter. Two minutes later, his pint arrived and after a couple of sips, he nodded in approval. He sat back, crossed his legs, and laid his arm across the top of the back seat cushion behind Quinn. She shifted a little, nestling into his side and the arm that curled around her shoulders. If he was going to sell the happily married couple thing, so would she.

"Before we get too far into this," Gemma said, "I have a caveat. I know quite a bit about manuscripts and have read and studied hundreds. That being said, I am in no way equipped to authenticate, date, or establish the origin. That will require the services of a different kind of expert."

"We understand, right, Quinn?" James gave her an encouraging smile.

"Mmm-hmm." When it became clear he wanted her to continue, her confidence returned. His thumb lazily rubbing a spot on her upper arm wasn't terrible either. "We know it will take some time to date the parchment and assuming it's organic, the ink, too. I'm sure there are experts here at Oxford, but I have a friend at UCLA who can do that, so we'll wait to tackle that when we get home."

"You mentioned you found it amongst your grand-mother's things. She never spoke of it?"

"No. We have a couple of theories." Quinn launched into what she and James cooked up on the train in case her ersatz grandmother was mentioned. "Her father, my great-grandfather, was in France during World War II. We think he might have run across this manuscript and brought home a 'souvenir.'"

"And kept it hidden so no one would know he had a pil-fered manuscript," Gemma supplied.

"Exactly." Quinn smiled up at the server when she set their plates down in front of them. "The much more mun-dane theory is that Grandmamma bought it and for some reason kept it a secret."

Quinn dove into her fish and chips with gusto. The first bite of delicate whitefish with the crunchy coating nearly had her swooning.

"What about your grandfather? Is he still alive to ask?"

"No. He died when I was a baby. My grandmother was an independent sort. She never remarried and took care of herself."

Quinn reached over, picked up James's porter, and took a sip. It was strong and had a bite, yet she detected a hint of sweetness. It was the best beer she'd ever tasted. For a second or two, she regretted not ordering one for herself. But when she remembered that drinking an entire pint would leave her weaving and dizzy, she knew she was better off satisfying her taste buds with an occasional sip from James's glass.

As they ate, they chatted about the weather, Christmas plans, and Gemma's husband the physics professor. Once the dishes were cleared away and they washed their hands of all destructive oils, James removed the manuscript from his briefcase and handed it to Professor Dudley.

Quinn watched the other woman closely as she turned the book over in her hands, examining the cover and then opening to the first page of text. Her green eyes darted back and forth as she read down the page.

After twenty agonizing minutes of watching Gemma turn page after page, her lips occasionally pursed and eyebrows puckered, she finally said, "This is the story of a knight's travels and exploits." She turned to the first page. "This is how it starts, 'The most noble and esteemed son of Johannes,' which is Latin for John," she interjected, "'was strong and well born and called Eugenius.' His name today would be Eugene Johnson."

"Eugene Johnson isn't quite as majestic as Eugenius, son of Johannes, is it?" Quinn said. She relaxed, now that she knew the professor could help them.

"Not really, no," Gemma said with a small smile before she continued reading. "'Born in the new town soon after invaders from the west were vanquished, he was destined to be a great warrior. Unmatched was he in size and bearing and his face did shine like the glorious sun. Eugenius did battle both the hated empire to the west and the infidels of the mountains to the east.'"

"'Infidels . . . to the east,'" Quinn repeated, turning the words over in her mind. "Do you think he was a Crusader?"

"That was my first thought," Gemma answered with a nod. "While he was in the east, he was kidnapped and held captive. Eventually, he made his escape with the help of a sympathetic local. The rest is his exploits from town to town as he journeyed home."

Quinn absently spun the wedding and engagement rings on her finger. "Eugenius must be the knight in the miniatures."

James hummed his agreement. "From what I read, these

kinds of heroic stories weren't uncommon. But I'm under the impression they were usually written in the vernacular so family and friends could read about their great feats. Why Latin?"

"Perhaps to make it appear more regal," Gemma said.

"Are the places where Eugenius, son of Johannes a.k.a. Eugene Johnson, traveled to mentioned specifically?" James asked. "Or any other people? Maybe his parents or a king?"

"That's an odd thing about the text, actually. Usually, these stories are very precise. It's all part of the bragging you mentioned. In this case, however, people and places are only alluded to with opaque descriptions. For instance, rather than saying outright to whom Eugene holds his allegiance, it says he served 'the great lion' and then 'the lion's successors'."

"In one of the miniatures, the knight is depicted kneeling before another man." James said. "Lion in Latin is Leo, right? A king named Leo? Or a duke? Or pope?"

"I know there have been a number of popes with that name," Gemma said.

Quinn squirmed in her seat, her brain buzzing as every synapse fired at once.

James narrowed his eyes at her. "I recognize that look."

"If we assume Eugene was a Crusader," Quinn said, practically vibrating with exhilaration, "we might be able to figure out which Crusade it was if there was a pope, king or duke Leo, Leon, or Leopold, something like that, involved. That would give us an approximate time when Eugene lived." She bolted upright and her eyes burned with inspiration. "Oh! Richard the Lionheart." She fought the urge to whip out her phone and start her research right there at the table. What she missed was the amused look that passed between James and Gemma.

"What about the places?" James asked. "That would help narrow it down, too."

Gemma skimmed several pages of the manuscript. "Here's one that's wonderfully vague. There's a place called 'blizzard village.'"

"'Blizzard village'? That's helpful," Quinn said sarcastically and slumped back. She touched her fingertip to her lips as she contemplated various scenarios. "Maybe he got trapped in a huge snowstorm on top of the Alps on his way to or from the Middle East." More to herself than her tablemates, she said, "He went east instead of west and ended up in the Himalayas. 'Wrong Way Eugene.'"

While Quinn ruminated, James took a notepad and pen from his briefcase and slid them across the table. "Could you write down all of the descriptive Latin phrases for the people and places, their translations and the pages where they're located for us? Quinn can take it from there. Her tenacity is second only to her intelligence. She'll figure it out."

"No doubt," Gemma said. "I can see the steam billowing from her ears." For the next thirty minutes she wrote down the requested information. While they waited, Quinn and James shared the rest of his pint and quietly chatted about their research plan of attack.

When Gemma finished, she set the pen down and pushed the paper back to James and Quinn. "Obviously, the pages in the manuscript aren't numbered, so I referenced them by their folio number, then recto and verso." To demonstrate, she turned to the third leaf in the book. She held the page straight up gripped between her thumb and forefinger. "This is folio three, or f. 3." She pointed at the front of the sheet, and said, "Recto, written f. 3r," and then the back. "Verso."

"F. 3v," Quinn said.

"Precisely." Gemma closed the book, refastened the

clasps, and handed it back to James. He promptly returned it to his briefcase.

"We can't thank you enough for your help," Quinn said. She leaned into James and whispered, "We should pay her a consultation fee."

"You'll do no such thing." The razor-sharp tone warned Quinn that arguing would be an exercise in futility.

"Okay," James said. "But please let us pay for your dinner."

"That I will allow. Thank you. You can also repay me by letting me know what you learn about the manuscript." She handed Quinn a business card she'd retrieved from her bag.

"You can count on it," Quinn replied and tucked the card away in her pocket.

Their business now concluded and the hour growing late, James said, "We really should get going. Can we walk you to wherever you're headed next, Gemma?"

"Thank you, but that's not necessary. My husband is coming here to collect me when his meeting is over, which should be any moment now." She paused and considered first Quinn and then James. "I hope you'll forgive me if I speak out of turn. But I have to say this. When you look at Quinn, James, I see in your face the same enthralled, amused, and bemused expression I've seen in my husband's for the past thirty-two years. Therefore, it is with good authority that I tell you your life with Quinn will never be dull." She narrowed her eyes and added, "But you already know that."

James nodded. "I can honestly say it's been a nonstop adventure since the day I met her."

"I could say the same thing about you," Quinn said, bumping him with her shoulder. Her stomach fluttered as they held each other's gaze for a brief moment.

James smiled and then glanced at his watch. "We'd better get going. If we hurry, we can catch the next train." He tossed enough pound notes on the table to adequately cover the tab. All three stood and shook hands again, then Quinn and James offered Gemma a final thanks and farewell.

They walked through the maze of rooms toward the front door. Quinn was happy when they stopped here and there long enough to look at the displayed Inklings memorabilia.

Out on the sidewalk, the chill in the air penetrated Quinn's overcoat like it was made not from wool, but from a thin layer of gauze. She turned up her collar to combat the cold.

"It's a bit nippy." James looked up and down the mostly deserted street and frowned. "I should have called a taxi." He turned and started back toward the pub. "I'll do it now. We can go back inside and wait."

Quinn gripped the sleeve of his coat and tugged, stopping him. "No, let's walk. We don't know how long it will take to get here and we don't want to miss the next train. Besides, if we walk fast, the exertion will keep us warm."

"You sure?"

"Yes. Now come on." Quinn turned on her heel, lowered her head, and marched off at a brisk clip. James jogged to catch up and then fell in step.

After walking for a couple of minutes, James put his arm around Quinn's waist and pulled her close to his side. He steered her toward a brick wall to their right.

"What are you doing?" she asked.

He didn't answer. When they reached the wall, he turned her toward him, lowered his head, and kissed her. It wasn't a chaste peck on the lips, but a full-mouthed go-big-or-go-home kind of kiss. It all happened so fast, and she was so startled by it, for a second her brain went numb. When it kicked in again, her body was already fully engaged, kissing him back. Any thought of "this is opening a big ol' can of worms" that tried to edge into her consciousness was beaten back by the sensation of his lips, his body pressed against hers. She slipped both arms under his open overcoat and around his waist and melted into him.

James broke their kiss, but kept his face only inches from hers. His smile was slow and sexy and his voice was deep in his chest when he said, "I've wanted to do that for a while." He cupped the side of her face with his hand and brushed her cheek with his thumb. "I finally found the perfect excuse." He closed the gap again and grazed her lips with his.

It was a good thing she was trapped between James and the wall. Otherwise, she would have crumpled to the sidewalk in a heap. "Excuse?" Why were they talking when they could be kissing?

"Mmm-hmm. I needed to be sure, and the only way to know was for us to stop walking. Once the idea of stopping to kiss you came to me, I couldn't think of anything else."

Her brain had turned to oatmeal, so it wasn't a big shock she had no idea what he was talking about. She searched his face, mostly hidden in the shadow cast from the glow of the street lamp behind him. "Be sure about what?"

His head turned a fraction when his eyes pegged all the way to the right. "Don't look and don't panic." His gaze returned to her and he gave her a swift, yet incredibly sensual kiss. "But we're being followed."

Chapter Twenty-Two

One minute James's warm kisses had curled Quinn's toes, and the next she was ice cold with dread when he informed her they were being followed by an unknown stalker. "What?" she asked in a strangled whisper. Her head jerked, but she refrained from whipping it around to scope out their tail.

"There's a guy behind us. I'll explain it all later, but right now you have to do exactly as I say."

Her stomach tightened. "Okay." She kissed him again and hoped it conveyed the confidence she had in him.

Based on his smile, she could tell he received her message loud and clear. When they started walking up the sidewalk again, he appeared to be helping her stay warm by wrapping her in the left side of his coat and keeping her snuggled to his side. Her arm remained under his coat and around his waist. "Unholster my Sig and hold it by my hip."

"Okay."

She kept her gaze fixed on the glowing stoplight at the intersection ahead and lifted the hem of his shirt. When her frigid fingers brushed against his warm skin, he grimaced. "Sorry. My hand is cold."

"No worries." He hugged her closer and kissed the side of her head. Was it for her benefit or the guy behind them?

That would have to be sorted out later. She curled three fingers around the grip, gave it a tug, and lifted the pistol from the holster. Careful to keep her index finger away from the trigger, she pointed the barrel down and off to the side, away from James's body.

"Got it."

"Good. And thank you for not shooting me in the ass." She knew he was kidding, but she didn't miss the slight strain in his voice.

Despite their dangerous circumstances, a number of highly inappropriate responses regarding James's backside flooded her brain. She judiciously pushed them aside and instead replied with a simple "Mmm-hmm."

"If he runs up to us before we get to the corner up ahead—"

"He'll wish he hadn't." Amped up on a gallon or so of adrenaline and the lingering effect of James's kisses, she knew she could put a bullet in their stalker without breaking a sweat.

"Once we're around the corner, give me the Sig and you take the briefcase. Then go find a doorway or a pillar or something to hide behind. Got it?"

"I want to be there to help if you need me."

"I know you do, but I've got this." He looked down at her, his eyes pleading. "I need you safe. I can't bear to lose—"

"You won't." As she uttered the words, though, she realized as much as she wanted to help, she couldn't allow her actions to distract him or cloud his judgment. She needed him to be safe, too. "I'll hide."

His anxiety faded and determination settled over his features. "Thank you."

Quinn's senses sharpened as they reached the corner

building. They turned the corner, stopped, and switched briefcase and gun.

"Go."

She scanned the area for a place to hide. The wall ran another twenty yards down the sidewalk to two squat pillars marking the entrance to a courtyard. That was exactly where James would want her to go, but she rejected it as too far from him. The same went for the hotel across the street. She eyed another spot, an offset in the wall of the stone foundation. It wasn't much, but it would do. She raced to the niche, wedged herself into it, and flattened herself against the wall.

The rough texture of the stone scraped at the back of her head. She stared up at the sky and controlled her breathing. Fifteen feet to her left, James had his back pressed against the wall. He ratcheted back the slide of the Sig, chambering a round and waited to pounce on their stalker.

First she heard a grunt, then an "oof" accompanied by the sound of a body slamming against the wall. Quinn peeked around the edge of the stone. In the shadows, she could just make out the dark form of a man pinned to the wall with James's forearm on his throat. Edward Walker was a Girl Scout compared to James.

"Why are you following us?" James's growl was feral and frightening.

"I'm not," came the strangled reply.

"Yes, you are. When we stopped, you stopped. Why are you following us?"

When he didn't answer, James rammed his knee into the guy's gut. He gagged and coughed.

"This is your last chance. Why are you following us?"

"I was at the Bird and Baby and saw you with an old book. I reckoned I'd nick it from you and sell it for a few quid. That's all."

"I don't like it when people lie to me, mate." James shoved the muzzle of the Sig against the man's cheek. "Try again."

Quinn heard a click when James cocked the pistol's hammer back. "I've got all night," he said, adding more pressure to the man's throat. The guy clutched wildly at James as he fought for breath. "You, on the other hand, have got thirty seconds."

Unintelligible noises came from the stalker.

"You're going to tell me the truth this time?" He eased up at the nod. "Talk."

The guy sucked in a rasping lungful of air before croaking, "You're barking."

"And you're dead."

The finality of James's words did it. "It was my uncle," he blurted. "He rang me and said he'd pay me to follow that professor lady around."

"Why?"

"I don't know."

James lowered his shoulder and rammed it into the stalker's chest. "Why?"

He expelled a weak groan. "I don't know. I swear."

Quinn believed him. James must have, too, since he dropped the question and asked, "When did he call you?"

"This past Sunday."

"What exactly did he tell you to do?"

"Follow the bird around. If she met up with anyone, I was to follow them to wherever they went and report back to him."

"Why you?"

"I do odd jobs for him sometimes. My mum's always on him to help me pick up a few quid."

"What's his name? Your uncle."

Silence.

"What's his name?"

After another bout of choking, he said, "Maltman. Hamish Maltman."

"Who does he work for?"

"I dunno. Some bloke by the name of Fitzgerald, Fitzroy. Something like that."

Quinn felt the blood drain from her face.

"Did you tell him you saw us?" The fury in James's voice had turned to panic.

Silence.

James grabbed a fistful of the stalker's jacket, jerked him away from the wall, and slammed him against it. "Does he know about us?"

"Yeah." Despite the abuse he was taking, Quinn could hear the sneer in his voice. "I sent him a few snaps of the both of you from my phone." He turned his head and spat on the pavement. "You're a lucky bastard. That blonde you were snogging back there. She's a looker. I wouldn't mind taking a turn—"

James smashed him in the face with a fist. The guy crumpled to the sidewalk.

Quinn bolted from her hiding place and sprinted over to James. "Are you okay?"

"Yeah." He decocked his pistol and returned it to its holster. "We gotta secure this punk and get out of here." He glanced up and down the street, weighing their options.

She looked down at their stalker. He was a skinny kid with light brown hair that looked like it had been cut with a weed whacker. She guessed he wasn't more than twenty.

"I think you busted his nose," she said. Quinn had the feeling the bend in it hadn't been there a minute before.

"Yeah, well, he's lucky that's all I busted." James knelt down and rifled through the pockets of the kid's jeans. He left the ring of keys but took the flick knife and dropped it in his coat pocket. James hauled him over onto his stomach, took his wallet from his back pocket, and checked his ID. "Ethan Burns, London."

In his other pocket was an Oyster card, a train ticket, and his phone. "He took the train from Paddington this morning and got here around nine. That part of his story checks out." James stuffed the ticket and card back in his pocket and clicked on the phone. It was locked. After shoving it back into Ethan's pocket, he jerked his head toward the courtyard and asked, "Can you help me drag him over there?"

"Yeah. He doesn't look very heavy." She knelt on the other side of Ethan and followed James's lead by hunching over, draping a limp arm around her neck, and gripping his wrist. When James counted to three, they stood. She was right. The kid was a flyweight.

Ethan's chin hung to his chest and his feet dragged behind him as they lugged him down the sidewalk. The black wrought-iron gate into the courtyard was locked, so they dumped him in the dark corner where the fence was secured to a short pillar.

James opened his briefcase and took from it a pair of disposable zip-tie handcuffs. He stuck Ethan's hands through the fence on either side of one of the metal posts and tightened the cuffs around his wrists. Ethan wasn't going anywhere.

Before standing, James took the small pistol from his ankle holster, pointed it at Ethan's thigh, and pulled the trigger. A tranquilizer dart stuck up from his leg. "We don't want him waking up and making noise before his ride comes." He grabbed the briefcase and jumped to his feet. "Let's go."

As they walked at a near jog away from Ethan, James took his phone from his pocket, stabbed at the screen with his thumb, and placed a call. "Homefront, this is Buffalo Bill," he said, and rattled off a string of letters and numbers. "I have a guest who needs an escort to our resort. I'd like him to have the full spa package. Pickup location is the front gate of the Ashmolean Museum. Also need feeds scrubbed from that intersection and a covert protection detail for Dr. Gemma Dudley. Annie Oakley and I are on our way back to the ranch. Full report to follow." After a brief pause, he said, "Roger that. Out."

He looked over at Quinn. "We need to catch that train. Are you up for double time?"

"Always. Just don't make me chant any cadences."

"Next time," he said as they set off.

It felt good to move and not think, to concentrate on her breathing and the sound of their boots on the sidewalk. Soon enough, her head would be flooded with questions and attempts to sort through the implications of everything that had happened that evening. Until then, she'd run.

A few minutes later, they arrived at the train station, warm and panting from exertion. They walked straight onto the nearly empty platform to wait. James's gaze flicked from face to face to door to bench to shadow, never resting on anything for more than a few seconds.

Quinn found herself noticing every movement and every sound, too. What if Fitzhugh had sent men to intercept them? The idea of a shootout at the Oxford station made her a bit woozy.

Fortunately, they only had to wait a few minutes before their train arrived. They boarded the last carriage. James led them past the compartment's only other occupants—a couple of amorous teenagers—to the very back row of seats. That way, no one could come up on them from behind. Quinn took the window seat and James sat on the aisle.

When the train pulled away from the station, James relaxed, but only slightly. She knew he would remain extravigilant until they were safely back in their hotel room.

"Do we need to move to a different hotel?" she asked.

"At this point, that's not necessary. Fitzhugh will recognize me as someone who stole from him. He knows I—we—are in

England now, but he can't possibly know where we're staying. And no one else is trailing us now."

"Are you sure? One of Fitzhugh's men would be better at it than that little snot Ethan."

He bristled. "I know when someone is shadowing me."

"I'm sorry. I didn't mean . . ." She closed her eyes and rubbed her hands over her face, fighting to maintain her composure. Her throat tightened and she could barely speak when she whispered, "Never mind."

His head bowed and he heaved a sigh. "I'm sorry." He slipped an arm around her shoulders and gently drew her close. "I shouldn't have taken that personally. Of course you're concerned that we're still being followed."

She shifted, turning a little to nestle into his embrace. "It's okay. It's been a really long day."

"It has."

Neither seemed interested in discussing manuscripts or Latin or Crusaders. There would be plenty of time for that when they returned to London. Instead, they rode in comfortable silence. The movement of the train and the steady rise and fall of James's chest calmed her.

Quinn's mind wandered until it tripped over something she'd heard him say earlier. "James?"

"Hmm?"

She turned her head and looked up at him. "Why are you Buffalo Bill?"

His crooked smile nearly did her in. When she realized her lips were only a couple of inches from his jaw and all she could think of was kissing him, she forced herself to face forward again.

"I graduated from the University of Colorado in Boulder," he said.

"That's where you're from? Colorado?"

He nodded. "A Denver suburb."

Quinn sat forward and twisted to look at him. "Wait a

second. The waitress when we went to dinner in Santa Monica. Molly. She really did recognize you, didn't she? She said something about Colorado."

With an embarrassed grimace, he answered, "Yeah. I think she was in one of my classes at CU."

"That's pretty funny that she knew you after all." She settled against him again. "Buffalo Bill. Please continue."

"Right." He shifted so that her shoulders were solidly resting against his chest. "CU's mascot is the Buffaloes. Some genius at the agency thought it would be hilarious to call me Buffalo."

"Not Ralphie?"

"Of course you would know the name of the actual buffalo that runs across the football field," he said, chuckling. "And yes, Ralphie was floated. I got them to compromise and call me Buffalo Bill. It helped I could claim there's a Buffalo Bill museum not too far from where I grew up."

"I think buffaloes are pretty majestic, although technically they're bison."

"Of course you know that, too. Also, they're shaggy and smell bad."

"Yeah, there's that. I guess I'm Annie Oakley because she was in Buffalo Bill's Wild West Show?"

"Mmm-hmm, but it's mostly because I bragged about your gun-handling skills in a report, and word got around fast."

She looked up at him again. "People at the agency know about me?" Of course Aldous Meyers, James's superior, knew about her, as did the brass that had approved of her accompanying James to England. It was weird to think that she'd shown up on anyone else's radar.

"They do."

"But you've never even seen me fire a weapon. I might be a terrible shot."

He snorted. "You may not be able to do all the trick shots

Annie Oakley did, but you're still the daughter of a Marine, a Marine who taught you how to shoot."

"True." Mollified, she faced forward again.

An easy quiet fell over them. Now that the adrenaline was gone, she felt like a wrung-out dish towel. She stared trancelike out the window at the darkness.

"Quinn?"

"Hmm?"

"We need to talk about what happened earlier."

"You'll have to be a little more specific than that."

He sighed. "You're not going to make this easy for me, are you?"

"No."

"Fine. I mean when we stopped and I kissed you."

"Ah."

"Maybe I should have handled it differently. It's just that I knew I'd only get one chance to make a first impression and I wanted to make a good one."

Heat crawled up her neck and spread across her cheeks. "Yeah, um, you definitely did that. Made a good first impression, I mean."

"That's good to know. And in case you were wondering, so did you."

Now her entire head flamed hot. She wondered if he noticed the crimson scalp under her blond hair. "I'm glad."

"But as amazing as it was, the thing is—"

"We need to put the brakes on. We're deep into this op and need to stay focused." Not to mention the temptation of engaging in a hot and heavy make-out session in a hotel room.

"Yeah. Are you okay with stepping back to where we were three hours ago?"

"Sure, as long as you and me sitting like this is okay."

"This is definitely okay." After a moment, he said, "Who knows? If we're lucky, maybe we'll be followed again soon."

She giggled. "Fingers crossed." She fiddled with a button of her overcoat and said, "It's too bad you're sure we don't have someone tailing us right now."

He rumbled a low growl and his arm squeezed her tight. "You know, now that you mention it, I'm not so sure after all. I think those teenagers a few rows up turned around and looked at us a minute ago."

She was pretty sure they had never once even come up for air. That wouldn't stop her from playing along, though. "They do look pretty dangerous."

His lips grazed her ear when he whispered, "We need to take evasive action in the face of this credible threat."

Every inch of her body tingled. "Who am I to argue with a professional?" She twisted, slipped her hand behind his neck, and pressed her lips to his. Their first kiss had been unexpected and confusing and powerful. The deliberate, slow burn of this kiss was equally thrilling.

The urge to intensify it swelled. She angled her head and deepened the kiss.

The arms cinched around her rolled her body into his.

His mouth slid from hers and left a trail of kisses along her jawbone to her ear. He kissed the sensitive spot behind her earlobe and smiled against her skin when she softly purred.

She was so engulfed by James she didn't notice when the train stopped at the next station.

The doors slid open and at the first sound of boisterous laughter, James tensed and lifted his head. She looked up and watched the four twentysomething men who boarded flop into seats three rows ahead.

James shot Quinn an apologetic smile. "Duty calls." His eyes darted between her to the new passengers.

"I understand."

He made no move to release her from his embrace and

she had no intention of pulling away. She rested her head on his shoulder.

An unexpected sense of peace fell over her. Perhaps it came from the knowledge they were safe, if only for a little while, isolated on a train rolling across the dark English countryside. Perhaps it was the security of knowing a highly skilled CIA operative watched over her. Perhaps it was knowing the man she cared for deeply felt the same way about her. Whatever the reason, she embraced the momentary tranquility, closed her eyes, and drifted off to sleep.

Chapter Twenty-Three

The train jerked to a stop. Quinn woke, lifted her head, and groaned.

James rubbed her back. "Come on, sunshine. We're at Paddington. Time to go."

She yawned and rubbed her eyes. She grabbed her bag, exited into the aisle behind James, and stumbled along toward the open doors.

They strode away from the train and toward the escalators to the Underground. James went into full spy mode again, his body tense and his gaze continuously sweeping the area as they walked. Quinn found herself doing the same, scanning the station, taking mental snapshots of the faces they encountered and noting the different escape routes available in any given area.

Once they were speeding along in the Tube, Quinn finally spoke. "Level with me, James."

He glanced at her, eyebrows lowered.

"Did I snore?"

He smiled. "Nah, although you were breathing pretty loud."

"Kill me now," she groaned and dropped her head back against the window with a clunk.

"Don't worry. I enjoyed being your pillow."

"I have to admit getting a nap in was nice," she answered. "So we start on the manuscript as soon as we get back to the hotel?"

"Not exactly. After I write up a quick report and check to make sure our friend Ethan got a ride to the resort, I'm going to work on the manuscript. You're going to bed."

"What?" Her head snapped toward his. "That's crap."

"It's not crap," he replied evenly. "It's been an incredibly long day and you need to get some sleep."

"Yeah, and I will. Eventually. But right now, we need to figure out what's going on with that manuscript and it needs to happen sooner rather than later."

"Right. That's what I'm going to do." He was clearly baffled as to why she was so animated.

"So am I." She ground her teeth. "I'm not eight, James. I'm a grown woman. I take care of myself—have been for years now. I don't need you to tell me when to go to bed."

He stared up at the ceiling and blew out a breath in exasperation. "I understand that. I'm just looking out for you."

"I know. And I'm telling you that's my job, not yours." The edge in her tone was sharp.

He crossed his arms over his chest and practically drilled a hole in the floor where he pinned his glare.

The announcement came over the loudspeaker informing them they were approaching Earl's Court.

The second the doors slid open, Quinn stomped out of the car and charged full steam ahead toward the stairs and the way out. James loped up next to her and gripped her by the elbow. She stiffened, but allowed him to bring her to a stop. When they started to walk at a normal pace, he said, "You're right. I was out of line telling you what to do and I'm sorry. I'll try not to do it again. But I won't stop looking out for your physical safety."

Her stomach dropped. She glanced up at him, his face

strained and his eyes darting about. In her irritation, she'd blindly stormed off, completely unaware of her surroundings. Chagrined, she replied with a soft, "Okay. I'm sorry, too. I wake up grumpy from naps."

"It's okay."

Although they walked in silence, the tension between them had dissipated. By the time they hurried up the marble steps at the front of the hotel hand in hand, rain had begun to spit down.

Once they were safe in their room, Quinn hung up her coat, grabbed her CIA-issue pajamas, and changed in the bathroom. She wasn't going to bed yet, but she might as well be comfortable.

She tossed her clothes on top of her suitcase, removed her laptop from the safe, and made her way across the mattress. She rearranged the pile of pillows behind her, settled back, and opened the computer.

Taking a cue from Quinn, James rifled through his suitcase, snagged some clothes, and marched to the bathroom. A couple of minutes later, he emerged wearing a pair of plaid flannel pajama bottoms dotted with brown moose, and a long-sleeved T-shirt.

She looked up and grinned.

"Don't start with me," he said and dumped his dirty clothes in his suitcase. "I didn't pick them."

She held her hands up as if in surrender. "I didn't say a word. Honestly? I think they're pretty adorable."

He smiled. "I can live with that." He took the manuscript and Professor Dudley's notes from his briefcase and handed them to Quinn. Then he set up his secure computer on the desk, sat down, and got to work.

She bubbled with anticipation as she reviewed the notes. She had no idea how any of the information there or in the manuscript could possibly connect to Yevgeni Dobrynin, Ben Hadley, Roderick Fitzhugh, or a stash of hidden weapons.

Still, it seemed Ben had given the manuscript special scrutiny. She was bound and determined to figure out why.

She thought through her search strategy. She decided to start with "*Eugenius filius de Johannes*" and go from there. That exact phrase returned nothing in her first search. Removing the quotation marks garnered links to a few ancient charters with the names Eugenius and Johannes sprinkled throughout, but nothing helpful. She decided to search the research databases available through the Westside Library. There, she found an interesting journal article about the papal patronage of musicians. She also learned there had been a number of popes named Eugenius, the fourth and last was elected in 1431. Had Eugenius been the pope, and not Leo as they originally surmised? From the text Gemma translated, there was little chance that Eugenius had been a pope.

She switched gears and decided to see what she could learn about the popes named Leo. The first was called Leo the Great, which tracked with the exact words in the text of the manuscript. The problem was he lived much too early to be connected with any of the Crusades. She didn't dismiss him, though. Eugenius being tied to a Crusade was just a hunch. They could be wrong.

Quinn opened a blank text document and made some notes about Leo the Great. More research revealed the second Leo was only pope for a couple of years. The third was noteworthy because he'd crowned Charlemagne emperor in 800. While interesting, it didn't seem pertinent to her search.

The fourth Leo had a problem with the "Saracens," a synonym for "Muslims" in medieval Latin literature. He warranted a closer look. She made a note and moved on.

Poor Leo V, upon becoming pope, was almost immediately tossed in prison by an antipope. He wouldn't have had anyone bowing before him, so she moved on. Leo VI hadn't even made it a full year as pope before he died, and Leo VII's fate wasn't much different than the previous two Leos. His papacy only lasted three years. She snickered when she read what the article said about the unofficial circumstances surrounding his death.

James twisted in his chair and gave her a look. "What are you snickering at?"

"Rumor has it the seventh Pope Leo died of a heart attack while, ah"—an eyebrow rose suggestively—"his mistress rode the papal bull."

He busted up laughing and shook his head. "Not the most pious way to go, is it?"

"It's really not."

He turned back toward his computer and said, "Bet they were never able to wipe the smile off his face."

Quinn beamed.

"Nice research, by the way," he said, his tone playful.

"Hey!" she replied in mock offense. "I don't go looking for this stuff. I go where the trail takes me."

"Uh-huh."

She was tempted to bean him with a pillow, but they'd decided to keep it professional—she chalked up their make-out session on the train as a momentary, albeit spine-tingling, lapse—so her only retort was a mild "Uh-huh."

Quinn sat straight, raised her arms up over her head, and twisted her torso first one way and then the other. Then she hunched forward and elongated her upper body similar to the way she'd seen Rasputin do it a thousand times. When she got back to L.A., even if she had to take out a loan, she'd spring for her and Nicole to get massages.

She flopped back against the pillows and found the duet of James tapping on his computer keys and the rain pelting the window to be rather soothing. She couldn't allow herself to get too complacent, however. There was still a mystery to solve.

Back to the popes, Leo VIII was another with an incredibly short papacy, so she moved on to Leo IX. German by birth, he eventually ended up a hostage in southern Italy after a defeat by Norman mercenaries. The manuscript indicated that Eugenius had been held captive as well, so maybe there was a connection with this Leo. She typed up her musings and kept at it.

She skimmed the entries for the rest of the Leos. Other than the pope who'd contended with both Martin Luther and Henry VIII, nothing was especially noteworthy.

Now finished with the popes, she reviewed her notes. Seven on her list warranted closer inspection if the rest of her research was a bust.

She mentally changed lanes and decided it was time to find out more about Richard the Lionheart. She really hoped to stumble across a Eugenius, son of Johannes, who had gone crusading with him.

She went back to the encyclopedia in the reference database and started reading the article on Richard I of England. When she got to the section about the various attempts by Richard's parents to arrange a politically advantageous marriage for him, Quinn's eyelids drooped and the words swam on the screen. She checked the clock. It was 1:30.

"I'm so fried I can't see straight," she told James. She closed her laptop and set it on the nightstand. "My brain is mush and I'm afraid I might miss something."

He turned and asked, "Will it bother you if I don't come to bed right away? I have a little more work to do."

A shiver raced through her. She knew what he meant. But his question sounded so routine, like they were an actual married couple who usually went to bed together every night. She slid off the bed and fussed with the covers. "No. That's fine."

His gaze remained on her while she rearranged her pillows. "How's the Leo research going?"

"I have about a half dozen on my list of suspects. I also might be on to something with Richard the Lionheart. During his traipsing about on the Third Crusade, he got into a spat with Leopold V, Duke of Austria. He imprisoned Richard in Dürnstein Castle for a while."

"It checks the 'held captive' box. And Austria has plenty of places that could be called a 'blizzard village.'"

"That's my thinking, too." She slipped under the covers and switched off the lamp. "I'll dig into it again in the morning."

"I have no doubt of that." The pale glow of James's computer illumined his smile. "Good night, Quinn."

"Good night." She was out the moment her head hit the pillow.

Quinn woke in the exact same position she'd fallen asleep six hours before. She became aware of the steady breathing from the other side of the bed, flipped over, and found James asleep, lying on his side with his back to her. He was actually under the covers this time.

She allowed herself to enjoy the moment. The warmth, the quiet intimacy—waking up next to James was something she could definitely get used to. At the same time, it stirred in her physical longing. The memory of their heated kisses the night before sent warmth spreading through her body. She yearned to breach the space between them, to roll him on his back and crawl atop him and kiss him senseless and . . .

She drew in a sharp breath. Her mind and body had led her deep into dangerous territory. She couldn't go any further.

"Keep it professional, Quinn," she whispered and abandoned the bed.

She peeked through a crack in the curtains. The world outside was wet, gray, and dreary. It was just as well they would most likely be spending the day indoors trying to unlock the mysteries of the manuscript.

She grabbed some clean clothes and stole a glance at the still-sleeping James on her way to the bathroom. At the flare of heat, she realized her shower would have to be on the colder side. By the time she left the bathroom, she'd wrestled her thoughts away from James, mostly anyway, and on her research. And to preserve this frame of mind now that he was awake, she studiously reviewed her notes while James showered and readied.

After a quick breakfast together, Quinn reassumed her position on the bed with her computer perched on her lap. James mirrored her, the open manuscript on his. Gemma Dudley's notes sat on the bed between them.

While James scrutinized the illuminations and maps, Quinn stared at her laptop screen, deep in thought. She still had plenty of research to do regarding Richard the Lionheart, but something had occurred to her at breakfast. They'd assumed the term "great lion" meant the name Leo or some variation of it. But she didn't know what Eugenius meant.

With this new tact in mind, she opened a browser and searched "Eugenius name meaning." She clicked on one of the links and read what she already knew. It was the Latin form of Eugene. She read further and learned it came from the Greek word "*eugenes*" which meant "well born." She remembered hearing Gemma read those very words in the opening text.

She sighed in frustration, not having learned anything new. She was about to click the tab closed when a name on the page caught her eye. She cocked her head and stared at it. There was a nearly audible click in her mind when the puzzle pieces fell into place. To test her theory, she typed the name John into the search box at the top of the page. When she saw the results, a prickly sensation crawled over her scalp. She managed to keep her tone measured when she said, "James?"

He turned a page in the manuscript and didn't look up. "Hmm?"

"Dobrynin. The Soviet general. Was his middle name Ivanovich? Or maybe his father's name was Ivan? Maybe both?"

"I don't remember. Let me check his file." He bounded off the bed, grabbed his laptop, and returned to his spot. After a half minute of typing, he narrowed his eyes. "How did you know his middle name was Ivanovich?"

"Because Ivan is the Russian form of John."

"Right, and Ivanovich means son of Ivan. That doesn't answer my question. How did you know that was Dobrynin's middle name?"

"Because a Russian form of Eugene is Yevgeni."

James's eyes widened.

"I think Eugenius, son of Johannes, is Yevgeni Ivanovich Dobrynin."

Chapter Twenty-Four

Quinn and James sat on the bed and stared at each other, completely dumbfounded. Had she really connected the manuscript directly to Yevgeni Dobrynin?

She picked up the manuscript and turned the pages. "This is going to sound crazy, but I remember reading somewhere a lot of times the person who commissioned a manuscript would have a miniature of themselves inserted into it somewhere. Do you have a picture of Dobrynin?"

"Yep." James tapped at the keyboard and swiveled the laptop so she could see the black-and-white photo on the screen. Broad-faced and scowling, Dobrynin glared at the camera from under caterpillar eyebrows.

She located the miniature of the knight supplicating himself before his liege and held up the book next to the screen for easy comparison. He had the same dark hair combed straight back and the same thick eyebrows. "He's the knight."

Inspiration flamed in James's eyes. He started typing. "Find that initial with the noblewoman in the middle of it."

"On it." Quinn flipped to the page and when she compared the woman in the large, fancy letter with the one James called up on the screen, she said, "Holy crap! It's the same woman. Who is she?"

"Dobrynin's wife, Svetlana."

Quinn felt like she was about to come out of her skin. "Who's the guy Dobrynin's kneeling in front of? The 'great lion'? Leo? Leopold? Leon?"

"In Russian, it'd be Leonid."

They looked at each other and at the same time said, "Leonid Brezhnev."

James checked his computer. "Dobrynin was born in Novgorod in 1947 and joined the army in 1965."

Quinn had already pulled up information on the former Soviet supreme leader on her laptop. "Brezhnev came to power in 1964." She looked at James. "His loyalty was to Brezhnev, and then 'the lion's successors'."

"He was born in 1947." His voice grew more excited when he quoted the manuscript. "'Soon after the invaders from the west were vanquished.'"

"The Germans in World War II." She tilted her head in thought. "You think the 'hated empire to the west' is the U.S. during the Cold War?"

"Yeah, although I wouldn't be surprised if he lumped all of Western Europe in there. He also fought in Afghanistan."

She nodded. "'The infidels of the mountains to the east.' Let me guess. He was captured at one point and escaped?"

"Yeah." James covered his face with his hands and his head thumped against the headboard when it fell back. "Oh God, Quinn. I'm such an idiot. I'd read Dobrynin's file. I should have picked up on the parallels right away."

"You're not an idiot and why would you have picked up on the parallels?" She pulled a hand away from his face and held it with both of hers. "A twentieth-century Soviet general has his life story written so that he comes off as some random Crusader knight running around Europe in the Middle Ages. The story is scribed onto parchment in medieval Latin using all kinds of vague imagery and then turned into a manuscript, complete with authentic-looking illuminations and a wood-and-leather cover. Of course you wouldn't assume the story was about Dobrynin." Incredulous, she added, "Who even does that? It's insane."

James bolted upright and blurted, "Novgorod."

"What?"

His eyes were wild, like a mad scientist about to reanimate the dead. "Novgorod. Dobrynin was born there. It literally means 'new city' in Russian."

"Yeah? So?"

"They didn't use Novgorod in the manuscript, they used the literal translation of it instead. If they used Novgorod, we would have known he was Russian right away."

"Okay," she said slowly.

"What if they did the same thing for all of the places mentioned? Do you remember when we were driving to LAX and were looking for clues in the letter? You had the idea that maybe Summerfield should be translated into Russian." He jabbed his finger at Professor Dudley's list. "Right idea, wrong document."

"Blizzard village," she said. "What's that in Russian?"

"Blizzard is '*buran*.' Add the suffix either '*ovo*' or '*ovka*' and that makes it village or town."

"Got it." Mentally crossing her fingers, she opened a map website and as she began to type '*Buranovo*' into the search box, that very word appeared as a suggestion. She clicked on it and when the little red flag appeared on the map, she stared in disbelief. "It's a town in Russia, about five hundred miles or so due east of Novgorod." Unblinking, she gazed at James and said in awe, "Holy smokes. I think we figured it out."

"I think so, too." He picked up the notepad and put his finger under the next entry. "'Great John's Town.' Try '*Bolshoi Ivanovo*.'"

She typed it into the search box. "It wants it to be spelled with a 'y.' Either way, nothing."

He frowned and thought for a moment. "Okay, try '*Bolshaya*.'"

"How does '*Bolshaya Ivanovka*' grab you?"

"Works for me."

"The closest city is Volgograd. It's seventy, eighty miles south of Bolshaya Ivanovka."

Over the next twenty minutes, they worked together and located the other three places on the list. Two were in Russia, although they were closer to Mongolia than Moscow. The final town was in western Kazakhstan.

Quinn studied James's face as he stared at the screen of her laptop. "This is it, isn't it?" she asked. "The rumors about Dobrynin coding information about some mysterious weapon or weapons in his art collection are true. We found it."

"I think so. We can't spike the football yet, though. We might know where the weapons are hidden, but we don't know what they are. These could be anything from secret labs that were developing nasty bioweapons to huge stockpiles of conventional munitions."

"Would whatever it is still be there twenty years later?"

"With how remote these towns are, I don't see why not." He slid the computer from his lap and opened the manuscript again. "The answer's got to be in here somewhere."

"If it's in the text, we'll never see it," Quinn said. "We'll need to get a complete translation of the Latin." She shook her head. "Although I gotta think Gemma would have mentioned it if she'd run across something really off." She blew a raspberry. "On the other hand, if Dobrynin and his scribe used the same vague language for whatever kind of weapon he hid, Gemma might not have noticed. An AK-47 could be 'an apparatus that used exploding Chinese black powder to expel small projectiles of ore at high velocity from a long metal tube.'"

While Quinn carried on her one-woman argument, James squinted at the illustrations in the manuscript. "It might be in the text, but if Dobrynin put himself and his wife"—he pointed to a miniature with a squire and a young maiden speaking with the knight—"and probably his kids in the pictures, he might have hidden intel there, too. We can't rule that out."

He turned to the page with the castle tower. Quinn wouldn't have been surprised if thin wisps of smoke curled up from a tiny hole burned in the parchment from the way James's eyes lasered in on the picture.

At his sharp intake of air, she jerked. "What?"

Wordlessly, he handed off the book to her and set the computer on his lap again. His lips were a thin line as his fingers pounded at the keyboard.

She hated not knowing what had triggered his flurry of activity. But she knew she wouldn't want to be distracted if she were in his position. She forced herself to be patient.

Goose bumps prickled over her skin when his fingers stopped and hovered over the keyboard. His face had turned a chilling ashen gray. She rested a hand on his arm. "What is it?"

He swiveled the computer so she could see the screen. It displayed a photo of what looked like the turret in the manuscript. Only, it wasn't a turret. It was a missile.

Her entire body went numb. "Nukes?"

"Yeah. This ICBM is what the Soviets called an RT-23. An SS-24 Scalpel to NATO." His voice was hollow when he said, "The ice-cream cone at the top of the missile houses the warheads."

A wave of nausea washed over her. "Warheads? Plural?"

"It's a MIRV. Instead of one warhead, the missile can deploy ten reentry vehicles, or RVs, each with a warhead targeted to hit a specific location."

"And Dobrynin got a hold of these intercontinental ballistic missiles and what, just left them in their underground silos?"

"That's a definite possibility. SS-24 Scalpels had the

ability to be deployed from railroad cars, too. The miniature of the guy pulling two caravan wagons makes me think Dobrynin was hinting at trains."

"So he could have had these missiles trundled off on the railroad to a spur line in some little town out in the middle of nowhere and hid them."

"My guess is that's exactly what he did."

"Those missiles have to be at least fifty feet long. How in the world did Dobrynin think he'd be able to deliver an ICBM or two to some random terrorist group? FedEx?"

James shook his head. "They wouldn't take delivery of the entire missile. He probably planned to sell the locations of the missiles to a terrorist group or rogue nation. Then they'd strip them for parts. The targeting and guidance systems, even old Soviet ones, would be way beyond anything those groups could have developed on their own. Then there's the solid rocket fuel, although the fissionable material in the warheads is where the money's at."

"James!" Another puzzle piece fell into place. She flipped to the next page with the diagram of concentric circles. "That's not the medieval solar system. It's an atom." She grabbed the hotel pen and notepad from the nightstand. Starting at the innermost ring and working her way out, she wrote down the letter at the center of each sphere on each ring. CCXXXIX. "Two hundred thirty-nine."

"It's the isotope Plutonium-239—what's used in most nuclear weapons."

They sat unmoving as the magnitude of what they'd discovered settled over them. Eventually, Quinn said, "Now what do we do?"

"I call Meyers and tell him what we figured out. He'll take it from there."

"And they roll out a squadron of HALO-jumping CIA commandos under cover of night? Will you need to go?"

The thought of him taking off and leaving her alone in London didn't sit well with her.

"No." He shook his head. "They've got other people who can secure the missiles."

The chirp from a phone atop the desk drew their attention. It was the "James Lockwood" phone he'd kept with him in case Ben tried to contact him. James scrambled off the bed, glanced at the screen, and showed it to Quinn. Blocked caller. He slipped into his British accent and said, "This is James Lockwood."

As he listened, his entire body stiffened. At his reaction, Quinn's blood ran cold. His gaze settled on her and he said, "Yes, I can do that." James crossed to the bed and sat next to her. He lowered the phone and pressed the speaker icon. "Go ahead."

"Good morning, Ms. Ellington. Roderick Fitzhugh here. I'm delighted to speak with you." His accent was polished and aristocratic. "My associate whom you met on Saturday, Paul Shelton, tells me you are highly intelligent and charming. And from the photos taken last night in Oxford, you are exceptionally lovely as well. You and Mr. Lockwood make quite the handsome couple."

Blindsided, the only words that came to Quinn's mind were "Thank you."

"You're very welcome." He paused for a moment, shifting gears. "Mr. Lockwood, Ms. Ellington, I've no doubt you have an inkling as to why I am ringing you. You see, I am rather disappointed to find I have become a target of your systematic thievery."

"I have no idea what you're talking about," James said.

"Come now, James. May I call you James?" He didn't wait for an answer. "I know you took the letter you found in the secret drawer in the clock you examined at my home in Los Angeles. No doubt you are aware of my attempts to retrieve it." What could they say? No one but Quinn, James, and Paul knew about the letter. When neither of them responded, Fitzhugh continued. "Your lack of a rebuttal supports my assertion. And now you and your cohort, Mr. Baker, have stolen my manuscript." The joviality in his voice was pushed aside by a more sinister tone. "I want them back."

"You have no proof we have those items in our possession," James responded. "And even if we did, I think we'd deserve a hefty finder's fee."

Fitzhugh released a mirthless laugh. "You do, do you? However, I have something in my possession you may be willing to trade for them, if you had them, of course."

James frowned and cocked his head in question.

A male voice, weak and croaking, said, "James. Don't do it. Just leave."

Bile surged up Quinn's throat.

The voice belonged to Ben.

Fitzhugh came back on the line. "Your partner in crime has been most uncooperative in telling us where my manuscript is. This makes me think it's of great value. With that in mind, I'm sure you can understand why I'm eager to get it back. I do hope you believe a man's life is more valuable than a book filled with pages of old parchment."

"I do," James replied.

The cheeriness returned to Fitzhugh's voice. "So you do have my items. Excellent!"

"I have the manuscript. The letter is still in Los Angeles."

"That is troublesome, but not surprising. I'm sure you know where my estate in Northamptonshire is located. Be here at four o'clock. We can enjoy afternoon tea before we complete our transaction."

"And if I refuse?"

"Your colleague will meet a most painful and unfortunate end."

"I'll be there."

Quinn scowled at James and whispered, "What about me?"

"Oh dear," Fitzhugh said with feigned distress. "I'm afraid I've given you the wrong impression. I apparently failed to mention it is only Ms. Ellington who is invited to tea. You see, Mr. Lockwood, I no longer trust you will not attempt to steal me blind while you are inside my home. Additionally, I believe you will be on your best behavior until she is safely returned to you."

"No way," James stated flatly, while at the same time Quinn said, "Agreed."

James's head snapped up and he shook it, glaring at her. She glowered right back at him with an eyebrow arched.

"Pity. You two seem to disagree."

"I agreed and I meant it," Quinn said.

James's face reddened.

"You said you don't trust James inside your home. Fair enough," she said, ignoring James. "Here's the thing, Mr. Fitzhugh. From here on out, James won't let me out of his sight, so there's no way I can get to you even if I wanted to. Let me propose a compromise. James is allowed to travel with me until I get inside your home. Otherwise, believe me when I tell you, you won't get your manuscript back."

After a brief pause, Fitzhugh said, "I agree with your astute assessment of the situation, Ms. Ellington. But I have two conditions of my own. One, I'll have a car waiting for you both at the train station. My team will keep Mr. Lockwood company while we have tea. Two, if at any moment I am informed anyone is lurking about my estate during our meeting . . . Well, let's just say you don't want me to finish that sentence." He paused before finishing. "When I have my manuscript *and* Paul has succeeded in securing the letter, you three can be on your way. Agreed?"

Quinn gripped James's free hand and looked into his face, eyes pleading with him. His shoulders slumped in defeat. "Agreed."

"Agreed," she said.

"I look forward to our time together, Ms. Ellington. Good-bye."

James tapped the screen with his thumb, dropped the phone, and leapt off the bed. "What the hell were you thinking, Quinn?" He glowered at her as he stalked back and forth. "That you'll have a nice cuppa with an arms dealer and then you and Ben will just waltz out and that's that? That Fitzhugh will live up to his end of the bargain? We can't trust him."

"I know, but what other choice do we have? If we don't go, we may never get Ben back. Besides, we don't need the actual manuscript anymore. We can take pictures of every page right now, e-mail them to your analyst buddies at the CIA, and let them pore over every word and miniature. He can have the letter, too. We know it's not important."

"Of course I'll send pictures of the manuscript to Langley. I'm not worried about that. But how am I supposed to let you go in there by yourself? That would be an incredibly dangerous thing for a trained operative to do, let alone a civilian. This isn't paintball." The knuckles on his clenched hands turned white. "You can't go in there. I won't let you."

"Then you're signing Ben's death warrant."

"What if I'm signing yours, too? I can't—" He closed his eyes and shook his head, battling his emotions. When he opened them again she had crawled off the bed and on her feet in front of him. Wordlessly, she slipped her arms around his neck. They stood there for a long moment and simply held each other.

She leaned back, rested her hands on the sides of his face, and tipped it down so she could look him in the eyes. "I'm gonna be okay. I promise."

"You can't promise that."

"No, I can't," she admitted with a sigh and placed her

palms flat on his chest. "The train could derail along the way and we could both be hurt."

"You know what I mean," he said, frowning.

"I do, but you know I'm right." Her gaze never wavered. "You know I have to do this. Never leave a man behind."

He regarded her from under lowered eyelids. "Do you promise to play nice with Fitzhugh and do exactly what he says? No heroics? No channeling spy novels? No Edward Walker or Chance Stryker?"

She drew an *X* over her chest with her finger. "Cross my heart."

"I'm not convinced. If Fitzhugh looks at you funny and you bust in his cranium with a first edition of *War and Peace,* we could all be in a lot of trouble." He leaned in and gave her a soft, languid kiss. She sank into it. He said in a gruff voice, "Hopefully that's a bit of incentive for you not to do anything crazy."

So much for their taking a step back, she thought. "Incentive, huh? You're pretty sure of yourself."

"You think you need more than that? It could be arranged."

She shook her head and bunched his shirt in her hands. Up on her tiptoes, she yanked him to her and kissed him, hard. The pressure from his hands linked at the small of her back mashed her body to his. The kiss left them both panting and her weak in the knees.

"Is that some incentive of your own?" he asked.

"Mmm-hmm. Did it work?"

His emphatic nod came swiftly. "Your wish is my command."

She smiled. "Good. Now let's go save Ben."

Chapter Twenty-Five

Quinn squeezed the hand that gripped hers during most of the train ride. "I've got it, James." They shared the carriage with several other passengers, so she spoke in a hushed tone. "We've been over this five times already. I go into Fitzhugh's house, have tea, give him the manuscript, and tell him where the agency said they stashed the letter for Paul to find. Once he has what he wants, he lets us go and we're out of there."

"Good. And remember, you're not alone." James leaned closer and kept his voice equally low. "I'll be able to hear everything that happens through your earwig. I won't be free to talk to you; I'll keep the mic on my comm muted so whatever is going on with me won't distract you. But I'll be listening no matter what. Okay?"

"Okay." She unhooked a strand of hair from behind her ear and let it fall loosely over the inserted communication device. "You're sure he won't know it's there?"

"Positive. It won't be picked up even if he's paranoid enough to sweep you for bugs or recording devices. But I don't think he'll do that. He thinks we're a bunch of thieves, no more, no less."

"Right."

"There are officers on standby not far from the estate. Fitzhugh won't know they're there; we have backup if needed."

"Okay."

"And don't try to get him to say anything incriminating. We'll go after him another time. This is only about rescuing Ben."

"I know."

"Just be yourself. Quinn Ellington, not Riordan." The lack of rings on her finger reminded her of that. "You got this." James's knee bounced, a bundle of jittery, nervous energy. He turned and peered out the rain-streaked window. "You'll be great." He'd uttered those three words so many times in the last half hour, they had turned into his own personal mantra.

She checked her watch and noted they were scheduled to arrive at the train station in about five minutes. The butterflies that had been fluttering around in her stomach since they'd boarded the train turned into the Blue Angels zooming around in F/A-18 Hornets.

A few minutes later, the train pulled into the station and came to a stop. Quinn rubbed her clammy hands up and down her thighs, psyching herself up and drying her hands on her jeans. With her mind focused, she stood and shouldered her bag with the manuscript in it.

James stood when she did. "You'll be . . ."

Her gaze rose to meet his when he stopped.

Looking her dead in the eye, he said, "You *are* great."

The conviction she heard in his voice bolstered her confidence. She flashed a smile and gave him a sharp nod.

After he responded in kind, they disembarked. It wasn't long before a hulking man and an equally intimidating woman approached them. The man towered over Quinn like a redwood tree. The thick wool of his coat was drawn taut across his shoulders and strained against his bulk. There was no doubt in Quinn's mind he could snap her in half with his giant, meaty hands.

The woman, while not as physically imposing as her partner, was just as menacing in her own way. Her expression remained neutral as she approached, but Quinn knew the dark eyes were assessing the threat level they posed. Quinn threw her shoulders back in a posture of confidence. She couldn't intimidate the other woman even if she tried; this looked like a woman who knew two hundred different ways to put someone on the ground while not dislodging a hair from her tight ponytail.

"Ms. Ellington, Mr. Lockwood?" the woman asked. When they nodded she said, "Mr. Fitzhugh sent us to collect you." Her gaze flicked from Quinn to James and back. "Before we go any further, I need to ensure you have the item."

Quinn complied by opening her purse and holding it out for inspection.

The woman peered into the bag. "Very good. This way, please."

They strode toward the exit, with Quinn flanked by the woman on one side and James on the other. The giant man walked on the other side of James.

Once outside, they headed directly toward a grand, stately car. With one glance at the winged hood ornament atop the iconic grill, Quinn knew it was a Rolls-Royce.

"Is that a Phantom VI?" James asked in his James Lockwood accent. Quinn suppressed a smile at the mixture of excitement and awe she heard in his voice.

"It is," the woman answered. She opened the back door and looked at Quinn. "Ms. Ellington."

Quinn slid into the backseat as directed while the man she'd dubbed "Bruiser" in her head opened the front passenger door for James. In quick succession, the doors closed. Bruiser strode around the front of the Rolls and took his place behind the steering wheel. "Ms. Badass" sat in the back with Quinn.

She hardly heard the engine turn on and didn't feel a bump or bounce as the dark car glided out of the parking lot and onto the road.

As they drove through Northampton, James peppered Bruiser and Ms. Badass with questions about the car. They obliged and went on to compare the V-8 engine with the 6.75 liter engine. When Quinn ran her hand over the soft leather seat and mentioned she thought the car was fit for the queen, she was informed that Her Majesty had two in her fleet. Of that, Quinn was not surprised.

James managed to turn what could have been an unbearably tense and awkward car ride into an amiable drive to the country. Quinn didn't know if it was due to his innate enthusiasm for exotic cars, if he was attempting to disarm the guards, or if it was all for her benefit to keep her distracted and relaxed. Knowing James, it was probably all of the above. The reasons didn't matter. His easy manner had indeed calmed her nerves. Her admiration and affection for him deepened.

It grew silent inside the car as Bruiser turned off the two-lane road and stopped in front of a tall, black wrought-iron gate. After a few seconds, it swung open and the car slowly passed between two stone guardhouses. The Rolls cruised along a narrow lane that cut through a sprawling expanse of green grass dotted with copses of tall, leafless trees. A mile later, they entered a large, gravel-covered courtyard. Pebbles crunched under the tires as the car slowly approached the house.

It had stopped raining, but the air was still cold and damp when they exited the Rolls, which did nothing to help the chill of nerves that shot through Quinn. When the massive front door swung open, her knees nearly buckled.

James kissed her cheek and gave her an encouraging

smile. "I'll be here when you come out." His smile turned wistful. "You'll be great."

With a fleeting smile, she said, "See you soon." She left James to wait outside with Bruiser and was escorted by Ms. Badass to the entrance of the house.

Standing just inside the doorway was an older gentleman in worn brown corduroy slacks and a wool sweater. "Ms. Ellington. Roderick Fitzhugh. I'm so pleased you agreed to meet with me." She shook his soft, warm hand in greeting. He then swept it toward the house, inviting her inside.

"I do hope the inclement weather didn't hamper your travels," he said, as he closed the door behind them.

"No, it was fine, thank you." Her first impression of him was that he looked more like an emeritus professor than a nefarious weapons dealer. She'd expected him to be more like a smug, soulless James Bond villain with a nasty scar over one eye, not a genteel country squire who reminded her of her grandfather. "Rain is what I'd expect in England in December."

"Indeed."

Directly in front of them was a central staircase that split and turned both left and right at the first landing. On either side of the staircase were hallways that went farther back into the house. He led her, with Ms. Badass following at a discreet distance, down the left hall. At the first open doorway, they turned into a large family room. The walls were tan with white wainscoting and crown molding. Rustic paintings of bulls and horses decorated the walls. The furniture was homey, comfortable-looking, the exact opposite of his house in Pacific Palisades. Quinn detected the faint scent of evergreen in the air and immediately spotted a tall Christmas tree in one corner of the room. It was all very cozy and frankly, disconcerting.

"I hope you don't mind, but since you are a librarian . . ." After a brief pause, he asked, "You *are* a librarian, aren't you?"

"Yes, I am."

"Very good. As I was saying, since you are a librarian, I thought you might enjoy taking tea in the library."

"That sounds lovely, thank you."

They walked through another door in the back corner of the family room and into the library. Quinn almost gasped at its size and beauty. Dark wood shelves packed with books covered one entire wall from floor to ceiling. Although it was dusk outside, Quinn could imagine the natural daylight streaming into the room through the two windows in the adjacent wall.

"From the admiration shining on your face, I see you approve of my humble reading nook."

"I do. I could see spending days in here, curled up with a book and a cup of tea."

"Something I myself have done on many occasions." Fitzhugh motioned to two burgundy leather wingback chairs situated in front of the fireplace. "Please, sit."

She sat on the edge of one of the chairs, slipped off her coat, and set her bag on the floor next to her feet. "Is it wrong to admit one of my life's goals is to one day own a library that needs a rolling ladder to get to the top shelves— like the one you have over there?"

"Not at all," he said with a chuckle. He picked up the silver teapot from the small round table between them and filled two porcelain teacups. "Feel free to fix your tea as you like," he said, indicating the milk and sugar. Crumbs tumbled down his sweater when he picked up a biscuit from a plate and took a bite. "This yearning for a large library of your own. Did you plan to use my manuscript as the cornerstone upon which to build your collection?"

"Absolutely not."

"I must confess, you don't look the part of a hardened criminal." Fitzhugh settled back in his chair, crossed his legs, and sipped his tea, a signal to her things would move along according to his terms. "Tell me, Ms. Ellington. How does a young librarian come to be a part of a syndicate of thieves?"

How she got mixed up with James was a perfectly believable story, so she decided to tell the truth, minus the part about the CIA. "I work at a library in Los Angeles. A couple of weeks ago, a man came in with a picture of a brooch and asked me to help him find out more about it. As my reference interview moved along, he told me he worked for a company that insured an art collection. He wanted to make sure the valuations the appraisers gave him matched up with his independent research." She shrugged and brushed at a strand of hair falling across her forehead. "What he said made sense. I didn't question it and helped him."

Fitzhugh nodded thoughtfully. "Yes. It was about that time my business associate, Paul Shelton, mentioned to me Mr. Lockwood was spending a lot of time at a library."

"James and I enjoyed working together. The research was challenging, and great fun for me. Then he asked me to go to your house in the Palisades with him on Saturday morning to examine some pieces there. That's when I stumbled across the ring and the letter hidden in the drawer in the clock."

"You didn't know he'd taken them when you left my house that day?"

"No. I didn't know anything about any of this until we got back to my apartment after dinner that night and found two men rifling through my stuff. One tried to steal my laptop and the other had my great-grandmother's cameo shoved in his pocket."

Fitzhugh's nose wrinkled, like he'd just caught a whiff of rotting fish. "Contractors." After another sip of tea, he said, "I suppose you wanted to ring the authorities and James stopped you?"

She nodded. "That's when he told me the truth."

"So you ran. With him."

"Yes."

"Aren't you furious with James, that you're now involved in criminal activity?"

"I was." The memory of her anger at the cabin flared in her mind. Her scowl was very real.

"And now you're not," he stated.

"No."

Fitzhugh smiled and picked off a piece of lint from his pants. "No, it's clear your feelings toward Mr. Lockwood are anything but negative."

Quinn dropped her gaze and stared into the fire.

"Now you find yourself here, more deeply entrenched than ever in this plot gone wrong."

"I'm hoping once everything gets straightened out, I can go back to my normal life."

"With James?"

"I don't know." She turned her face away from the fire and looked at Fitzhugh. "Perhaps."

He gave her a look of sympathy, or pity. "Oh, my poor dear girl. I hate to be the one to tell you, but I don't think that will happen."

"What? Why?" This genuinely surprised her. A rock lodged in the pit of her stomach.

"Because he continues to lie to you. He's not a thief." Fitzhugh waved a hand dismissively and said, "Well, yes, he is a thief. He is also a member of a black market weapons organization."

Tea sloshed over the rim of her cup and splashed on her jeans when she bolted upright in her chair. "What? What are you talking about?"

"I'm British Intelligence. MI6."

She stared openmouthed at Fitzhugh and the hand holding her half-empty teacup began to shake. Had James been playing her? She set the cup down, closed her eyes, and took a deep breath. No. James had a badge. She spoke to his boss. They got her a fake passport in just a few hours. But a large criminal syndicate could probably do the same thing. Was she the most gullible person on the planet? She blinked and gazed at Fitzhugh, her eyes blurred with tears. "I don't understand."

"I'm very sorry to be the one to tell you this, but it's true. James and Ben are looking for a rumored secret weapon of some kind. If it exists, information about its location is believed to be hidden somewhere in the art collection I recently purchased. That's why they didn't steal something infinitely more valuable, like my Fabergé egg."

"They think something is in the manuscript, or the letter," she finished for him. She slumped back in her chair, dropped her chin to her chest, and rubbed her fingers over her forehead. It couldn't be. Had her feelings for James blinded her to the truth all along?

Then it hit her. MI6 would never allow items with such valuable intelligence out of their control. They'd be kept under lock and key in London with a cadre of analysts studying them. No, it was Fitzhugh who was lying to her. The fact she'd doubted James's veracity for a split second compelled her to say, "I'm an idiot."

"No, you were dazzled," Fitzhugh said, clearly believing she bought his load of crap. The burning logs in the fire-place crackled in the silence. Finally, he said, "Tell me, do you think James learned anything after your meeting with the professor last night? Once you were alone, did he ask you to find any hidden meanings in the manuscript?"

She'd play the naïve girl he thought her to be. Her cheeks pinked and she dropped her gaze to her hands. "We didn't discuss it at all. Once we got back to our hotel, we were, um, busy with other things all night."

"Ah, I see," he said with a perceptive smile. "Well, you can set things right by helping me find this weapon. Tell me everything you may have learned about the manuscript during your time with James."

"I want to know what will happen to him."

"He's a criminal. He is currently being detained by my associate, Joseph, and will later be handed over to the authorities."

"Detained. A nice way of saying he's tied up somewhere?"

"Yes."

Her stomach dropped to her shoes. It was clear if they were going to get out of this alive, it was up to her. What she was about to do was gutsy, but it was her only play. "From what I heard from the professor last night, I'm pretty sure what you're looking for is in the manuscript." She shifted in her chair to look at him dead-on. "I'll help you under one condition."

"I don't have to meet any conditions. If you don't help me, I'll charge you with the same crimes as James—or worse."

She thought back to Ben's weak voice on the phone and Fitzhugh's promise to hurt him further if they didn't give up the manuscript. She knew he was fully prepared to follow through with his threat. "Killing me won't get you answers."

"Perhaps, but you witnessing Joseph breaking James's fingers, one by one, should be sufficient motivation."

Her stomach churned. "Look, you don't have to hurt him. I'm willing to help you. All I want in return is for James, Ben, and me to walk out of here, free and clear. No arrests. No charges. No physical damage."

"You're willing to put your freedom, your very life on the line for a blackguard? You do realize you are doing this for a man who has lied to you and used you."

"Yeah, I know. And the stupid thing is I still love him anyway."

She stared back at him impassively as he considered her for a moment. The affable Roderick Fitzhugh returned.

"The things we do for love," he said with a mock sigh of defeat. "Agreed. Now, tell me what you learned."

Quinn removed the manuscript from her bag and handed it to Fitzhugh. He eagerly took it and immediately began to turn through the pages. "It's the story of a man, a knight, who goes to war, is captured, escapes and then has adventures on his way back to his home kingdom. The places he traveled to aren't mentioned specifically, though. For instance, one is called, 'Blizzard Village.' Last night at the pub, we thought maybe the knight was a Crusader. Now I wonder."

Fitzhugh leaned forward. "You wonder what?"

She had to make it seem to Fitzhugh she didn't already know the answer, but she also wanted to tell him what he wanted to know as soon as possible so they could get out of there. Her gut told her it probably wasn't going to be that easy. "Could the locations mentioned in the text be some kind of secret code as to where these weapons are hidden?"

His eyes flashed with interest. "Where are these places?"

"See, that's the problem. Everything is in medieval Latin. I don't know what country it's talking about." She stopped and thought for a moment, trying to figure the best way to lead Fitzhugh to the answer. "Like, if I knew the knight in the story was in California and the text said he was at 'the beach of the king,' I'd know it meant Playa del Rey. It's right by LAX."

Fitzhugh sat so far forward in his chair, literally on the edge of his seat, Quinn thought he might slide off and end up on the floor.

He wasn't there yet, so she fed him another line. "The other thing is, I don't think we're talking about a stash of trebuchets. So it must be the manuscript is referring to something and someplace modern. We haven't been able to date the manuscript, so we could be completely wrong, but it's just a hunch."

His eyes widened, apparently putting everything she'd been saying together. "It might be the former Soviet Union. The man who owned the art collection before me was Russian."

Finally. "Hmmm. That might be a good place to start."

Quinn jerked when James's voice came through her earwig. "Try not to react," he said. *Too late*, she thought when Fitzhugh shot her an odd look. Trying to cover for her jump, she said, "I just thought of something. If you could find me a piece of paper and a pen, I'll write down the names of the places Professor Dudley told us about. We can go from there."

Fitzhugh stood and went to the large desk in front of the windows.

As Fitzhugh searched for her requested items, James said, barely above a whisper, "I'm not tied up and I found Ben. There's no way Fitzhugh's gonna let us go once he gets the locations. We have to make a break for it. Clear your throat if you copy."

A noise rumbled from the back of her throat.

"Good. We're on our way to get you. Just hang tight until we get there."

She cleared her throat again as Fitzhugh returned with paper and pen. She took a sip of tea, and patted her chest. Pen in hand, she wrote the location names as slowly as possible, pretending it was hard for her to remember them all.

"Do you speak Russian?" she asked Fitzhugh.

"No, but I believe I have a Russian-English dictionary."

He doesn't speak Russian? *MI6, my ass,* she thought.

They both rose and she followed him to the wall of books. She tipped her head back and stared openmouthed at the hundreds of books before her. "Do you have them organized at all?"

"Not really. Most of these books came with the estate when I purchased it from an impoverished earl."

The librarian in her wanted to cry.

"We'll have to hunt about," Fitzhugh said. When they'd first entered the library, Ms. Badass had crossed the room and taken her post at a second door that led to the hallway. She'd stood there during the entire confab, stone-faced and motionless. Now, Fitzhugh addressed her. "Lucy, if you could assist us. We need to locate a Russian-English dictionary."

"Yes, sir." Lucy moved to the section of the bookcase closest to the door. Quinn took the middle, next to where the rolling ladder stood while Fitzhugh, his hands clasped behind him, scanned the books at the far end.

Quinn was about to check to see if the four volumes in the set of Winston Churchill's *A History of the English-Speaking Peoples* were first editions when she heard shouts and the crack of a gunshot.

In her earwig, she heard James yell, "Run, Quinn! Run!"

Chapter Twenty-Six

At the sound of the gunshot, Lucy whirled toward the door to the hall and reached for her firearm. Quinn grabbed the ladder and yanked on it with everything she had. It flew along the front of the bookcase and crashed into the back of the bodyguard. The force sent her sprawling. Her pistol skidded across the Oriental rug when she hit the floor.

Quinn bolted for the door that led to the family room.

"Stop her! I'll get the gun," Fitzhugh shouted.

Quinn was most of the way across the room when Lucy, having scrambled to her feet, lunged at Quinn's lower legs and wrapped her arms around them like a defensive back making an open field tackle.

The floor raced up toward Quinn's face. Her hands shot out instinctively to break her fall. Pain raced up her left arm and exploded in her shoulder when it took the brunt of her fall. Her chest and stomach slammed against the floor, forcing the air from her lungs.

Her eyes clamped shut and watered in pain as she gulped for air. She rolled onto her side and kicked to break the death grip Lucy had on her ankles. She jerked one foot free and blindly kicked in Lucy's direction. She caught nothing but air. Quinn drew her knee up and opened her eyes. Target sighted, she drove the heel of her boot into the center of Lucy's face. There was a sickening crunch followed by an indignant cry. Blood gushed from Lucy's nose as wild-eyed, she let go of Quinn's ankle, rolled onto her back, and cupped her hands over her face.

Quinn scrambled to her feet and sprinted toward the door. She grabbed the door frame with a hand and slingshot herself into the family room. She darted across the room, dodging furniture, and burst into the hallway.

A gunshot rent the air and the large vase on the table next to her exploded. She ducked and dove for cover. Crouching, she peeked around the end of the bench she hid behind and saw Fitzhugh coming toward her with Lucy's pistol in his hand.

Quinn lifted the hem of her jeans and grabbed the Baby Glock from the holster strapped to her calf. When James had handed her the firearm he'd told her to only use it in case of emergency. She figured this counted as an emergency.

She whipped the Glock around the end of the bench and fired off a shot in Fitzhugh's direction. He let out a surprised bellow and disappeared through the doorway of the family room.

"James! Fitzhugh has me pinned down in the entryway."

"On our way!" James replied through the earwig.

Fitzhugh popped into the hallway and squeezed off another shot. The bullet ripped into the wall behind her, raining down bits of plaster.

James appeared from behind the staircase with another man, his arm slung over James's shoulder. Quinn couldn't see his face well, but it had to be Ben. James leaned him against the newel post at the base of the stairway and let go of him long enough to spin around and fire off two rounds down the hall from which they'd just come.

"Quinn! Go! Wait for us in the car out front!"

"No! There're shooters in both hallways. You can't hold

them both off and get you and Ben out the door. You go. I'll cover you."

"No way." James jerked his head back when a bullet zinged past. He fired again at the same time as Quinn shot at Fitzhugh who'd popped his head out from the doorway. "You go! Now! Be safe!"

"I'm not having this argument with you again," she growled.

James expelled a frustrated snarl and grumbled a few choice words. "Fine. Don't move. I'll be right back to get you."

"Copy." She instinctively ducked her head when part of the railing nearest her exploded and sent splintered wood flying in all directions.

James sent two more bullets down the far hall just before he and Ben headed for the door. At the same time, Quinn pinned Fitzhugh down by squeezing off four rapid shots. Ben staggered as they moved, but did so mostly under his own power. It was only a couple of seconds before James threw open the door and they ran outside.

The man who had been following James and Ben burst from behind the staircase and bolted for the front door. He was halfway across the entryway when Quinn took aim and fired. She missed, but the shot sent him swan diving to the floor.

While she was busy with the new threat, Fitzhugh came out from his hiding place and advanced down the hallway toward her. Quinn swung her pistol back toward Fitzhugh and squeezed the trigger. The bullet caught him in the shoulder. He jerked and dropped to the floor.

Quinn thought that hallway was now clear, but Fitzhugh's shouts had roused Lucy. The woman stumbled out from the library and lurched down the hall. Blood covered her hands and a murderous rage darkened her face.

Quinn couldn't wait around for James to come back for her. With one guy crawling across the floor like a commando for the safety of the staircase, Fitzhugh down, and a bloodthirsty Lucy soon to be but not yet armed, it was her only chance to make a break for the open door. By her count, she had seven rounds left in the Glock. No problem.

She stood and fired twice down the left hallway, forcing Lucy to plaster herself flat against the wall.

As Quinn moved toward the front door, she fired at the commando guy and sent him skittering for cover. Her firearm was trained on him when movement to her left caught her eye. She glanced over to see Lucy raise her gun.

Quinn ran for the door. She tore out of the house right before a bullet embedded itself in the door frame. She didn't look back and ran as fast as she could.

She ran to James. He stood next to the open door of a silver sports coupe parked twenty yards away. When she yelled his name, he spun around and his eyes widened. He looked at her and then his focus shifted to something behind her. "Duck!"

She hunched, but kept her feet moving. He stepped away from the open car door as he repeatedly fired his Sig at the front of the house.

Lungs burning, she sucked down the cold evening air and sprinted for the car. She dove into the front seat, scrambled over the center console, swung her legs around, and hunkered down in the passenger seat.

James climbed in behind the steering wheel and handed her his Sig.

He hit the ignition and the engine growled to life. He popped the clutch and smashed his foot on the accelerator. Bits of gravel sprayed up in rooster tails from the spinning rear tires. When they gained traction, the car launched forward. At the end of the driveway, Quinn braced for the upcoming high-speed turn. Pain erupted in her shoulder when her elbow pressed against the door. She hissed when she sucked in air through clenched teeth.

"Quinn? What is it? Did you get shot? Oh my God! You're shot!" James sounded absolutely panicked. The back of the car slid when he cranked on the steering wheel and turned onto the lane, casting a glance at her at the same time.

"I'm not shot." Despite the adrenaline coursing through her, she tried to keep her voice calm. "My shoulder got jammed when Ms. Badass tackled me. I'm fine." After safely stowing the Sig under her thigh and returning her Glock to its holster, she grabbed the seat belt. She yanked it across her chest and clipped herself in.

James peered over at her, his face tight with concern. "You're sure you're okay?"

"Positive. You okay?"

"Yeah." He glanced into the rearview mirror. "Check around for a remote control or something to open the gate. This car can't smash through it."

She'd have to find it fast since they were almost to it and James had to slow the car. The center console was empty as were the storage bins in the doors.

From behind, a rasping voice said, "Try the sun visors."

The car was almost to a complete stop when Quinn spotted the small box attached to the visor above James's head. Quinn reached over and pressed the button. The gates jerked and began to swing toward them at a frustratingly unhurried pace.

"Come on, come on," James urged under his breath. In the rearview mirror, they could see the headlights from a car racing up behind them. He stomped on the gas the second the gap in the gate grew wide enough. The car flew through the opening and careened onto the main road.

Quinn craned around to look over her shoulder at the man wedged into the tiny backseat. She smiled. "Hi, Ben."

Even in the dark, she noticed his once-white dress shirt was filthy, torn, and splattered with blood. One eyelid was puffy and partly closed, the skin around it purple and mottled with red. Dried blood was caked at the corner of his mouth and clinging to several days' growth of scruff. She winced at the way two of the fingers on the hand resting limply on his lap were swollen and bent in unnatural positions. Bruiser's handiwork, she assumed. The thought of the pain he must have endured turned her stomach. Despite it all, he smiled at her a smile that reached his eyes. "It's great to finally meet you in person, Quinn."

"You too." Her heart soared to have him safely with them.

James cut in. "It's great you two have finally met and all, but we still have Fitzhugh, or at least one of his flunkies, on our tail."

Quinn turned forward again. "Probably not Fitzhugh. I put a bullet in his shoulder."

James's head snapped back.

"Ms. Badass might be riding along, but I doubt she's able to drive. I'm pretty sure I broke her nose when I smashed the heel of my boot into her face."

"Marry her," Ben said to James.

She chuckled and hoped the darkness hid her blush. "Actually, we are married. Well, sort of."

"What?"

"It's a long story," James said. "We'll bring you up to speed later." He lifted the phone from his back pocket and handed it to Quinn. "Bring up a map and figure out where we are exactly, would you?"

She did and said, "We're headed northwest and about five miles east of the M1. If we stay on this road, it'll take us right to it."

James shook his head. "We don't want to do that. Too exposed, too dangerous to other drivers." He glanced up in the rearview mirror again. "If they're in the Lamborghini, we can't outrun them."

She did a double take. "You passed up a chance to drive a Lamborghini?" One glance at the small logo that looked like a set of pilot's wings in the center of the steering wheel told her they were in an Aston Martin.

"The Lambo only has two seats. The DB9 at least has a tiny backseat."

"Oh."

James downshifted when they raced up on the glowing red taillights of a much slower car ahead. The Aston Martin's tires squealed in protest when they made a hard right turn onto a narrower road.

Once she was upright in her seat again after being pressed to the door during the violent turn, Quinn asked, "Do we keep driving until one of us runs out of gas?" She peered out the back window. The headlights reappeared behind them and seemed to be edging closer. Not good.

"What if it's us?" James answered and shook his head. "We can't chance it. We've got to disable them somehow."

"I take it this thing doesn't have the James Bond premium package, complete with machine guns installed in the bumpers and exhaust pipes that squirt oil slicks," she said.

"Seriously, James. Marry her."

James smiled and glanced at his partner in the rearview mirror. "Sorry. No grenade launchers that I know of. We need to use the darkness to our advantage. Doing something unexpected that will stop them long enough to give us time to get away."

British operative Edward Walker's car chase in *Target São Paulo* sprang to mind. "Like have them end up in a sheep pasture?" she asked.

"Yeah, like that."

Quinn studied the map and spotted something that looked promising. She switched to the satellite view and nodded in approval. "How do you feel about a road that comes to a T at a pond?"

"I like it. Get us there."

"Okay. At the next road, make a left. We'll go about a quarter mile and make a right."

Fortunately, they were on country lanes with no traffic. At the impressive clip they were traveling, it didn't take long to execute her directions.

Focused on the blue dot moving across the tiny screen, she said, "After the second roundabout, take the first right." When they'd done so, she checked behind them again. The headlights were so close they practically filled the back window. She spun around again. "This is the road. It's a straight shot. The end is in a mile."

"Roger that," James said. The tension in the car ramped up as they hurtled down the lane. "Tell me when we're two hundred feet from the pond."

"Will do."

"Ben, you strapped in back there?" James asked.

"Yep. Let 'er rip."

Quinn's gaze was glued to the map. "Three hundred feet. Two-fifty," she said, her voice growing louder with each announcement. "Two hundred!"

The engine whined in protest when James downshifted. "Hang on!"

Quinn braced her feet against the floorboard, pressed her back into the seat, and white-knuckle gripped the door handle.

James flicked the steering wheel a touch to the left, stomped on the brake, and then snapped the wheel to the right. The tires skidded and squealed when the back of the car kicked out and spun around one hundred eighty degrees. It came to rest only a few feet from a clump of reedy trees.

Their pursuer's car flashed past them in a yellow blur. By the time the driver hit the brakes it was too late. The two beams of light from the headlamps wobbled up and down in the darkness as the Lamborghini bounced over the uneven ground. Then they disappeared completely.

Not wasting any time, James slammed the car into first gear and sped off.

Quinn's every extremity buzzed. She slapped a trembling hand to her chest to keep her heart from hammering its way out of her rib cage.

"You okay?" James asked.

She took in a deep breath, held it, and then blew it out slowly. "Yeah, I'm good. You'll be happy to know you're a much better driver than Madison. He did a turn like that once with me in the car. Only, when he did it, it wasn't on purpose." Quinn looked over her shoulder at Ben. "Do we need to get you to a hospital?"

"No, I'm okay. We need to clear out, right, James?"

"Yeah. With a bullet in Fitzhugh, he'll probably have to go to the hospital and the police will get involved. It won't be long before the three of us are wanted for all kinds of bad stuff, including stealing this car. We need to ditch it and take a train back to London."

"You don't want to hook up with our backup?" she asked and opened the map application on James's phone again.

"No. Fitzhugh doesn't know we're CIA. We want to keep it that way. Right, Ben?"

"Right. I didn't tell him anything."

"I have a question about that," Quinn said. She paused and examined the map. To James, she said, "The closest train station is Long Buckby about five, six miles due south. The next left will take us straight there and keep us off the main roads."

"Perfect," James said. A half minute later he made the turn and checked the mirror. "No one's behind us. I think we're good."

All three relaxed and the tension inside the car disappeared. James slowed and drove at a less conspicuous pace.

"If you're not up to talking right now, or you can't say in front of me, that's fine," Quinn said.

"I'm okay talking," Ben said. "It's moving that I'm having some trouble with."

"Well, stop me if you get too tired," she said. "Here's my question. Was Fitzhugh bluffing when he told me you and James were part of a weapons organization trying to find Dobrynin's stash?"

"No, he really believes it. The whole thing went pear-shaped when I was at this party he threw at his place in Notting Hill Saturday night. I didn't want to go, but I knew Ben Baker the insurance guy would go schmooze the rich and powerful to drum up business. So I'm working the room, pressing the flesh, and I recognize one of Fitzhugh's guests. The minute he sees me, I know he's pinned me as part of a weapons ring—I'd been undercover in one during an op in Chechnya."

Ben stopped for a moment to catch his breath before continuing. "He goes straight for Fitzhugh to tell him I'm not an insurance agent but a weapons guy working for a rival syndicate and I take off, knowing Fitzhugh will immediately connect what I'm doing with the Dobrynin rumor."

"What did you do?" Quinn asked.

"I grabbed a cab and headed for Victoria Station. I sent the e-mail with the coded ISBNs to James's account on the way. Two of Fitzhugh's goons caught up with me before I could catch a train to Destination Anywhere."

"It must have really hit the fan when Fitzhugh realized the manuscript was missing," she said. "How'd it end up at the library?"

"So you found and deciphered my research notes. Good. I figured you would if I ever got in a jam. I left the manuscript there in case it turned out to be important. I'd done it before with other items. I didn't want to take the chance of Fitzhugh taking something that might be important before I'd cleared it. The big guy, Joseph, was with me Saturday. He's not the sharpest knife in the drawer and never bothered to check to make sure the manuscript was in the briefcase before we left."

"Weren't you afraid someone in the library would find it before you came back for it?"

"I always made sure to be the last person there when they closed and the first one there the next time they opened."

"So you stashed the manuscript Saturday afternoon before the party and planned to be there when the library opened Monday morning."

"Yeah."

"But you were exposed and captured on Saturday night and couldn't be there."

"Exactly. I wish I could've seen Fitzhugh's face when he opened the briefcase and found an old Bible instead of the medieval manuscript. He must have gone ballistic since he had Joseph and Hamish beat the crap out of me to get me to tell them where it was."

"Hamish was the one chasing us after I found you tied up in the cellar?" James asked.

"Yeah. He's a real charmer."

"I'm sure," Quinn said. "We're familiar with his nephew." Her nose wrinkled at the memory of the delightful Ethan. She pushed aside thoughts of that little weasel and asked, "Why didn't they search your flat for the manuscript?"

"I thought they did."

"Nothing was out of order when our guys got there to look for you," James said. "Your phone was there, too."

"They must have done that to make it look like nothing was wrong, to keep my people from looking for me."

"It worked, sort of," James said. "We knew you'd gone off grid because of the e-mail, but we didn't know what had happened to you until Fitzhugh called us today."

"We thought maybe you were sipping mai tais on a beach somewhere," Quinn added.

Ben chuckled and then groaned. "I wish."

James slowed the car as they drove through a tiny village. "They must have looked at the calls on your phone and figured out who Professor Gemma Dudley was. That's how Fitzhugh knew to have her followed. He assumed we'd find the manuscript and take it to her like you were going to."

"He guessed right," Quinn said. "Ben, how did you know the manuscript was connected to Dobrynin?"

Ben shifted in his cramped seat. "It was? I didn't know for sure. If I had, I would have taken it straight to our station in London. Something was hinky about it. I just didn't know what. I figured talking to Professor Dudley would be a good start. So it really had important stuff in it? You're sure?"

"Mmm-hmm. Dobrynin tucked away some SS-24 Scalpels," James said. "The agency is mobilizing to verify and intercept."

Ben blew out a low whistle.

"The text in the manuscript gave us the locations. Quinn figured it out," he said, turning the Aston Martin into the train station parking lot.

"No," she said. "*We* figured it out."

"Okay, *we* figured it out," he said with a smile. "Ben, we'll tell you more about our adventures later," he said as he parked the car. "Right now, we need to get on the next train out of here."

After shutting off the engine, James took the sleeve of his coat and wiped it over the steering wheel. Quinn did the same with the door handle she'd touched. James jumped out of the car and pushed a lever on the seat. The seatback folded forward and Ben slowly maneuvered himself out. James had already shrugged off his coat and was helping Ben's arms into the sleeves when Quinn joined them. She handed James his Sig, which he promptly returned to its holster.

Ben tugged the coat closed and walked gingerly across

the parking lot with Quinn and James flanking him on either side. A gust of cold wind cut through her sweater, sending an icy chill through her. She was bummed her beautiful CIA-issue wool coat was forever lost to Roderick Fitzhugh. She pictured Lucy using it for target practice. "You're going to leave the key in the ignition?"

"If someone takes it for a joy ride and it ends up in Birmingham, all the better for us," James said.

The station wasn't much more than an outdoor platform. James bought the tickets from a vending machine and the trio slowly climbed the stairs. They took refuge in a small covered shelter on the platform. It was of little comfort. Quinn shivered on the cold bench and pressed her hands between her knees in a vain attempt to keep them warm. She really missed her coat.

They waited ten agonizing minutes for the train to arrive, and when it came to a stop, Quinn was off the bench like she'd been shot from a cannon. She hopped on the train as soon as the doors opened. It wasn't exactly a sauna, but it was infinitely better than being outside.

She knew where James wanted to sit, so she walked toward the last row of seats in the car. As she did, she noticed the furtive looks sent Ben's direction from the passengers already seated. She couldn't blame them. He looked like he'd gone ten rounds with a boxing kangaroo. Ben didn't seem to care since he was asleep within a minute of the train rolling away from the station.

An hour and forty-five minutes later, the train arrived at Euston Station. As they walked down the platform, James said to Quinn in a low tone, "I need to help get Ben cleaned up some." He steered them toward the closest place to sit. "I'm gonna go to the pharmacy over there and pick up a few things."

Quinn nodded, sat down with Ben, and watched James hustle off. Five minutes later, he returned, bag in hand.

The three walked to the men's room and just before James and Ben went inside, James took out his money clip, peeled off two twenty-pound notes, and handed them to Quinn. "Can you go next door and buy some food and water?"

"Sure," she said, and plucked the money from his fingers. "You trust me to go it alone?"

"You'll be okay." A wink accompanied his smile. "I happen to know you're still armed and dangerous."

She flashed him a grin. "I am."

Had she looked over at Ben, she would have seen him smile, roll his eyes, and shake his head. Instead, she spun on her heel and walked toward the convenience store while he and James disappeared into the men's room.

A few minutes later, she exited the store with a bag loaded with three large bottles of water and some prepackaged sandwiches. She walked toward James who stood alone near the bathroom's entrance. When he caught sight of her, he smiled. She noticed his entire body go slack in relief. "There you are," he said.

"I was only gone for five minutes." She glanced around. "Where's Ben?"

"He had some business to take care of that a man's gotta do on his own." He opened his arms to her and she didn't hesitate to accept his invitation. Arms around each other in a comfortable embrace, she rested her head on his chest. It vibrated when he said, "And maybe you were only gone for five minutes, but the last time you went someplace by yourself, you ended up running from a hail of bullets."

She tilted her head back and looked into his face. "I'm not sure it was a *hail* of bullets. I think it was more like a smattering."

His lips only twitched before his face clouded. "Do you know how terrified I was when you were being shot at?"

"I have a pretty good idea since you were dodging bullets, too."

A smile appeared. He'd caught her meaning and an impish twinkle sparkled in his eyes. "You were worried about me even though I'm a blackguard and a liar?"

She winced. "You heard that, huh?"

He nodded and raised his eyebrows in amusement.

"I was playing along with what Fitzhugh said about you being a bad guy. I wanted him to believe I was okay with you lying to me because I was in love with you and would do anything for you no matter what, including telling him about what was in the manuscript. Betrayed Quinn was in love with blackguard you. Not James you." She was powerless to stop the panicky rambling. "Not that I don't lo—erm, care about you, because I do. Or wouldn't do anything for you. I would. Well, I mean, there *are* things I wouldn't do, but you know what I mean. Anyway, I thought they had you tied up somewhere and that it was up to me to save you. You, James, you. Not blackguard, you. And Ben! To save Ben, too. And that was why I said what I said." She closed her eyes and dropped her forehead against his chest. "You're going to abandon me here in this train station, aren't you?"

He laughed and squeezed her tighter. She smiled despite her embarrassment. "Not a chance."

"How did you get away from Bruiser, anyway?" she asked, looking up at him again. "Fitzhugh told me he had you tied up."

"Bruiser, huh?"

She lifted a shoulder and smiled.

"I like it. It fits. I was never tied up. The door had barely closed when you went into the house with Fitzhugh and Ms. Badass . . . is that what you called her?" When her smile broadened and she nodded, he chuckled and continued. "Anyway, the minute you were inside, Bruiser had his gun pointed at me. After I wrenched it away, I hustled him off to the garage."

"Don't believe a word he tells you, Quinn," Ben's voice said from behind James. "This guy's full of crap."

At Ben's return, Quinn expected James to release her. To her surprise, he didn't. Instead, she remained firmly in James's embrace and he replied with a mild, "She already knows that."

"And she's still here with you?" To Quinn, Ben said, "I'm disappointed in you. All this time, I thought you were smarter than that."

"What can I say? He knows how to show a girl a good time. Technically, we're still on our first date."

They turned and started toward the Underground section of Euston Station. James draped an arm around her shoulders and she slipped one of hers around his waist. She looked up at him. "Or did it end when you shot me in the back with a tranquilizer dart?"

"He what?" Ben asked, sounding both amused and incredulous.

James grimaced. "You're never gonna let me live that down, are you?"

"Nope," she said. She shifted her gaze to Ben. "You feeling a little better?" He looked better. The nasty purpling around his gray eyes was still prominent and his gait remained slow, but the dried blood on his face had been wiped away and the previously unruly brown hair had been tamed with a comb. In the light, Quinn noticed the flecks of gray at his chin in his four-day-old stubble. When she'd first seen him in the backseat of the Aston Martin all battered and bruised, he looked seventy. At least now he looked forty again. His previously contorted fingers were now taped together. She didn't want to think about what Ben had endured to straighten them.

"A little, yeah. Thanks. The painkillers will be kicking in

soon. And don't change the subject. I want to hear about my boy, here, shooting you on your first date." He scowled at James and teased, "What's the matter with you?"

Quinn opened the bag she carried, took out a bottle of water, and unscrewed the cap. She reached across James and handed it to Ben. He took it and greedily chugged down half the bottle in one go.

"We'll fill you in on our adventures after he finishes telling me how he found you inside Fitzhugh's house," she said. She prompted James. "You just relieved Bruiser of his weapon and marched him into the garage."

"Right. I found some rope and secured him. At first, when I asked him where Ben was being held, he wasn't very forthcoming. With a little persuasion, he told me Ben was in the cellar and how to get there. He failed to mention Hamish was skulking around. We ran into him as we left the cellar. That's when I told you to run, Quinn."

"Persuasion?" Ben asked.

He stiffened, slid his gaze toward Quinn, and then forward again. "Lug wrench."

To be confronted with the brutality of James and Ben's world made her queasy. She knew James to be funny and sweet and kind and brave and smart and protective. And yet, in a world filled with dangerous and violent people, at times he had to be dangerous and violent himself.

In a flash, it hit her that she was no different, really. In the fluid situation inside Fitzhugh's house, she'd put a bullet into another human being and broke another's nose. When the reality of her injuring others hit her full force, the world tilted and she stumbled.

The arm around her shoulders steadied her. "Quinn? What's wrong?" James asked. His voice was strained. "You're pale. Do you need to sit down?"

They stopped and Quinn felt him lift the bag she carried

from her hand. A bottle of water was pressed into her hand. "Drink," James's voice commanded.

The cool water cleared the fuzziness from her head. She blinked and James's face, inches from hers and tight with worry, came into focus. Her voice was hoarse when she said, "I . . . I shot someone today."

James's arms engulfed her and crushed her to him. There was no condemnation, only compassion in his soft reply. "I know."

She was vaguely aware of people rushing past them. The only thing she truly comprehended was the hand drawing soothing circles on her back. When James spoke again, his tone was filled with understanding, but firm with conviction. "You only did what you had to do. You only shot at them because they shot at you first, right?"

She thought back on the moment when Fitzhugh's bullet blew that vase to smithereens. Had she not been armed and returned fire, things would have turned out very differently for her, and for James and Ben. She nodded against his chest.

"If you hadn't done what you . . ." He paused, cleared his throat and started again. "It was your only option." His hand gently caressed her cheek, lifted her head, and turned her face to his. "I want you to remind yourself of that whenever you start to beat yourself up over this." With a raised eyebrow, he added, "Because I know you will."

She nodded mutely and gave him a watery smile.

His thumb lightly rubbed her chin. He closed in and gave her a gentle, lingering kiss. It was so heartfelt and filled with tenderness, the tears that had been threatening finally squeezed through her lashes and trailed down her cheeks.

Their kiss ended and James wiped at the wetness on her face with his thumbs. "I hate to push you, but we really need to keep going."

She swallowed hard, breathed deeply, and gritted her teeth. "I'm okay." They released each other from the embrace, and immediately took each other's hands. She glanced over at Ben who had moved a discreet distance away to give them some privacy. "Sorry about my little breakdown, Ben."

His sympathetic smile came quickly. "Are you kidding? You're a warrior," he said as he joined them and they started toward the escalators. "Anybody else who'd been shot at like you were today would be curled in the fetal position, rocking back and forth, and talking to their hand."

"He paints quite a picture, doesn't he?" James said.

She sent Ben a smile, grateful for his words. "He really does."

James's phone chimed as they stepped onto the escalator. He glanced at the screen. "Our ride home tonight is lined up."

"Wait, home home? Like me going straight back to L.A. home? Tonight?" She was in no way mentally prepared to simply wave good-bye to James in an hour and fly off alone.

James scowled and shook his head. "Oh God, no. All three of us are flying to Virginia together." He gave Quinn a meaningful look. "My boss needs to talk to you."

Apparently *debrief* was not a word James wanted to utter in public.

"Oh, okay. That makes sense," she said, relieved.

"What's our time frame?" Ben asked. "Can we swing by my flat? I need to change my clothes and grab a few things."

"I think so. We have to be at the heliport in an hour. A copter will fly us to the RAF base in Suffolk where we'll hitch a ride on a C-17. Just don't take too long. Quinn and I need to grab our stuff from the hotel, too."

Ben winked at Quinn and said, "Hang on, James. Are you saying we don't have time to box up all my books and bring them with us? I'm not sure I'm okay with that."

Quinn grinned while James huffed a breath in feigned exasperation. "You librarians are all alike."

They stepped off the escalator and walked toward the platform. Quinn slipped her arm around James's waist and said, "If you mean we're all kickass, then yeah, we are."

He hugged her to his side and kissed her head. "That's exactly what I mean."

Chapter Twenty-Seven

Quinn took another sip of tepid coffee. It tasted awful, but it was caffeinated, which was all that mattered. She'd grabbed a few hours of sleep during their flight, using James's shoulder as a pillow, but it wasn't nearly enough. Her eyes were dry and gritty.

She sat across the table from Aldous Meyers in a conference room inside CIA headquarters and watched him jot another note on his yellow legal pad. When he finished, he looked up at her. His eyes were as red as hers. It was little wonder, given her debriefing had begun at 4:00 A.M.

"Were you planning on helping Fitzhugh decipher the locations of the missiles?"

"Not if I could help it. James warned me Fitzhugh wouldn't let us go once he knew. Plus, my idea was to feed him enough hints for him to eventually figure it out, but have him take long enough that you could locate the missiles and put each installation under surveillance until Fitzhugh showed up at one. Then you could take him into custody for unauthorized possession of nuclear material." She shrugged. "Or whatever laws he'd be breaking."

"Catch him in the act as it were."

"Right. But since I shot him, the point might be moot."

Her gaze dropped to the scrawl-covered pad. "He's not, um, dead, is he?"

"No. Our sources indicate he's recovering from surgery and is in good condition. He told the local constabulary you and James invaded his home to rob him and shot him in the process."

Fitzhugh had shot at her, so her returning fire was justified. Still, she was relieved to know she hadn't killed him. She gave him a rueful smile. "Sorry I mucked up the plan."

He waved off her apology. "You did what you had to do. And you didn't muck it up. It may push back the time line a bit, but it gives us that much more time to implement your plan."

Her plan.

Meyers glanced down at his notepad. "I think we've covered everything." Looking at her again, he asked, "Are there any other details about Fitzhugh, his people, or home you'd like to add?"

"Not at the moment, other than he had a pretty cool library. If I think of anything else, I'll let you know."

"Fine. You have my e-mail." He screwed the cap on his pen and set it on the notepad. "You are not to discuss any of this with anyone, not even your immediate family—your parents, your brothers, no one. No one can know the true nature of James's occupation, what his business was in Los Angeles, or the events in London. The nondisclosure agreement you signed remains in effect in perpetuity."

"I understand. I won't say a word to anyone." Then it hit her. Her adventure had come to an end. She couldn't even contemplate what that meant for her and James's budding relationship. She swallowed down her swelling sadness and said, "I guess it's time for me to go home." The thumb of one hand rubbed into the palm of the other. "I don't want to sound presumptuous, but you think you could get me a ride the rest of the way?"

"We already have seats on a commercial flight booked for you and your escort. It's scheduled to leave for LAX in a couple of hours."

Her heart fluttered in her chest. "My escort?"

"With Fitzhugh and his people still at large, there remains the risk they could come after you. A twenty-four/seven security detail is in place for your protection until the matter is resolved."

"Oh, right. Okay." Her pulse quickened. "Will James be a member of my detail?"

"Jurisdictional considerations dictate your protection be carried out by the FBI."

The attempt to hide her disappointment with a smile was a complete failure. "Thank you for looking out for my safety."

"It's the least we can do." Meyers stood and tucked the notepad under his arm. "James will escort you from the building and hand you off to the FBI. There are special agents waiting to drive you to the airport."

She rose from her chair and slipped on the oversized coat she'd borrowed from Ben's closet before they left London. "Great. Thank you," she said and shook the hand he offered.

"You're welcome." He released her hand and opened the door. "Anderson, you're up," he said to James waiting in the corridor. Meyers turned and walked down the hall.

James was at her side in a flash. "How'd it go?"

"Fine. Told him everything I knew. He admonished me to keep my mouth shut about this in perpetuity." She lifted a shoulder. "About what I expected."

"Good. I'm glad it wasn't so bad." They left the conference room and as they walked the corridor, James took her hand and laced their fingers together. "And now I have the honor of walking you out." His tone was cheery and his smile encouraging. But they couldn't mask the sadness lurking behind his eyes. "Just so you know, I volunteered to escort you to L.A. and be a part of your security team." He breathed a quiet laugh. "Actually, I requested to be your full-time bodyguard."

She smiled.

"But they denied my request because of—"

"Jurisdictional considerations," she finished for him.

"Yeah. And I need to be here and work on bringing Fitzhugh down."

"I understand. I have to get back to work, too."

They turned the corner and walked to security. Once her bag was scanned, she signed out and turned in her visitor badge. As they walked through the empty lobby, Quinn glanced at the Memorial Wall where stars were carved in the marble honoring agency employees who died in the line of service. One of those stars was for Claire. She felt a profound sense of respect for the woman who gave her life serving her country. At the same time, her heart ached for those, James included, who grieved her loss. On the chance he, too, was thinking of his fallen partner, she squeezed his hand. Together, they walked across the iconic CIA seal inlayed in the floor and out the door.

The sky was still dark and the air was cold and miserable. It perfectly mirrored Quinn's mood.

They walked a short distance to the parking lot where two men in dark overcoats stood stoically next to a black SUV. The shorter and slightly older of the two stepped forward and offered a gloved handshake. "Ms. Ellington. I'm Special Agent Turner. I'll be your escort to Los Angeles."

"Nice to meet you."

James used only his first name when he introduced himself. "I need a couple more minutes with Ms. Ellington."

"Certainly." Special Agent Turner returned to his position next to the vehicle and clasped his hands in front of him.

James led Quinn a short distance away and into the shadows. He faced her and held both of her hands in his. "This sucks." Their breaths mingled in the frigid air like puffs of smoke.

"It really does." She gazed into his face and blinked at the stinging tears. "Will we see each other again?"

"Do you want us to?"

"Yes."

"Good. Because I'd have a hard time staying away since I'm in love with you."

Her jaw dropped.

He stepped closer and wrapped her in his arms. "It's true. I love you." His gaze held hers for a brief moment before he lowered his head and kissed her.

She closed her eyes and drank him in, memorizing the way his lips moved over hers, the feeling of his arms holding her, the myriad powerful emotions behind that kiss.

He loved her.

She broke the kiss and rested her palm on his cheek. "I love you, too."

She smashed her mouth on his. It was the fiercest, deepest, most passionate kiss they'd ever shared, one that indelibly branded the moment on Quinn's heart.

As much as she wanted to stay like that forever, reality pushed its way in when one of the special agents cleared his throat. She reluctantly pulled back and blew a sigh. "I have to go."

"I know."

"How is this going to work? We live on opposite sides of the country."

"We'll figure it out. I mean, I could leave torrid love notes in the secret drawer of an antique clock, but I think the Internet might work better."

Grinning, she cut her eyes up at him. "Smart aleck."

He gave her one more kiss before releasing her. Arm in arm, they sauntered toward the awaiting SUV.

"I'm going to miss you," she said. "A lot."

"I'm going to miss you, too."

As they drew closer, Special Agent Turner pulled open the door to the backseat.

"Let me know how things are going along the way home. I can't have my cell phone inside the building, but I'll check it as often as I can."

"I will." She gave him one final kiss and whispered, "I love you."

He pressed his forehead to hers. "I love you, too."

She nodded, gritted her teeth, and broke away. She climbed into the SUV and gave James a little wave. Her throat constricted. "Bye," she croaked.

James's smile faltered as he raised a hand. "Bye."

Special Agent Turner shut the door and took his place in the seat in front of her.

The SUV pulled away from the curb. Quinn kept her gaze pinned on James until the vehicle turned a corner and he was no longer in sight. She faced forward, sniffed, and rubbed her fingers over her wet eyes.

Now she'd *really* gone and done it.

She'd fallen in love with a spy.

Chapter Twenty-Eight

"Nope. *The Chronicles of Narnia* should be read in the order Lewis wrote them, not the bogus rearranged way," Quinn typed into the chat box at the corner of her computer screen. While she waited for Nicole's response, she read the next reference query in her in-box. It was another question about Valentine's Day. She sighed and glared at the red-and-pink heart garland strung across the top of the doorway of the Bullpen. She'd be really happy when it was over and they could move on to questions about St. Patrick's Day instead.

She'd fielded this question before, so she typed, "Yes, Saint Valentine was a real man and no, he wasn't killed in the St. Valentine's Day Massacre of 1929." After copying and pasting a couple of elucidating paragraphs from an online encyclopedia, she hit the send button.

Her computer binged, informing her Nicole had replied. "But why not read them in story order? It makes more sense."

Quinn checked her phone, and immediately chastised herself for doing so. It had been three weeks since she'd heard from James. He'd warned her he was about to drop off the face of the planet for an unspecified amount of time.

It still didn't make it any easier. And could she help it if she'd been spoiled by their consistent contact during the six weeks prior to his disappearing act? They'd texted every day and talked on the phone several times a week. Their dates consisted of video chatting while eating dinner or streaming the same movie. It wasn't ideal, but it made their separation bearable. Now she was suffering from withdrawal.

"Because the first introduction any reader should have to Narnia is through the wardrobe," Quinn replied.

"I wish I could argue that point, but I can't. Smarty pants." Quinn smiled at Nicole's response.

"Such language from a children's librarian!" Quinn typed back, grinning.

"Bite me."

Laughing now, Quinn tapped, "Speaking of bites, it's almost time to go. You still want to grab some dinner?"

"I can't," Nicole answered a half minute later. "Something just came up."

She frowned and was about to ask if Virginia Harris, library director, was breathing down her neck when Ed pushed the Bullpen door open and stuck his head through the gap. "Quinn, there's a patron at the desk you assisted a while back. He insists he'll only let you help him."

She groaned. "It's not Kumquat Dude from last week, is it?"

"No, it's not Kumquat Dude," Ed said with a chuckle.

That was a relief. That guy had a serious problem when it came to exotic fruit. "Okay. I'll be right there," she told Ed and typed on her keyboard, "brb."

Her relief was short-lived when Nicole responded with, "I doubt it." Her friend must have spied whoever waited for her at the desk and knew she was in for it.

Quinn pulled open the Bullpen door and started for the reference desk. When she saw who waited for her, she stopped in her tracks.

A brilliant smile lit up James's face the second he saw her. He came around the end of the desk and started for her, his long legs halving the distance between them. She managed to get her feet moving again and when they met next to the Valentine's Day display table festooned with paper hearts and a bunch of romance novels, he kissed her cheek and said, "Hi."

Given that James standing before her had reduced her mental capacity to that of a hamster, "Hi," was as eloquent a response as he was going to get. She decided that he'd somehow grown more handsome since they'd said good-bye outside CIA headquarters. "What are you doing here?"

"I'm here to see you, of course. What did you think? I'm here for Virginia?"

She gave him a sly smile. "I don't know. I'm sure those pantsuits of hers are hard to resist."

His eyes sparkled with humor before they shifted left then right. He lowered his voice and said, "I hate to disappoint our audience, but is there someplace we can talk privately? Can I take you to dinner or do you have plans?"

Quinn shot a look toward the children's section and glimpsed Nicole peeking over the shelves before she ducked away. "My plans mysteriously fell through a couple of minutes ago." Her gaze slid back to James. "Come with me to get my bag."

She turned and tugged him into the Bullpen. At her desk, she stooped, and as she opened her bottom drawer, she glanced at him over her shoulder. "You didn't come all this way to dump me, did you?"

His face twisted into a scowl. "No."

"Good. Then you won't mind if I do this." She straightened, put a hand behind his neck, pulled him down, and kissed him. Her feet nearly lifted off the floor when he snatched her up in a tight embrace. She basked in the taste of his lips, his familiar scent, his arms crushing her to his chest. When she tilted her head and deepened the kiss, he groaned, bunched the back of her shirt in his hand, and kissed her harder.

He tore his lips from hers and moved them next to her ear. His hot breath made the hairs on the back of her neck stand up when he growled, "God, I missed you."

"I missed you, too." She relished the feeling of him in her arms. "Why didn't you tell me you were coming?"

"It was kind of a last-minute thing. Plus, I thought it'd be fun to surprise you."

"You certainly surprised me, but I'm just glad you're here."

James said, "We really need to talk, but we can't do it here."

"Right." They parted, albeit reluctantly. Quinn snagged her purse from the drawer and kicked it closed. "Do we need to tell my protection detail who you are or do they already know?"

"Your detail has been dismissed." At her raised eyebrows, he said, "I'll explain everything when we can talk."

"I can hardly wait."

His eyes flick down to the gold eagle pendant she wore around her neck. He'd sent it to her as a Christmas present with a note that read, "*I saw this eagle and immediately thought of you. Merry Christmas. James. P.S. They didn't have one with a baby being carried in its talons. Sorry.*"

He smiled. "Nice necklace."

"Thanks." She fingered the navy blue Lamborghini necktie he wore. It had been half of her Christmas present to him. He wore it loose around the unbuttoned collar of his white dress shirt. Jeans and a leather jacket completed his supremely sexy look. "Nice tie." She gave it a firm tug and drew him down until their lips met again. "Decided against wearing the Aston Martin one I gave you?"

"I wear this one on special occasions. Getting to see you today qualifies."

"Smooth talker," she said with a crooked smile. It dropped away when his gaze turned intense and the muscles in his face grew taut.

The unadulterated desire emanating from him stoked the flames already burning inside her. Like a roaring inferno, they kissed again—urgent, hungry, abandoned. James shuddered when she wrapped her leg around the back of his and slid her hand under his jacket.

The specter of Virginia walking in on them crept into Quinn's blissful haze. She slid her mouth across his cheek to his ear and dragged her nails across his back. She nipped his earlobe for good measure before whispering, "We need to go . . . talk." She picked up her purse from where it had dropped to the floor and hauled him by the hand toward the back door.

A trail of hastily shed jackets, shoes, jeans, shirts, and firearms led from the door of Quinn's apartment, across the living room, and into her bedroom. They'd crashed onto the bed and ravished each other, wild and uncontrolled. At the moment they'd come together, Quinn knew what it was to explode like a supernova.

Sweaty, spent, and satiated, Quinn lay snuggled against James, her head resting on his shoulder. Rasputin, having apparently decided it was safe now that the fireworks had ended, jumped up on the bed, padded across the comforter, and curled up at their feet.

Quinn's fingertips leisurely brushed back and forth over James's chest. "I noticed you weren't using your accent at the library."

"I don't want to be James Lockwood around your friends and coworkers anymore," he said, his tone low and drowsy.

"Now I'm James Anderson, American. I was on assignment for the U.S. government and that's all anyone needs to know."

"Works for me."

An easy silence stretched, during which James lazily twirled a strand of Quinn's hair around his finger.

Eventually, she said, "Not that I'm complaining you're here, because *wow*, am I glad you're here. But what's so important you had to talk to me in person?"

"Do you have any plans for Valentine's Day?"

She tipped her face up and gaped at him. "You flew out here to ask me that?"

He peered down at her. "Just answer the question, Ms. Ellington. Do you have plans?"

"Well," she started dramatically, "since the incredibly sexy spy I'd want to go out with had apparently been abducted by aliens, I'd planned a rousing evening for Rasputin and me. First, I'd dine on spaghetti made with sauce from a jar while my feline companion feasted on the finest cat tuna money can buy. After cleaning his litter box, I thought I'd round out the festivities by doing some ironing."

"You sure know how to party. Do you think Rasputin would mind if I cut in on his action?" He glanced down at the cat dozing at the foot of the bed before looking at her again.

"Nah, we're good. If he was upset with you being here, he'd have thrown up by now." Rasputin had been in her apartment for all of five minutes after she'd picked him up from Rick's place when he vomited on her freshly cleaned carpet. It made for a memorable homecoming. "What do you have in mind?"

"I've got two tickets to tomorrow night's UCLA basketball game at Pauley, center court. And a Double-Double with your name on it."

"Throw in some fries, a chocolate shake, and a whole lot of sexy time, and you've got yourself a valentine."

"Great," he said. "And no, I didn't come here just to ask you out for Valentine's Day. There are some less important things we need to discuss." He paused for a beat as if to build up anticipation. It worked. She was about to explode with curiosity when he finally said, "We caught Fitzhugh."

"You did? That's fantastic! Congratulations." She pushed herself up and kissed him. "Is that why you went dark three weeks ago?"

He nodded. "It took some time for Fitzhugh's shoulder to heal and for him to figure out where the missile sites were even with the clues you gave him."

"He's clearly not as brilliant as we are," she said wryly.

"Clearly." His tone was equally droll. "Anyway, we took your idea and embellished it. Before Fitzhugh knew exactly what he was dealing with, we set up a sting. We had our contacts feed Fitzhugh information saying there was a terrorist group looking for some weapons grade uranium-235 or plutonium-239. When Fitzhugh realized what he had in those missiles, he offered to sell us—the fake terrorists—one or all of the missiles. Our guys met him in Yasnaya where two Scalpels were stored. Once we transferred ten million dollars to his account, we busted him."

She flipped onto her stomach, folded her arms over his chest, and rested her chin on her fist. "You weren't part of the group that met him in Yasnaya, were you? He'd have killed you on sight."

"I was there, but he didn't see me until he was in custody. It looked like a vein was gonna bust in his head when he realized I was CIA."

"I bet. Was Ben there, too?"

"Yup. And Fitzhugh was there with our favorites: Hamish, Bruiser, and Ms. Badass. It took some time to take down the entire organization, but we did it. Took Paul Shelton in this morning."

"The threat to me is gone. That's why my detail was removed." Her eyes lost focus for a second when his hand settled on her hip. Their skin-on-skin contact was intoxicating.

"Exactly."

"I'm sure those FBI agents will be glad not to have to sit in the library and watch me work anymore."

"Hardly. I heard they all said it was a sweet gig."

"They definitely caught up on their reading," she said with a smile. "I'm glad you were there when Fitzhugh was taken into custody. You were the one who made the connection between him and Dobrynin's art collection in the first place. This was your op." She cupped his face with a hand. "I'm really proud of you."

He kissed her open palm, sending a thrill hurtling through her. "It wouldn't have happened without you."

"That's sweet to say, but I doubt that."

"That's not what my bosses think."

"Really?"

"There's another reason I'm here. They sent me to personally ask you to come work for the CIA."

Her head jerked up. "What?"

"They want you to come work at headquarters in Langley."

"As a librarian." It was the only thing that made sense.

"To start with, yeah. But they also want to train you to become a covert operative."

She stared at him, dumbfounded.

"I know this is a huge thing, so you don't have to answer right away."

"Leave my job? My friends? My parents in San Diego? Living in California is all I've ever known. I'd be starting over in a place I don't know if I'd even like." She eyed him.

"How do you feel about this? I'd be in dangerous situations if I became an operative. You can't be happy about that."

"To be honest, it terrifies me." He heaved a sigh. "But I'd love for us to see each other all the time."

"That would be really great." She shook her head in disbelief. "Are they sure they want me? I mean, I might suck at being an operative. I'm just a librarian."

"They're sure," he said. He slipped out of bed long enough to retrieve his phone. "Now that I've given you the offer, I've been instructed to make a call."

"To who?"

"Codename Buckshot. He's a legend at the agency and has been around for a gazillion years. He's a retired operative who does recruiting and gets called in to consult on ops."

"Have you worked with him at all?"

He shook his head. "Not that I know of, anyway."

"So cloak-and-dagger."

James tapped at the screen and held the phone up to his ear. After a pause, he said, "Good evening, sir. This is James Anderson. I'm here with Quinn Ellington. Yes, sir, I spoke with her."

Quinn could hear a voice through the phone's earpiece, but couldn't make out the words.

"No, sir. She hasn't decided. Leaving her job and moving across the country away from family and friends are huge considerations. She's also concerned she may not be right for the agency."

She marveled at his ability to be so diplomatic.

"Yes, sir." He held the phone out to Quinn. "He wants to talk to you."

She sat up, clamped the sheet under her arms, and took the phone. Sounding more cautious than confident, she said, "This is Quinn Ellington."

"Hello, Quinn," the warm voice said. "Let me assure you the agency would not be making this offer if we had any reservations about your candidacy, nor would we make it capriciously. We've been aware of your potential and have been watching you for quite some time."

Wide-eyed, Quinn stared at James in complete and utter shock. She'd immediately recognized the voice. She tried to speak, but couldn't make a sound.

"These things tend to run in families, you know."

The phone almost slipped from her hand before she finally found her voice.

"Grandpa?"

Can't wait for more of
Quinn and James's adventures?
Keep reading for a sneak peek at

A COVERT AFFAIR,

coming soon from
Susan Mann
and
Zebra Shout.

"Don't move," the voice said from directly behind her.

The library book nearly jumped from Quinn Ellington's hand. Standing alone in the stacks, she'd been so absorbed in its pages she hadn't perceived her stalker's movements. While she chided herself for being caught unawares, she was pacified by the knowledge that had she not immediately recognized the voice, its owner would be doubled over and gasping for air after ramming her elbow into his gut.

Two arms slid around her waist and cinched her tight. She smiled and said, "Now why would I do a stupid thing like that?"

Chills raced through her when James Anderson pressed his lips to her ear and whispered, "Then I've got you right where I want you." He kissed the ear before he lessened his hold on her and straightened. "Ready to go?"

"Almost." She spun around, gripped his tie, and pulled him into a lingering kiss. She went nearly cross-eyed when she pulled back and looked at him nose to nose. "Now I'm ready."

He pinned her back against the metal shelf with his body and gave her a kiss that had her knees buckling. He lifted his head and gave her a lopsided smile. "Me too."

Once assured her legs wouldn't give out from under her, she pushed away from the shelves and led him through the stacks to her desk. She set the book down, straightened her top, and slipped on the jacket of her pantsuit. She couldn't wear jeans to work anymore, something she greatly lamented. It was one of the trade-offs when she accepted her grand-father's offer to work for the CIA.

James peered down at the book. "*Women of the OSS*. That looks interesting. What are you working on?"

"I'd tell you—"

"But then you'd have to kill me. I know," James finished. "I'm pretty sure you can tell me without getting in trouble."

"Yes, yes, you're right, Mr. I Have-A-Security-Clearance-And-You-Don't. For the record, I'm working on something pretty cool. One of the recruiters who visits college cam-puses is preparing a presentation that highlights some of the women who worked in intelligence in the past. She asked me to find some interesting stories."

"It won't be long before you're one of those women who has her own interesting stories."

"We'll see. It'll be a while since I . . ." She was going to say, *Since I've only been doing unclassified training here and haven't gone to the Farm yet,* but stopped. Only a hand-ful of people within the agency knew the plan to train her to become a covert operative. With the exception of the head librarian, none of her library coworkers knew. To those within the agency, she was a librarian. To those outside the agency—her family and friends she left behind in Califor-nia—she worked for an unspecified governmental agency.

Quinn smiled as she thought back on when she'd told her best friend and former coworker at the Westside Library, Nicole Park, about her move to Virginia. Quinn had said she wanted to serve her country. Nicole had guffawed and replied, "Yeah, and living near James had nothing to do with it."

James nodded. "No matter what happens in the future, you already have one good story under your belt."

"That's true."

On their way out, Quinn stopped by her boss's office and knocked lightly on the door. When she heard a muffled, "Come in," she pushed it open and poked her head through the gap.

Linda Sullivan looked up from the stack of papers on her desk. "Quinn, what can I do for you?" When Quinn joined the staff six weeks before, Linda told her it would be the most challenging, rewarding, and important library job she'd ever have. The information they collected, maintained, and provided to agency directorates was vital to national security and the safety of Americans around the world. By the time she left Linda's office that first day, Quinn was ready to do anything asked of her.

"I wanted to remind you I'll be away from the library for an hour or so," Quinn said.

"Thanks for the reminder. You have an escort?"

"James Anderson." Without her clearance, she wasn't free to walk unaccompanied around the secured CIA headquarters. She always felt like a nuisance whenever she needed to go anywhere.

"Excellent. I'll see you when you get back."

"Yes, ma'am." Quinn pulled her head back and gently shut the door.

Quinn and James left the library and strode toward the elevators. "I hope Linda doesn't find out about us goofing around in the stacks," she said. "I don't want her to think I'm not taking my job seriously."

They reached the elevator bank and James punched the up button. "No, it was my fault. I started it. I should have just walked up to you instead of sneaking around. If there's fallout, you can throw me under the bus." He sighed. "Again."

"Don't worry," she said, smirking. "Throwing you under the bus is always my go-to plan."

After a short elevator ride, they walked down a long corridor to their destination. They stepped into a front office and were met by a young man behind a desk. "Ms. Ellington, Mr. Anderson. Go on in. He's expecting you."

"Thank you," Quinn said.

Supervising Officer Aldous Meyers, her and James's Clandestine Services boss, sat behind his desk scribbling notes in a file. He glanced up. "Thank you, James."

"Yes, sir." He gave Quinn an encouraging smile before he stepped out and closed the door.

Meyers indicated a chair in front of his desk. "Have a seat."

Quinn did as told and waited, the acid roiling in her stomach about to burn a hole in its lining.

He dropped his pen on the desk, folded his hands in front of him, and looked at Quinn with a penetrating gaze.

"I hear from your instructors you're doing well in your unclassified training."

She resisted the urge to slump back in her chair in relief. "That's good to know. Thank you."

"So well, in fact, I want to see you in action. I have a minor op for you this afternoon."

"Oh, okay." She paused. "Yes, sir."

"You sound hesitant," Meyers said. "Is there a problem?"

"No, sir. It's just that I thought we weren't allowed to run ops on U.S. soil."

Meyers's lips twitched. "Yes, that's true. I've already cleared this with the appropriate domestic authorities."

"Of course." She could kick herself for questioning him.

He picked up a folder and held it across his desk. "Your task is to follow this man."

She took the folder and opened it. The man pictured on the top page appeared to be around sixty years of age. His hair was gray, as were his eyes and bushy beard. With his thick-rimmed, black glasses, he was rather monochromatic.

"His name is Karl Bondarenko, a Ukrainian weapons engineer. Our intel indicates he's developed an honest-to-God death ray and is here in D.C. to meet with a potential buyer today. We need to know who that buyer is. All we need you to do is follow him and take pictures of whomever he meets with. Once we get pictures of a face or two, we have other officers who will take it from there."

"That doesn't sound too difficult. Follow him and take pictures." She studied the photo. "Will he have the weapon with him?"

"We don't think so. We believe the meet is only to discuss a deal, not deliver a product. If he does have a working prototype, he most likely has it stashed somewhere."

"What if he has it with him and hands it off to the buyer? What do I do?"

"Operatives in the field can't call in every time they're faced with a decision."

That wasn't a helpful answer.

"Any other questions?" he asked.

"Where is he now?"

"He's registered at the Elegance Hotel in Georgetown. You'll start there. Also, do not discuss your task with anyone. Good luck." He held out his hand indicating she was to give him the file, which she did.

He set it on the edge of his desk, opened a file, and began to write in it. Taking the hint, she stood and walked out the door.